ALSO BY JERRY JAY CARROLL

Top Dog

Dog Eat Dog

Inhuman Beings

The Horror Writer

End Times

The Great Liars

PRAISE FOR *THE GREAT LIARS*

"This meticulously constructed thriller from Carroll delivers healthy doses of political conspiracy, paranoia, and pulse-pounding suspense. Oral historian Harriet Gallatin gets into deep trouble when recording former Navy Lt. Lowell Brady, who uncovered a terrible secret about Pearl Harbor... Cantankerous, lewd, vulgar, and skillfully rendered by the author, Brady is as warm as he is infuriating... Carroll has crafted a crowd-pleasing page-turner."
—*Publishers Weekly Starred Review*

"But the plot is secondary to the book, which is a madcap collection of reminiscences of Brady's interaction with the rich and powerful before and during the war. The humor is the real draw—and, as noted above—it stems largely from the witty way in which the protagonist recalls his recollections.'
—*William Wallace on Amazon*

"The writing style is witty and fun and my husband and I fell in love with the characters and couldn't wait to find out what was going to happen next... The Great Liars has it all. History, international intrigue, suspense, mystery, humor and romance. Carroll's novels never disappoint. If you haven't read it yet, I would recommend it." —*Amazon reviewer*

"The Great Liars takes readers into the 1930s...a Jeopardy category, of course!...but turn off the TV, read it page by page and be your own TV learning channel." —*Pat Sullivan on Amazon*

"This book is so engaging that the reader is gripped by the older Brady telling his story and the young Brady enacting the tale. This format is wonderful. The reader is kept enthralled by Brady's wit and the wild audacity of his young life as his older self tells all to the tape recorder." —*Betsy Ross-Edison*

"The most disappointing part of the book is that it is only half of Lowell's story. Both his WW2 adventures and the 1953 action are broken off almost literally in the middle. I want to hear more, if only Mr. Carroll will provide it." —*Ron N. Butler on Amazon*

"Great read." —*Amazon reviewer Cheryl B. Dale*

THE GREATER
LIARS

JERRY JAY CARROLL

Swaggering Press

Published by Swaggering Press
992 SE Portlandia Avenue
Hillsboro, Oregon

ISBN: 978-0-9898269-3-8

To my darling wife.

AUTHOR'S PREFACE

THERE IS NOTHING IN HISTORY THAT COMPARES WITH THE SECOND WORLD WAR. Tens of thousands of books have been written about its vast scope and unparalleled evil. The modern mind shrinks from the enormity of its horrors in confirmation of Stalin's icy maxim that a single death is a tragedy but a million is just a statistic.

Rounding off from what records were fished from the rubble, it is estimated from 75 million to 100 million lives were lost in the global conflict that raged from magnificent cities, where the riches of ages adorned palaces, squares and museums, to sodden, fever-ridden swamps and jungles in permanent twilight where pestilential insects waited with disease and death in their bite.

Tank wars threw up towering dust clouds on fly-blown, sun-scorched deserts in North Africa while on the Eastern Front the endless vistas and winter lowered the spirits of German invaders looking through field glasses after a victory that led to the next battle and the one after that until at last the colossal tide of war turned against them and vengeful Russians sacked their cities. Submarines glided beneath icy northern waters and through warm tropical seas, sending thousands of ships and their crews to the bottom until improvements in technology and tactics turned the subs into steel coffins.

Most victims of the war were civilians killed in obedience to the precept settled on by general staff planners and their political masters that war was too important to be limited to the traditional battlefield. An era had dawned of total war without mercy; everyone in theory was on the front line from babes in arms to the elderly too deaf in their beds to hear the bombs falling.

Huge armies of conscripts were massed for the struggle that had begun with political murders in sordid alleys and escalated to population extermination as mad schemes of revenge and world conquest played out on a gargantuan chessboard where countries were pawns and individuals no more than motes in a hurricane. Hitler, the insane hysteric with a sour stomach, and the coldly sinister Stalin combined with Mussolini and Japanese militarists to bring to the world cruelty never before imagined on such a scale. Entire armies were enveloped in battles fought for days and weeks on end. Hundreds of thousands soldiers on the losing side were disarmed after surrendering and shot at once or forced behind barbed wire at gulags and concentration camps to slowly die of starvation, disease or exposure. The tortures, beatings-to-death, rape and other crimes against humanity were beyond calculation. The modern mind is numbed by the enormity and would erase all trace if that were possible. Although strong interest remains in a niche audience, the war is rarely studied in schools and military historians do not rise in the academic hierarchy.

I was nearly two years old in 1941 when the war became truly global with the attack on Pearl Harbor. I remember as years passed how adults seated around the domed radio in the living room gravely discussed battlefront developments. I lay on the floor and drew pictures on butcher paper of American planes shooting at the enemy, little dots showing bullets striking tanks or aircraft. "Aieee" or "Arghh," said the little dialogue balloons I put over the stick figures that were our enemies, the Krauts and Japs.

All the women in my family were Rosie the Riveters types. They worked at a vast Firestone plant making truck tires and rubber fuel tanks for bombers. My lanky, laconic uncle who fought in the Pacific wrote to my mother to say that he had come to the realization that "people are no damned good." I don't think he meant just the ones on the other side. Like most men who saw combat, he didn't talk about it when he came home. He had spells of malaria for years when the whites of his eyes would turn yellow. He despised the Red Cross to the end of his life because it had charged soldiers coming off the front lines a nickel for a doughnut to go with the free cup of coffee. That would be like 75 cents in today's money for a Private First Class who earned only $50 a month.

It is natural that the war stayed with me and over the years I have read hundreds of histories, biographies, auto-biographies and other source material including Winston Churchill's war papers, a Brobdingnag work of thousands of pages, and made countless notes with the idea one day of adding my own two cents to the vast cataract of words. It always struck me as improbable that America could be taken by surprise at Pearl Harbor, particularly when our ambassador in Tokyo warned eleven months earlier that planning for such an attack had begun in the Imperial Japanese Fleet.

Breaking Tokyo's a secret naval code and high-level diplomatic codes coupled with radio intelligence stations that monitored Japanese traffic from the Philippines, Bainbridge Island in Washington, and Hawaii, and knowledge of a spy operating from Honolulu, made it unlikely that a fleet of 20 ships forming a box 18 miles wide could steam undetected across two thousand miles of the North Pacific.

Both the FBI and naval intelligence knew of the spy sending his telegrams via RCA and other commercial carriers that gave Tokyo a map grid of what warships were berthed or anchored at Pearl. Tellingly, the invaluable air craft carriers that would revolutionize how war at sea would be fought slipped out to sea a few days before the Japanese struck. In the haste, Army planes and fliers had to be unloaded when it was realized they could not operate from carriers

Sixty years after the attack, an Englishman named Peter Shepard wrote *Three Days to Pearl*, his account of a drunken Japanese engineer he encountered in a bar in what is now Vietnam boasting about his work preparing the fleet. The engineer drew a sketch of how planes on the six aircraft carriers had been fitted for shallow running torpedoes. Shepard, then a young airplane mechanic, told his base commander of this upon returning and was ordered not speak about it to anyone except the two British intelligence agents flown in to interrogate him. They uttered another warning against repeating what he had witnessed and disappeared. Shepard kept his secret for six decades for fear disclosure would harm British-American relations.

His book was written before the last of nine Congressional investigations into the attack, whose success was originally blamed on the negligence and incompetence of the Pearl Harbor military and naval commanders. Only later was it learned they had been denied access to critical intelligence known to the White House. Instead, they were given cryptic and baffling messages about being on guard. Whether London told Washington about Shepard's warning is unknown, but skepticism about the official story deepened as the years passed and some files suspiciously disappeared from the archives. General Walter Short having died, Admiral Husband Kimmel was exonerated by a 52-48 vote of the Senate in 2000.

As a journalist all my adult life, I am aware governments at all levels hide what they don't want the public to know; only occasionally are they caught out. Sometimes the only way to get nearer to the truth hidden by the official version is through informed guesswork and imagination. That is what I have tried to do with this novel and the predecessor, *The Great Liars*.

JERRY JAY CARROLL

THE GREATER
LIARS

CHAPTER 1

Virginia Beach, 1953

IT TOOK MY NERVES A LONG TIME TO GET OVER THE SHOOTOUT AT THE AUTO COURT between the government agents sneaking up on our room. We always kept the Plymouth packed and pointing to the road for just this sort of get-away. I left the pancakes on the griddle just ready to turn. In the slow-motion clarity of the moment that strangely was fixed in my mind.

"Another royal screw up," my husband yelled over the engine as we tore off like the famed Bonnie and Clyde. The men at the car that partly blocked the way were running to where the shots had been fired; Lowell ignored their order to stop and we went through the small gap they left at the gate.

"One was FBI for sure and my guess is the other was the spooks. It happened all the time in the war, the FBI not knowing what the OSS was up to."

He was grinning delightedly, picturing the bureaucratic war about to start. It was understandable in light of his persecution, but I was sick with horror. Like many men of his generation and profession, Lowell Brady was accustomed to seeing men die, hardened to it is closer to the truth, and quickly put the event out of his mind. But I thought about it obsessively in the weeks to come and suffered from terrible nightmares. As I looked out at the early light from the kitchen window, they had jumped up in the long beach grass surprising one another. *Pop. Pop.* The gunshots were almost simultaneous.

A movie kept running in my head afterward of those two men falling after firing, collapsing like puppets whose strings were severed at a single stroke. Two human beings with families and friends to mourn them, dead in the blink of an eye. Dry, brittle leaves left over from fall gamboled in our wake as we sped along thin country lanes, my eyes on the rearview mirror to watch for pursuit.

"There'll be a hot time in the old town tonight," Lowell said ten hours later as he turned into another auto court after a journey winding through timbered hills and small Virginia towns still mired in the Depression despite the postwar boom. "They'll be up all night tryin' to think of a way to blame the other side." He looked at me with exasperation. "Hell's bells, you've been crying and blowing your nose all day."

"What do you expect?" I burst out, "I'm not the Sphinx you know."

I explained in my earlier writings how Lowell, a Navy lieutenant attached to the White House, learned that President Roosevelt and a small circle of advisors knew the Imperial Japanese Fleet had put to sea to attack Pearl Harbor. He had failed in a quixotic attempt to warn the Pacific command and afterward narrowly escaped the many attempts to silence him for good.

The men in the conspiracy knew the United States must enter the war before England gave up and we faced the Axis powers alone with our tiny and untrained military. They also knew the public outrage and indictments for treason that would follow if their acts were revealed.

We had been married for only six months at the time of the shootings and were still getting to know one another. The truth is it was not in his nature to understand a woman's emotions as there had never been any need. We were like a floral spray from which he could select any bloom he liked. I myself serve as a prime example of his magnetic allure. Had it not been for a charm and presence I can only call engulfing, I would not have been spun into his tumultuous life as helpless as a bird in a high wind.

I sometimes look back with longing to when I was safely moored in the quiet anchorage of the Smithsonian Institution. Personally on the timid side as the reader knows from before, I avoided attention in the belief there was little to set me apart me except for a diligence that finds satisfaction in expanding a footnote to correct an error or to sharpen the understanding of a point in a dense work clotted with academic jargon. But our cross-country odyssey revealed to me unsuspected personal reserves of courage, boldness, fortitude and, I must confess, a kind of animal cunning at times. All of these in addition to luck are required for success as a fugitive.

Bluff and direct himself, the complexities of female nature mystified Lowell at times to the point of baffled silence. But he always rallied and I was not surprised that hearing "Sphinx" reminded him of a story, this one about North Africa and the famous Averill Harriman. Lowell told it with the customary relish and mastery of detail his phenomenal memory gave him.

Randolph Churchill, the prime minister's son, had been cuckolded by his teenage wife Pamela and Harriman, the immensely rich railroad magnate and diplomat twenty-eight years her senior. Unaware of this, as was Winston, Randolph was assigned to escort Harriman on an inspection tour of defenses with Lowell traveling as a minor aide.

"I came close to letting the cat out of the bag a dozen times when I found out just to see the look on the snotty bastard's face," Lowell told me. "We'll write that story down someday." He gave me a comradely clap on the back as we walked in the dusk to register at the dreary auto court (they were not yet called motels) under one of our family aliases, Henry and Dorothy Brown, from Massillon, Ohio.

Everything reminded him of a story that invariably had him at the center. Born to a leading family in Georgia, Lowell Brady was an intriguer, adventurer, spy, gambler, womanizer…but survivor above all. No one knew this better than I, Harriet Brady, née Gallatin, a Boswell to his Doctor Johnson. Not that he had heard of either of those august literary figures, being the opposite of a bookish man.

"What has that got to do with the price of tea in China?" he said when I explained, in too much in detail I'm afraid, the relationship of biographer and subject.

A scoffing chuckle, cleared throat, or fingers lightly drumming were signals a conversation had drifted from him as the subject and it was time to return. Though the printed page with the exception of sports in a newspaper held no interest for him, he was vain enough to want a record of his role when momentous history was being made. This sounds severe put that way and fails to capture the truth that I hung swooning on his words in a young wife way that I would not have believed possible when I was a scholar immersed in the linguistic roots of Southern folk music.

I had never met anyone like him in my humdrum life; I was like a butterfly freed from the pale chrysalis of uneventfulness. Our hasty vows were said before a beaming country parson in our early days as fugitives. As it was a dry county, we celebrated by clinking bottles of Dr. Pepper, Lowell shaking them up for a foaming champagne effect. He could make me laugh even in the worst times.

He was so handsome he was offered leading man work in Hollywood by the famous director Howard Hawk, who promised he could teach him acting in a couple of weeks. "Less if I was willin' to work weekends." Before that he had been steered into the White House job by his stepfather at the command of Lowell's mother, a famed Savannah society beauty who typified the Steel Magnolia strain of females. From what I understood from diaries, memoirs and other published and unpublished sources that I have consulted, she had wiles to rival history's most famous courtesans.

She dominated her husband, a powerful Senator from Georgia, a man feared by cabinet officers, generals and admirals. Her vaulting ambition for her only son was at odds with his natural indolence and the eye he had for the easy way out of things, work foremost among them. Her zeal had the ironic effect of thrusting him into dangers he would have evaded if not for fear of a court martial for cowardice in the face of the enemy. "A firing squad or a lively jig at the end of a rope was the strong possibility for that back then," he said. I wrote about this in my earlier manuscript which, like this present work, is meant to correct false or misunderstood events in recent history.

As related before, the pivot point in his life was that impulsive decision to warn Pearl Harbor of the Japanese fleet, an act of selflessness that in all candor I must admit could not have been more at odds with his true nature. The sacrificial acceptance of that attack was essential to pushing the United States into war before the Germans joined with the Japanese to turn their all-conquering juggernaut our way.

That Lowell was aware of White House treachery—to view "treachery" only in its narrowest sense—made him the target for elimination. He was shuttled from one hopeless war front to another in the belief by the conspirators that the enemy would kill him for them. It is a moral fastidiousness that seems antediluvian in our more cynical times.

Even with Franklin Roosevelt and his closest aide Harry Hopkins long dead, there were great reputations at risk. We became objects of a Javert-like hunt when my scholarly work on an unrelated subject inadvertently revealed that Lowell had survived the war and was living under an assumed name in a home for indigent soldiers and sailors.

He lay now on the creaking iron bed, the only kind auto courts seemed to have, with ankles crossed and hands behind his head, fondly observing as I unpacked our suitcases and manhandled the heavy reel-to-reel tape recorder to the electrical outlet. He waited as usual until the spools began to turn before speaking.

LET'S SEE, where were we? Okay, yeah, the Sphinx, I got a look at it in Egypt on that trip. Nothing much to see if you ask me. To pass the time, Napoleon's troops blew the nose off with artillery fire. You have to keep men busy or they get in trouble, every petty officer knows that.

Harriman was a pal of Hopkins, which is how he got that big Lend-Lease job in London. Averill was tall and good looking but, ahem, not as tall and good looking as me. Hawr, hawr, hawr. No, seriously, he wasn't; people said so. Where he had me was the hundred million bucks inherited from his father. The old man built the Union Pacific Railroad by being smarter and meaner than the rest of those robber baron bastards. A load of dough makes up for plenty of drawbacks. You can be a hunchbacked dwarf and still get a beautiful woman if she hankers for the high life, which I expect is true of just about all women if you dig deep enough, not countin' present company of course.

Old Harriman must have turned over in his grave when his son went to work for Roosevelt, the class traitor as he was called. Averill was a Wall Street banker himself but knew Republicans were going nowhere fast and wanted a cut of the political action. The papers say he sees himself in the White House one of these days. I met a lot of men like him back then. Rub shoulders with enough politicians and you start thinking your gardener could do the job better with less whiskey spilled.

Hopkins didn't tell him Roosevelt had sent me to London as a go-between with Winston, so Averill treated me like his flunky. I was career Navy and he thought I must not be very good at the work, still being only a lieutenant. But promotions came slow in the peacetime Navy, even if you had juice like me. You learn your place fast in the services. It's yes sir this, and no sir that. Polish the right apples and you end up a fleet admiral. Winston used to hide a wink when Averill was being high and mighty with me.

Any more of those hot dogs we got at that crossroads dump? I can eat 'em cold. I ate far worse, including mule in Siberia in the dead of winter, old ones as tough as cured hide. If you didn't have good teeth and strong powers of digestion, you'd get so weak you dropped to the snow and that was that, you never got up again. The men behind just stepped around, being near the end of the line themselves. I saw many men go that way with the wolves like shadows in the trees. Before we got far we'd hear them snarling and fighting over the body. Looking back wasted energy, so we kept staggering through snow knee deep and up to the hip sometimes.

We'll go someplace nice tomorrow if we can find one. It's plain vittles in this part of the country, not what we were used to when the government picked up the check. I'm lucky I didn't get crippled up with gout from all that rich food we took on board talking about the war. Gout runs in the family on my mother's side, the big toes mainly. I'm just goin' along free flow like you told me to when we started.

The British upper class likes a man with a good seat on a horse and Harriman was a top polo player, so that opened doors that even his fortune wouldn't have. We spent five weeks back in the summer of '41 looking over the situation. Winston wanted him to see how poorly equipped his military was though they weren't as bad off as Norway when they got shipped over in such a hurry the troops had no knives, forks or mugs for their tea.

But weak as they were in North Africa, the English sent the Italians yelping when the shooting started. The Eye-ties had 600,000 troops to 100,000 English, but Italy is Italy. The Ministry of War in Rome closed up shop at two o'clock sharp every afternoon. Joke at the time was a German field marshal was asked who'd win the next war.

"Madam, I cannot tell you that. One thing I can say is whoever has Italy on his side is bound to lose."

Another one: A lackey says, "My Führer, Italy has entered the war."

"Send two divisions, that should be enough."

"No, my Führer, not against us but with us."

"That's different, send ten divisions."

That got a smile out of you. Lordy, what would we do in life without humor? Mussolini turned down the offer of two German armored divisions in the early going, which would have made all the difference in the world. It didn't seem to penetrate that shiny, bald head of his he'd be fighting a European army instead of skinny Ethiopians in flapping gowns armed with swords and muskets. Pride goeth before the fall. That's in the Bible I believe.

Somebody totaled up the miles for that inspection tour and it came to better than sixteen thousand. The RAF flew us some of the way and we sailed on warships, but a good part of it was overland on rutted roads no better than camel tracks. The sun beat down like we were ants under a magnifyin' glass. There's not a boy born who doesn't think that's great sport; I spent many a happy hour outside holes frying red ants to a crisp as they came out to fight the black ants we sprinkled on them to stir things up.

Even the Bedouins complained how unusual hot it was, but it beat the Blitz and a bomb coming through the roof. You dove under a table and prayed hard when you heard them screaming down. A lot of underwear had to be wrung out when the plaster was done falling from a near miss. People stopped being embarrassed about it, war being the great equalizer as Winston said.

The Savoy Hotel had a nightclub underground called the River Room with a dance orchestra playing so loud you didn't hear the bombs or the ack-acks blasting away in the park. Waiters wore tuxes, elevator operators were in wing collars, bellboys in gray uniforms, everybody keepin' up standards.

You went outside into pitch blackness where the cables up on the barrage balloons sang like wind in a ship's rigging. It was nice until you remembered why they were there. Thousands got run down by cars in the blackouts. Or you tripped over something and fell so hard the next stop was the hospital. Noses broken or teeth knocked out, people coming to work wearing casts or bandages—a very common sight.

Harriman talked to everyone, including the Colonel Blimp types with faces red as bricks standing at ease in baggy shorts with swagger sticks behind their backs, teeth gritted, barely hiding how they hated us Americans. They were still peeved we took our time getting into the Great War where they lost the flower of a generation and afterward listened to us crow that we won it for them. A secret poll the government took showed they liked the Russians over us and even the Italians who were at war against them.

The colonels marched us into sweltering tents with maps spread on a camp table and "put us in the picture" in that clipped way they talk. "Over hyah, you see," whackin' the map with a stick. Lots of broken-down equipment was laying around, and some of the trucks had tires worn so thin you could just about see the air in them.

The British tanks were undergunned and had thinner armor than the Germans. The word was they needed a two-to-one edge to have any chance in battle. One of my jobs at these meetings was taking Harriman's sodden handkerchiefs and passing him a fresh one to wipe away the sweat. This gave the colonels an idea how I stood in the scheme of things and the looks my way showed it.

We traveled in a long convoy that threw up a huge cloud of dust, me in a truck way at the back eatin' grit even with a bandana over my face like a bank robber. Roll up the windows to keep out the sand and the cab got hotter than the hinges of hell, so we had to let it blow in. You raised a blister if you touched a hood or fender at a rest stop, it was that hot. Gulp down a canteen of water and it was all sweated out in fifteen minutes.

When we sighted soldiers camped around a well they seemed floating in the heat waves. Harriman always ordered a halt to talk to the Other Ranks for an idea of their morale. We call 'em enlisted men but by any name they were bitter and surly, all sunburned and scratching at flea bites.

They were mostly skinny little fellas raised in the slums and wearing khakis washed-out by the sun and sweat between the shoulder blades. Their hair was bleached white from that sun. Bully beef, biscuits and canned fruit was all they had to eat unless an Arab sold them a stringy old goat for the pot that cost ten times what it was worth. They brewed tea in old gas cans and it tasted like it.

Flies by the millions from first light until darkness, the sand always in your mouth, hair and clothes. Any shade was worthless because the wind in the afternoon was like a furnace. The tanks were 120 degrees or more inside.

Open the hatch to gasp for air and you let in the sand and flies. That white light blasting down got your last nerve on edge.

Bad it was, we heard the Italians had it worse. The ordinary soldier got thin soup, bread and a little jam, maybe a lemon now and then. Their officers enjoyed pasta and wine at their messes and mineral water flown in from Italy. In the dugouts that got overrun, they had clean sheets and chests of drawers with fine clothing and parade-ground uniforms that had gold braid and embroidered capes down to the ankles. They left cologne and fancy silver brushes and mirrors on the dressing tables.

Even the dumbest peasant sees what's going on and puts his hands up first chance he gets. The Italian salute we called it. The English bagged them by the tens of thousands when hostilities commenced. Dagos made the most cheerful prisoners of all. They got three squares a day and put on theatricals and opera in camps instead of running for their lives from planes strafing them or seeing Crusader tanks coming over the horizon already firing.

We'd drive on more hours to an air strip to talk to pilots and mechanics. Give Harriman credit, he asked a million questions and noticed everything. There wasn't near enough ships to bring the troops what they needed or trucks to carry it from the ports if there was. The brass hats put up a brave front in the briefings, but standards were below Mexico let alone Germany. Having worked for his pappy's railroad growing up, Harriman could see how pitiful things were between the services. The RAF required forty-eight hours notice for infantry support, which is like writing a letter to the fire department when your home catches fire.

At that, it wasn't as bad as on our side. I told you how the Navy had to get permission from Washington to borrow a paper clip from the Army just down the street in Manila. Inter-service rivalry—every country suffers from it. General MacArthur treated Pacific Fleet admirals like foreigners he wasn't sure he trusted.

Everybody looked down on everybody else. Our general staff said the British army was good at brushfire wars but wasn't set up for large-scale operations so no wonder the Krauts were winning so easy. Both us and the Germans noticed that it didn't bother them to give up in a battle when things looked bad.

I don't know if Harriman let on to Randolph what he was thinking. It didn't take long to see the son couldn't hold his liquor, not like his old man. He chattered away after throwing back a couple, all friendly like, and then a line was crossed and got meaner than a copperhead snake. One of the men in our party said Randolph bragged he'd be prime minister sooner than William Pitt the Younger, who you might have heard of but I never did up to then and still don't know more.

When he'd put away half a bottle of whatever was handy, people looked at their watches and said my word, is it that late? Cheerio. Ta-ta for now. After surgery for a benign tumor, some writer friend of his said the doctor took out the only part that wasn't malignant. Even his mother hated him, that's what he told Pamela. He realized it when she slapped him in front of the boys at his public school. No doubt he had it coming.

Randolph talked his cousin the future duke into dumping a chamber pot out a window on a prime minister when he came to Blenheim Palace. Duff Cooper—I'll tell you about him later—slapped him twice over something. He must have caught him with the backhand. *Whap-whap.*

What I heard was when Randolph was sent off to Eton, Winston asked the headmaster to spare him beatings but no soap, he got them anyhow. They would've straightened him good out at the Ironwood School for Boys up in the Michigan woods where the Senator sent me. They didn't fool around there.

With the war coming, the sons of the ruling class knew they had to get going on heirs. Randolph asked eight women in a row to marry him until he dropped down to Pamela. She was the daughter of a baron with some land in Dorset but no money to speak of. She still had her baby fat when I met her. The fast Leeds Castle crowd she ran with called her "the dairy maid."

Quite the beauty though, and she slimmed down later. Thick red hair half way down her back and blue eyes sparkling with fun. Knockers out to here. Her and I gave one another the eye a couple of times, but nothing came of it. She hoped to pick off a peer of the realm or some rich businessman with land for riding to the hounds; they said it wouldn't matter if he was as ugly as a sack of genitals. She only got half the deal in Randolph, though; the Churchill's were one of the great families going back centuries but were the poor cousins. Like his father, he scratched out a living in Parliament and writing for the papers and was always in debt up to his ears.

When even Harriman saw enough of the desert, we flew in a Blenheim to Cairo where you'd never guess a war was going on. The stores were full of butter, sugar, eggs, oranges and dates and so on. Hills of beans and cauliflowers and cabbages bigger than any I ever saw. What with bombers setting the cities ablaze back home and U-boats sinking the shipping, Londoners were already wearing patched clothes and shoes down at the heel. And hungry? I'll say!

Oranges in London were so rare that if you walked down a street with one like I did after an embassy breakfast, tossing it one hand to another, people stared like it was a human head. Everything else was rationed; they ate things they wouldn't dream of before, like crow pie, pig's brains and cow udders. There was muck called sheep's head broth if a man was hungry enough. You could go days and not see somebody fat. I'm losing track here.

After a long soak at Shepheard's Hotel to get the desert grit out, I joined the towel heads taking in the Cairo air, which is mostly exhaust fumes and dung with a dash of raw garbage. The blue haze over the streets burned your lungs if you took in a deep breath. Old Thorneycroft buses belching out smoke edged past carts pulled by donkeys with heaps of fresh vegetables that would make English housewives cry. Those women stood in line hours with their ration books hoping what was being sold didn't give out before they got to the front.

The donkeys in Cairo had long strands of blue beads hung around their necks to ward off the evil eye and so did buses on the mirrors. Now and then you'd see a European in a Fiat or Austin lay on the horn to get through the crowds and sheep herded to be butchered in the open air. Flies on them like blankets as they were cut up. If that bothered you or the blood underfoot, you didn't belong in the souks. Muslims, Copts, Jews, Syrians, Lebanese, French, Italians, Maltese, Cypriots, Greeks—all jabbering away at each other. It was Babylon…Babel is the word? Well, I say if you can't learn something new every day there's something wrong.

Beggars with bare feet black as coal and in those flimsy nightshirts they wear were everywhere; them Arabs pump out swarms of kids like you wouldn't believe. Every man takes as many wives as he can afford and even if he can't. A family of ten—nothing at all unusual. They live on top of each other in mud hovels outside the city. No sewers or running water it goes without saying.

Some kind of plague from the Middle Ages comes down reg'lar as clockwork;

it sweeps folks away by the thousands and nobody turns a hair. It's been like that since the pharaohs I believe; even before, probably. In the cities they whine for piasters for the sake of Allah, and it takes a strong man not to walk past without a look. Little kids "guard" cars for a few coins. If you don't cough up, the tires are flat when you come back. I turned in at the Turf Club after a five-minute walk, glad to get out of the stinking crowd. Native police with long sticks beat the beggars back at the gate for you.

I had trouble with the porter, the place being only for Englishmen and colonials that passed muster. No Aussies though, the Egyptians got their fill of them in the Great War and they weren't even allowed in the country. The Aussies are unruly people with beer in them, everybody knows that. An officer just behind me stepped forward when the porter turned down a bribe that was damned generous given his attitude. I got signed in as his guest and he showed me to an office where I got a visitor's pass good for a month.

"These people are living in a dream world," he said when I bought him a drink at the bar.

Captain Addison Revere was a thin, intense fellow in khaki shorts and blouse, as they call shirts. All elbows and knobby knees and dark hair doing a quick about-march up his long head. I'm glad I never had to worry about getting bald. He was quiet but mad as hell.

"They threw me out of the Continental Hotel because I wasn't dressed properly. I told them for God's sake I'd just arrived from London and shouldn't allowances be made for war? I'd spent seven days flying here with the Luftwaffe a threat to shoot us down any minute. An insufferable brigadier said I had no right to an opinion in the matter and I was told to leave."

As he blazed away at his countrymen, I looked around the posh room, which had a colored glass dome high overhead, famous according to what was said. The terrace where we set up camp had wicker chairs and tables. People were drinking and laughing and having a merry old time.

"I proposed a radio broadcast describing the gallantry of Londoners under the Blitz," he said. "Draft after draft was turned down by another brigadier with some propaganda job who said the men would be upset to hear their families were undergoing those trials and would give a bad impression to the natives."

"Bad show," I said. I'd picked up some English talk.

There was a grand staircase going up with tall caryatids of brass on the sides. Drunken officers buffed their breasts as the evening got on, a local tradition. I have to admit I did it myself a few times, grinnin' down at the crowd yelling approval. The marble bathroom in the lobby had pharaohs and cats on the ceiling. The place was so huge it echoed and a fart sounded like a pistol shot.

After a couple of pegs, Captain Revere and I strolled around with our cigars. The grounds were immense. Gardens, a polo field, a golf course, race course, cricket patch, squash courts, croquet, tennis courts, and a swimming pool by a clubhouse. Nannies with shouting children gathered at a playground under the trees. A lawn smooth as a billiard table ran down to a wall where the Nile River was on the other side.

You name it and they had it, first class all the way. Say what you will about the English, they make themselves comfortable wherever they go. They take a bit of home along and it's always the best neighborhood. No wogs except servants and the local sheiks or maharajahs or whatever they call themselves.

Revere was disgusted by it all, saying it reminded him of the old Roman Empire when the hungry barbarians came out of the dark woods up north and put an end to all the luxury and corrupt ways with sword and torch.

With the blinding glare of the desert behind me, I was actually warming to Egypt. Cairo looked like a place where a man could settle in and have a good time.

"You have to have connections for a spot on a staff here," Captain Revere said. "An aristocratic family with influence or a personage on the Imperial General Staff will do. This lassitude and condescension has to be seen to be believed." He tapped a cigarette on a thumb nail before lighting up.

"They seem to see the desert fighting as an event on their sporting calendar. There are musicales, improving lectures, river cruises, tours of the pyramids, everything to wile away the time. Dinner is at Fleurents or the St. James, followed by dancing at the Duck Club or the Kit Kat Club. Meanwhile, the bombs drop on London and anti-aircraft guns bang away without any effect I can see except perhaps to sustain civilian morale."

"How'd you swing the transfer?" I asked to change the subject. You never knew when you might pick up something about fiddling rules the higher-ups won't catch. A man has to be cunning to come out of a war with his hide in one piece.

"It's only temporary, they made that clear," he said. "I used to be a Reuters correspondent in Cairo and know this part of the world pretty well. The War Office is desperate that some kind of offensive spirit be shown here. For every poor beggar sweating 'up the desert' there are twenty men in uniform kicking their heels in Cairo. General Ritchie himself doesn't like roughing it in the field; he sends his shirts back here to be laundered. HQ asked if I had any ideas when I got here."

The spy in me put up ears at that.

"I explained to the chief of staff in some detail what London had in mind to get things moving, but he said thanks awfully but they prefer to do their own planning." He gave me a hopeless look. "It's always been like that. Every important decision in Egypt has to be approved by up to six departments in London, meaning the Middle East command is effectively independent in all but the most important strategic matters."

That told me his ideas were peanuts; cutting off roads, blowing up rail lines, raids on dago outposts—pin-prick things. Why stir up the enemy? Let sleeping dogs lie is my philosophy, and plenty more you meet on the battlefield go along with that. But down the chain of command from the fire-snorting busybodies come the orders.

Captain Revere was a sincere type; in war that's the most dangerous except for the glory hounds who want to ride to the sound of the guns with you alongside whoopin' and hollerin' like you're having the time of your life. Anything less and they think you're yellow. Don't go near a man who dreams of glory, that's the best advice I have for anyone thinking of a military career. It ends with you in a shallow grave and him with medals on his chest brushing away tears at Taps.

You know what, I bet that old woman that registered us would heat the hot dogs up in her kitchen if you ask her nice. I'd do it myself but for this damned cold that's got me barking like a seal. I never have recovered full from those days we spent hiding in the cave. She also might have some beer she'd sell; it never hurts to ask. A couple of bottles unless you want some yourself. I'll lay here and listen to the radio news to see if they mention the shootings. I doubt it, but you never know.

CHAPTER 2

WE CONTINUED DRIVING THE NEXT MORNING WITH LOWELL AT THE WHEEL AS always, keeping to dirt roads as we headed deeper south into a greening spring past small farms with outbuildings weathered gray and animals grazing in fields. We asked directions at small general stores that I guessed seldom saw strangers from the open stares from idlers. Sometimes we found ourselves behind a horse and wagon with no room to pass.

"Hell," he said in exasperation, "they're so backward here I wouldn't be surprised to see a coonskin hat or somebody with a flintlock on his shoulder."

We had been on the run so long I had forgotten what it was like to have a real home, an unhappy state for someone who treasured order in life and the stillness of the library stacks with a barricade of books to say do not disturb. I always had writing paper and a row of sharpened pencils close at hand and a nice sandwich in wax paper in my purse for lunch.

Travel is wearing even when for pleasure and far more so when one has a nervous nature like mine. My heart leaped painfully at a patrol car on the outskirts of Mangohick. Oh, how hard my imagination worked devising dire scenarios! Jail, a trial, and then years in prison with violent prisoners further maddened by their confinement. I was afraid looking straight ahead like I was a statue might be suspicious enough that a bored policeman would pull us over just on a hunch, or maybe because he was behind in his ticket quota. I didn't dare look in the side view mirror for fear our eyes met and he saw guilt in mine.

Lowell scrupulously complied with every traffic law. "Neither too fast nor too slow," he'd say in a sing-song voice as we approached a little cross-roads town.

He had told me if we were caught he would be made to vanish after a secret court proceeding, if bureaucratic punctilio allowed him even that, but argued somewhat unconvincingly I would be freed. "They'd see you were kissed off as a crazy lady if you went to the newspapers."

I knew one of the men who was shot, an FBI special agent named T.E. Hawley who tried to pressure me into telling where Lowell was hiding when I was still at the Smithsonian. He was tall and heavy-boned, hard-eyed and with a thick, ox-like body. It would take strong men to lift his coffin.

We stayed that night at an auto court that smelled of mildew after dinner at a cafe called Uncle Phil's Chowhouse. We sat among poor farm people, tired-looking women and men who ate with their hats on. Looking around, Lowell whispered, "You and me have more teeth than the rest put together."

He was pleasantly surprised by the food shoved before us by an over-worked waitress with a red face and untidy hair. "Say, this fried chicken's ain't bad, is it? The biscuits are the way I like them, soft and fluffy." He slathered butter on them.

I picked without appetite, the tragic event strong in my mind.

In my earlier writing, which I titled "The Great Liars," I told in some detail about how Lowell, a liaison officer for naval intelligence at the White House, tried to warn the Pacific Fleet at Pearl Harbor of the coming attack. That event and the terrible years that followed are long in the past, but sometimes they seem like just last week. Wise men over the ages lament how swiftly time passes. For what is your life, the Bible asks. "It is a vapor that appeareth for a little time, and then vanishes."

But some things must be remembered, including facts powerful people would hide from History. That earlier document in his own words like this one, with explanations and extrapolations by me where necessary, is under lock and key in the secure place where this will go when complete. The tapes and transcriptions will join them in storage until the last of the actors in the vast tragedy no longer lives.

The treason and other crimes they were complicit in were surely justified by the peril we would have faced had our isolationism continued. If

President Roosevelt had not allowed the fleet at Pearl Harbor to be attacked with the loss of only a few obsolete battleships, most of which were refloated, England would have followed France and the rest of Europe into defeat or cowed neutrality.

My research told me that with no Western Front to worry about, the Third Reich would have defeated the unprepared Soviet Union before the next year's winter, leaving the even more unready United States on its own. Our Army was small and the new draftees marched with broomsticks on their shoulders for want of rifles. Half the ships in our Navy were World War I vintage or older. So in the end it was the country's good fortune that my husband's attempt to warn Admiral Kimmel failed. To remind the younger, he is the scapegoat who lost his command as well as his reputation in the aftermath.

"In a lot of countries the secret police would have taken me to the basement and put a bullet in the back of my head," my husband told me, "so I was lucky they only sent me to war zones, though it sure as hell didn't seem like it at the time."

He was never able to clearly articulate why he threw away his career and nearly his life to warn Pearl Harbor. "It sure wasn't like me," he admitted, smiling ruefully and running fingers through his thick salt-and-pepper hair. Time has been kind despite his trials and he remains strikingly good looking, but of course I am prejudiced.

I have wondered if the Freudian analysis so popular today could explain that sacrificial aberration in a shallow life which up to that point was devoted to Byronic solipsism. He admitted his goal in life was no loftier than to marry a rich woman and travel the world in style. "Looking out for Number One" was his creed and his trouble began when he departed from it.

Passing young sailors marching in formation a month before the attack and seeing their faces alight with patriotic resolve was the epiphany that plunged him into danger and hardship that would have broken many a man professing nobler values. Did some incident in childhood unconsciously trigger that response?

Once in response to my questioning he said, "I saved a sack of puppies a farmer threw in the river when I was ten, is that what you're lookin' for? I swam with the bag in my teeth and didn't think I was going to make it in the strong current. The Senator hit the roof when I brought them home. He'd had enough of farm dogs nipping at his hocks for something they sensed in him; they circled with hair up or walked stiff-legged, growling and showing teeth. I bet I was on the road ten miles on foot looking for kids who'd take them for a quarter a pup. That was good money for then and I was poor for a considerable time."

The Senator, Lowell's stepfather, was Josepha Brady, the powerful committee chairman who lost his eyesight from the bite of a poisonous snake when touring Europe with his wife Eliza, Lowell's mother, the toast of Georgetown society as she had been in her native Savannah.

The mystery of who placed the serpent in their room in Venice was never solved. In part it was because the Senator's high and mighty manner as an important Congressional committee chairman created enemies during their travels, which were conducted in an imperial manner with fawning ambassadors and consular personnel smoothing the way. He had gone out on the balcony one evening to berate gondoliers about their singing, which he found too loud, and was violent on another occasion with an Italian nobleman who flirted with Eliza at a glittering gala. An investigation led nowhere and our embassy protested its perfunctory nature.

Lowell said upon meeting him in person that voters didn't like the Senator any more than farm dogs, but his portrayal in the newspapers back home as the plucky blind man looking out for them in treacherous Washington made him unbeatable in elections. The publishers, who were his cronies, saw to that. Researching the papers from that period, I saw that reporters seem to have settled on "white-maned" and "florid-faced" to describe him, never mentioning the milky eyes that my husband said "gave people the willies."

The Senator was the sledgehammer Eliza used to flatten anyone who stood in her son's way. Admirals and generals bowed and scraped because of his power over budget spending. Although they might be lions in battle, they feared her honeyed Southern voice on the telephone. Lowell's entry into FDR's circle and the friendship struck up with Harry Hopkins in the mid-1930s led to his secret role with Churchill.

The lady with white hair in a bun who was the wife of the owner of the auto court charged me twenty-five cents to warm the hog dogs in her oven, but sharply said she had no beer to sell and wouldn't if she did as it was against a local law to which she had not a single objection as a church-going woman. She had a shaming manner and pointedly looked at my hand fore a wedding ring. "You can buy one of those at the dime store," she said under her breath as she turned to the stove. I was meant to hear that.

As we ate our humble meal with glasses of water from the bathroom faucet, I thought about the relationship between Randolph and Pamela. How could Lowell possess such a wealth of detail about them, including that Harriman moved her into a luxury flat with a car and driver with gasoline rations from the embassy petrol account on top of a yearly allowance of three thousand pounds? With a sheepish look when I put it like that, he told me to start up the tape recorder again.

◾◥◾

AS LONG as we're getting at the straight truth, not holding nothin' back except (coughs) some of the *amore* you wouldn't want to hear anyways, I have to go back to Sir Peregrine Colville who lost an arm in the Battle of Jutland. Fourteen British and eleven German ships were sunk in that action and hundreds and maybe thousands drowned. Winston introduced us at Belvoir Castle at one of those country weekends where the upper crust shoots pheasants and grouse from the sky by the hundreds.

It's a huge place on a hill, more than three hundred rooms and a hundred inside servants at the prime. They loaned me an over-and-under and I brought down my share and then some of the birds the beaters drove to our guns. If you're a boy and not handy with firearms in the South people think something's wrong. Why aren't you wearin' a dress they say, or would you like a dolly to play with?

I liked the shootin' end of the visit—it was getting toward the end of August and the trees were colorful—red and gold and so forth—and the air was nippy enough that the whisky flasks passed around were damned welcome another time when we were waiting to spur off after the next fox to break cover.

But on the other hand you had to change clothes five times a day and were expected to bring a valet, which used to be the tradition before the Great War made standards drop off. I had the clothes, including tails for dinner that

Winston warned me to bring along, but no man servant because the Bureau of Supplies and Accounts would never go for that.

The old butler couldn't have been more amazed when he looked around and saw I was alone except for the driver dragging my luggage from the taxi from the train station. He might admit things had gone to the dogs, but to him this was as primitive as showing up wearing a grass skirt with a bone in my nose and a necklace of human ears.

Hobbes was his name, a tall, grave man like the dean of a cathedral. A long, pale face, dark suit, wing collar and tie. He walked at a slow pace like in a church procession, me holding to the same speed and nodding and winking at the titled folks in their tweeds and plus-fours, it being before they changed for tea.

They were wondering who this stranger was acting so familiar, some of them even offended from the looks they gave, so I left off from that and kept eyes straight ahead as we passed through big rooms. There was a great library with thousands of books on the walls and ladders to reach those up high enough that I reckoned they might not be touched from one lifetime to the next. Those people are all related one way or another or went to the same schools so it's rare to see somebody they don't know or heard of.

The butler and me went up a grand staircase big enough for eight men shoulder to shoulder, up other flights and down corridors. Each floor was more narrow than the one below and the ceilings got lower. We reached nearly to where the servants were quartered, the ones not down in the basement.

"Your room, sir," he said. "A footman will bring your luggage and unpack. I trust you will have a pleasant visit." Some of the worst snobs over there are butlers, more even than the lords and ladies they work for. I wasn't up to scratch by his way of thinking.

The narrow room had a window more like a slit for an archer, bare walls, a cupboard, and a narrow bed with a thin mattress and blanket. Wheezing from the climb before the cocktails hour, Winston said it looked to him like a cell of a man who had renounced the world for religious reasons.

He offered to fix it up with the Duke of Rutland for another room, but I told him I was used to roughing it. You got worse billets in the Navy and you're in there with others, some not so clean in their habits. With him was Sir Peregrine, also pretty winded.

"I haven't been this high up a castle tower since I was a young man," he said. "I believe the flagpole can't be far." He was a short, trim man, a widower with red hair turning gray at the temples. The empty sleeve of his houndstooth jacket was pinned up. "I don't think there is the smallest danger of being over-heard here, Winston." Sir Peregrine had sharp features like a fox and people joked that he should be appointed Professor of Cunning at Oxford. He…well, I'm beating around the bush, I guess.

What I'm getting at is I've been letting on the intelligence I sent to the White House was from Churchill's meetings with big shots, generals and politicians and so on where I played fly on the wall. And some of it was, but to be honest ninety percent came from Sir Peregrine, who you called Percy if he knew you well enough.

Winston told me he realized the only way to get past our suspicions about the British Empire was to be totally open and let us know not just what the cheeky newspapers said but what was going on behind the scenes. Isolationists here at home well remembered the English whipping up feelings in our coun-try before the Great War with how the Hun beasts were raping nuns and toss-ing babies on bayonets.

So figuring honesty was smarter this time around, he told Colville to clue me in extra from what I learned eavesdropping going to the parties and din-ners in high society, which as I say wasn't all that much.

The man was a real charmer, everybody's friend from the First Lord of the Admiralty to Silas who slides the pint down the bar at the village pub. Five minutes with him and it was like you'd been pals since the nursery. The Queen Mother laughed and tapped him with her fan for his wit, and salty old sea dogs roared at his stories when women weren't around about bordellos in Singapore and other ports when he was a young officer.

What I'm saying is the man fit in everywhere like he was greased with bacon fat, nobody really noticing the missing arm except when he played billiards. Some let him win a game here and there, but not me so he wouldn't think I was going easy out of pity. I heard later the holier-than-thou types—they're a plague everywhere you go—said it was unsportsmanlike.

But my opinion was Colville wanted to be treated normal. In his shoes I would've asked to be spotted two or three balls, but we played even-steven and he always paid up with a smile. He might say before a game that ten pounds was a little rich, how about five, but I always talked him around. He played good enough with the one arm that he would have skunked me with two, but nobody says life is fair.

Colville was invited everywhere and heard all the gossip along with the military and diplomatic stuff people let slip with wine and he passed the good things on to me. "You mustn't tell a soul," he'd say with that foxy look, knowing of course I would.

I told you before that Roosevelt liked nothing better than hearing about bed-hopping amongst the upper class, so that was always the cherry on top of the stuff I sent home in letters to the Senator, sometimes in the diplomatic pouch when I wanted to beat the newspapers.

Hopkins got the best of the inside stuff when he came across the pond to put his head together with Colville, but I had that advantage of detached duty and living in Churchill's flat, people thinking I was a cousin from the lower branch of the family across the pond. So, to make a long story short, that's how I know the nitty-gritty about Randolph and Pamela, and there's plenty more where that came from. Too bad Colville didn't write a book like we're doing.

I'll give an example of what I mean. The top man at Belvoir was John Henry Montagu Manners, the ninth Duke of Rutland and one of the richest men in England. The family history goes back to William the Conqueror, who ran things a long time before we were even a colony, how long I couldn't say without looking it up but it was considerable.

"Tell him the story," Winston said to Colville. He sat down on the edge of the bed making the old springs screech like they'd been hurt and touched a match to one of his long Cubans. "I know it well and can attest to its veracity."

"Lord Manners is as peculiar a man as you'll ever see," Colville said to me. "He is remarkably fierce looking, six-foot tall or better and very thin. He's sharp with people except for social occasions such as this where with great effort he manages a cold and distant civility, a man doing his duty and no more. He is a fanatical collector of things; there are thousands of bird eggs here and even more bits and pieces of pottery from Roman times he dug up over the years. People remember his handshake because he keeps the nails on that hand an inch long; they're curved like talons for scraping dirt and mud off old tiles.

"His diary in the library is opened to the day in February of 1923 when he and his friend Lord Carnarvon were the first to see the inside of Tutankhamun's tomb. He wrote that the sight of this was worth it even if a man never did anything else with his life. Whether that fostered his interest in the occult is unknown. He exhumed eight tombs in the crypt of St. Mary's Church in Bottesford where the earlier dukes are buried, supposedly looking for evidence that the fifth earl of Rutland was Shakespeare."

"I know the story, but not in such detail," Churchill said in the growly way he had. "A strange hobby, fooling around with old bones and relics. It's not healthy."

"He has also spent considerable time looking for where the heart of King John is buried."

"But this is not the point," Winston said. "Get on with it, Percy."

"The air is blue from your cigar, is it possible to open the window?"

I told him it was stuck shut, probably since the Middle Ages.

"Then let me show you the chapel, which figures in this story." He led the way and Winston and I followed. "John became the heir when his older brother, the apple of his mother's eye, died when both were children."

"I remember; it was tuberculosis," Winston said. "There is still a regrettably high incidence of the disease in the warrens of the cities. The sanitary conditions…"

"Tuberculosis was the story in the newspapers."

"Meaning the truth is elsewhere?" Turning to me, he said, "What Percy doesn't know is rarely worth knowing."

Colville smiled and said surely that was giving him too much credit. I warned myself again to be careful what I said to him; he was so smooth and almost hypnotic with his eyes that you'd be willing to spill your guts just to keep him listening.

That chapel was something to see. It was at the end of a circular passage, and the first thing you did when you stepped inside was throw your head back and look up with open mouth. The room went clear to the top of the castle with windows in the rafters for light on the huge tapestries that hung down.

"Scenes from the Bible," Winston said.

Plain white walls and a black marble floor and the figure of a boy in marble on a tomb smack in the center. "Lady Violet spent forty-two years on that," Colville said. "It had to be as perfect as her child."

Forgetting Winston hated the sound, I gave a whistle.

"I recall she had a reputation as an artist," Churchill said with a hard look at me. "Not in a professional sense, of course, as women of her class were not encouraged to develop such skills too highly, but good in a hobbyist way. Pen-and-ink drawings of heads, that sort of thing. But it appears she was quite a good sculptress. Such a pretty little boy with his curls." We looked at it in silence.

"Grief is natural, but not of that duration," Winston said. "It is suggestive of obsession."

"Heddon was the favorite of both the duke and duchess," Colville said. "As the younger brother, John was jealous of the attention lavished on him. Heddon died on his ninth birthday, not of tuberculosis as the plaque says and the newspapers reported, but of an injury suffered six days earlier. The child was unable to eat or drink and was in extreme agony until death. You can imagine the suffering of his parents. At his funeral, the local militia in full dress uniforms and brass helmets formed a guard of honor for the procession to the family mausoleum a half mile away. They reached it when the tail was still leaving the castle."

Colville shook his head. "The ducal establishments were vastly more impressive before they were ravaged by our confiscatory taxation. The servants were led on the sad march by the various heads of departments, including the house steward, the housekeeper, the head forester, the stud groom, the coachman, the duke's factor, the French chef. Then came the outdoor servants in order of precedence, the huntsmen and the whips of the Belvoir hounds in their scarlet hunting coats, the grooms, stable lads, dairy maids, mole catchers, millers and so forth. Thousands of voices counting friends and neighbors joined in the hymns."

Colville paused like in a drama on the radio; the man was a born storyteller. "There was one conspicuous absence...it was our present host John, the younger son. He watched from a window in the castle and then was taken away to live with a bachelor uncle and not allowed back for years."

"You mean it was fratricide?" Winston gasped.

I'm an only child myself, but I know there's as much brotherly hate as brotherly love and maybe a heap more. The Jenkins boys were always fighting, drawing blood more often than not. They'd kick the other when he was down. I expect it goes back to Cain and Abel, which they talked a lot about at the Ironwood School where bad boys were sent to learn good behavior by working our tails off in the fields or sawmills from before dawn to after sunset. We didn't have a speck of energy left to get in trouble.

"The details were not generally known," Colville goes on, "but Heddon's cause of death was a twisted gut from a fall of considerable height. If it was only an accident, would John have been sent off so brutally and forbidden to return all that time?" His look gave away what he thought about it.

After drawing on his cigar, Winston says, "That's very interesting, but it's not the story I had in mind."

"No, but it's connected," Colville tells him.

He turned to me. "In 1914 when the war broke out, the seventh Duke of Rutland, John's grandfather, rode about the estate in his barouche making rousing speeches and urging men to enlist in the regiment he served as honorary colonel. As they were employees and tenants, it didn't require great powers of persuasion. He promised their jobs would be waiting after the short war that everyone expected and wages would be paid as usual to families less their military pay. Seventeen hundred men, a fifth of the population on the estate, most of who had never gone beyond the thirty-odd villages on Belvoir land, marched off with the Leicestershires to the great adventure. John rode at their head on a prancing horse as one of the regimental officers."

"Although a terrible thing," Winston said in that growly voice, "war is a great and exalting thing that calls to men to be braver and finer than is possible in civilian life."

Colville's look said he didn't go along with that—not all the way anyhow. "I remember the rubbish said about how the flashing of the unsheathed sword was needed to cut away the rot in this country, but the Great War was a great slaughter over nothing and laid the seeds for the one fast approaching."

Winston looked down at the floor. "There were blunders," he admitted. "I was in the trenches myself for a time. The chateau generals…"

Corville didn't let him finish. "Nearly three hundred Belvoir men were killed when the Leicestershires were on the line at the Western Front in 1915. John was on home leave when they moved up after four months in reserve. He was shooting partridges the day a quarter of his battalion was mowed down by machine gun fire. The irony is he had a staff appointment that would have kept him safely in the rear. It seemed quite shameful, that extra margin of safety. There was muttering in Parliament."

Winston thought this over for a little while. "It was no doubt a question of the family line. Of the heirs of military age to the thirty dukedoms in the realm, only ten were on the front lines for that reason. The rest were in the Home Service or HQs behind the lines. If John had been killed, the estate would have passed to another branch after his father died. His mother and sister would no doubt have been left destitute and dependent on the favor of the new heir."

"There is yet more to the story," Colville said to me. "His sister is Lady Diana Cooper."

He acted like I should know who that was so I said, "Ah." He must have suspected I was blowing smoke. "She was on the cover of Time magazine," he said.

"The most beautiful woman in England at the time," Winston explained, "and I would say she is still in the running."

"Not only beauty but the highest intelligence," Colville said. "She was and is at the very zenith of English society, more than once at the time mentioned as a possible wife to the Prince of Wales. Sadly, there was no chemistry between them. I was surprised to see her downstairs; she and her brother have been cold to each other for years—and for good reason."

He put his eyebrows up waiting to be asked why and Winston muttered, "There is no need to draw this out."

"Her mother, Lady Violet Manners, a great beauty in her own time," Colville went on, "forced her into prostitution to keep John from the front lines."

Winston was knocked back on his heels. "What!" He wouldn't believe it, he said, not for a moment.

Colville smiled thinly. "Do you recall an odious man named John Gordon Moore, a Canadian many assumed was American because of his crassness and vulgarity?"

Yes, of course, says Churchill. "Before the Crash there was no escaping him, his disappearance was one of the few good things to come of that calamity. A man infinitely wealthy, but most disagreeable in manner and appearance."

"Moore didn't discourage rumors that he was the bastard son of King George," Colville said. "The fabulous wealth he flaunted was said to come from mining, railroads and utilities in several countries. He was heavily into munitions on the eve of the war…I say, it's damned cold in here, why don't we make our way below to a fire? These corridors are like the Arctic in deep winter," he said as we walked. "A heavy coat, hat and muffler are needed to go from one room to another.

"Moore was mad about Lady Diana, not only for her beauty but for her connection to one of the great families of the realm. He was someone who didn't know the meaning of no, a very powerful and magnetic man as you might imagine, dynamic—no barrier too great to scale. He was said to be the model for the rich man in the Gatsby novel. He had ten thousand acres around Carmel in California where his neighbor was Robinson Jeffers, the poet, through whom he gained access to Sara and Gerald Murphy's Villa America on the Riviera, where Pablo Picasso, Ernest Hemingway and F. Scott Fitzgerald and other leading figures in the arts were familiars."

"I have heard that Gatsby comparison made of others," Winston said. "The American Tommy Hitchcock for one, a much likelier possibility. Do you know him? Married a Mellon heiress. He was with the Lafayette Escadrille in France and shot down two Germans, winning the Croix de Guerre, before being downed in German territory. While being taken by train to a POW camp, he stole a map from a sleeping guard and walked a hundred miles to Switzerland. He was the best in the world at polo in his time, without question; he gave the sport its popular appeal with the masses."

"Moore seemed to know everyone of consequence," Colville said with a look that said polo didn't count much with him, and Winston could have the masses if he liked. "He met General Sir John French on the liner carrying them from America, and they became such fast friends that he invited the general to share the huge mansion he had taken at Lancaster Gate. Both had wives they neglected."

"The field marshal was the commander of the British Expeditionary Force sent to France," Winston said to me. "Like many high-ranking officers, he was susceptible to the allure of aristocrats. I met him in Egypt when we vanquished the dervish hordes to avenge General Gordon's beheading. He was a turbulent man, insubordinate at times, but cool under fire. He had a reputation for womanizing and came close to being forced to resign his commission because of personal bankruptcy. Only a loan from a fellow officer saved him from disgrace. He and Lloyd George undermined Lord Kitchener in the shell shortage crisis. It was a case of..."

"If I may continue, Winston," Colville said smoothly. "Her mother in despair pleaded with Lady Diana, who had rebuffed Moore's advances from physical revulsion, to reconsider for her brother's sake. Diana called him Little Chief Big Head because of its disproportionate size in relation to his body; he had a flat face and combed his black hair straight back. Her friend Raymond Asquith showed me a letter where she described Moore's advances as 'sullying, mutilating and scarring.'

"She found his boundless energy distasteful. She confided to friends that he perspired beyond even a very strong cologne's power of amelioration. Mind you, this is a woman whose beauty with her creamy skin and cornflower eyes were so extolled that her later wedding to Duff Cooper required mounted police to control the crowd. George Gordon Ghastly, she called him. But finally, in response to her mother's endless importuning, Lady Diana agreed to ask Moore to approach the general on John's behalf. He said he would, but of course there was a condition: she must surrender to him."

"You mean crawl in the sack?" I said.

Colville didn't know how Americans don't beat around the bush. He cleared his throat. "Physical intimacy is what I refer to, yes."

I later found out what "ameliorative" means, sounding it out over a dictionary with a woman in the castle library who took an interest in me, but I don't think I'll go on more about her. Moore must have worked up a quite a sweat doing the Charleston and Bunny Hop back then.

He held balls in his mansion called the Dances of Death on account that the young officers on leave knew what waited for them back in the trenches. "Eat, drink and be merry for tomorrow we shall die." Being smart about books, you probably heard that one before. Ragtime music one night, Hawaiian the next. Colville said the ballroom was decorated different for every dance, a circus look one night, the Wild West the next, Ballet Russe after that.

"They were on a preposterous scale," Colville said.

The way he said it the tables were works of art with hot house flowers and so forth, ice statues and other stuff. What they ate was impossible to find unless you were filthy rich; avocados, terrapin and soft shell crab to name a few dishes the common man can only dream about if he's even heard of them. Rivers of expensive booze, including that stuff called absinthe that makes you go loco. In short, a rippin' good time was had by all. "Hectic nights of oblivion," was how Colville put it.

They carried on until eggs and bacon at dawn or Diana got tired of Moore slobbering over her. When that happened, he threw up a hand and the music stopped and people cleared out. I don't like to think of the hangovers those poor bastards took back to France. Death must have seemed like a friend.

"There was a very worrying increase in all manner of vice at that time," Winston said. "Hashish, which makes parts of the empire sluggish and without ambition, made its first appearance."

"And morphine and cocaine," Colville said. "Sheets of gelatin paper impregnated with it were bought from the local chemist and sent to the boys in France. Savory and Moore in Mayfair advertised in the papers that they made a useful present for friends at the front, and civilians used it as a catchall for insomnia and anxiety. It was reported in The *Evening Standard* that in the ladies' cloakroom of a certain establishment two bucketfuls of small circular cardboard boxes were found by the cleaners—discarded cocaine containers. That drug percolated to the lower orders, though, thank God, not the opium smoking of the bohemians in the West End."

They talked about, the general moral decay of the nation, et cetera, I'll tell you more if you want to know, and then we changed into tails for dinner and went downstairs followed by Inspector Thompson, Winston's bodyguard. He was pulled out of retirement at the grocery store he bought when he left the Special Branch with a pension. He'd had the job with Winston for years and picked up right where he left off at five pounds a week and was never far from Winston from then on.

"I see the man every time I turn around," I heard Clementine say.

When we reached the bottom of the stairs, I noticed a big change. Instead of the down-the-nose looks before, being seen with Winston and Sir Percival raised me in the general opinion, that and my shooting which already gave me a leg up with the sportsmen. I hadn't been properly introduced when we were gunning down the birds, so they had just given me nods and a few "I say, good show" as we blazed away.

Winston was a coming man again with the German threat getting worse while Coleville was Coleville, everybody's favorite. So the dukes and lords and ladies, the marquis, viscounts and so on down the line to the rich businessmen who knew their place but hoped to improve it stuck out their hands like they just now noticed me. "I don't believe we've met."

I was all grins and howdy-do myself. The ladies complimented me on my Southern accent even though it had a bad reputation thanks to Wallis Simpson from Maryland, who enslaved the king with her sexual wiliness learned in the Far East. Why, thank you, ma'am, I told them, it's the only way I know how to talk. They tittered at that and called me a rare wit. I admit I like flattery as much as the next man and was having a fine old time.

We stood around throwin' back cocktails until called in to dinner at a table long enough to need three chandeliers for people to see what they were eating. An oak ceiling and paneled walls, candles galore, and footmen in livery and powdered wigs. The Duke of Rutland was like Colville described; he could have been eating alone for all he said.

I was put between two ladies who asked me about the United States and was it true the president didn't have the use of his legs? They wanted to know something about me personally, so I said the family money was from hog growing, slaughterhouses and meat packing. It was the cover story Winston thought would work best as it sounded as dull and draggy as a Sunday sermon on a hot day down South. Sure enough, they didn't ask much after I began to explain the salting process.

"Oh, look, Adele," the woman on my left said to the one on my right, putting a hand on my forearm to quiet me and leaning toward her, "Lady Diana is wearing the smartest outfit, isn't that velvet top just the loveliest thing?"

There must have been forty people at the table and we put away a wagon load of groceries. We had brown soup, trout, quail, saddle of lamb, pudding and pears with cheese. Sherry with the soup, white and red wine from France was poured with the other dishes. Seconds and thirds if you wanted.

The ladies left after coffee and us men smoked cigars and drank port for an hour. Some blew out their cheeks and someone joked about being windy later.

"Later," another shouts out, "what about now?"

That got us all laughing and we headed for the drawing room in good spirits for bezique, backgammon or bridge according to what we were partial to. I was looking forward to it, cards being second nature before my fingers stiffened up, but Winston called me over to where he stood with men looking grim.

"I have had a telephone call from a spy in Whitehall," Winston told me in a low voice. We followed him into a sitting room with a crackling blaze where he stood warming his backside at the fireplace and I guess thinking about what he was going to say.

"How bad is it?" asked a man who came in a minute later. It was Anthony Eden when I got a better look, who I told you about before; the man was as handsome as a movie star except for his crooked teeth.

Bad teeth kills you in Hollywood because of the close-ups—Howard Hawks told me that when he was trying to talk me into resigning my commission to take up acting. I opened my mouth for a look when he asked and I passed inspection okay. Some big names had theirs yanked for dentures. Wallace Berry's face looked like a caved-in pumpkin when he'd had a few drinks and took them out clowning around, but you couldn't tell from the movies with them in.

He'd been a big shot in the Foreign Office—I'm back to Eden now—but was on the outs with Chamberlain and hoping to ride Winston's coattails back to power. "Chamberlain's indecision has allowed Hitler to steal a march," Winston said. "Von Ribbentrop is to go to Moscow, no doubt to sign a treaty of non-aggression," A stunned silence hit the room.

"We have a military delegation there headed by Admiral the Hon. Sir Reginald Aylmer Ranfurly Plunkett-Ernle-Erle-Drax," Eden said at last. "And General Doumenc for the French."

"The admiral's resounding name fools no one in Moscow," Winston growled. "His is a low-level delegation with little authority except to string out a conversation that the Russians rightly suspect is going nowhere. Stalin and Molotov are practical men uninterested in talk for the sake of it. The Germans know time is of the essence with winter and its mud approaching.

He paused to relight the cigar that had gone out and he eyed us one by one as he puffed to get it going. "Their negotiators fly back and forth on airplanes while we sent the admiral and the French delegation on an old packhorse from the merchant marine. It took them eleven days to reach Russia; these day ships cross the Atlantic in less time; and then it was another day's train ride to Moscow. How else could they interpret this except as a delaying tactic?"

"Damn the Poles," said a slim man with a soup-strainer moustache looking into the fire. "It's their fault we're in this blasted fix. They're an arrogant people and will not listen to reason."

"There is more than enough blame to go around; no reason to single out the Poles for obloquy," Churchill said, "The root of the trouble is the harsh terms of Versailles."

"It was meant as a cage to contain the innate bellicosity of the Germans," another man said. "War is in their blood, the Romans said so a thousand years ago."

"It was a goad rather than a cage," Winston said, "and the result is Hitler."

"The German territorial demands are not excessive," Eden said.

"You sound like Chamberlain," Winston said. "He thought Czechoslovakia would be enough, but Hitler doesn't nibble at hors d'oeuvres, his ravening appetite requires a full course meal."

"I was opposed to that as much as you," Eden said.

"That's all water under the bridge. Even Chamberlain will realize his blunder if the Germans and Russians reach agreement with who knows what secret protocols. Hitler sized him up like the wolf does a sheep and is convinced he will take the pacifist's way out and abandon Poland as he did the poor Czechs."

"Public opinion wouldn't allow it," Eden said, "he must know that."

"Hitler snaps his fingers at public opinion. He thinks the French are degenerate and that we're decadent. We talk big for the press and other such fools, but he believes we will submit to his will rather than go to war over Poland and the public here be damned. I have studied the man and that is how he thinks."

"The Poles!" cried the man at the fireplace. "They rattle a sword without realizing a sword is all they've got. An army of men on horseback with lances, what a joke! A few obsolete airplanes, a small number of tanks no better than tin cans yet they strut like Napoleon after Austerlitz. They believe the Germans will rise against Hitler if there is war and the Polish army will be in Berlin not long after. Absurd! The Wehrmacht will make horse meat out of their gallant cavalry."

That made everyone quiet again and then Eden said, "The Polish bravado is because they know the French and the British Empire stand behind them. Our frontier is no longer the Rhine but the Vistula hundreds of miles to the east. That agreement encourages the Poles in their delusions."

"Never before in history," said Duff Cooper, "have we left in the hands of the smaller powers the decision of whether or not Great Britain goes to war." He was small and fussy-looking man with a toothbrush moustache. You'd take him as a bank clerk, but he won a medal for bravery in the war, so you can't always go by a man's looks.

"The Rumanian foreign minister told me Poland is the least moral country in Europe," he said. "Their foreign minister is a common drunk."

"That story is spread by the French, who detest Colonel Beck," Churchill said.

"Everyone detests Beck," said the anti-Pole, "even the other two colonels who run the country with him. I disliked him on sight and believe this is common. Only in Poland could a man of such deep stupidity rise so high."

Churchill said stupidity began when the Garden of Eden closed up shop and would still be with us when Gabriel blows his horn.

As they talked, I began to follow things from the nods Winston gave me to pay close attention at this point and that. Russia was on one side of Poland and Germany on the other. The Poles could mock the Huns because England and France were backing their play to show they had learned a lesson from selling the Czechs down the river.

But the two countries needed the Russians with them as Germans feared another two-front war, which they'd had in World War I and were still sorry about it. But the Poles hated Russians on account of how they treated them through history. The Russians didn't like the West and that went double for the Germans because they knew Hitler was just waiting for the right moment to smash them to bits. The West would welcome war between them, especially if both sides fought to the death. But you had to be a real optimist to think that would happen.

Germans had a low opinion of Slavs, thinking they were subhuman. They didn't believe anyone was their equal except maybe the English if the point was stretched. The Japs, to bring them into the picture, laughed at that. *Everyone* was inferior to them on account of them being the offspring of gods. The rest of us were no more than dogs.

Long story short, Russians were willing to join the West to defend Poland so long as they didn't have to fight their way through the Polish army to get to the Wehrmacht. That meant an okay for them to pass through Polish territory, but the Poles knew the Russians like a cat knows a dog. They'd never leave once they were there.

The way it stood, the English and French would have to declare war on Germany to make good on their promise to protect Polish independence, which the Germans gambled they didn't have the guts for based on what happened with Czechoslovakia.

Chamberlain stepping off the airplane and fluttering that piece of paper, peace in our time—remember that? In the end, the Poles ended up with the worst of all worlds when Hitler and Stalin signed their agreement. The Germans came at the Poles from the west and the Russians from the east and the country got carved up like a Christmas turkey. I could talk the night through on the what-ifs and if-onlys if I wasn't feeling so peaky, but that's the story in a nutshell.

A footman came in to add a log to the fire and when it started spitting sparks we pulled our chairs back. Winston told him to bring brandy and glasses and make sure it was from Sir John's cellar and not the sideboard. That there might be fit for hostlers but not for gentleman like was sitting around this room.

"The exhaustion of this government can be seen in the matter of Birger Dahlerus," Eden said. "Does anyone know the name?" People shrugged or looked blank. "I thought not; he is either a saint or a master plotter."

It turned out Dahlerus was a Swede who admired Britain and but was also an old friend of Hermann Göring, who was in the newsreels a lot at the time as the Number Two man in the Nazi party—big, fat guy, stood out from everybody in his white uniforms.

"The Foreign Office have been bypassed through Chamberlain's use of this man Dahlerus, who evidently believes he can bring peace by chatting up people on both sides," he said. "So as it stands, the prime minister is allowing a foreign national to conduct very sensitive and secret negotiations regarding Poland for His Majesty's government. It appears neither the French nor the Poles know about it."

"Extraordinary!" busted out the soup-strainer-moustache man. "If the Foreign Office is in the dark, who knows of these machinations other than Chamberlain and his flunky Horace Wilson?"

"Ambassador Henderson in Moscow might know," Eden said, "but the closest he has come to sharing inside information is that Hitler's breath knocked him back a step at their last interview. He attributes it to the Fuehrer's nervous stomach. It also causes windiness, which everyone is warned must be ignored."

"Henderson is not a first rate man; his attraction to the Fabians is evidence of that," Churchill said, patting his coat pockets for another cigar although the one he put in an ashtray was plenty long. "I wonder if his theories have changed by observing socialism in practice." He put a match to the new one and drew on it in the silence. "He is a frail reed on which to rest such grave responsibilities as the hour now presents."

AS ALWAYS when remembering the past, Lowell's eyes had turned inward as he pictured scenes and remembered conversations. If asked, he could have told me how many cut-glass crystals were on the chandeliers overhead at the dinner or described the clothes and jewelry each woman wore. His total recall pulled up answers in as much detail as I wanted, even the weather on a particular day years before and what he'd had for breakfast that morning.

In the Southern style, one story led to another in a leisurely way and he sometimes jumped forward and backward in time. Future scholars will have to unravel his recollections to put them in chronological order. But as I wrote before, this phenomenal memory did not necessarily entail analysis or even reflection on events that he witnessed. You asked and he answered; like a film editor he could produce a scene on demand.

Now his green eyes came back to me and I switched off the tape recorder.

"Joltin' over these backroads wearies a man; I don't know how truckers do it, it has to be almighty bad on the kidneys. There's a ghost story goes with the castle that will curl your hair, but I'll save it for later; your nerves are strung tight enough as it is. I hope you don't scream like last night, I sprang up out of bed like I was touched by an electric wire." Yawning, he began to undress and said the noise wouldn't bother him if I wanted to type.

I worked on the rough draft of the transcript for a couple of hours to the sound of his stertorous snores and put on my nightgown and climbed into bed. I pushed him on his side and he slept quieter, but the restless trees kept me awake for a long time. Then I was being interrogated again by Special Agent T.E. Hawley.

His red, meaty face and peppermint breath were close enough that I smelled the bourbon it was supposed to hide. He was sure I was about to break. "Where can I find him?" he demanded again in that bully's voice I knew so well.

I woke up screaming, "You're dead!"

CHAPTER 3

WE RENTED A SMALL COTTAGE IN ATLANTA BEHIND AN OLD MANSION IN A SHAB-by-genteel neighborhood that had known better days and would see worse as people bought the new homes farther out. The white-haired old woman on a cane who shuffled to the door was frail and sparrow-like. Her blue eyes were faded but there was no mistaking the spark of sharp intelligence.

"Dear lady, we've come about the ad in the paper," Lowell said in the stagy Southern manner he could put on. If he had a planter's hat he would have swept it from his head to his chest with a bow.

Eleanor Rowan's face lit up in a smile at this courtesy from an earlier time and she invited us to a sitting room I thought had seen little change since the Confederacy. It had heavy furniture with thick legs, dark green patterned wallpaper, and lace curtains at tall windows. She ordered coffee when a plump, aproned woman with a rosy face came in answer to the little bell she tinkled.

"Where all y'all from?" Mrs. Rowan asked. She wore a gray shawl over her flowered dress even though the day was warm.

"We're from…" I started to say.

"I guess you could say from all over," Lowell interrupted. "But chiefly Virginia where I an in the peanut business. Our sales could use some firmin' up in these here parts, so I'm looking round for more retail stores. Do you like peanuts, ma'am?"

"I liked them well enough when I was young, but they're hard on me at this time of life." It seemed she was going to pat her stomach but thought better of it. They are very ladylike with strangers in the South.

"We also deal in other members of the legume family, of course. Walnuts and pecans and so forth, but our principal interest is peanuts. The soil and climate of Virginia grows 'em best of all. Your average peanut…"

"I see," she said with a nod, her interest in the subject evidently not strong. "My late husband was a vice-president of the Illinois Central System, which hereabouts was the Central of Georgia Railway before it was taken over by Yankees. That's his picture over there." A hard-faced man with mutton chops glared furiously from the frame as if saying, "How dare you!"

Warming her up with little courtesies and his natural charm, Lowell effortlessly spun a story. His company had the pleasure of doing business with her husband's railroad before pulling out of the soybean market on account of declining profitability for that commodity. "I'm sure those who went before me must have known Mr. Rowan personally."

"I'm sure they must have," she said. "Vanover made a point of being on good terms with our customers. That picture makes him look stern, and I admit he could show his temper pretty regular, but he also had a side most never saw. I sent out I don't know how many cards at Christmas time, each one hand-addressed with a personal note that he dictated to me." The coffee came on a tray in delicate bone china with a pretty floral pattern.

Quite forgotten, I listened to them chatter on like old friends. Speaking of nuts, Lowell said, the chestnut blight is a terrible thing; nobody knows how many trees have gone down but they must be in the millions. She responded by saying the change from steam locomotives to diesel was a source of grief to her and she imagined many others.

"I loved to hear that lonesome whistle," Lowell agreed. "I believe there's a song with them very words."

"I wouldn't be the least surprised," Mrs. Rowan said. "Hearing the whistle just leaves a kind of ache in the heart, doesn't it?"

"I have often felt it, ma'am."

They continued on until Mrs. Rowan remembered I was there. "What a fortunate young woman to have such a nice husband," she gushed. "Would that my daughters had done as well. They…well, never mind. How long have you been married?"

"It's been five years now, hasn't it, dearest?" Lowell said, answering for me.

"I robbed the cradle and it was worth it."

Oh my, Mrs. Rowan said, aren't you funny?

I asked if we could see the house out back and she hobbled on her cane to a drawer. "Take your time," she said, giving the keys to my husband. "I know you'll love that little house. I only rent it to people I think are right."

It was a small museum of times past, charming in its way. "It sure beats hotels and auto courts," Lowell said. "Good news," he said from the kitchen, "it's got a Kelvinator instead of an icebox."

It was furnished throughout with antiques that Mrs. Rowan no doubt thought of as just old things. "Maybe at one time this was for the coloreds and Servant Quarters stuck as the name," Lowell said as he tested the four-poster bed. "They wouldn't waste this on hired help; it must have been for family when they didn't all fit in the big house."

"What a whopper you told," I said. We hadn't made up a story, so what he said to Mrs. Rowan was made up on the spot. "Peanuts and chestnuts, how did you ever come up with that?"

"The fugitive life teaches a man cunning; anyhow most people aren't as suspicious as you. Remember when you didn't believe a word I said until you started checkin' around? That's what led the FBI to me, not that I'm complaining, far from it. Aside from making it through the war by the skin of the teeth, you're the best thing that's happened to me."

He went to the window to look out as I was bathed in warmth and tried to hide a smile; Lowell didn't pay compliments as often as a woman might like, but they came from the heart when he did.

"It's going to get hot before long here and we'll have to raise the windows at night. I wonder if this is far enough away so she or that other one won't hear you when you go to sleep. Those screams you let off curdle the blood even if you're used to 'em."

We'd had a scare one morning when a man at an auto court office said he almost called the police because his wife thought I was being murdered. "He didn't want to get his lazy butt out of a warm bed," Lowell had said as we drove away. "Maybe next time we won't be so lucky."

I thought the strain from worrying all day about the police stopping us caused my sleep problem and we should get off the road for a time and this little home fit the bill perfectly. We moved our few things in and the next morning Lowell ran a finger down the listings in the Southern Bell directory.

"Here's somebody who specializes in neurasthenia and female problems."

Gray is the color Dr. Wirtz brought to mind in his office in the back half of a residence on a leafy street. His hair, the carefully-trimmed Freud-style beard, his slacks, shirt and sweater were all gray, even his soft voice seemed in some way gray. He asked what doctor referred me, and I said my husband, who was in the next room reading the sports pages, looked him up in the Yellow Pages.

The answer seemed to disappoint him, but he straight off began asking about my medical history, taking notes in a small, fussy hand. He went through my childhood, my education (he said I struck him as an intelligent woman), my health, my diet, and any unhealthy attachments I could think of. I answered his questions as fully as I felt I should.

"And so when did these nightmares start?"

When I told him, Dr. Wirtz said it was unusual that I should be as exact as to the date. "Was there some traumatic event on that day?"

I said yes, but I preferred not going into detail. That made his eyebrows go up, but we passed on to other things. Then suddenly in a very loud voice: "DOES YOUR HUSBAND BEAT YOU?"

"Certainly not," I said indignantly. "I wouldn't put up with such a thing."

The soft voice was back. "I have had patients deny it as angrily as you, but further in the course of treatment it develops that the moment of trauma was a slap in the face, a kick, or a knock down by closed fist. It is only when this event is acknowledged by the conscious mind instead of continuing to fester in the subconscious that the healing process commences."

"You'll have to come up with another theory," I said coldly.

"He is a very handsome man despite his years; women have been drawn to him all his life I should think. Wives confront husbands on the issue of fidelity and violence frequently ensues. Out of a misplaced sense of shame, they shrink from telling others. Do you mind if I ask him?"

"Are you joking?" I said. "Why would he admit it if he did?"

"I'm a trained observer of human reactions, highly trained if I may say so. I'm not deceived by even the most practiced of dissemblers. Eyes shift, feet shuffle, the rate of respiration increases, all of these I observe. Others in my profession might approach the question differently, but I believe time is gained by directness. Going to the horse's mouth so to speak."

"I was hoping for a prescription for sleeping pills."

"They would merely mask underlying problems and the possibility of an addiction must be taken seriously."

I was torn between laughing in his face and walking out. Instead, I sat back in the chair. "Okay, go ask him." He rose and silently left the room. He returned with cheeks flushed.

"He said he beats you like a drum." He paused, hesitant. "But I had the sense he was being humorous. Then he used an expression I haven't heard before. What does it mean to beat someone like a rented mule? He was joking, yes?"

"Obviously."

"I didn't understand the reference, but perhaps it is not important."

"If you don't own the mule, you don't care about it as long as the work gets done."

"Ah, yes, I see now – that would be an example of rural humor." He shuffled papers on his desk and peeped at me from under his eyebrows—gray, of course. "I am told I can be too serious at the expense of…" He cleared his throat. "Still, jokiness can be a mechanism for distancing the individual who jests from the person who…" Doctor Wirtz saw my impatience. "But to return to your sleep problem."

"Thank you," I said, hoping not to sound hard; he struck me as a man with a sensitive nature. We finished the session and he walked me to his door, not looking at Lowell.

"He's so quiet he took me by surprise," Lowell said in the car. "I'm reading along about Mickey Mantle's heel spur and his face comes over the newspaper and he says, 'Do you beat your wife?' Like a drum, I say automatically. He turns away and I say, 'Like a rented mule' to his back. Laughing by then, of course."

"He believes something terrible happened to give me these nightmares, which is true. He's trained to catch people in falsehoods, but he seemed sheepish when he came back."

"I bet you regret the day you first set eyes on me," Lowell said, strangely downcast.

"Come here, you," I said, hugging and kissing him. "What you said about the best thing that ever happened to you goes double for me."

"We'll get through this and be free as birds," he said.

But that kind of life was the last thing I wanted, natural as it was to him. Restless movement from here and there was the pattern for the greater part of his life. First, as a child shuffled from one boarding school to another, and then as a career naval officer. When he smuggled himself back from Europe after the war—we haven't progressed here that far in his reminiscences—he was continually adrift and even a hobo for a time.

Then he went to ground as he said for five years on a farm owned by a reclusive miser without family after Lowell, bearded and unshorn like John the Baptist, had arrived on his doorstep in a storm. He was given room and board in return for laboring in the fields.

When the old man suddenly died, Lowell dug up the money he had buried, assumed his identity as a retired commodore, and turned to life as a rake and gambler until his luck turned bad. It was then that he ended up at the retirement home where I met him.

THE BRANDY Churchill called for was too valuable for a footman to handle, so Hobbes the butler came in with the dusty bottle on a tray, carrying it like it was something holy. He waited for Churchill's nod to speak. "Gentlemen," he said in a voice like he was in church, "this was bottled in 1789, the year of the French revolution; the Bastille was being stormed as it left the cask." That made several of them sit up and take notice.

"How many bottles are left?" Churchill asked, looking round the room for reactions. "Only nineteen, sir," Hobbes said.

"Does the duke know we're availing ourselves of this treasure," Churchill asked.

"It requires a special key, so yes His Grace knows."

As Hobbes went round pouring the brandy he was startled to find me. "Sir," he said in a humble voice, looking sorry he hadn't been aware of my high standing. I nodded, showing I was big enough to forgive a man an honest mistake.

"To the king," Winston cried and everyone took sips, except I took a good swallow. Grand stuff for a simple sailor.

"Good Lord," said William Strang, a diplomat type, as he held his glass to the light to look at the color, "it's beyond praise." Nobody else spoke as they rolled the brandy around on their tongues. Sir Robert Vansittart closed his eyes like a man praying. He was a lean and good-looking fellow, a cousin of Lawrence of Arabia it turned out. He wrote poetry but otherwise seemed all right. He worked for Chamberlain in some important diplomatic job before he got kicked upstairs so nobody would pay any attention to him.

"Truly the nectar of the gods," Churchill said at last. "Napoleonic, the name for brandy of this superb vintage, was not yet a word that struck terror into the heart of man even as Hitler does now." Hobbes was heading for the door. "Did you want him to leave the bottle?" I said alertly, "it's probably half full."

Winston had a big smile. "Our young American friend has put our thoughts to words." He had introduced me to the few men I hadn't met already as his cousin from America who has the ear of certain people in Washington he could not name. "Yes, leave the brandy and express our deepest thanks to the duke, as I shall do when I see him." After more praise for its mellowness and so on, the serious talk started up again.

"That first Munich meeting was a fiasco down even to the superficial details," Colville said. "It was a mistake for Chamberlain to take such a small party. The two of them, a bodyguard from Scotland Yard and a female secretary. Even that fool Horace Wilson now admits as much. They were met at the airport by a throng of Prussians in full uniforms and chests full of medals. The road was lined to Hitler's mountain residence by SS troops in jackboots and their sinister black uniforms; they leaped to attention and presented arms as the car passed. Chamberlain hasn't let on what he thought except to say Hitler struck him as 'the commonest little dog,' but Wilson was thoroughly cowed. I read his notes on the meeting. He wondered if they would come out of it alive."

"The value of first impressions with Germans cannot be overstated," Churchill said. "I would have taken a regiment of civilian and military aides, the latter in uniform wearing the medals awarded for vanquishing the Huns in the Great War."

Vansittart swirled the brandy in his glass. "They flew off into the blue with the bright faithfulness of two curates entering a pub for the first time; they did not know the difference between a social gathering and a roughhouse; nor did they realize that the tough guys assembled neither spoke nor understood their language. They imagined they were as decent and honorable as themselves."

Strange said quite right. "It was the first time Wilson had been on an airplane and only the second for Chamberlain. They seldom visit Europe, speak a foreign language, know what Europeans are like, and don't have the slightest conception of the enormity of Hitler. Their whole upbringing conspires against understanding that such people could exist. Beyond that, the prime minister has an ill-judged and naïve belief in his judgment and powers of persuasion."

"I said at the time," Winston said, "that the government had to choose between shame and war. They chose shame and they would get war." Neville was a good enough mayor for the Midlands, he said, but in over his head when it was more complicated than drains or road work.

"He didn't think much of the Czechs as a country or a people," Eden said. "Not out of the top drawer, he said, or even of the middle. It didn't help that President Benes was recorded calling him a 'Nazi bootlicker.' The ambassador's language was even worse."

"I read the transcript the Germans very thoughtfully sent," Vansittart said. "Jan Masaryk said Neville 'is longing to lick Hitler's backside,' and Wilson 'is nothing but a jackal.'"

Churchill said if it were up to him he would assign Wilson to a lower place in the animal kingdom. "The Czechs were under a great deal of mental strain, rightfully fearing the worst, and I think a charitable view should be taken of conversations that were meant to be private."

Eden sadly looked back. "How it must have wounded President Hacha to return to Hradcany Castle from his meeting with Hitler and be directed then and in the future to enter through the servant's entrance."

Colville said the Germans had a genius for humiliation that couldn't be matched by any other people

"You would have gotten on better with the prime minister if you hid your brilliance a little more," Vansittart said to Eden. "He was forty-nine years old when elected to parliament and you were only twenty-six. That alone was enough to cause resentment, but you compounded the offense by becoming foreign secretary at thirty-eight."

"It wasn't so much that," Vansittart went on, "as the habit of flaunting your superior intelligence and connoisseurship. I'm reminded of your many corrections during cabinet meetings. 'But, prime minister, I take it you can't know the Franconians when you say that. Now, when I was living in Nuremberg...' That insufferable manner gets under a man's skin, even someone as cold and impassive as Chamberlain."

"I would not say that was my manner, but his ignorance on many matters is provoking," Eden said. "The prime minister believes Mussolini and the Italians are a real power to be reckoned with, just to choose one example. His brother assured him that was so. That is why he refused us permission to protest when Italian ships sank our foreign flag shipping during the Spanish civil war. The fact is Mussolini and the Italians are paper tigers. As for my 'brilliance' if it can be called that, it won't be a problem when you are at Number Ten, Winston."

Churchill tipped a long, gray ash from his cigar and said a good many facts were fastened to the strong memory he was blessed with. "But the future holds many imponderables."

"The taunting and mockery of the Poles, and Colonel Beck boasting that the Germans know Poles are not Czechs and that he has won the war of nerves have thrown Hitler into ungovernable rage," Eden said. "Hitler was prepared to like the Poles at first because they hated Jews as much as he did, but turned against them when they refused a corridor to Danzig. The Poles think they are not only a great people but a great nation, the equal of Germany, France and England, and greater than Russia."

That stirred 'em up.

"What rot," one said.

"The very idea," another said.

"Well, the Poles might be right about Russia," a third chimed in, "but I wouldn't want to argue that case before a judge." There were a few chuckles around the room.

Eden stayed serious. "Hitler says the German minority in Poland is being brutally mistreated, including castrations. It is something one always hears from him at the height of these crises. 'They will see! They will see!' He shouted and pounded his fist into his palm. There is a reliable witness of that scene."

Colville looked up from his glass. "The Viennese doctors would say he has a castration complex. Do any of you know Burckhardt, the former League of Nations High Commissioner in Danzig? No? He is a dapper, smart, fresh-colored Swiss aristocrat who speaks the most beautiful French. He told me that on some days Hitler is the most profoundly feminine man he has ever met, and there are moments when he becomes almost effeminate. He thinks he has a dual personality, the first being that of the rather gentle artist and the second a homicidal maniac. He has never met any human being capable of generating so terrific a condensation of envy, vituperation and malice."

I never got around to learning the name of the man with the moustache, but he looked like he knew what he was talking about. "When Wilson was sent back to Germany for further discussions, Hitler flew into one of his rages. He said, 'The old Scheisshund must be mad if he thinks he can influence me that way.' When Wilson said the prime minister was not mad, only interested in peace, Hitler lashed out in a vile way.

'The observations of ass-lickers,' he shouted, 'do not interest me. All that interests me are my people in Czechia who are being murdered and tortured by that foul sodomite Benes. I will not stand it any longer. It is more than a good German can bear! Do you hear me, you stupid pig!'"

"When I was still in the government," Eden said. "I attended a briefing where Hitler's hysterical outbursts came up. A source told an M6 agent the Führer is attended by a Dr. Morell who injects him several times a day with vitamins and Pervitin, a drug that is pervasive throughout German society. It allows one to work long periods without fatigue and gives a feeling of power and confidence. It is how he can give that stiff arm salute in cold weather so long wearing only a shirt to impress the public with his strength. President Benes collapsed from a heart attack when told to sign the surrender document, but an injection by this Doctor Morell brought him around and a pen was put in his hand."

"Such a thing would surely have military uses," Winston said, "allowing an army to fight on after the enemy is exhausted and requires rest on the second or third day of battle. Do our people know about this wondrous drug?"

"Our military are an incurious when it comes to that sort of thing," Eden said. "The Americans have something called Benzedrine, but apparently Pervitin is far superior."

"Hitler is said to be impotent and that is the reason for the castration fixation," Vansittart said. "He orders fabricated stories put in the newspapers reporting such atrocities and then is outraged when he reads them. Force is the only thing Hitler understands. The German races must rule and others will only be tolerated, which will be called 'the state of peace.' They will not strike at combatants only; they will massacre women, children, old men; they will pillage and burn. The idea will be to destroy towns, villages, and the whole population."

The room was silent except for the crackling from the fireplace. That went on until I asked what about another touch of that there old brandy? Everybody agreed what a good idea and Churchill did the honors, winking when he gave me a splash more than the others.

What with the heavy meal and wines and that brandy nearly as old as the U.S. of A., I was half-dozing when Hobbes came in with a frozen-looking dispatch rider with frosted-up goggles pushed high on his leather helmet. He peeled off a fur-lined glove to take an envelope from his shoulder bag and and handed it to Winston. Hobbes escorted the man out before Winston opened it and read it twice.

"A source in French intelligence says Chamberlain has offered Germany a bilateral treaty that would nullify the guarantees we have given Poland and offered the loan of a million pounds to sweeten the deal." People jumped up talking, Eden loudest of all.

"It is a disaster. Hitler will see it as contemptible, a cheap attempt at a bribe," he said. "The French will know we've gone behind their backs and the Russians will be glad they decided to sign that treaty. It gives them time to prepare for Hitler's inevitable attack."

"It is worse than that," Vansittart said. "Hitler will gamble he can invade Poland and neither we nor the French will lift a finger. The Russians will be boiling with anger because this proposal says Poland is the worthier ally. The Rumanian foreign minister says Poland is the least moral country in Europe."

"Another loan!" Colville cried. He was normally cool as a cucumber, but he looked like steam was about to come out his ears. He banged a fist on a table. "We and the Americans have already granted loans far in excess of the reparations they were to pay but never have for the damage they did to Europe."

I listened to them rave away a while longer and then slipped out; I had more than enough for my letter to the Senator. Roosevelt didn't want his personal spies like me using official channels, I told you that before; he and Harry were afraid somebody at the White House might steam open a letter with a Royal Mail postmark. Cordell Hull was the Secretary of State and you'd expect him to have an oar in the water with war on the way, but nobody told him anything that wasn't already in the papers. The Senator told me if Hull showed up at the White House without an invitation he'd have to prove who he was. Roosevelt would be too busy to see him anyhow.

That room had been so toasty warm what with the brandy, the fire, and all the bodies throwing off heat, I had forgot how cold the rest was. You were born and raised in Montana, but us Southern boys take time to adjust to that kind of weather and some never do. Hobbes was standing just outside the door and saw me shiver in a draft like it just came off an iceberg.

"Sir," he said, "I moved you to a more comfortable room; a servant will guide you when you retire." I thanked him and went into the ballroom where a lively orchestra played and people twirled round working off that big dinner. Women wore furs over their bare shoulders and men standing to the side blew on cupped hands. A handsome woman came up to me, forties, early-fifties, quite the beauty when young if I was any judge.

"Are they deciding the fate of the world in there?" she said, hooking my arm with hers and looking up into my face with what Colville later said were her "practiced arts of allurement."

I can't say, ma'am, I said, being just an ordinary fellow enjoying your fine country. She said never mind, she'd find out later as her husband was in there. "I understand you are Winston's cousin from America." One hundred percent correct, I told her.

"I've known him forever," she said, "and more and more he reminds me of the good little pig who built his home of brick." I haw-hawed and asked who she might be.

"I'm Diana Cooper," she said, surprised. "I'm so used to everyone knowing me that I never introduce myself anymore, isn't that just *too* conceited?"

On the cover of *Time*, I said.

"Oh, that," she said. "I hope there's more to me than what they wrote."

Riot police at your wedding, I said. I hadn't read the article or picked up the magazine more than once or twice in my life, so I didn't think I should run on too long on the subject.

"My," she said, drawing back amazed, "you *are* well informed. I suppose you know I was on Broadway in your country." I didn't, but nodded. "Do you think I look religious; the show business people thought I did. I played Madonna on stage and was quite famous for a short time and then I was a nun in a film. Heaven knows I'm not religious, not in that way, but people will have their ideas, won't they?"

'Deed they will, I said. There's no stoppin' them.

She said come and sit with me and we went to an empty table with a candle. Women her age like that kind of lighting; men don't care about it one way or another unless there's a newspaper they want to read.

"Tell me all about you," she said. Well, ma'am…I began, but she cut me off.

"You could be in Hollywood films yourself you know, a man of your appearance, and your voice is right; so many of the silent screen idols sounded lispy and queer and their careers ended when sound came in. But the problem is you're too big and strong; all the men in Hollywood are small and resent those who are your size."

I told you I saw that myself when the president sent me out to Hollywood with Bill Stephenson to talk the studios into making movies to put the English in a good light and the Germans look evil.

"Are you an American spy?" she asked, cocking her head to one side.

No, ma'am, I told her, Winston had kindly invited me over to get acquainted with the cousins on this side of the pond. "Like Randolph?" she said, making a face. "I don't envy you; the man could pick an argument with a chair." Folks seldom wasted time giving me their opinion of him.

"Are you from the Jerome or the Hall side of the family?" she asked. I was about to flip a mental coin when she called out to a passing man, "Mr. Winant, join us."

John Winant used to be a governor in New England; I couldn't tell you what state. Roosevelt saw him as a future ambassador and he was here to size up things.

"Do you know your fellow countryman...?" she asked. "I'm sorry; I didn't even ask your name!" She put her hand to her forehead in a hammy way.

Lowell Brady, sir, I said. Winant stuck out his hand and smiled sadly, the only way he ever did that I saw. He reminded people of Lincoln; he even looked like Honest Abe a little, shaggy eyebrows and hair, a lean, long face. He had a way of slowly searching for words; he gripped and ungripped his hands when he did it. That made for pretty long gaps in the conversation; you'd think he'd finished talking and then he started up again. On the receiving end of this, as I was a few times, you looked at the floor and wondered if time stopped. When he did it in a speech, you could see men and women in the audience straining to keep from calling out words. People at the embassy looked like cornered animals when he headed their way.

We chit-chatted a bit, Lady Diana smilin' brightly through his silences, and then he excused himself to go put the brakes on some other conversation going on. He might have known the effect he had, but there wasn't a thing he could do about it.

"Poor man," Lady Diana said, "he suffers so. He's been in love with Sarah Churchill since he came over; she's a saucy little flirt but he took it seriously, earnest man that he is. They're both married so it makes matters difficult."

She asked if I'd met my Cousin Sarah and I said I hadn't had the pleasure as yet. "She's married to a comedian of all things. Winston hates him, but he's really quite funny, poles apart from worthy but dull Mister Winant."

There's a little something for Roosevelt, I thought; as I told you the president loved gossip, the spicier the better. Harry Hopkins told me he sprang it on people to watch their mouths fall open. They asked how he could possibly know that, whatever it was, but the chief would just smile and say a little bird told him. It added to the feeling people had that he knew more than anybody, and maybe even something about them they didn't want to be general knowledge.

Women mostly rest up during the day at these shooting weekends so they can shine in the evenings, but being out in the cold all day and then all that food and booze—well, I started yawning and couldn't stop for the life of me.

"I can see I'm keeping you up," Diana said huffily.

"No…no," I said, trying so hard to hold another back that my eyes watered. She stood and walked away. I guessed her pride was hurt.

I started climbin' the stairs and took some wrong turns down the long corridors and backtracked till I was on course again. There was no electricity, meaning full time jobs for who knows how many people. They went through the castle twice a day lighting or putting out candles in lamps and replacing ones burned down to stubs; there were hundreds and maybe thousands of them. And the lamp chimneys had to be cleaned, a lot of work right there. They were a different gang than the ones who lit the fires and cleared out ashes in the fireplaces. One ranked higher than the other, but I never found out which.

I stopped on a landing to draw breath—Winston and Colville must have had to sit down more than once on the climb—and saw a young footman at the door to the better quarters Hobbes had assigned me. His back was to me as he peered toward the darkness at the end of the corridor.

"Thank God you're here, sir," he said in a trembling voice when I heaved alongside. The man was shaking like a leaf. What's wrong, I asked. "It's the ghost," he says, "don't you feel it?"

You hear a lot of those stories in the South where the nigras are great believers in haints, and quite a few white people for that matter, but I never paid no mind to them. It was cold enough before but now I saw my breath in the air and felt hair standing straight up on my scalp. Something pure evil was headed our way.

The footman shot off real sudden but I caught up and passed him going full bore. He gave out a scream from behind and I was just about flyin' down the stairs. You work up heat running flat out like I was, but the back of my neck was getting even colder. Up the next corridor, down the flight of stairs at the end, arms pumping like pistons, knees high like Jesse Owens at the Olympics. I rounded a corner and snatched open the first door, slammed it shut, and crawled beneath a high four-poster to the head of the bed next to a chamber pot.

I've been scared plenty of times in war, but this was different. When things are blowing up or bullets clip past close enough to feel the breeze, it's plain luck whether you get hit or not. But this darkness or evil force or whatever you want to call it had a will to do me personal harm, I knew it as sure as you're sittin' there. But it seemed it couldn't see around corners and passed on by. I knew because the faint light under the door blacked out for a couple of seconds and came back. I lay cowering like a farm dog waiting to be beat for killing chickens. Maybe fifteen minutes passed and I was starting to screw up my courage to crawl out when the door opened and a couple came in and lighted candles.

My wits were still somewhat froze up by fear otherwise I would have rolled out, claimed I was in the wrong room and I'd been looking for a cuff link. But you've got to do that straight off to be even a little believable—searchin' for something in the dark is hard to swallow in the first place—and I'd already waited too long for that unless I blamed it on being dead drunk. So I lay still whilst they got ready for bed, thinking I'd clear out when they dropped off, which I hoped wouldn't be long. I saw her feet at the dressing table and he was sitting above me on the four-poster. His trousers dropped to the ankles and he peeled socks off skinny, hairless legs as white as a bar of Ivory Soap.

"Tell Harvey tomorrow to press these," he said. An older man to judge by his voice. He massaged his foot like it hurt.

"Tell him yourself, I'm not your slave." She was up in years too and cranky from the sound of it. He gave out a long sigh like he put down a heavy load. "Can we please maintain a small level of politeness?"

She said nothing and he walked across the room in bare feet to a closet. The purple satin dressing gown there reached nearly to his matching slippers. "I don't know why Manners bothers with these parties. He is the least companionable of people; the man scarcely says a word and always looks like there is a bad smell nearby."

"For their children," she said. "They have to see and be seen and if they are to have a life in society."

"It's overrated if you ask me."

"I didn't."

"What?"

"I didn't ask you."

A long silence. "He wants something from the government," she said.

"Who does?"

"Who are we talking about? The Duke of Rutland, of course."

"Silly me, I thought we'd moved on."

"Like the rest of the earls he doesn't want troops quartered in his castle smashing things up if there's war."

"There's not going to be war," he said sounding like he'd never heard anything so dumb. "Poland!"

"Alex Hardinge told me he wants Belvoir used to store government records. Why do you think there won't be war? Did you see the looks on the men with Winston after dinner? No, of course you didn't, you were with Vickie Holland."

He sighed.

"When you have too much to drink you think you're invisible."

"I didn't have too much to drink."

"You fell asleep at the table!"

"I did not!"

"I suppose I should be grateful to Vickie for sobering you up. Tell her next time you see her she's too old to dress like a trollop, years too old."

"There's no point talking to you when you're like this." The candle was blown out on his side of the bed.

"She's put on weight, too. Did you notice?"

Silence.

"On her bum."

"Oh, for God's sake, do shut up! It was years ago."

The candle on her side went out. From the mattress sags, they lay on opposite sides. That's married life for a lot of people, but not you and me. Give us a kiss, sweetie! So I lay there a long time waitin' for them to doze off, pinching my nose because the maid didn't empty the chamber pot.

Then he stirred a little. There was enough light from the crack under the door to see his feet slide into the slippers. There was a swishing sound—I guessed the dressing gown—and he tiptoed to the door and slipped out. She didn't move a muscle so I thought here's my chance. I waited a minute to be on the safe side and slid out silent as a snake through grass. I reached the door and she spoke in a voice like ice.

"Vickie isn't receiving company tonight...or did someone get there first?" I didn't envy that old boy when he sneaked back.

CHAPTER 4

WE SETTLED INTO A QUIET ROUTINE IN ATLANTA THAT SUITED ME BUT MADE MY husband fidgety as spring moved toward summer. He hankered for the open road while I was happy to sit with a book in my lap and enjoy the dogwoods in bloom. "Don't get too comfortable," he kept reminding me. He worried inactivity would dull our edge; our bags were ready for us to leave on a minute's notice. "The feds have sorted this out by now and they're back on our trail."

But my feeling was surely the shootout must have caused them to wonder why continue this travesty. Lowell wouldn't be moved, however. "Don't kid yourself, Hoover never forgets and he'll keep the pressure on the field offices. The stakes are the same as they ever were and maybe more because of the blunder. They'll find a way to blame us and add more charges to what they cooked up in the first place."

With time for unhurried thought, I began to wonder if Lowell craved excitement the way the addicted person does his drug. He had spent time in the rarified company of the dazzling Roosevelt and Churchill circles and then was engulfed in the maelstrom of war. All those narrow escapes and hardships followed by years of living by his wits and expecting the knock on the door at any moment—or more likely battered down by men with guns drawn.

It would be strange if his brain hadn't become conditioned to overactive alertness and find quietude hard to bear. I also had the leisure to worry about this account straying from its purpose—the transcription of his unique perspective on great events of a tumultuous time—into these diary-like wanderings of its transcriber. But I know a future historian will know which passages to excise, leaving my personal remembrances to the exegesis of some poor doctoral candidate as yet unborn.

Lowell kept himself busy most mornings doing fix-up work on Mrs. Rowan's house, unsticking drawers and doors, repairing leaks, and doing a myriad of other repairs needed from years of neglect. In the afternoons he was gone, supposedly to drum up business for the peanut company, but in reality he played penny-ante poker at the American Legion hall.

"They invited me to sit in on the big game in the back, but I learned my lesson."

His work on her house endeared him to Mrs. Rowan; she often had him in for tea and cake and to show him off to lady friends from church. One was an amateur musician, and he sang "I'll Be With You in Apple Blossom Time" as she played the spinet in the sitting room. "He's as good as Bing Crosby," Mrs. Rowan said proudly. That was hardly so, but I smiled and agreed. My exhaustion from lack of sleep and the dark circles under my eyes made her think I suffered some illness we did not want to talk about. She was the very soul of kindness to me.

I continued to see Dr. Wirtz twice a week. I talked lying on a leather sofa and he listened in his various ensembles of gray that made me think of a film negative. He maintained a Delphic silence during our fifty minutes, only taking notes from time to time. I never saw any other patients enter or leave and the receptionist there at first disappeared after my first few visits. She was a severe older woman with a heavy bosom and hair parted in the middle pulled back so tightly it gave me a headache to look at her.

Dr. Wirtz must have listened for me thereafter because he came out right away to escort me into the inner sanctum. I didn't have screaming nightmares anymore, to Lowell's relief, but I still woke him with my thrashing about.

"This 'friend' you mention from time to time who has difficulty remaining in one place," Dr. Wirtz asked, "it might be that he is running from something?"

I was startled because I didn't remember mentioning this, but much of what I said was free-association babble he encouraged in the hope a diagnostic nugget would turn up.

Noting my surprise, Dr. Wirtz said, "Sometimes the patient is not aware he or she says something revealing or that a 'friend' is sometimes a proxy for one's self. Perhaps a traumatic experience occurred to your husband that led to his compulsion always to be on the move. Many men came home from the war with psychic wounds hidden even from themselves. I have had considerable experience in cases where standard treatments do not work and a new approach is necessary."

"He's not the one having the bad dreams," I reminded Dr. Wirtz.

"No," he said, "but at a certain level perhaps there has been transference." I'm sure my doubt showed. "You mean if he has a problem, it's causing *my* dreams?" I said.

He rested his chin on one hand as he looked at me; yes, he said, even though the layman might think this absurd. "You wouldn't necessarily be aware of this transference, but the mind is a strange and complicated mechanism that we are only taking the first baby steps to understand. Would you be willing to undergo a procedure I have in mind? It is one I have performed very successfully but has become the subject of misrepresentation and controversy and as a result has been overshadowed by dubious experimental methods like electro-convulsive shock treatment and hydrotherapy. It's called a transorbital lobotomy and I have personally performed it more than two thousand times. Changes for the better have been experienced by many of my patients, and they often go home to their families the same day. I can do it right here in the office, no hospital involved. You have spoken of the dread you feel before going to bed. Wouldn't it be wonderful to return to deep, restorative sleep?"

Oh, how I long for it, I told him.

"I enlarged my professional emphasis when I realized, like others in my field, that although psychoanalysis can give gratifying results in many cases, certain problems lay beyond conventional treatment. But two approaches combined can be more effective than either alone." I asked him to tell me more about the procedure.

"To be a successful wife is a career in itself, requiring the abilities of a diplomat, a businesswoman, a good cook, a trained nurse, a schoolteacher, a politician and a glamour girl. You have assured me your husband is not prone to violence, but if he were I would counsel avoiding arguments; indulge his whims, help him relax, and share his burdens to foster domestic harmony."

Lowell and I got along pretty well, I told him. Dr. Wirtz seemed to hesitate before continuing.

"I induce sedation with two quick electric shocks to the head. I then roll back one eyelid and insert an instrument smaller than a pencil into the patient's head. Guided by markings that show the depth of penetration, I tap the instrument with a small hammer and its point enters the frontal lob. It is then manipulated back and forth in a swiping motion."

He glanced at the window, not seeing my shudder. "I learned the technique at the Athens Asylum in Ohio under the direction of the great Dr. Freeman, who trained under Egas Moniz, who won the Nobel Prize for Medicine in 1949 for inventing the procedure and who has himself—Dr. Freeman, I mean—performed more than three thousand lobotomies. If you wish to contact him as a reference, he will attest to my skill and how common the procedure is."

I said I would have to talk to my husband before going any further. "You may encounter some resistance," Dr. Wirtz warned. "The average person has a superstitious dread of brain surgery, seeing it as a desperate last resort when as I have said it is quite common. If you like, I will speak to him."

Lowell turned off the baseball game and put down the sports pages to listen when I got home; he laughed when I finished. "That'll teach us to look in the Yellow Pages for a doctor." He looked at me more closely. "Hey, wait a minute! You aren't seriously considering this?"

Seeing his astonishment, I realized the enormity of what I had drifted into like a ship blundering toward rocks in a fog—the insidious gray fog of Dr. Wirtz's soft voice. "He said I'd be able to sleep better," I said weakly, feeling my cheeks burn. How could I have given this even a second's thought?

"For crying out loud, that's like putting a gun to your temple because of a headache," he said. "What about sleeping pills, what happened to them?" I said Dr. Wirtz feared the possibility of addiction. "What about the possibility of losing your mind?" he demanded. "What about that?"

He looked at his watch. "There's a doctor who drops by the legion hall every day to knock back a couple and shoot the breeze. Nice guy. I'm going to ask him about this character." He came back a couple of hours later. "The guy's a quack. My pal doesn't know anyone who refers patients to him. He says this operation is known in the profession as 'psychic mercy killing.' He guesses Wirtz is pushing it because he needs the money; he heard the guy's receptionist quit because he was a month behind on her salary. I went into the phone booth then and there and called Wirtz to say you won't be seeing him again. I used some pretty salty language on him."

Just after dinner two policemen came to the door. "Yes?" I said, opening it with a pounding heart as Lowell listened from another room. "We're looking for a man named Henry Brown," one said.

"My husband isn't here. What's it about?"

The older policeman said they had a complaint from a man threatened with bodily harm over the telephone. The officer read from his notes. "The suspect said he was going to come over and knock the man's fuckin teeth down his fuckin throat."

My husband doesn't use language like that, I said, you're at the wrong house. He tipped his hat back on his head and asked if I was Mrs. Brown. I said yes. "Well, we'd like to talk to him for his side of the story. Mind if we come in?"

I said I most certainly did mind and knew my rights. "Come back when he's home."

He asked if I was a patient of a Dr. Wirtz.

"I never heard of him," I said and closed the door. They talked in low voices on the porch for a moment and left.

"They're not going to waste a lot of time on something this petty, but it's time to hit the road," Lowell said, his voice happy.

We drove south to Valdosta and spent the rest of the night there. I slept well and strangely wasn't ever bothered by those dreams again. It was if something in my mind that had come loose was knocked back in place again.

HAVE YOU got that thing turned on, I can't see from here. Okay, where was I? Oh yeah, sneaking down the corridor. A castle full of guests and servants, but I don't think I ever felt so alone except when I was stalked by a tiger in Siberia. When people think of Siberia, they think of the bears. There are plenty of them, but it's also got lots of tigers to make life even more interesting. You can generally hear a bear coming, but with tigers...there I go, off the track again. I didn't have the sense this time there was an evil force in the vicinity, but what guarantee was there it wouldn't come back? I hustled downstairs to where the party was going strong. The ghost experience did the same for me as dancing did the others and I was as sharp and alert as a huntin' dog with a bird in sight. Colville was looking at his watch when I hauled alongside in the library.

"What on earth have you been doing?" he asked. "You're covered in dust."

I gave him the cufflink story smooth as butter, no hesitation at all. He tsk-tsked and said it was a pity maids didn't take as much pride in their work as before the Great War. "They used to be proud of being in service as their forbearers had for generations, but I fear that is a thing of the past now like so many traditions and customs." He told footmen to bring a clothes brush and I was soon shipshape in Bristol fashion as they say there. "If there is that much dust under your bed, the same must be true of others; the housekeeper ought to be informed, but it is not for us to do. The poor woman would be mortified."

I let time pass and as then as casual as can be I said you hear crazy stories about these old castles being haunted and did Belvoir have one he knew about? "Oh yes," he said, "they've all got them. The one here is supposed to be particularly malevolent; an ancient family curse they say. Two eldest ducal sons died in childhood due to witchcraft; I believe two women were put to death for it. That was some time before Heddon, also a first born. The servants in their cottages below the castle still bury containers of urine and fingernails beneath the hearth to ward off evil. I suppose the duke has had his own encounters, which would explain his morbid interest in the occult." He gave me a quick look. "Why do you ask?"

I didn't want to own up to being scared by a ghost; it ain't manly in the best light. Officers in the peacetime Navy were happy to pass around stories to make the other fellow look bad if it got them moved them up the ladder; I did it myself more than once. "One of the footmen mentioned something," I said with a laugh not quite as hearty as I was shooting for.

Lady Diana, who came in looking for a book, joined us. "He's looking rather more alert now than earlier," she told Colville. "I was boring the handsome dog to where he couldn't stop yawning."

Dear me, Colville says, that's hardly gallant. "Retiring so early, Diana? I saw your husband leave for London with the others, the affairs of state I presumed."

"Yes, and leaving me all alone, she said," shooting me a smoking look.

Not to be critical, far from it, but aside from shooting birds or tearing across the countryside after foxes, rutting was the point of those weekends; I believe I already told you that. And the big meals, of course; I don't think the royal family ate as well, though from the paintings of old King Edward, Victoria's son, he didn't push away from the table until the last pea on the plate was gone. People came from the villages the next day to take home leftovers and there were plenty.

The Senator didn't believe in charity; he had ours thrown to the hogs. He was a close man with a dollar and told people who he was sure wouldn't repeat it—that's strong Bible country and people vote in every election—that the ancient Jews must've written it down wrong about the rich man and the eye of a needle. A lot of them couldn't read nor write properly, he said, so mistakes were bound to happen. Why would God let a man make money in this life and punish him for it in the next one? Didn't make sense to him. His hogs were famous for their flavor and won him a wall full of blue ribbons. He said feeding them those leftovers good enough for people to eat was the secret.

"There's Ed Murrow," Colville said, "I must have a word with him."

"Who is he?" Diana asked as he left at a dog trot. Beats me, I said. That was before Murrow got famous broadcasting in the Blitz. "He's an American and important or our friend wouldn't be heading for him at such speed," Diana said.

Murrow is a lanky guy with dark hair, always with a cigarette in his hand. He's on TV a lot these days. A couple of his fingers were yellow from them; he'd light a new one from the one that burned down to the end. Lucky Strikes was his brand, but he'd smoke Chesterfields. He brought his wife with him from New York when he opened up the first CBS bureau in a closet at the BBC. Janet was a nice woman, not glamorous exactly, but not bad looking either. She didn't care much for the big shots and wives he mixed with in England.

"Unless you are important in some way, you aren't very welcome," she told me at a reception where Ed was the center of things and we might as well been invisible. "Abigail Adams was right when she said that studied civility and coldness disguise their malignant hearts." I didn't ask who Abigail was, not wanting to seem ignorant in case she was famous. It looked like Ed and Colville were having a serious talk.

"Are you coming upstairs with me?" Diana asked out of the blue.

I didn't know it then, but upper class Englishwomen could invite men to their boudoir, not for hanky-panky as we might think, but to talk away like they were in the parlor. Nobody thought a thing about it, it being an old custom as you might say. You couldn't get away with that here without gossips getting their jaws going. When we reached her room, considerable warmer than the rest of the castle by the way, she told me to take a seat and she'd be right back.

Preparing herself for *amore*, thinks I, loosening my shoe laces, but instead she comes back in a fuzzy robe and a maid who proceeds to comb out her hair as Diana sits at a vanity and puts cold cream on her face.

"Do you think there will be war?" she asked.

Not a chance, I said. I was peeved at the maid being there, which I think is understandable—a man with a man's appetites and so forth. I thought of saying don't look for us to bail you out again—fool me once, et cetera. But I feared getting a sorehead's reputation and not being invited to dinners and parties and stuff. One word from a duchess would close every door in society.

"The Great War just about ruined the country and another one would finish us off," she said.

The maid gasped, "Oh, please don't say that, Your Ladyship."

"Hold your tongue, Gretchen."

Diana's eyes blazed at her; the newspapers and magazines always mentioned how blue they were. "Cerulean" is what one wrote, another word I had to look up. They called them azure in another paper. I met the famous newspaper publisher Lord Beaverbrook that weekend by the way. He looked like a monkey dropped from a tree, but the man was a dynamo; Winston looked up to him like an older brother with plenty of money who liked to spread it around. All the other newspaper owners inherited their wampum, but Beaverbrook swarmed up from below thanks to genius and the sweat of his brow. I heard him say that a dozen times. He was not a man to hide his light under a bushel, and that monkey face of his rubbed people the wrong way. You didn't see words like cerulean or azure in the *Daily Express*; his paper was for the common man eating fish and chips with his pint .

The maid left and Diana dropped her robe and slipped under the covers of her bed, which was as big as the Conestoga wagons the pioneers rode in. Now we're cooking I said to myself, thinking I'd be waved over, but she kept talking, not missing a beat.

"I've been thinking about writing a memoir even though Duff says I would have to pay people to read it. Why are men such bullies? In a way I'm a link to times unchanged since feudalism; surely that would be of interest to the general reader." I said there's no doubt; I'd read it myself, though personally I wasn't much for books.

"My grandfather's work, if you could call it that, was to ride around the estate every afternoon on a fat, white horse named Perfection with my father or the private chaplain, who was also the captain of the castle's fire brigade and wore spurs under his cassock. An old groom in blue with silver buttons and a top hat jogged behind for these inspections. If it wasn't Perfection it was the landau, the victoria or the barouche." She didn't like these expeditions because of the horse smell and the dung they dropped.

"A huge coachman with a red face was in the box and a footman in a coat almost to the ground sprang up and down to open and close the gates. Tourists lined the road and Grandfather tipped his hat to honor the ancient bond between the nobility and the lower classes."

I said it was rare to see people tip hats back home, though I understood it was common once upon time. That didn't catch her interest either.

The castle was open to visitors free some days. "The unwashed masses is not just a phrase; they brought a smell with them so strong some of the ladies held handkerchiefs soaked in cologne to their noses. They brought their lunches and beer and took off their boots in the garden, where they picnicked and napped afterward." Sunday was when the old man toured his realm with the family, riding in a dog cart with a groom at the pony's head. It was a three-mile walk with the ladies gathering long skirts in their cold hands.

"My Aunt Kitty, having no ability at life, put on all her jewelry one day and drowned herself in Belvoir Lake."

I said I was sorry to hear it and moved my chair closer to the bed.

"One uncle was a correspondent in the Boer War with Winston. He threw himself under a train when he was eighty, another died of fits at a young age, and third of tuberculosis. Uncle Bobby, who won a DSO fighting the Boers and was Master of the Belvoir Hounds, was forty-five and in the Sixtieth Rifles reserve when he was killed in the Great War. These are interesting stories, don't you think?"

I was going to say maybe for another time, not wanting to get her nose out of joint, but she was too quick for me.

"The fox hunting seemed always to be in bitter weather. The ladies wore top hats or billycocks with very black veils pulled tight around their fringes and buns and cold noses. The men wore pink coats and glossy white leathers and drank cherry brandy for warmth. The horses pawed and snorted; some wore signs on their tails that said 'I Kick.' They came home at twilight and fell upon tea and boiled eggs like wolves until it was time to dress for dinner."

They had a man with a white beard down to his waist who shuffled the corridors three times a day beating the gong to announce meals. "We had water men, immense and silent, who trudged through the castle with a wooden yoke on their shoulders supporting huge containers of water on either side for the jugs, cans and kettles in the bedrooms."

Them and the coal men knocked at the doors before coming in, she told me. Is that so, says I, working as best I could to seem interested.

There was a Betsy born in the castle that lived to be a hundred and got a grand funeral. Never learned to read and write and was always laughing, which tells me she wasn't all there. One story after another she gave me. Lots of deaths at the castle, there being so many people living there, and she told me about a good many of them.

"Deaths made me pensive to an unhealthy degree as a child. I was afraid my mother and father would die in an accident and prayed to God that I would be taken before them even though I found the thought of death terrifying."

She fell down a lot as a child and one day her mother noticed she couldn't raise her arms over her shoulders. The doctors said she was bad off and would die young, so her parents decided to make her as happy as possible.

"I no longer had to climb stairs like a stooped gnome, but was carried in a chair."

The result was just what you'd think, a spoiled child who growed up to be a woman who always thought of herself first. I met a lot of them types in my life.

Diana had been on her elbow looking me in the face with those huge eyes, but now she lay back on the pillow yet keeping me in her sights; her voice got kind of slow and dreamy.

"We young girls were raw and shy with shapeless hair held by crooked combs. The gloves we wore above the elbow to balls got dingy as the season went on. We poor creatures suffered great humiliation, for between dances we stood in a sort of slave or marriage market at the door, and the unfortunate ones with few friends or who had been betrayed by a partner, or were victims of muddling the sequences of their dances, became cruelly conspicuous. Those who found such shame unendurable like me could only sneak downstairs to the cloakroom, ostensibly to have dresses mended, and hope not to meet fellow wallflowers in the same predicament."

I'm sure that you...

"I was still forbidden to be alone with a man unless by chance in the country. A married woman had to bring me home from the balls. I could go to the Ritz but no other London hotel." By and by, she grew into her looks and heads turned. Marrying a well-born man with a fortune was her mother's goal for her, but the eligible males were a dull lot and she fell in with a wild set.

"I was part of a madcap group the vile newspapers called the Corrupt Coterie. There were stories about orgies and such nonsense, but we never paid attention. We drove fast in racing cars and flew in aeroplanes; Lady Dudley looped the loop and Sybil Cooper, Duff's sister, took two piglets aloft with a pilot to show that pigs could fly."

Ha-ha, I said, that's funny. I once...

"Faster, madder and different were the thing," she continued, "something bad was bound to happen as one looks back. Someone said what a lark it would be to have supper on a river barge at sunset."

A string quartet from the symphony was hired and off they went.

"Denis Anson was in the rigging straight away and climbing around like a monkey to impress me. Who suggested taking a dip in the Thames? It may, it *may*, have been me. Oh, how I have prayed it was not." The young buck gave her his coat and watch and went into the river and that was that, he drowned along with a musician who dived in to save him. It seems the Thames current is like a tidal bore. There was a big stink in the newspapers and her mother pulled every string so Diana didn't have to testify at the inquest.

I was wondering how long she was going to go on before we got down to business, but next up was the war. Diana and her mad crowd thought they'd better tone things down when causalities got high and soldiers came back with missing limbs and so on. She trained as a nurse and went to work at Guy's Hospital where nobody cared that she was a lady.

"There was a mad woman who had to be walked to the light department and it wasn't easy, more like driving a pig, which I suppose you are familiar enough with. She lay on an iron slab, between four old men, syphilitic, I guess. They were half-naked and pale as bladders of shining lard. Their four noses had apparently drawn all the blood to them that their bodies held and their scalps were as white and hairless as china. Sometimes she managed to swim out of her craziness for three minutes and groan and say 'poor, poor brain—it's that that's gone I know it has.'

"There was a vast woman lying in her own dirt who had a disease called foetid bronchitis. To tend her it was necessary to burn incense near her bed or wear a mask. Every few hours she put on a gas mask snout filled with the strongest disinfectant and breathed it for an hour. She thought it was a part of treatment but it's only for the staff's sake. All the fluid in her lungs despite all her spitting had gone bad inside her. Could anything be worse? You look a little queasy so I won't speak of that anymore.

"A man twice my age named George Gordon Moore from Detroit or some such place showered gifts on me, including an ermine coat to the ankle chosen by my mother and a monkey with a diamond waist bell and chain. Boxes big as coffins came twice a week full of flowers. He was married with children but said he would give up all for me." He began throwing the parties that Colville mentioned. "Those eaten up with envy because they weren't invited called them the Dances of Death," she said.

The young bucks from Oxford were crazy for her--a dozen or so I reckoned from the names she threw out were killed off one by one.

"I would have happily married any of them with the joyous approval of my mother and father, but it wasn't to be. The war went on and on endlessly. Then it was over and someone, I can't think why, said I had the makings of a stage actress. Oh, dear, you're jiggling your knee; I suppose more of your cruel yawns are next. Good night, then; tell my maid she can go to bed."

She turned to her other side and that was that. The maid peeked her head around the corner.

"Is Her Ladyship resting?" She led the way to my new quarters.

I didn't get much shut-eye what with one thing and another running in my mind and must have looked it to Colville, dishing up kippers from a silver chafing dish in the morning room.

"A strenuous night?" he asked with an amused smile.

I thought of giving him the wink guys do, the ones who don't Yee-haw and do a hip grind so everyone knows they hit the jackpot. But he'd dig out the truth if he thought it was worth it, so I admitted I struck out.

"Don't feel bad," Colville said as we walked to a table with a servant following with our plates, "many are called but few are chosen."

We got busy with our knives and forks; fear gives you a tremendous appetite, at least it does me, and I went for seconds.

"She is terrified of being alone," Colville said, "as with her brother, there has always been an unstable side, unreasoning fears, and spells of melancholy and threats of suicide. It's odd given her beauty and delightful personality and family background. So she takes morphine and talks to willing ears until she drops off. Duff doesn't approve of the drug or use it himself, but doesn't object to her using it for the calming effect.

"He was the last man still standing in her set after the war and he realized his great luck. In the ordinary course of events, a man of good family but lacking a fortune could never aspire so high as Diana despite his first-class mind, a medal for bravery in the war, and political acumen that have carried him far. Not foreseeing that outcome, her parents fought the marriage tooth and claw. Remember, she could have married Edward and been the queen had the mutual attraction been stronger. The Royal Prince confided to her how unhappy he was, but that was as far as their intimacy went.

He put his fork down. "I fear the Polish business has taken the wind out of our shooting party. Bundles of telegrams are arriving and generals and colonels are returning to their regiments and admirals and captains to the fleet. There's another batch."

We watched a servant deal out five to men who took them with a stiff upper lip. "Oh, dear," Colville said. "He's headed our way now; it is unlikely it is for me so you must be the lucky one."

I tore open the telegram. "Hell!"

The Navy Department ordered me to proceed to Portsmouth and *HMS Dahlia* to observe sea trials for the Bureau of Construction and Repair, what the Bureau of Ships was called at the time. Every now and then the bastards found a way to stick it to me; it was a game they played. There were plenty of eager-beaver naval aides at the embassy who'd jump at the chance for some fresh sea air in their lungs, but the brass hats were sure I had some dodge going and it made them sore.

"I don't envy you," Colville said when I told him. "The new Flower Class corvettes are basically jumped-up trawlers that are to be used for anti-submarine and convoy duty; the Pekingese of the ocean they call them. I'm told they're damned uncomfortable and would roll on grass if it was wet enough. Small shipyards are turning them out as fast as they can, which usually means corners are being cut."

Dahlia was putting out to sea early the following morning so I took a train to London to pick up my sea bag and push on to Portsmouth, where I spent the night at the Admiral's Head. The rats in the wall enjoyed a high old time scratching and squeaking; the man at the desk the next morning said the building would have to come down to get rid of them.

"They're prodigious breeders, sir, big and fearless when they get their full growth; your average cat is scared of 'em. They come right at a man if you catch them by surprise. Smart, too, they won't go near the poison we put out. People say a trader brought them in the 1800s from a Pacific island famous for the buggers; no doubt he was a Frenchman or maybe Spanish, anyway one of them foreigners we was always fighting. They gnawed their way through a wall when they left the ship, killed off the local rats, and been here ever since."

I told him don't expect any more business from me, and he wasn't a bit surprised. "My wife won't even come into the building." There I am, steering off course again.

Somebody with an evil sense of humor must have named it the Flower Class because Dahlia was as dumpy looking as anything afloat if you don't count garbage scows. The captain, Ronald Blair, a short guy with sandy hair with a lot of gray in it, returned my salute and we shook hands at the top of the gangplank. He had a jolly way and a ruddy face with the lines and wrinkles you get from outdoors work.

"Heavy weather on the way, so this promises to be a real adventure," he said in the laughing but mean-bastard way that says you're not going to like something. He led me around, pointing out this and explaining that. The ship was two hundred feet long with a thirty-three foot beam and a complement of ninety men.

"Why is the mast in front of the bridge?" I asked.

The way he took his hat off, rubbed his head, and put it on again showed he was stuck between diplomacy and telling the truth.

"You'd have to ask the people at Smiths Dock Company in Middlesbrough." He gave me a wide grin. "My guess is incompetence of the grossest sort, which would also explain that squatty funnel and the crew quarters in the foc'sle with the galley aft, making a dog's breakfast of the messing arrangements."

He showed me the depth charger rails that ran over the stern where they hauled in the whales in the civilian version; there were two mechanical throwers and forty depth charges.

"There's no forced air ventilation, so we're hot in summer and cold in winter. An old whaler I met in a pub told me they're natural bastards in any kind of seaway; he said they bounce like a pea on a drum. Sounds like fun, doesn't it?"

We climbed down to the engine room where the black gang was getting up steam.

"A double acting triple-expansion reciprocating engine with a pair of fire tube Scotch boilers. She has twenty-seven hundred horsepower giving a top speed of sixteen knots, hardly a barn burner but good enough for convoy work. Keep it down to twelve knots and she's got a range of thirty-five hundred miles."

We went topside again to inspect the armament, a four pound gun, two twin fifty-caliber Vickers machine guns and twin thirty-caliber Lewis machine guns. "Lightly armed is the word for us." We climbed a couple more iron ladders.

"You will have noticed the open bridge from shore." He was grinnin' again. "The naval architects denied us any hint of luxury; we stand out there in good weather and bad."

The grin left and his face turned as mean as King Kong. "My hope is they roast in hell, the lot of them." He ordered lines cast off and a bosun's mate showed me to my quarters.

It was just big enough to turn around in if you didn't have a cook's gut; the rack was as narrow as a plank and nearly as hard. Our ships are as spartan as jails, but the British take it a step or two more. By bringing my knees part way up to my chest, I just fit without my feet dangling over the end. The stateroom was the second-in-command's, so there was no hope of talking my way into better quarters. Yet it was a rajah's palace compared to what the other had The officers doubled up, the petty officers were four to a stateroom, and below decks the ordinary seamen slept in rows stacked five high. Later they added crew so men had to sleep on table tops or lockers.

We were passing the Southsea Castle Light on the port side when I joined Blair on the bridge with Lieutenant Paget, his second in command.

"Bad weather from Cornwall is headed for the North Sea," Blair said cheerfully. "Gale force winds." The water was already choppy when we cleared the harbor and a wall of dark clouds rose on the horizon. An hour later we were in the storm.

Blair had to yell over wind screaming through the rigging. "Steer oh-six-five." Fortunately, he had a voice as strong as a tenor that needs to be heard when the fat lady cuts loose. The officer of the deck repeated the order, yelling so hard veins stood out in his neck.

Blair stepped closer to me and bellowed, "It will be dangerous as hell out here when we got ice underfoot."

His new grin made me wonder if he was fooling with me; another possibility was he wasn't a full hundred percent upstairs. My eyes and lips already burned from salt spray that slashed at us on the horizontal.

True to the warnings, the ship blew around like it was made of feathers and string, twisting and rolling sickeningly as we hung on for dear life as the masts plunged and rocked in a wild arc. The motion was endless, up and down, a forty-degree lean to one side and then forty to the other. Every dip of the forecastle brought a huge wave down on us that made the ship pause and shudder like it had walked straight into a punch. Seawater roared and foamed past like river rapids aft to the well deck amidships.

I began to think about the changes in its design, weight shifted from one place to another by someone working with blueprints in a warm, dry office. The old design was seaworthy enough when chasing whales, but this was a new warship configuration. These were huge waves, a mile from crest to crest, that bent the bridge and funnel as that wind screamed and clawed at the rigging. Two men disappeared overboard without a trace.

Day after day of this. A sea trial was supposed to identify the bugs, but what if one of them was it sank like a rock in a storm like this? The Admiralty would worry when radio contact was lost, and planes and ships would be sent to search when the storm blew itself out. Maybe a bit of wreckage would be found or a dead man in a life jacket. Something's a bit off in our design, they'd say—Jones, it looks like your mistake. Back to the drawing boards, lads. Jones would hang himself in the garden shed after work. Life would move on.

Men were at action stations—we call them battle stations—because the Admiralty wanted Blair to make the sea trial in combat conditions with a U-boat believed sneaking around for an opening. That meant tight turns and the same drenching at the action stations that the flying bridge got. Cascades of seawater poured into the interior decks from hatches open to get to the ammunition. Another skipper might have said to hell with the Admiralty and rode out the storm battened down, but if Blair wasn't crazy he was one of those blindly obedient types thick as fleas on a dog like with the Germans. They said it was the Prussian influence. "Just following orders."

I'm not saying that's wrong, mind you; it's a smart way to shift the blame if it looks like a court-martial is shaping up. I fell back on it myself more than once.

Back when I was quietly collecting names from the younger officers on who the deadwood and mossbacks were so they could be retired early or moved where they couldn't do any harm, Admiral King himself called me to his office. The man was famous for his foul temper; he woke up mean as a wasp and stayed that way until he had enough booze in him after quittin' time to mellow out and make a pass at another man's wife.

"Are you doing the White House's bidding?" he said in a voice like a whiplash.

A silent lieutenant commander sat in a chair looking like he'd rather be chipping barnacles off a ship bottom with his wife's nail file.

"No, sir," I said.

"My information is that you are," the admiral replies.

"With respect, the information is incorrect, sir."

He kept me standing at attention while he badgered me. "*I'm* doing just fine identifying incompetence in our senior ranks because personally I saw the war coming faster than anybody else," he said. "I don't need the White House's help to smoke them out."

That told me he'd heard something and believed he could force it from me. If I was caught in a lie, that would be a court-martial offense and the man in the chair was his witness. But I was acting on the orders of someone even higher than the chief of naval operations, to wit the commander-in-chief himself, who thought the Navy Department wasn't bringing in new blood fast enough. That was my defense if push ever came to shove, which thank God it didn't. King was a ruthless man and he'd have found a way to get even with me even with the White House in my corner, which as you know by now from what I said that a man couldn't count on with someone as slippery as Roosevelt.

When I left the *Dahlia's* flying bridge nearly frozen and my teeth chattering, they gave me a cup of tea that I could hardly feel in my hands. The men were talking about how everything was wet below deck because of seawater down a ventilator.

"It was like a waterfall," one man said.

The mess was a hell of overturned food and dishes, and spare gear washed around underfoot. A messenger staggering from the engine room to the bridge told a petty officer as he passed me that rivets were loosening and there was worry about the steering gear. "It could go out at any time."

The passageways were like climbing a hill as we rose on a wave and then went down putting you into a dead run if you didn't grab hold of something, all the while bouncing off bulkheads like a billiard ball. Condensation dripped from the overheads nonstop, making it slippery going; the wardroom furniture was lashed down in a corner so it didn't bash itself to pieces. As I made my way aft, a shout came from the head. A reverse flow of cold water from the straight pipe that emptied in the sea spouted geysers in the toilets, catching a man taking a…answering a call of nature. There was swearing you could hear even over the storm.

Cooking was impossible so those that could hold it down ate cold sausages and stew from cans, hard biscuits and tea. I pride myself on good sea legs, so no problem for me. Some guys never do get over the sea sickness that comes on them in heavy weather. Even if they finish at the top at Annapolis, a lot go into another line of work because promotions come from ship command.

A lot of *Dahlia's* crew, maybe half of the poor bastards, mostly reservists, spewed their guts out until there was nothing left but dry heaving. The Frenchies call it *mal de mer*; it sounds nicer that way, don't it?

It took me a half hour of being thrown around in the stateroom to peel off my oilskins, dig my long johns from the sea bag, and get everything back on. When I got back to where you pass from the superstructure onto the flying bridge, a gigantic sea was running from the beam and the captain and a yeoman were lashed to the rail. The ship rose up on a wave like an elevator, teetered at the peak that gave a terrifying view of whitecaps and heaving sea and then dropped into the trough with its wicked, sideways roll. I waited to put my shoulder to the heavy door, not being in a hurry for more tips the captain shouted on the finer points of ship handling in heavy seas. He and the yeoman were cowering at the sight of a wave even bigger than the one before.

The door slammed shut the little I'd opened just before tons of water beat down with a huge boom. Blair and the other man would have been swept away if it weren't for the safety lines. They struggled to their feet spewing water after it passed with another on the way; that was enough even for the captain and he signaled a change of course downwind.

"Thank God," a midshipman said, "I thought we were gonna turn turtle that time."

That means the ship rolls over and sinks, dear girl, all hands lost. Who knows how many lives Neptune has taken over the ages, but it's thousands and thousands. Two crewmen pushed on the door and Blair and the yeoman staggered inside gasping and streamin' water, the hoods and top half of their oilskins torn off. When the captain stopped coughing out seawater, he caught my eye with that grin of his.

"A bit brisk out there." He retched out more water. "They can't say I haven't put her through her paces, now can they?"

In the days it took for the storm to blow itself out *Dahlia* traveled eighteen miles—but it was sideways. Nights were the worst. Sudden waves crashed into the ship in the dark, jarring her end to end. She dove into the troughs, shipping tons of water and sounding like a house collapsing, and then slowly, slowly rose to meet the next one. I wondered each time if she would make it back up before we were buried for good. Sailors are superstitious people and think ships give up just like humans when life gets too much. I'm not saying I believe that and I'm not saying I don't.

People got beat up pretty good from all the jerkin' around; steel doors hit us as we left cabins or people got thrown out of their racks when sleep relaxed their muscles. There were cracked ribs, smashed kneecaps, bruised legs and shoulders, cut lips and foreheads, sprained ankles. If I hadn't mashed my sea bag against the bulkhead, I would've broken a bone or worse. If you snatched five minutes of sleep you were lucky, and just imagine the dreams. I almost wished I was back at Belvoir Castle. The ship was all busted up when we limped back to Portsmouth. The captain had a knot like a pigeon's egg on his head but was still grinning when we said our goodbyes at the gangplank.

"Come back anytime," he called down to me when I was on solid ground. I don't think he heard what I said.

The newspapers on the streets had big headlines about Poland and people on the street looked glum or angry, a lot of 'em depressed as hell. The Germans were massed on the border and ready to let 'er rip. Winston, rushing off as I arrived at his door with my seabag over my shoulder, said Chamberlain and the French were trying to skip out on their promises to Poland. They were begging Mussolini to ask Hitler for more time to palaver—that was Winston's word—but nobody knew if Duce would go along.

"They already offered Hitler everything he demanded, but as I said the Fuhrer has the bit in his teeth. Tell your people I'm making every effort to deflect us from this shameful course." I started to remind him it took awhile for my scuttlebut to get to Washington, but he waved me off. "No time, no time."

I went to the American embassy with my notes on the shakedown cruise to write my report for the Navy Department. I showed it to Admiral Deveral because he eyeballed high-priority cables so traffic didn't get jammed up with run-of-the-mill stuff from people trying to impress the other side of the Atlantic with how important they were; there's a lot of that goes on in the services because if you're not tooting your own horn people think you're slacking off.

The admiral was a tall, beaky man with slit eyes who wore his full uniform at all times, even at his desk. He was so buttoned up I wouldn't have been surprised to find out he had his underwear starched and ironed; his arms barely oved when he walked. Tight as a bull's ass in fly season. I judged him a born paper pusher, the kind that always floats upward in bureaucracies where dotting every "i" and crossing every "t" is what counts.

Like a lot of the Navy brass, he didn't like the way I drifted around with the hazy status I had, free to come and go pretty much as I pleased. They felt it wasn't right to not know what a man in their command was doing. It got up their nose as the British say.

Admiral Deveral found me with my feet up making time with a good-looking secretary from Wisconsin, the cheese state; he told her to clear out and close the door behind her. I stood and put a friendly look on my face.

"You need to make some changes," he said. "Begin by changing questionable seaworthiness to unquestioned seaworthiness." He handed my report back. "You're already in the soup with some important people, I wouldn't dive any deeper. We've ordered twenty Flower Class bottoms from British shipyards."

I felt like I'd been chewed up and spit out. "Before the sea trial?" I said. "Then what was the point of me..."

He cut me off. "We accepted the British assessment of the class because time is of the essence. We have to get ships in the water faster than before in naval history and anti-submarine ships are a priority. If they have the defects you claim, we'll fix them as we go, but it sounds to me that *Dahlia* took a lot of punishment but still got back to Portsmouth safe and sound."

She barely made it, I said; it would take weeks before she's seaworthy. So many rivets worked loose they pumped day and night, even at that there was an inch of water in the engine room. Neither that nor them two hands lost overboard mattered to him.

"It was approved by three committees. This report as sent would question their competence; is that your intention, Lieutenant?"

No sir, I said, not at all.

"Make the changes," says he, "and get it back to me. Delete your reference to the skipper's mental competence, that's none of our business."

Yes sir, no problem, I said.

He lingered at the door. "Nobody gets what you do around here, Brady. I mentioned your name to someone in a position to know and he never heard of you." He paused as if wondering if I'd spill my guts.

"I'm not allowed to say what I am doing, Admiral," I said, "but I can ask permission to put you in the picture."

He had obviously heard the rumors about me and the White House and knew I was the stepson of a powerful Senator. He was too smart to get mixed up in that.

"No, I don't want to know and that's an order."

He flashed a mean smile. "My guess is someone put you on that shake-down cruise to even a score, and I very much doubt they're sorry you ran into a storm so bad men were lost or carried off on stretchers."

I made my lower lip quiver like I wouldn't jump over a nickel even if a dime was waiting on the other side. I told him I sure didn't know what I did to deserve this here treatment.

"Save that act for someone who might fall for it," the admiral said. "After I see your amended report, I wash my hands of this whole business."

When he was gone, I told the switchboard to put me through to Senator Josepha Brady in Washington. It took more time in those days for a call across the ocean and I got busy changing the report so it read like the vessel was top-notch except for a few minor things that might need looking after. I wrote: "It is strongly recommended by this officer after observing a sea trial that the Flower Class be approved by the Navy Department."

There's that look again, darlin'. A man does what he has to get along in this wicked world.

Admiral Deveral looked over my changes in the report and said, "I'll take out how much you admire the foresight and wisdom of the committee members."

I hope God forgives me because a lot of men won't, the ones who got knocked around in heavy seas before the new destroyer escort class came along. Not that those were any picnic; somebody called them the Buckin' Bronco Class. The admiral and I saluted smartly, no one did that better because of my practice in front of mirrors, and he left for the cable room with the report which of course no one would bother to read with the decision made.

When the phone rang with the connection to Washington, I barely made out the woman through the static. "Hello, can you hear me? This is Senator's Brady office."

I asked to speak to him. "He's meeting with constituents."

That meant a lobbyist was finding out how much a vote cost because the Senator would walk a mile to avoid a voter except at election time. Then he put on his false smile and went to county fairs, pancake breakfasts, dinners of grits and greasy possum he could hardly choke down, and the greets-and-meets in muddy fields and old barns swarmin' with flies on the the manure that need to be shoveled out. Someone held his arm to guide him, usually me in dress uniform to awe the backcountry folks.

He would pick up the phone at election time and get me on detached duty no matter where I was or what I was doing. Superiors who objected got straightened out by the CNO's office faster than green grass through a goose.

"I can't spare Lieutenant Brady at the present time because…yes, sir. I'll get right on it."

So you see the prejudice against me wasn't entirely for something I might've done…not all of it anyway. A victim of circumstance is how I'd put it. I told the secretary to say his loving stepson is calling from London.

"Oh my, from all that way? I'll go right in and tell him."

A few minutes passed and the Senator came on the line. "This better be important," he said, not bothering with hello. A man we both know asked me to pass on a message, I told him through the crackling static.

"There's a lot of snow in the passage," is what the Senator heard.

"What the hell are you talking about?"

I went over and closed the door and said it more loudly into the phone.

" Betty, come over here and see if you can understand him." Betty's timid voice came on. "The Senator didn't understand, can you say it again?" I said the man we both know is going to be the First Lord of the Admiralty. There must have been a burp of distortion on her end because I heard her tell the Senator the Good Lord is going to praise us.

"I'm glad to hear it as I have always followed the Word," the Senator replied, "but he better not be calling just to say that." I repeated it to her again and the Senator came on the line. "Has that been made public? No? Good I'll go straight over to...the place we both know to tell you know who." This was to stump anyone listening in.

He hung up and I pictured him telling Betty to order the car so he could get to the President before the newspapers got hold of it. Being first was a way to keep a spot in the circle unless you had some other value to Franklin, but I mentioned that before.

What say we knock off now? I saw an Italian restaurant down the road and I feel like spaghetti tonight. I hope the Chianti is decent; the Italians fob off raw wine on us because they think Americans don't know any better and they're right. They know their tricks in Europe and they can't get away with it there.

CHAPTER 5

WE WERE SUDDENLY IN DANGER OF RUNNING OUT OF MONEY. WE HAD DRIFTED down to Florida until the heat and humidity got unbearable and were on our way to the Southwest when I was informed at a bank in Little Rock that a transfer of funds could not be made from my account. Astonished, I telephoned the Frontier Bank in Missoula, where my family had done business for a generation. Mr. Rodrick, the kindly old assistant vice president who used to give me lollipops when I was a child, was very apologetic. He said the account and those of my brothers were frozen at the request of the federal government. "We assumed it was trouble with the IRS."

"Why now?" I said. Oil and natural gas had been discovered five years ago on property we owned in Wyoming, and Standard Oil paid royalties quarterly, which we divided. "Your brothers went to court to unfreeze their accounts; there was a story in the paper their lawyer put in. You know how folks here feel about government."

Those who didn't work for government disliked our haughty overlords in far off Washington; many employed by federal agencies felt the same but didn't think they should say so outside of family or close friends. I asked why my account was still blocked, but Mr. Rodrick didn't know.

"Where the hell are you?" my oldest brother Buck said when he took my collect telephone call. "You used to give us a ring once a year reg'lar as clockwork." He thought it was funny to exaggerate; the truth was I called often before I entered the fugitive life and Lowell warned me about phone tapping. I told Buck I was traveling in the South and he guffawed. "Let me guess, you can't say more because it's a big, dark secret."

Nashville if you must know, I said snippily.

"And my quiet little sister is an outlaw, is that right?" I pictured his taunting grin; oh, how my lanky, red-haired, big brother loved to tease.

"Have your fun," I said.

We talked about family and farm matters for a bit. Beau, the middle brother, had a leg broken when he was kicked by a horse he was leading from a trailer; the winter snowpack had been thin and there hadn't been enough rain; a two-headed calf had been born up Darby way. I formed a mental picture of the Bitterroot Valley as we spoke and felt a pang of homesickness; it is never lovelier than in the late-arriving spring.

"Why did you say I was an outlaw?"

"Are you?" he shot back, his joshing manner gone.

"What have you been told?"

"They want to talk to you," he said, "and the FBI is in the picture. Rod Troutman told us that off the record; he's back in private practice now." He was a former U.S. Attorney who resigned to run for governor but lost to the incumbent, who wore a bigger silver buckle on his belt. Buck's opinion was that was the deciding factor. "He's still got good connections in law enforcement…what the hell is going on anyway?"

I told him the story as briefly as I could.

"I gotta tell you this is hard to believe," he said when I was done.

Maybe you need to live it to believe it, I retorted.

"You *married* this guy? Sorry for saying it and no offense, but he sounds like a wacko."

Does that make me one too? I said.

"Hang on, don't get huffy."

Hang on? I fired back, I'm about to hang up. "No, no, c'mon," he said appeasingly. "This is a lot to spring on me out of the blue. It's just that…" Then his voice got firm. "The family is behind you whatever's going on."

Unexpectedly touched—we do not know how to handle emotion in my family, preferring to hide behind jokes—I said you don't know how much I appreciate that. I asked if he could get my account unblocked as fast as possible.

"Depends on what you mean by fast," he said. "It took us three weeks and that's only because Troutman goes hunting and fishing with the judge. We weren't the ones they wanted anyhow; they just threw out a net the judge said was big enough for a whale. Luckily, the government decided not to appeal. It'll take longer for you I'd guess, maybe months or a year unless you do what they want. Which, I guess, is talking to them about your new husband."

They want me to lead them to him so they can hush him up for good and I won't do it, I said fiercely, not in a million years.

Buck blustered back that no man was more suspicious of the government than him. "You know that much about me."

But he couldn't believe they would get rid of Lowell, lock him up in some faraway prison or even kill him for something so long ago. I reminded him that J. Edgar Hoover was just one of the big names with reputations on the line.

"Yeah, I see your point," he admitted. He said he would drive to town the next day to see the lawyer. "How do I get in touch with you?"

I'll get in touch with you, I said, half way expecting another cloak-and-dagger joke, but he surprised me again.

"You take care of yourself," he said in a husky voice.

"How much do we have left in the kitty?" Lowell asked as we sat in the clubhouse at the Oaklawn race track in Hot Springs. "Four hundred and three dollars, counting the fifteen dollars and twenty-five cents you won on Rebecca's Dream in the last race," I said. He watched through binoculars as the racehorses with jockeys in gaudy silks caper and dance sideways in the post parade.

"Zeus is takin' a dump, that means he's ready to run," he said. "Post Haste is the favorite, but he's got his front legs bandaged; never bet on a horse with that, same with one that's wearing blinkers for the first time and there's a couple of them in this race. King's Daughter has her mane braided, which means the trainer thinks she'll get her picture in the winner's circle, but I'm going with Zeus."

Zeus won the race easily and earned us fifty-four dollars. "The ponies are fun, but it's hard to make steady money on them," Lowell said. "I'm feeling lucky so I'm going to look up where the poker game is. At every track there's at least one for high rollers at a hotel or some joint in the neighborhood; you just have to know who to ask. I'll start with the bartenders."

Women gave him admiring glances as he made his way to the clubhouse bar; he could have made a living as a dashing older man in slick magazines ads. As I wrote before, he was offered a job as a model for bespoke clothes in New York City, but the peacetime Navy did not look with favor on outside work.

"You'd get dinged in your file," Lowell said, "and promotion passes by without a second look."

It was marvelous to be outdoors in a milling crowd enjoying ourselves under a bright blue sky instead of in the car or a room taken for the night. The women in pretty sundresses and the men in short sleeve shirts had heads together over the racing form and tip sheets with losing tickets underfoot everywhere you looked. Lowell came back with notably improved spirits after two more races. He said joking around and a few generous tips had made him friends with a bartender.

"He was leery at first because he was suspicious I might be an undercover cop; the local ones don't bother gamblers because they're paid to look the other way, like the mayor and anybody else who matters, but they have to look out for the feds and the state police. The poker game is every night at the Southern Club; a hundred bucks just to get into the back room, which is pretty steep from what I remember. He says Al Capone's Chicago mob runs the show from the Arlington Hotel, but gangsters from all over are welcome."

What a fund of information, I said.

"Bartenders are almost as plugged in as barbers. He says Hot Springs is a truce town. The crooks agree to behave so they don't have to watch their backs all the time like at home."

"A hundred dollars is a lot of money," I said hesitantly, "and there's no guarantee you'll win it back."

Lowell gave me a flat look. "That's why you don't see women in high stakes games, they start worrying about losing. You have to think you're going to win or you might as well forget it."

"I was just…"

"Never mind," he said roughly, "I don't want whatever's bothering you rubbing off on me."

A side of him I had never seen was in that quick, angry flash and I quailed before the violence of suppressed feeling it showed. It was if a curtain had been yanked open giving a glimpse of the harder man, the one who had passed through horrors that would have broken the spirit of other men.

He had been in the early Blitz, survived a ship sinking in the Solomons, endured bombing and shelling on Guadalcanal, escaped with General MacArthur from Corregidor, and just now was getting around to his wartime experiences in Russia. He'd had enough adventures for a dozen men, none of which he wanted; to the contrary, he made every effort to avoid exposure to the front lines. He often shook his head over the irony.

He had expected a drowsy stateside billet in a nice climate, the duties not burdensome and the hours reasonable, where he would safely see out the war. He had imagined one of the naval bases in Southern California with palm trees would be about right. Having acquired a taste for naval ceremony in his Annapolis years, he saw himself in charge of welcome-home parades for ships returning from combat.

"A brass band playing, flags flying, me marchin' at the head of a smart body of men all spit and polish—why, it would give the boys coming home a big lift, show them the Homefront was behind them one hundred percent." Then missteps that swept him into the winds of war.

"That's the way it goes in life," he said, "you plan one thing and get another." He was not one to ponder deep matters for long. I wondered if his many trials had laid down a layer of fatalism as the underside of his usual sunny nature, hidden as was the steely resolve that showed itself at times.

Lowell's manner changed in the blink of an eye. "Don't you worry, Harriet, I'm going to bring home the bacon."

When the day's racing was over, I tucked $540 of our winnings in my purse and we checked into the Arlington with a crowd of high-spirited winners and sour losers from the racetrack. It was evident in the lobby this was the hangout of gangsters in flashy clothes and two-tone shoes and hard-faced gun molls with penciled eyebrows and beehive hairdos.

All eyes turned to Lowell as usual, passing over me like I was the commonest brown sparrow. He showered and changed into casual but elegant clothes beautifully tailored that would show this crude set what a well-dressed man really looked like. He kissed me goodbye like he was off on another wartime adventure from which he might not return.

"Wish me luck."

I simmered at first—it was *my* money after all, not counting the winnings at the track—but then began to worry. If you believed the stories in the newspapers, the radio serials, and the motion pictures that glorified violence while seeming to deplore it, he would be rubbing shoulders with brutes who didn't think twice about using a blackjack on a man, shooting him dead, or slitting his throat as an example to others in the underworld.

For distraction, I began a slim history book about Arkansas that was on the nightstand. Like most, I didn't know much about the state; it exists on the fringe of national consciousness, doesn't it; a shape on maps one must pass through to get from one place to another, a space between Frenchified Louisiana and sinful New Orleans and the wide open spaces of the braggart Lone Star state.

The slimness of the volume testified how little of consequence had occurred since it was acquired as part of the Louisiana Purchase; what notice taken of Arkansas was of a derisory nature. I read that a train brakeman named Thomas W. Jackson wrote a book of puns and corny jokes titled *A Slow Train Through Arkansaw* that fixed the public impression that the state was peopled by slow-witted, no-account whites and shuffling, grinning Negroes of the minstrel sort. It sold seven million copies, making it the best selling joke book in American history. The first line shows the level of its sophistication:

"You are not the only pebble on the beach for there is a Little Rock down in Arkansas."

Another of the state's claims to a certain kind of fame was the knife fight in the state's House of Representatives between its speaker, John Wilson, and a fellow legislator named Joseph J. Anthony. The House was discussing where bounties should be paid on wolf scalps when Anthony, who had been charged with cowardice in the War of 1812 but resigned his commission before going to trial, made a slighting remark about Wilson, who pulled out a Bowie knife and went for him.

Anthony produced his own Arkansas Toothpick, another name for the blade, and they fought. Wilson won when he drove his steel into the larger man's heart. He was indicted for murder but the charges were dropped when the case was moved to the neighboring county. They were rough-and-tumble times, but these events shocked the whole country. As interesting if discrediting as the state's history was, my anxiety over Lowell made me set the book aside and go down to the lobby to ask at the front desk where the poker game was. I didn't know what I would do, knock at the door perhaps and ask to see Lowell even though I knew it would anger him. What if he was on a winning streak, which he once told me cooled off as fast as they came?

"What game are you talking about, ma'am?" The man at the front desk was a slight, narrow-shouldered man with a sharp nose, thin lips and red hair and stick-out country ears. Jug ears, we call them in Montana. He had been smiling before, a small duty smile, but it left his face.

"The card game," I explained, "my husband is playing in it."

"I don't know what you mean." His manner was icy now. "There is no card game in this hotel." He paused and added in a sanctimonious voice, "It would be against the law."

He would hold to that story even if dragged off in handcuffs; no doubt the hotel staff had been instructed in the relevant parts of the criminal code and how to behave under questioning. I did not reply and returned to my room, feeling his pale eyes on my back. Fifteen minutes later, the phone rang.

"Hi," Lowell bellowed into my ear, "what's going on…sounds like a party." In a low voice, pretending to listen to my reply, he said, "Get packed and meet me at the car in ten minutes. Keep the stuff to a minimum and don't forget the keys. Start now!" He went back to his loud voice. "Yeah, put him on." As I put down the phone I heard him talking to a make-believe person. "So what if he did?" he said aggressively.

I threw a few things into a single suitcase and slipped out of the room. I took the service elevator to the basement where a janitor in coveralls sat in a little office bent over the radio laughing at something on *Amos 'n' Andy*. I went to the parking area and started the engine to warm it up. No more than a minute later Lowell was at the driver's side.

"Shove over," he said, "we're gonna make tracks." We pulled out of the parking lot with a wave to two policemen in a patrol car.

"They're lookouts for the mob," he said. "They'll get a call in a minute to pull us over if they see us."

He turned at the first street and then again at the next, and we were traveling really fast in the opposite direction from the hotel. "What happened?" I asked.

"I'll tell you later," he said, "I got to concentrate on driving."

As if he had memorized a map of Hot Springs—which he had, he told me later—we weaved in and out of unlit streets past houses where faint lights showed until we reached the state highway.

"Man alive!" he said. "That was something."

"When do you plan on telling me?" I said coldly.

"When we stop for the night; I want this on tape just in case."

In case of what, I asked.

"In case they try to get a judge to issue a phony warrant, we'll have the story down from soup to nuts."

We drove on through the night to a town so small it never got around to naming itself. We found a tiny cabin with a faded For Rent sign leaned against the porch by the general store and gas station. The barefooted owner in an undershirt and trousers he was still pulling up didn't like being turned out so late but was glad for the three dollars.

"It pains me somethin' terrible," Lowell said, "but I left eleven hundred dollars on the table when I went upstairs to straighten out the guy on the phone." He meant the pretend caller.

He got up in his pajamas, making the old springs twang, and went to his coat and pants on a hanger. "I guess I forgot to mention this." Grinning, he began pulling currency from pockets and piling it on a table.

"Fifty-two thousand, give or take a couple of hundred. The biggest pots I ever saw—who says crime don't pay?—and, boy, was I on a streak. They expected me to play through the night so they'd win some back, which is the way with these guys. It's an unwritten law chiseled in stone if you know what I mean.

"I called you when I got way ahead. They figured I'd be back, leavin' that much on the table and my new friend Owney Madden watching it for me. A New York showgirl named Vickie introduced me to him, quite a beauty. Her, not Owney, hawr, hawr, hawr. Low-cut dress with skinny straps that kept slipping off her shoulders and long blond hair like Veronica Lake. They had a bar and bartender, the guy from the racetrack, and she was drinking bubbly. She waved me over as soon as I coughed up the C-note at the door."

"At last,' she said, "a new face." She pointed at the chair next to her so I sat down. "Where you been all my life, you handsome devil, are you a friend of my Owney?"

I'm not sure I know Mr. Owney, I said politely, but if I did I'm sure we'd be friendly.

She threw her head back and laughed like it was the funniest thing ever said. Vickie was the only woman in the room and the tough guys at the tables looked over through the cigarette smoke to see what's so funny.

"His name is Owen Madden," she says, "but his friends call him Owney."

Feeling my way to get the lay of the land, I tell her now that I think about it, I'm pretty sure I haven't met said gentleman.

"He's no gentleman, believe you me, she says." "He was in the newspapers before I was even born."

She talks a mile a minute, that woman; she'd been bored stiff watching the mugs in the Little Game, the Big Game being in the other room. Turns out Madden owned the Cotton Club in its heyday, which I'm sure you've heard of, and was called The Killer from putting so many men in the ground.

Three guys from another mob put eleven bullets in him in an ambush. He's on the floor leaking blood when the cops get there and ask who did it, but Madden won't say. I'll take care of it myself, he tells them. Code of the underworld, you know. They didn't push it because they figured he was on his way out, but he survives and the guys who tried to kill him had nice funerals as soon as Owney was back on his feet.

She tossed her hair and laughed as she tells me. Tough of nails, she was. He shot a store clerk for making a pass at one of his girlfriends—he had plenty, she tells me, but she's the only one now—and the victim told detectives who did it. They arrested Owney, but the guy croaked from his wound before the trial and the cops couldn't get any witnesses to testify. It was in all the papers and I could look it up if I didn't believe her. He got convicted for his next killing thanks to stool pigeons and spent nine years in Sing Sing.

Lowell said the Irish gangsters had been forced out by the Italians by the time he got out on parole, so he went into another line of work. He bought the Cotton Club and became a boxing promoter, meaning he fixed fights, including the big one between Max Baer and Primo Carnera. He heard Hot Springs was easy-going on gambling and prostitution, so he ends up here. A runty guy who needed more chin but was a real natty dresser, comes up while she's telling me a story about how George Raft was his driver before he went to Hollywood. 'Owney,!' she says, jumping up and giving him a big kiss.

"'Who's your friend,' he says in this cold voice, pushin' her away and giving me a look even colder. The room goes silent and I'm remembering the store clerk. On a sudden inspiration I jump up and said Captain Lowell Brady, United States Navy, retired, glad to meet you. During the war a guy in intelligence, who transferred in from the FBI told me, funny as it sounds, the underworld has great respect for the military; they're as patriotic as the next guy, most of them, and sorry their criminal records didn't let them see action.

Owney's face changes friendly right away and he sticks out his hand and asks to see my academy ring. "You boys did great work,' he says. "I wish I could've been with you; I got experience that might've come in handy when you needed somebody to talk."

He and I sit down on the sofa, him careful about the sharp creases on his trousers and Vickie like she was invisible all of a sudden. He asks to hear some war stories, which I was happy to do; I got a million as you know. Maybe a half hour passes, with Vickie flouncing off, jealous I suppose, and Owney looks at his watch. You want in on the action in the Big Room, he asks. Sure, I say, I'm feeling lucky.

We go in, I get introduced around, Owney makin' it sound like this new pal of his personally won the war. I no sooner drag up a chair than it seems like I'm winning every other pot and guys at the table keep askin' for fresh decks. Nobody can believe I'm that good; there must be something fishy going on. Owney is lookin' as proud as a teacher with his prize pupil. A few more hands where I see my luck is beginning to cool and I say I got to make a phone call to my wife...and here we are.

I wanted to talk more, but Lowell rolled over and was soon snoring. How I envied that talent he had for dropping off. I couldn't sleep on that sagging springs and thin mattress that smelled of old sweat, but I wouldn't have on a feather bed in a deluxe hotel either, the way my mind raced.

When I fell in love with Lowell he claimed that he always looked for the easy way out of a bad situation, but perhaps the truth was something different. Did he court danger because it stimulated him? Maybe that explained his attraction to gambling where you could win big or lose all on the turn of a card. Was this the way our life would be, restless travel punctuated by terrifying events when boredom set in? The underworld was now after us in addition to law enforcement; I looked back with longing for that brief idyll in the little house behind Mrs. Rowan's. That was the closest we had come to a normal married life. I could see myself becoming a nervous woman scared of her own shadow if this kept up.

After he shaved and dressed the next morning, Lowell said he was going to talk to the general store man. A half hour later, he came back tossing keys from one hand to the next. "I traded the DeSoto even up for his Ford truck. I looked out the window.

"That old thing?" I cried. "Our car is worth ten times more."

"Yeah," Lowell said, "the guy thinks he really suckered the city slicker."

Well, I said angrily, why wouldn't he? "Does it have as many dents on the other side?" Lowell said he hadn't looked but supposed so. "It'll get us to Dallas where we'll buy something nice. He'll be who the cops pull over and haul off to jail until things get straightened out."

And so off we went in a rattletrap that needed water in the radiator every fifty miles. The springs were almost gone on the driver's side and tall as he was, Lowell had to sit up straight to see over the wheel. "Forty is the best she'll do," he said.

We lost speed on even the smallest hill and dirty looks were thrown at us by people who had to veer into the oncoming lane to pass. In downtown Dallas, the cool reception from the valet at the Adolphus Hotel warmed up with the five-dollar tip Lowell gave him.

"I'll take good care of it, sir," he said and pulled away belching blue smoke so heavy that a tour group approaching the hotel entrance put handkerchiefs to their faces.

"Take your last look at that junkheap," Lowell said cheerfully as he strode with me hurrying at his side into an elegant lobby with crystal chandeliers, substantial furniture covered in velvet, dark wood paneling, and heavy drapes. He flashed a Texas-size roll of currency and peeled off enough for two nights in one of its finest suites.

"I'm in oil," he told the man at the front desk. That's the magic word in Texas and we were treated like royalty. The next day we bought a tan Oldsmobile, Lowell deciding that a Cadillac with tail fins, which was his preference, would draw too much attention.

"There's too much of the wrong kind of excitement in our marriage," I told him when we were on the road again. He reached over to turn off the car radio.

"It has been mighty lively lately," he said in a mollifying way, giving a pat to my knee.

"You like it that way," I said accusingly. "Oh, no, darlin,'" he said, it's a quiet life for me. You watch, we'll find some nice place to hole up and get back to normal.'"

"That's the problem," I fired back. "A place to 'hole up' *is* what's normal for us."

He let a few minutes pass and then said he'd like to mosey out to the West Coast and a quiet beach town. "If that's okay with you," he said with a side-ways look.

I didn't say anything at first, but as the miles passed it sounded appealing; better than anything I could think of at the moment. The lulling sound of the ocean waves, the salt smell, the cry of seabirds… it would be so restful and soothing. We could concentrate on what brought us together in the first place, Lowell's role in World War II.

CHAPTER 6

WE TRADED THE OLDSMOBILE AND A THOUSAND DOLLARS FOR A BURGUNDY Lincoln Capri with a private party in New Mexico to avoid paperwork that could be traced by the FBI. Lowell was chipper; nothing about the fugitive life daunted him. His mind seemed to need the chase the way the knife needs the whetstone to stay sharp.

"It's got to be Hoover," he said. "He's held a grudge since that dinner when he tried pumping me on what Stephenson was up to. He wanted foreign intelligence under his tent but Roosevelt was too cagy for that."

"Why would he care after all this time?" I asked drearily.

"I don't know, ego maybe. Or maybe his boyfriend is behind it."

That was Clyde Tolson, the second-in-command at the FBI, who burst in on his boss and Lowell at a country restaurant in Maryland. In my earlier manuscript, Lowell related how the agent who chauffeured the director said Hoover singled out younger men he found attractive and got them drunk to seduce them.

"Or it could be Harriman egging him on," Lowell said. "He missed getting the Democrat nomination for president, but he'll try again and what I know about him and Pamela during the war would kill him in the Bible Belt if it got out. The Democrats can't win unless the South is locked up, I learned that when I was only knee-high to a grasshopper." He thought a while. "Hell, it could be any one of a dozen people in Washington, and that's not counting them in the shadows."

THE TIME I'm remembering now was when Winston was still at the Admiralty in April of 'Forty. Colville said Winston thought the war couldn't be fought unless a single man was both prime minister and defense minister. Norway showed that plain as a nose on a face.

Beaverbrook convinced him to go a step more and be party leader so as to keep parliament in line. A month later he was like a king. I passed all this on as it was happening and it seemed Roosevelt and Hopkins thought it was good news, which of course they would. A lot of people thought he was a dictator and Harry was his Rasputin. You know who that was, a Russki from back when? I should've known you would, smart as you are.

Colville spoke to Inspector Thompson after Winston met with the King at Buckingham Palace two minutes away in the Rolls. He said he wished he'd got the job in better times. "Winston replied, 'All I hope is that it is not too late. I am very much afraid it is.'"

That put Colville in the dumps again and he said right away, "Perhaps you shouldn't pass that on to your people." I swore I would never even dream of it, but I made a bee-line to the embassy as soon as I could.

The Senator's voice was waspish through the static. "He's afraid it's too late, eh? Sneak around in your way and see if they'll agree to send the fleet to Canada. The president mentioned it off hand just the other day." I guessed he thought he was paying a compliment with that "sneak around." Mother would've given him a good smack.

Colville and I had lunch at the Savoy a couple of days later, Welsh rarebit with a dry Riesling I drank most of it while Colville sipped and listened to me rattle away; being under his eye made me nervous. I was calculating how to bring up the fleet business when he suddenly said, "Winston would like to see you."

I choked on the bite of rarebit I just forked in, the last for me by the way—it's so cheesy it binds you up for days, at least it did me.

"Are you all right?" Colville said. "Your face is purple."

I took a long drink of water and then a longer one of Riesling. "Why does he want me?"

"Winston needs a sense of what is in the President's mind. I told him of the lengthy visit you had recently with him and Harry Hopkins."

"Lengthy?" I said, caught in the lie. "Well, yes, it was long, but the president rambles around, tells jokes and stuff from the past. Good luck trying to figure out what he's thinking; even Harry says he doesn't know half the time, which he thinks is doing better than the president himself."

I saw how Roosevelt operated when I worked at the White House. He'd give the same job to three or four people and see who did the best. The losers that worked their asses off weren't seen again. I told you about that before.

I was undressing after a so-so night of poker at Boodle's when there was a knock at the door. I opened it in my bare feet and two men showed me MI6 credentials and said Churchill wanted to see me toot sweet.

"It's almost two o'clock," I said, tapping the crystal of my watch.

"The prime minister keeps irregular hours," said the one decent enough to look apologetic. I put my clothes back on and they took me to the Cabinet War Offices underground at Whitehall. It was a cramped and crowded place with small rooms and narrow corridors.

We passed an officer I recognized from the newspapers as General Ironside, the new commander of the home forces that were supposed to turn back the invasion with knives on poles, hunting rifles, the few tanks left, and trucks with steel plates bolted on them.

"I've been to nine meetings today," General Ironside said bitterly to an aide as we passed. I was asked by the MI6 men to wait in the hallway as the word was the prime minister was running behind.

Winston was snappish to people who came and went through the door left open for air. I sat in a straight-back chair in the hallway and yawned, regretting the Veuve Clicquo I put away with a few of the club members waiting for the all-clear to push off to their country homes for the weekend. We were telling jokes and stories to keep up spirits, but they were as sad looking as dogs back home that get mixed up with skunks. They envied me that I'd be called home before the Hun stormed the beaches at Clacton-on-Sea and Ramsgate.

Clouds of blue cigar smoke drifted out of Winston's office pretty regular and people hurrying back and forth made it swirl. A young woman pulled a black handkerchief from a ventilator sucking in air from outside. "This was white when I came on my shift," she told me. "And to think we're breathing this." Time passed and my head started jerking. Then I heard Churchill say real sharp, "Where the hell is Lieutenant Brady? He should have been here long ago."

"I don't know, prime minister," a male voice said. "There's a man sitting outside, could that be him?"

I heard the scrape of a chair. "Someone will pay if it is." Churchill peered around the doorway. "Lowell Brady! Come in, old friend." The aide hurried out, shooting me a look of fear.

"Old friend" was on the strong side, but you know politicians. I followed him into a bare room with a low ceiling and patches of damp on the wall and took a seat in a chair as uncomfortable as the other. His desk had three telephones and was drowning in papers and files.

"I was not prepared for the sloth and incompetence at the War Office," he said, "but I should have known from the conditions at the Admiralty. I sent General Ironside on his way a short time ago after I had a look at his plans for the defense of our island. A 'thin crust' of defenders on the coast with fallback lines to be more robustly contested by what troops we have. They are to be assisted by mobile units of untrained volunteers astride horses or in private cars and double-decker buses. They'll wear armbands in lieu of uniforms. The way Ironsides has drawn it up, our airfields will be abandoned at once, giving the Luftwaffe dominion in the skies. You can imagine what they would do to those buses and men on galloping horses. I'm going to make Ironside a field marshal and send him off to retirement with a peerage. General Brooke will replace him; I believe you know him from France. He speaks amusingly about the encounter." He looked at me with a twinkle in his eyes as he relit his dead cigar, sending up more blue smoke to circle and drift for the door.

Then he got serious. "As before, I will be as open to you as to President Roosevelt if he sat in his wheelchair where you are. We've lost ten destroyers in eleven days to U-boats and other attacks. We can't continue the war at this rate. We can't feed ourselves without imported food and our convoys depend on destroyers to get through."

"That's hard," I said, shaking my head. I decided it was better to hold off mentioning moving the fleet to Canada. It was a damned awkward position to be in, a lowly lieutenant talking to the prime minister of the greatest empire in the history of the world.

"Hard?" he said, like he couldn't believe his ears.

I saw he thought that didn't do it justice. "Really hard," I said. "Awful."

"Despite all its riches, the English language doesn't have the power to describe our condition at this moment. 'Catastrophic' might come closest." He peered at me through the smoke as if he had misjudged me.

"It's terrible for sure," I said. I was straining forward like I was watching a runner round third who'd get home the same time as the ball. I think that more than any fancy word I might come up with convinced him I got the picture.

"Do you believe this feeling is shared by the White House?"

"They're plenty worried, I can tell you that."

"Worry is an emotion any casual bystander can feel. Do you think your country would give us scores of your destroyers in this our time of greatest need?"

I was about to say I doubted it, but then I had a flash of inspiration. "We've got plenty of four-pipers left over from the Great War in our reserve fleet, why not ask for them?" Then I blurted, "While we're on the subject, what about sending the Royal Navy to Canada if...you know...if it comes to that?"

Churchill glowered and it felt like the walls were closing in and the floor squeezing up toward the ceiling. "If it comes to what?"

I stammered in a high voice. "Well, you know, if...if...if the Germans looked like they were winning and...and..."

"Sending the fleet from our shores would be an admission of defeat," he roared, with a thump of his fist on the desk. "We would never, never do that. As I said in my speech, we would rather die choking on our own blood than surrender."

"Times change and nobody could blame you..." If my voice got any higher only a bat could hear it. It was nerves, of course. If I'm honest, that wasn't my finest moment.

He got that bulldog look you see in pictures. "Nothing has changed!"

He poured brandy into two tumblers and pushed one to me. "I think you need this." I gulped mine down as he diluted his with water from a carafe.

"I can formally request the destroyers through diplomatic channels, but

I would first like to determine if such a request would be received with sympathy in light of the power of your isolationist bloc. The President and I have had a few informal exchanges, but they have been little more than expressions of good will." I felt the presence of someone in the open door behind me; Churchill waved away whoever it was.

"I know the President is concerned about the upcoming election, but I wonder, Lieutenant, if you would be so kind as to privately and quietly plumb your well-placed sources in Washington. I would hate to have a request through official channels declined with every polite expression of sorrowful reluctance. The newspapers inevitably would find out and it would have a dampening and even fatal effect on the morale of our people. I possibly would be forced to leave office for someone more conciliatory toward the Germans."

The brandy steadied my nerves. "I'll ask as soon as they open up shop." I banged the desk myself with a fist. But then I realized I couldn't tell the Senator because he would be on the phone to his newspaper friends ten seconds after he told the White House.

"Let me know the answer as soon as you can." He drew on his cigar. "Action this day is our motto now." He smiled. "That is why you see dignified civil servants known for stately pace running in the corridors of the War Office."

"There are several people with appointments waiting, Prime Minister," said the voice behind me.

"Yes, yes, yes," Winston said impatiently. "Show the first of them in. God bless you, Lieutenant Brady, our hopes ride on your shoulders."

I squared them and marched out with one of Churchill's secretaries, a slender man in a wrinkled pinstripe suit, loosened tie and shirt he hadn't changed for days from its look. He was dead tired, almost out on his feet. Bags under his eyes, his pip-pip Old Boy voice gone hoarse.

"Good Lord," he said, looking at his watch, "it's almost four o'clock."

"How does he do it, a man his age?"

"A two-hour nap in the afternoon," he said wearily, "while the rest of us stagger on as best we can. We eat standing up and snatch a few minutes of sleep in a chair when we can. People are breaking down from the pressure. The worst is his shouting at us; Mrs. Churchill promises to speak to him." He took a deep breath of early morning air only a little smoky compared to others lately.

"Well," he said wanly, "back to the salt mines."

My hope was Harry Hopkins was back to work, but if he wasn't I'd have to try the Senator. He usually took his sweet time getting back to me. I had spent hours at the embassy chatting up girls with I admit pretty good success waiting for his call. He wasn't interested in most of the political developments that Colville told me were highly important.

"I get enough of that horseshit here," he said.

Lately, it was the next day that he called back, or even two days later. Never a word of apology for wasting my time. I could try to get through to the president myself, but I was sure to be blocked by Pa Watson, who didn't like me as I told you before. He guarded Roosevelt's time like it was the gold at Fort Knox.

I felt my way in the darkness for a long stretch being extra careful where I stepped until I found a pub that opened early for workers at a factory that made military uniforms. I had three cups of strong tea and ordered an old fashioned English breakfast.

"Pitiful, ain't it?" the young waitress apologized when she put the plate in front of me. "One banger, one egg and that a blessing, one rasher of bacon and a little bit of beans. The only thing wot's the same is the price. Well, we better get used to it and worse if I'm to guess." She said it with a tired smile, English pluck for you.

The night porter let me into White's and I caught a few winks in a leather armchair until the snap and rustling of newspapers by early risers woke me. I walked around outside and killed time looking at the shell of a bombed building. Its insides were opened up to show sitting rooms, bedrooms and toilets like stage sets in a theater; you expected an actor to pop through a door and say some drivel like in those modern plays nobody understands. The Marines opened the gate for me before the embassy opened and I put in a call to the White House. Luckily, I got one of the operators I knew and she found out Harry was awake.

"Hopkins," he said when he answered the phone.

"Harry, it's me, Lowell Brady."

"What do you want?" I told you he didn't spend much time on a phone conversation those days.

"I talked to Churchill a few hours ago. He wants to know if we'd give him some destroyers. He said scores."

Harry laughed.

"No, I'm serious Harry. We've got them in our reserve fleet."

"Those rust buckets? He wouldn't want them."

"They're desperate, Harry. They lost ten destroyers in eleven days, he tells me."

"Holy shit." He was silent for a minute. "We'd have to get something back for it. The stingy Yankee crowd up north will throw in with the isolationists if we don't."

"There's something else. Sending the British fleet to Canada? No deal, Winston says."

"How'd he hear about that?"

"My stepfather asked me to feel him out. Winston said no and he meant it; it would look like they're throwing in the towel."

"I'll run the destroyers past the President when I see him, and I'll tell Senator Brady to keep his bottle nose out of this. This town leaks like a bucket used for target practice."

That night I was at the Savoy dining with a shop girl I wanted to impress. She was saying I was the handsomest and best dressed man in the room when a moon-faced Marine lieutenant named Rod Howard came up to the table and asked for a private word. I introduced him to Miss Williams and we excused ourselves.

"Ambassador Winant told us to find you as quick as we could," he said at the bar. "Yes, I will have something, thanks. A double Scotch if it's on you; I'm off duty now that I've delivered the message. You're to call your stepfather as soon as possible; he's at home."

"How'd you know I was here?" I asked.

"Someone said go to the most expensive restaurants in London and you're bound to find him, and a bunch of us went out looking. I was just at the Dorchester Hotel." He looked around. "Impressive, but not as nice as this."

I asked would he mind seeing Miss Howard home and he said do monkeys shit in the jungle? She didn't have the time of day for me after that. Howard must have had a terrific personality because he wasn't much to look at. Ordinary is the best you could say, but homely was closer. A moon face, like

I said, and liver lips. Maybe I'm being too hard on the guy out of jealousy, but I didn't lose many gals and it pissed me off. When I telephoned the Senator, he asked straight off why I'd reversed charges. I explained the embassy was closed and I was calling from White's because it was urgent.

"Never mind, I heard at the White House today Churchill asked for some destroyers. The president was surprised I didn't know and it was goddamned embarrassing. I'm supposed to be giving him the inside stuff on what's happening over there."

"I told you Senator, don't you remember?" Mother had said his memory was starting to slip, but something this big?

"That's a damned lie," he said in a blustery way. Didn't want to admit the gap in his recollection, was my guess. I bet it was the moonshine they drank at the fish camps. Damn potent, that stuff.

"It's news to me, Senator, I'll find out right away."

"Don't bother, this will be handled by the Navy and the cookie-pushers at State and I'll be…" His poisonous tone changed to nice as pie. "Why, hello dear. Oh, no, it's nothing important. I'm talking to someone about a post office for one of our smaller towns." He whispered to me, "Get on the ball or you'll find yourself at the Buffalo dry docks."

If you've ever been there in winter with icy winds cutting through your clothes like you don't have any—well, it would put the fear of God in an atheist. I knew an ensign sent there as punishment who said a gust popped the buttons off his watchcoat and it billowed out and snapped behind him like a sail torn from the main. He was nearly pulled off the deck into the following sea and a watery grave. He…there I go, off course again.

A mass of military officers and diplomats was sent over to the embassy and kept coming; the British cleared out buildings in the neighborhood for offices. It was like a little village of Americans got turned into a mid-sized city right in the heart of London.

That meant the bureaucracy grew faster than a mushroom sittin' on horse manure. Helped along by people just like them at Whitehall, soulmates you might say, things slowed so committees could split up into sub-committees until something got talked to death and there was nothing to do but take action, which meant more meetings and more committees set up. Then there was the paperwork people had to put their initials on to show they'd read it. From bits of conversation I heard most would touch a match to nine out of ten reports stamped "Classified" for all they were worth. Seeing all these new people left no doubt we'd be in the war no matter what baloney the White House fed the people back home.

The destroyer deal went through in March, giving us ninety-nine year leases on British bases in the Caribbean and other stuff for the hulks in our reserve fleet. You could almost build a new one in the time it took to make them sea ready. Colville told me the bitterness was so thick at the Admiralty you could cut it with a butter knife. Screwed again by the Yanks was the feeling.

But Roosevelt in his devious ways built on the deal until it became Lend-Lease and the thousands of shiploads of weapons and food we sent saved the British; Harriman was sent over to run the show and lord it over everyone. I told you about that before.

One afternoon I met Colville to take a turn around one of London's squares some way off from the embassy. He pointed with his walking stick at the plane trees. "Each year I wonder if I will live to see their leaves change again."

We walked in silence, me wondering how to move the subject on to something more cheerful. "I'm changing next week from my summer wardrobe to the fall one," I said, meaning civilian clothes of course. He gave me the sort of disappointed look he did now and then as if he was wondering, I don't know, like was I a serious enough person for this work

Contrails made patterns in the sky way above. "The dog-fighting is at its highest pitch," Colville said. "All three air wings are up, leaving no reserves. The Germans are paying a heavy price in bombers to knock out our airfields, but captured pilots have that strutting arrogance of Prussians and say their detention will not be for long." It gave you a queer feeling watching those life-and-death fights going on like they were silent movies.

"The prime minister has written to the president to tell him the hour of decision is near at hand, but who knows what effect that will have? They are still in the feeling-out stage of a relationship. Our air defenses are buckling and reconnaissance shows a thousand barges in Channel ports waiting to bring the invasion. Our intelligence reckons about a hundred thousand battle-tested soldiers are ready for embarkation; if they get their panzer divisions ashore it will be the end for us. Winston says he won't be taken alive and has Clementine learning to shoot a pistol in the event Germans come over the garden wall."

"There's the Royal Navy to get past," I said. Even I didn't know things were this bad, let alone the White House. Maybe Colville had been holding out on me.

"Yes, the Royal Navy," he said sadly. "Who knew warships would be so vulnerable to air attack before this started?"

Nerves at the embassy were stretched tight as piano wire. A big new Stars and Stripes was ordered for the flagstaff so Germans knew this was American soil if it mattered when they came tearing across St. James Square. People were told to get sensitive files together for burning.

"Mine are up here safe and sound," I had said, tapping my temple. Joking around like that came back to bite me in the ass as usual. I found out when I wasn't allowed in the room with the scrambler phone. The man in charge, a middle-aged commander with a high forehead dimpled with old shrapnel wounds, didn't hide that this was fine by him.

"I've got an important message to get off," I said.

"Try the OSS boys, but get it in writing," he said. "There is a meeting tomorrow in the Secure Room at 0800 and you're to be there." I sent off five overnight cables to Harry via different companies with the same message. "We must talk. Urgent. B at breaking point."

The OSS people from the Ivy League schools made themselves stand out trying to look ordinary; trench coats and hats pulled low was what they came up with. The Britons had a good laugh at them. "They mean well but they are such innocents," Colville told me.

It felt like a courtroom when I was led into the Secure Room like a criminal from the holding cell. A fiftyish, pompous sort in civilian clothes sat in the chairman's chair looking so full of himself he'd burst if he took a deep breath and we'd all be ducking flying guts. I pegged him as an investment banker or Wall Street lawyer giving the government his services for a dollar a year. The embassy's naval and military intelligence bosses and their subordinates faced each other across the table with faces like stone.

He told me, "I'm with OSS" and motioned to take a chair. "Lieutenant Brady," he said, "who is your source in British intelligence?" His glance at the others said this was the question they'd agreed on. I learned more spooning soup with Colville than the OSS crowd did grubbing away for weeks. It must have stung more than I thought when questions were asked in Washington and repeated in London.

"I can't tell you that," I said nicely. "Orders."

"We understand you have learned that 'B,' as you call it, is at the breaking point. That obviously is the British and evidently refers to air defenses. Is this true and how do you know it?"

"I can't tell you," I said, beginning to feel uneasy at bucking the whole system. It came to me under their hard stares that if Harry faded away for good it would leave only the president in my corner and he'd give me up as easy as a pawn on a chessboard. "Orders," I repeated.

"Orders from whom; surely you can say. Captain Waters here was told by the CNO himself that he doesn't know whom you work for." Two "whoms" in a row; a simple sailor like me couldn't help but feel small.

"His information is essentially accurate," Captain Waters said in half-hearted defense. We Navy guys stick together, right? Nope. Everybody's out for his own. "But I think you should answer the question, Lieutenant."

"The fact is," Mr. OSS said, "nobody in the Navy is higher than the Chief of Naval Operations."

"There's the Secretary of the Navy," I said.

He brushed that off. "I understand you have had a very nice little life here, coming and going as you please and spending government money like it was water. I know that you are Senator Brady's son…"

"Stepson," I corrected.

"Very well, stepson. The Senator is a fine man and I have the utmost respect for him, but a patron, even as important as he, is not enough to explain the freedom with which you operate." He paused to see if I had an answer.

"You're right," I said. "It wouldn't."

"So then, the question is…"

At that moment like in a radio drama there was a knock at the door and a young Army shavetail stuck his head in. "Sorry, sir," he said to the brigadier at the table, "but there is an urgent telephone call for Lieutenant Brady."

"Inform them that Lieutenant Brady is at an important meeting and will return the call when it has concluded," Mr. OSS said, his jowls darkening. He wasn't a man used to being interrupted. The brigadier nodded okay at him and the lieutenant closed the door.

Mr. OSS looked at the ceiling to simmer down or get his thoughts together again. He cleared his throat and was about to speak when there was another knock and the lieutenant was back. "Sorry, sir, but it's the White House and he is to come to the phone right this minute."

I would have liked to stay a bit to enjoy the sight of all the dropped jaws, but I followed the lieutenant to the scrambler phone and closed the door behind me. "What's going on?" Harry said. "I got a strange telegram from you."

"Only one? I sent a bunch."

"I'm looking at the one that got through."

"The OSS is reading your mail."

"They are?" He sounded irritated.

"That's what this meeting is about. They want to know what the message means and how I know."

"*I* want to know what it means," Harry said.

"The RAF is almost out of fighter pilots."

After a long silence, Harry said, "That's very bad news."

"You know about the German armada across the Channel?"

"Yeah, we've known that for a while. Not about the pilots, though."

"I'm getting some heat, Harry. The OSS doesn't like our arrangement."

"How did they find out?"

"They haven't said but they're grilling me about it right now. There's a fat guy who didn't give his name, he only said he's with the OSS."

"Put him on the phone. Don't say who's calling."

I went back to the Safe Room. "They want to talk to you," I said to Mr. OSS.

"Who is 'they?'" he said, rising from his chair with indignation.

"I can't say," I said. "Orders."

I looked around the silent room with a pleasant smile after he left. He was back in less than a minute breathing deep and his jowls a richer burgundy color. Harry must have been pretty rough on him.

"This meeting is adjourned," he said, "thank you for your time."

This should have put me in deep clover, feared by both the Navy and the intelligence boys, but life seldom pans out the way you think it will. You could travel the world and not find anybody who knows that better than me.

A huge storm blew up in Washington over this two-bit event in the Secure Room. I told you J. Edgar Hoover was still trying like hell to pull foreign intelligence into his orbit and was being fought by Wild Bill Donovan and his OSS with the backing of Stephenson and M6, which did all the training of Donovan's agents in the beginning. They were thick as thieves, those two, with enough medals for courage between them for a whole division. Also in the fight were naval and military intelligence and even the spooks that worked at the State Department. It all came to a head in that little Secure Room in London where I waltzed out thinkin' I was king of the hill when I was no more important than a rooster crowing on a dunghill. The upshot was I was ordered home in a compromise that saved everybody's face.

"I suppose it's all for the best," Colville sadly said at our last dinner together. "I'm being shunted to the sidelines myself by young blades coming up who don't see much use in an elderly admiral poking his nose around where he shouldn't. Something to do with 'security concerns.' Winston was most unsympathetic when I approached him. 'The old gives way to the new,' he told me in a dismissive way. 'It will happen to me one day and I hope I go with equanimity before they use the hook like in the old days in the music halls.'"

"I did the best I could for you," Harry told me two weeks later when I was called to the White House, "but you were the one thing they could all agree on. Franklin did his soft shoe away from the fight like always. 'You boys figure it out.' I'd say if there was a winner, it was Wild Bill. The president is going to keep you on his bench for the odd jobs that come up if that makes you feel better."

Harry was in bed, pasty-faced and weak, eating bread dipped in milk; the man had strength hidden to the naked eye, to mine anyhow. He always looked at death's door, but it wasn't long before he was flying across the Atlantic with me carrying his bag of medicine to introduce him to Winston and then go on to meet Joe Stalin. You already wrote that stuff up.

CHAPTER 7

WE TOOK A LEASE FOR A YEAR ON A HOME AT LAGUNA BEACH, A LOVELY TOWN where we had a splendid view of the ocean and heard surf boom like a bass drum night and day. We walked hand in hand on the beach at sunset in our bare feet, sometimes not saying anything. It was the honeymoon we never had, lazy days and romantic nights. I caught up on my transcriptions so one fine morning we resumed the interviewing. A long extension cord let us use the tape recorder on the deck when it wasn't windy or overcast.

LET'S SEE, where were we? Okay, the Huns invade Poland and the Russians pile on from the east. Nobody but the Germans were ready to fight when you came right down to it. The Poles were beaten fast and then it was France and England's turn, except nothing happened for weeks and then months. People were itching for action at first and then that melted away into a kind of dull dread as one paper put it except for snorting bulls like Churchill who was sure England would win in the end and wanted the main event to get goin'.

People began to call it the Boer War, but those in the know were stunned how fast the Poles got flattened by dive bombers and armor working hand-in-hand with infantry. Nobody saw the likes before and the government began to have second thoughts—what's Poland to us, really, was the new line. Not for the record, of course. Winston tipped me off to the rumblings, which I passed on to the Senator. He never said what he told Roosevelt, but it wasn't his style to give anyone credit but himself. The newspapers at home began to mention him as a regular at the White House cocktail hour and he was even invited with Mother to Campobello for weekends, so I reckoned what I fed him had a good effect on his career.

General Brooke, who was a corps commander in the BEF in France, came over one weekend for emergency talks at the War Office. Winston invited him to dinner with a dozen important types—Colville on hand giving me his winks. Randolph went half-nuts when he found out he wasn't needed and slammed out of the flat after kicking the furniture.

Brooke looked every inch the professional soldier, squared away and solid, and it was like he hummed with energy. He'd won a Victoria Cross in the Great War, so were dealing with the real goods here. He was going bald and had a small moustache and what you'd call a piercing look that made me uneasy when it landed on me. He was another example of the man you want to stand clear of when the battle starts, the VC told you that. He'd slap you to sleep for slacking off and then slap you for sleeping—old Southern saying.

He said he was "unfavorably impressed"—his exact words—when he saw the French Ninth Army on parade. Faces got long around the table as he went on.

"Seldom have I seen anything more slovenly. Men unshaven, horses ungroomed, complete lack of pride in their units. What shook me the most, however, were the men's faces, their disgruntled and insubordinate looks. I could not help wondering whether the French are a firm enough nation to see this thing through."

I can tell you *that* started the buzzing.

"It is an army of more than two million men, a formidable force," Churchill said. He had a higher opinion of the French than most English you talked to. Their food might have been part of the reason, and he was real fond of the south of France for vacations. You laugh, but from what I've seen little things push history as much as the big ones they write about.

After a couple of hours it looked to me they were going to plow the furrow down to the bedrock, and I figured I already had enough for the Senator so I slipped out. I won fifty pounds playing cards at White's where, like I said, Winston got me a guest membership. Before the war a Yank like me would be no more likely to get through the door than mongrel dogs with ribs showing.

I have no doubt they've tightened the rules back to what they were. The dukes and royals like their own kind, which is why it was a great place for eating, drinking and gambling. The best of everything and no women allowed, not that I minded having them around. I think it was the private schools they were sent to as little kids; public schools they called them for some reason. Buggery was quite the thing, so Colville told me. As the twig is bent so grows the tree—old saying.

"Back in the old days, one of the lords bet another three thousand pounds on which rain drop would reach the bottom of the window first. That was the early 1800s, so we're talking about a fortune in today's money, a few hundred thousand according to the story. I suppose they had a lot of fine French wine warming their bellies, but a bet that size was peanuts to them. They were sitting at the table by the bow window, the place reserved for the first Duke of Wellington when he was alive, the one who beat Nappy at Waterloo. There I am, running off course again.

The barrage balloons went up over the city by the thousands and sandbags were piled against buildings everywhere. Moms and kids got shipped out to the countryside, but that didn't go over too well. The little ones from the slums were dirty and raggedy and didn't know how to use knives and forks. They ate when they felt like it, walking around the house gnawing on bread like they were back in the family hovel; they wouldn't touch soup or any vegetables except potatoes.

The moms got bored with nothing to do and walked to the village pub, miles if they had to. They got drunk and rattled on like empty wagons; the locals didn't care much for their swearing. So when nothing happening kept it up, the Londoners trickled back from homesickness and being looked down on as riff-raff by the country people. Couldn't blame either side, really.

The rich sent their cubs to friends or relations over here. I heard Lady Cooper and Duff sent their kid to New England. Rank has its privileges as they say; I had quite a few of them myself at the time and didn't give the matter a second thought. Of course, I was a different man than today; war changes people and not always for the worse.

And then after the war there were those years hiding out on Commodore Crockett's farm working as his farm hand and listening to him read from the

Bible when supper was over. We started it all over again when we got to the end of Revelations. He threw out his radio before I got there because of its ungodliness, the old fellow having a sharp eye for it no matter how well hidden to others.

He signed up for a telephone after I got there, but had them take it back because it was a party line and he heard blaspheming once or twice when he went to make a call. Everybody listened in though you weren't supposed to. Another of the devil's snares, he said.

So we were pretty much cut off from the rest of the world, which was one of the reasons he couldn't keep hired hands until I came along that stormy night begging for shelter—yes, begging with tears in my eyes. When you're a broken-down beggar there's not much farther you can fall, is there? Well, I suppose a dead beggar with the crows pecking.

I still think about those black days. Without the commodore's help, I would have breathed my last without a friend in the world. We dropped to our knees for prayers three times a day; if his timing was off and we got caught in the fields in the noon day sun, so be it. Sometimes his voice gave out before he got to the end of the longer verses, but I didn't stand until he did for fear he'd think it was showing ungodliness and send me back to a tramp's life.

He went to town only when he had to and brought back a newspaper for me when he remembered. He didn't look at them himself for fear they'd stir him up like the radio did before he threw it out. A couple of years after I got there, the police chief asked if he knew a man that matched my description; a government agent had drove over special from the capitol to check around.

"I told the chief I wouldn't talk to a man who left his lawful wife for another woman," the commodore said. "He wanted to know what's that got to do with anything, but I turned and walked away."

Of course, I had the beard and long hair at the time and I doubt even Mother would recognize me. I keep forgetting you like the little details from the war, the human touches as you call 'em.

I was walking to the embassy one morning when a bobby stopped us crossing the street because soldiers were marching to the railroad station. A cockney woman called out, "Look at 'im, girls. 'E should be at home wit his Mam. Never mind, son. You'll be alrigh'. God bless yer la."

We had a good laugh there on the sidewalk, but there were black looks from the soldiers. The Half-Asleep War was another thing they called it. Colville told me people went mad from the strain of waiting and were sent to the crazy house, though they didn't put that in the papers. In April of '40 Chamberlain crowed that Hitler waited too long and they were ready for whatever he threw at them.

"He missed the bus," he said. Famous phrase.

I bet he wanted that back when the ground dried out so the Panzers could roll and then it was Poland all over again. The French army melted away when the Germans went round the Maginot Line and took them from the flank, and the next thing we knew the English were falling back to Dunkirk in danger of being cut off. That was later though; everything in its time and place, no hurrying at my time of life.

Although he told people he was a charlatan, Chamberlain was forced to bring Churchill into his cabinet as First Lord of the Admiralty. The first thing Winston does is send troops over to Norway to block iron ore shipped from Sweden to Germany, which turned out to be a blunder nearly as bad as his Dardanelles stunt. He was kicked out of office and went to fight in the trenches, which he said was the honorable thing to do. I don't know more about that, not being much for history unless I'm in it. Hawr, hawr, hawr.

Those troops sent over to Norway were a rag-tag bunch without much training and no heavy weapons, transport or radios. A fair number were never on water before or seen ground higher than Ludgate Hill. General Hotblack, who was supposed to lead the expedition, dropped from a stroke on the steps of his club as he was leaving for the ship. How's that for an omen? Disembarking in Norway, the first thing the troops see is deep snow everywhere and a huge mountain looking down on them. You can imagine how spirits sank. Morale being lower than a snake's belly from the start. Lacking discipline, they looted stores and bothered Norwegian women when they came ashore. A Foreign Office man reported that drunk soldiers fired on fishermen during an argument.

You deal with raw recruits like they're criminals. Pick two or three and make examples of them, bread and water and chipping paint when they get out of the brig, that was my way. It puts the fear of God in all of them and they're better sailors for it, ask any seasoned officer. The English army acted high and mighty in Norway, as bad as the Prussians, and the Royal Navy was so suspicious they turned down the intelligence the locals offered even though they stopped being neutrals when the Germans invaded them. I wouldn't have trusted them either, the sneaking cowards.

The English didn't have snowshoes, so the troops had to stick to the roads, meaning they were targets for strafing and bombing whenever the Germans felt like it. French troops sent to help them raided English stores, and vehicles crashed into each other because neither gave the right-of-way to the other. Supply dumps were blown sky high almost as quickly as they got stacked up.

"The operation was like an expedition against the Zulus except we were the fuzzy-wuzzies," Colville said. His silence was thoughtful. "Winston has always had a weakness for rash and spectacular exploits."

Churchill was busy as you might think and I didn't see as much of him as before, so I depended even more on Colville for items for my letters, which I was now expected to write twice a week. He had a lord's taste and we lunched and dined at the Ritz and other prime places. Heavy silver plates with gold rims, beautiful crystal, dignified waiters, restaurants had to have all that plus mahogany walls and fine chandeliers before Coleville stepped across the threshold. I snapped my fingers and a waiter in white gloves was at my side. Coleville tried to grab for the tab a few times, but he was off balance because of the one arm and I beat him easy.

He wasn't the only one who fed and drank at Uncle Sam's expense. You'd be surprised how much information a glass of first-class champagne pulls from the ladies, not the old biddies with wrinkles and squints wise to the ways of us men, but the young second or third wives of the generals and admirals and cabinet ministers working themselves to death at the War Office trying to catch up because of those years of appeasement. Fine eyes, those women, some of them a-rovin' like the song goes.

They made me promise not to repeat a single word their husbands told them before the old fellows fell to snoring at the dinner table, worn down from their long hours. I swore I wouldn't, of course, and why don't we have another glass of the Ayala before we order? They always said they didn't dare, but mostly then they said yes. Afterward, we generally went upstairs…um, no need for that.

A colonel who won two hundred pounds off me at cards and hoped for another killing warned me a rear admiral known for a savage temper was after me on account of his pretty, young wife. The old devil was putting it around he would give me an old-fashioned flogging in public and carried a riding crop in hopes we'd meet on the street or one of the clubs. I went to earth as they say, wore a wig and false beard and so forth, ate meals in the embassy canteen. Compared to what I was used to, it was like dipping from the pot at a hobo jungle.

Explaining that my disguise was for undercover work was wearing a little thin at the embassy, and I was even thinking about asking to be sent home. Fortunately, that admiral was drowned when his ship took a torpedo in the North Sea. A damned shame about the ship's crew, of course—I don't even have to say it, do I? Fine men, no greater sacrifice and all that, so take that look off your face.

It was one of many close calls with husbands in war and peace, and a good many closer than that. I told you how I ran barefoot down an alley carrying my clothes and nearly lost a toe from broken glass.

I comforted the widow as best I could until Colville telephoned to say he was hearing talk, and of course he heard everything first. Every society I've ever seen has dirty-minded gossips, from savages with bones in the nose deep in the Solomons to society swells in New York City. Human nature, I suppose, no changing it.

I was getting troubles about my expenses from the Bureau of Supplies and Accounts. By their way of thinking, I should've sat on a park bench and ate fish and chips from greasy newspapers to entertain "your sources." They used quote marks to show they saw through me, but I never rose to the bait. Pissy runts in green eyeshades; no experience with the real world.

My normal routine was I dropped by the embassy twice a week for the skinny and to see if something came in for me. One gray morning with the damned sleet coming down again, Admiral Deveral sent someone for me to where I was having coffee in the cafeteria with a young lady. I could tell by his smile when he turned from the window that he had bad news for me. He held the cable like he wanted to squeeze out every drop of pleasure before he gave it to me; I noticed right away it had arrived six hours before.

"You're ordered to Belgium this afternoon on *HMS Amazon*," he said. "You are attached in observer status to the BEF Fourth Division GHQ at Lomme…if it's still there. If not, find it. There is a car waiting in front, you can just make it before *Amazon* sails." It was like being hit between the eyes with a ball-peen hammer.

"That will be all, Lieutenant."

He turned back to the window again and his shoulders began to shake. No, you don't understand, darlin.' He wasn't crying, the bastard was laughing. I would've done the same if some rotten shirker, which he thought I was, got transferred some place the odds were he wouldn't come back from, only I wouldn't hide it like he did. I'd grin and dust my hands, do something to rub it in; dance a clog step maybe, hands behind the back. Unprofessional conduct, of course, but his word against mine.

First thing that occurs to me is what if I can't make it before *Amazon* sails? That would give me time to reach Harry Hopkins or the Senator and get the order cancelled. The Senator knew there'd be hell to pay if Mother found out her darlin' boy was sent in harm's way and he'd get on the ball fast. Just turning the pages in the papers you could see things were bad. Three French formations fell apart around Sedan before "the German onslaught," as the *Times* wrote, and it didn't look like the Belgians had any fight in them at all. Like the Norwegians and Dutch and those other little pissant countries, they hoped staying neutral would keep them out of trouble, but Hitler had other plans.

A petty officer named Anderson was waiting behind the wheel at the curb outside the embassy. I told him to take me to Churchill's flat for my gear; he had moved with Clementine to the Admiralty House so Randolph and I had it to ourselves except for servants. I dodged him as much as I could because he gave up on strong hints and took to hollering, "When are you moving out?" I overheard him tell a visitor he was going to have the police remove me by force, but I put it down as bluff because of me being the pipeline to the White House. But that wasn't as important at that point because Winston was in a position to tell Roosevelt directly about England's dire straits. His cables were from Naval Person so if any fell into the wrong hands he could say it wasn't him.

The plain fact of the matter was I needed a place to stay because I had run up some pretty big bills at White's and Boodles and one or two other clubs thanks to a run of bad luck; too much doubling down on good hands that turned out to be second best. I began pressing my luck, which any good gambler will tell you is a mistake; it's a lesson I learned over and over again before it stuck.

I took my time packing my gear and then gave Anderson a few bum steers as to directions, so we were two hours and fifteen minutes late getting to the dock. I figured *HMS Amazon* would be long gone, but instead we're waved through the gate and led by a seaman on a motorcycle to the gangplank where the ship's officers stood in welcome—if you could call it that.

Captain Phipps-Howard did the introductions in the stiff wind blowing the sleet. Their looks were cold and not just from the weather; they gave me forced smiles of a half a second each, but I pretended not to notice and gave them all a big grip-'n'-and grin like I was glad to be there. Phipps-Howard was an ordinary-looking guy with a ruddy face, reddish hair going gray, medium height but holding himself straight as a ramrod so he seemed taller.

"We expected you some time ago," he said. He arm shot out to make a show of looking at his watch. I said the driver got lost because he was new and didn't know his way around yet. Phipps-Howard said "extraordinary," but I had the feeling he'd say more if he was free to; no doubt he had instructions to be nice to the Yank. The steam was already up, the lines were cast off, and the destroyer was underway in less than two minutes—it would have taken us peacetime sailors fifteen minutes going flat out—and was clipping along at thirty-two knots as we left the harbor with the weather freshening even more.

"You must have a very important mission," he said in his cubbyhole just off the bridge. "Or be a very important man to delay one of His Majesty's warships at a time like this."

Ordinarily, I'd puff up and say I wish I could say more and act mysterious for whatever benefit that might bring, but my spirits were too low. I said does liaison with the BEF Fourth Division GHQ sound important to you? I sounded hangdog even to me.

"Good Lord," he said, "what is the point of putting an American in the headquarters of an army being routed? You'd be in the way of everyone, and why a naval officer? It must be a terrible mix-up."

Nope, I said, orders straight from the top with my name on them plain as your nose.

"It's chaos over there, and how are you going to get to Lomme? How do your people know it hasn't already been overrun? The Germans are moving faster than anyone believed possible."

I couldn't think of anything to say, so I gave him a shrug.

"You poor devil," he said. "I'll do what I can, but I'm afraid it won't be much." He said he'd speak to the brigadier general in charge of the evacuation. *Amazon,* one of the Tribal class, a fine looking ship with a clipper bow that made for good seakeeping, was running a shuttle to evacuate rear echelon personnel and English civilians pouring into Antwerp. Looks of stark panic were on faces as we pushed through the crowds on the docks.

General Hensley was at a cluttered desk in a building that smelled of fish gone bad. Messengers in slickers were coming and going on motorcycles that they rode inside, phones rang constantly, and men yelled into them with fingers in the other ear. Airplanes roared overhead constantly and there was shelling. I didn't know how anybody could hear in that racket. The general pushed his glasses to the top of his head and gave my khaki work uniform an up and down.

"American? he shouted at Phipps-Howard. "What's he doing here?" The captain roared out my situation. "We have a convoy heading east he can ride with," Hensley yelled back. "Leave him here and someone will take care of it."

The captain and I parted with salutes and a handshake and I sat down for what came next. It was clear someone high up in the CNO's office pulled this off with Deveral's help, but the question was why?

Keep in mind I hadn't yet made the enemies I did later nosing out mossbacks at the Navy Department so Roosevelt could put livelier men in their place. With war coming, the regular promotion boards and bureaucratic folderol worked too slow for him. I could understand why people hated me after that; careers were ended or senior officers sent to shore jobs that led nowhere except early retirement and gardening with the wife.

People disliked me in London, jealous of the juice I had through the Senato… but enough to push me in harm's way? No, I just didn't see it. I figured someone was getting payback for what the Senator did through the power of the purse in Congress. Whoever pulled this off didn't know the Senator didn't like me. Well, hated is more like it. If it wasn't for Mother, he would've pretended he didn't know me even though I was his legal adoptee; she wouldn't marry him unless he came through on that. She had plenty of rich men chasing her after my real pa disappeared to look for gold in South America; though some said it was the ruins of a lost city. I told you all that before.

The convoy was four three-quarter ton trucks with medical supplies going east to the fighting, which depressed the Cockney driver and he wasn't hiding it. I rode in the passenger seat instead of in the back with the Other Ranks, another one of those officer privileges. He was a skinny guy named Shields who needed a shave and had a dirty uniform and a strong smell.

"It's bad innit," he said as we moved at turtle speed through the jammed streets.

I thought he was talking about the people packed so tight it was hard for them to get out of our way.

"No, I mean all this medicine and bandages and splints we're haulin'. Says to me we're taking more casualties than the masterminds expected. These crowds? Poof, they're nothin' compared to France where I just been. Get outer the way, bastards!" He leaned on the horn a long time. *A-Hoooooooga.*

"A mess over there in France, 'orrible mess. Masses of peasants on the roads acting dazed like. You say somethin' and there's no answer back, not a word, like they don't even see you. Shock, probably, and tired out. Whole families on the march pushin' prams with stuff piled high as their heads, the grandpas and grannies holdin' onto the kids and even carryin' babies. We seen beautiful horses pullin' wagons with furn'chur and trunks. The kids holdin' on to their little dogs or a canary in a cage. Pitiful! Some say it's the biggest migration in history. The army can't deploy on them roads even if it wanted to, which I doubt. The soldiers are pushin' their gear on bicycles with helmets and guns out of sight. There's no fight left in them by the look, sad and 'opeless is what I'd say. You sometimes saw the wankers changing into civvies in plain view. Move ya bastards!" More blasts on the horn.

We traveled fifty miles before the refugees began to thin out, letting us pick up speed. "I 'ope this don't mean the Luftwaffe's machine-gunnin' the road up ahead. They do it all the time in France; people run into the fields and woods when the twats come over. Germans! Can't tell me they don't get a bleedin' kick out of it."

A bulb went on over my head at that. The krauts would jump at a chance at a military convoy headed east. Grabbing my haversack, I asked him to stop under the beech trees up ahead so I could answer a call of nature. "I'll give yer five minutes," he said. I loped along so fast his honking was faint when the deadline came.

I hid in a ditch when I heard them coming. Their orders were to get to HQ as fast as possible, but mine was just to get there period. I could have explained to Shields the feeling I had—superstition I suppose some would say—that we were driving into trouble, but what would that do except waste time?

When I got the feeling trouble was shaping up back then I changed course whether on a battlefield or with a woman...you get that look whenever I say "women." That's in the past and you weren't even in the picture. Understood? Thank you.

I don't get that feeling anymore—what's it called, instinct?—which is why we were caught with our pants down at the auto court. Hell's bells, you're listening to a simple sailor so what you hear might not always be in good taste all the way. Were you raised in a convent or something?

Getting a bit nippy out here, what say we go indoors and you rustle up some chow? A drumstick from last night would be fine. A bottle of beer with it. All this talking makes a man thirsty.

CHAPTER 8

I EDITED OUT SOME OF LOWELL'S COLORFUL AND OFTEN DISRESPECTFUL ANIMAD-versions in our interviews without altering the general sense of what he said. Here are a few examples I retain in the appendix.

"Admiral Halsey was a brave man but so dumb he could throw himself on the ground and miss."

After weeks on Guadalcanal, "I smelled bad enough to knock a dog off a gut wagon."

"If Churchill was an inch shorter he'd be round."

A starving peasant in Siberia was so thin "if he turned sideways and stuck out his tongue, he'd look like a zipper." Lowell was so hungry himself at that point "my belly thought my throat was cut."

The wife of a Soviet diplomat was so ugly "a freight train would go off on a dirt road to get around her." Averill Harriman was so rich "he bought a new yacht when the other one got wet."

I toned down the jocose nature of his utterance because often it seemed to make light of a tragic era and his own dreadful experiences, but the jokiness gave me insight on how quickly he was on easy terms with people, an aspect of his personality which future historians must keep in mind. My job obtaining the oral histories of veterans at VA hospitals had brought me into close contact with withdrawn men who still suffered from the physical and mental wounds of the war. It forced me into an extroversion foreign to my nature to get them to speak freely, though many remained frozen and remote no matter how chatty I was.

My strain to simulate outgoingness showed how different Lowell and I were. He seemed able to make friends in the blink of an eye. Perhaps there is something to the theory about the attraction of opposites. But strangely, with few exceptions, he did not speak again of most of the people in his stories after the first mention; it was if a line had been drawn through them.

Being on the run all those years prevented the renewal of ties, of course, but did not explain how people in his narrative vanished so comprehensively, especially with someone who had his perfect recall. Colville was an exception, but he was more political intercessor than friend, and I'm sure both born charmers knew their relationship was of a utilitarian nature.

I loved my husband deeply and believed it was returned, but I was also aware this was not the same as knowing him, not fully anyway. Could he walk out of my life tomorrow without a look back as it seemed he had with so many people? Aside from the wedding ring, how was I any different from the women he'd been with despite his protestations that I possessed singular qualities?

"You're special," he insisted. How I wanted to believe that!

I PROMISE you this fog will burn off by ten and we'll have another beautiful day. Look, there's already people headed down to the beach with towels and picnic baskets. Let's see, okay. I walked quite a while on that dirt road where trees hangin' over both sides made it so you couldn't see very far. Not a single soul or farm animals in sight and no cars and trucks either. It would give anybody the willies; all quiet except for the wind and when the sleet rattled down; empty fields and orchards. I spotted a roof way back from the road and walked down the long drive. It was a solid stone house, two stories with dormers. Barn behind, ivy on the walls of both; the place was centuries old by my guess.

I knocked on the locked door and then hammered. Nobody at home, so I pulled off a shutter and went in through the window. Nice rooms, nice furniture, lots of stuff for the looters when they came. That's one of the few advantages of war, not that I got much chance to help myself being jerked around by the White House as I was. I noticed plenty of times that soldiers roaming free are too greedy; give them time and they load up with more stuff than they can handle. They'd leave a place bent double with loot and right away begin

132 | JERRY JAY CARROLL

throwing away stuff. You'd see all sorts of gear that got the heave-ho; I once saw a grand piano alongside the road. You had to admire the ambition. People with money lived in the farmhouse, but probably now were in that horde on the road. You have to be really scared to leave everything behind.

Of course, there was plenty of reasons to be afraid. A shot fired from a village meant the Germans executed every man there, the older boys too. Brutal bastards, the Germans. My stomach was growling like a pack of wolves were in there fighting to get out, so I helped myself in the kitchen to ham and a hunk of cheese on brown bread so stale I guessed three or four days passed since the owners ran off.

I was nervous about my uniform because it was a natural target for both sides. Looking in the closets told me the men were built like squatty beer barrels, but then I came to a room with pictures of a gigantic man with a jaw strong enough to hold up a bridge. He must've been seven feet or more, eight feet even, a real freak of nature, especially coming from this family. One picture showed him in a coffin built special, maybe two sawed apart to make one.

I suppose he'd been a family favorite, lifting them up from the ordinary, someone they could brag about, and the room was kind of a shrine. The pictures on the walls showed kings and prime ministers on their tiptoes to pin medals on his chest and to put sashes over his head. He must have done something besides just being big—raised money for the poor or some deal like that—but these people were Walloons so I couldn't read what he got the fancy certificates for.

The clothes in his closet were way too large, but staying in uniform upped the possibility of taking a bullet on the road. I picked a suit, midnight blue, expensive fabric, the same he wore in all the pictures. He wasn't just tall; the coat hung down to my ankles to give you an idea, and enormous everywhere else. I rolled the trouser legs up above my knees and cinched his belt around my chest with a hole I made with an icepick in the kitchen. There was nothing I could do about that coat. The shoulders sagged way down on my arms so I rolled sleeve cuffs above my elbows. His bad weather cape dragged on the floor like a wedding gown. I needed a hat to go with the outfit, but the smallest sat on my ears so heavy they bent over under the weight. In the mirror I looked like a kid playing grown-up, but there was no helping it.

A mule had showed up at the barn looking to be fed; he hee-hawed and trotted over smartly when I came outside. The Senator said they are more intelligent than other animals, and he had all kinds on his plantation. The farm horses had run off with no idea where they were going, whereas the mule reasoned there was a better chance of getting fed if he stuck around.

After I gave him oats in a bucket, I put on a saddle and bridle and we jogged down the long drive and turned on to the road to Lomme. It was windier and coming on toward dark when I saw a family that had been slow getting on the road, stubborn types most likely. They ran into a field when I raised my arm to show I was friendly. When it happened again with another group, I figured people must be scared by my outfit; the cloak billowed and snapped like a sail catching the wind. Something monstrous this way comes, that's what they must have been thinking, and raising my arm like I did was like I was sending an evil spell upon them. I would have run for it myself to be truthful; who needs more trouble with a war going on?

A little ways on I saw a vehicle on the road and thought what if it's a German patrol? It wasn't likely this far west, not yet, but they were always surprising us. I considered galloping across the plowed field to my left and jumping the ditch at the far end, but mules aren't as nimble as horses nor as fast, and they can have strong opinions about running and jumping. They stop on a dime if they feel like it and there you go, flipping like a coin over its ears. If it was Germans they might think it great sport to give chase and shoot me from the saddle. So I stayed put and saw when it got closer that the vehicle was an Austin, which the British used as scout cars before we gave them Jeeps.

It stopped and a soldier got out for a long look through field glasses. I waved both arms to show I was friendly. All that loose cloth caught the wind and nearly lifted me off the saddle; the mule danced and tossed his head up and down like bucking was next on the agenda. The man with the field glasses said something to the driver and the car eased forward slow and easy. They told me later they feared I was bait for a trap.

"Hello," I yelled, "I'm an American!"

"What in God's name are you dressed up as?" said a major with his sidearm drawn when he and his sergeant pulled alongside.

The officer was a middle-aged man with a dent in his forehead from the Great War; he and the driver both had red-rimmed eyes and looked like they would benefit from a solid twenty-four hours in the rack. "I'll need to see some military identification," he said tiredly. He holstered his pistol as I climbed down from the saddle and dug my ID out of an inside breast pocket deep enough that my hand went up to the forearm.

The driver immediately dropped off to sleep while Major Wentworth-Smyth studied my identification.

"The United States Navy?" he said puzzled-like.

He handed it back and rubbed his face. I told him I was looking for Fourth Division HQ.

"Did you see any German units back your way?" he asked, which gave me a good jolt.

Aren't they in front of us except maybe for scouting parties, I asked.

He gave out with a bitter laugh. "They're all over, breakthroughs everywhere. The Belgians are melting away, leaving our flanks bare-assed. I say, do you know how to operate one of these? The sergeant keeps falling asleep at the wheel and I'm knackered myself. We nearly ran into a tree a while back."

They were headed for their regimental HQ east off that road. The Austin was a two-seater and the sergeant shifted to the tiny space behind them and went back to snoring inches from my ear. I've been that tired myself; you don't have the strength to chew even if you're starving to death.

"Take the second right turn and stay on it four miles," Wentworth-Smyth said, "then we go left at the windmill. Wake me and I'll take over. Don't turn on the headlamps no matter what."

I unsaddled the mule and turned him loose and the major and I climbed aboard, him falling asleep as fast as the sergeant. He hadn't mentioned my weird getup again, showing how bushed they were. Traveling slow for some considerable time on account of the darkness, I saw flames up ahead putting out black smoke yellow and orange on the bottom, sort of beautiful in a hellish way. That was what was left of the convoy I was with.

"We didn't see them because they came out of the clouds," the major said. "Two Messerschmitt 109s; they passed us to get to the trucks."

He covered his nose with a handkerchief. "Those tires will burn for days."

He went back to sleep, and I woke him at the windmill. He took the wheel and gave the password, "Buggered," when challenged at two outposts.

"Someone's sense of humor, but it couldn't describe the situation better," he said half to himself.

The road became a trail and then petered out, and we traveled over rough ground to trees where officers stood under a tarp looking at a map with a flashlight; torches they call 'em. They stared in amazement when I got out of the car, lifting the giant cloak up for fear of tripping and walking careful so the cuffs didn't unroll. I must have seemed dainty, which is not the impression you want to give hard-faced men in war. There was laughter and remarks from the Other Ranks. Your common soldier is as crude as they come.

"I'm sure there is an explanation for this, major," said a precise voice I recognized; it was General Brooke, who gave the talk at that dinner Churchill put on.

"We found him riding a mule west of here, sir," Wentworth-Smyth said.

"Why is he wearing that strange costume?" Brooke asked. The major said he hadn't quite got round to that.

"Really? It would have been my first question." There was a chuckle or two, which I admit I joined in with. Brooke silenced us with a look.

"We've met, general," I said. Brooke's mouth fell open, he was that surprised. He said in this cold voice, "I have never met anyone of your appearance."

I took the big hat off. "It was at Winston Churchill's home in London where you talked to us about the war."

He put his torch on my face. "Yes, I recognize you now. Brady, isn't it? An American cousin of his as I recall."

I explained my orders from Washington and how I hitched a ride with the convoy that was in flames on the road; not going into the funny feeling thing, of course. The military mind is not open on some subjects. I said I'd been doing some scouting around on my own and we parted company a ways back. He asked the others if they knew about a convoy, and an officer said he believed trucks with medical supplies were due. That's the one, I said.

"A total loss," said Major Wentworth-Smyth. I explained the reason for my clothes and a few heads nodded.

"Many a man falls from friendly fire," someone said, "the hazards of war."

A staff officer with a red cap band and red tabs said when he was a kid he saw a giant man at a circus. "He was monstrous and I hid behind my mother's skirts. The ringmaster said the giant had no feeling in his legs and feet, which resulted in his shuffling walk that scared the bejesus out of us little ones."

Artillery began firing somewhere off to the east—I learned later five thousand rounds were shot over thirty-six hours in just one engagement in that area. A corporal came round with biscuits and tea in a bucket. They made a line and he slopped it into mugs, spilling as much as went in. I was impressed by how dirty everyone was. They had the original dirt on them, followed by mud, and then who knows how many more layers on top.

General Brooke tipped his head at me and we walked out of earshot. "Why are you here?" he asked. He was not a man to waste words, at least not on small fry like me.

I said all I knew was my orders were to liaison with his headquarters.

"Whatever for?" he asked. "You're in the American navy, I recall Winston telling me that, but even if you were an army officer I don't see the point. Is your country planning to send people over?"

I told him not so far as I knew.

"These have been desperate days and I'm not always in touch with the War Office, but surely some word would have reached me." He looked off in the darkness. "You will stay with us until I have clarification. Do you have something else to wear?" I explained that my uniform was in the scout car, but things happened so fast I didn't have a chance to switch.

"CHANGE AT once," he ordered and walked off to talk to a colonel; the subject was obvious from the looks that came my way.

As I was pulling on my trousers, a young corporal hustled up with field rations. "Colonel Nelson thought you was hungry." Canned ham, two kinds of biscuits, cheese, fruit pudding and other odds and sods as the English say. "Eat fast 'cuz the general and them is pushin' off back to Armentiers and Third Division lines double-quick."

I didn't want to seem ungrateful, but I wanted a look at the food in better light. I suspected they'd been in a warehouse since the Armistice, and my suspicion was vermin had been at the boxes over the years.

I rode with the colonel in an armored car with a driver and a sergeant carrying a Thompson submachine gun. Nelson was one of those spit-and-polish lifers at home anyplace where Reveille starts the day and the Last Post ends it. Chain-of-command, men marching on parade grounds, orders shouted, flashy salutes with foot stamps, gin after sundown, carry on sergeant-major, *Suh!*. You get the picture, the backbone of the professional army type, married to it actually. He'd served in nearly every godforsaken outpost of the empire, putting down revolts and marching troublemakers off to prisons they never came out of.

"We knew what to do with them, Lieutenant," he told me, "and the world was better for it."

He had a stone face, if he ever smiled I wasn't looking, and a raspy voice from shouting orders. He worked his way around to the real reason for inviting me to ride with him.

"I know what you told the general, but orders or not it doesn't make sense. A war front is risky place, as you know now if you didn't before."

I explained how I thought it might be revenge for something my stepfather did.

"A politician is he?" Nelson said. "I don't care for that lot, never did. Still, putting a man in danger because of a stepfather is hardly cricket. And the reality is he doesn't give a rat's ass about you?" He shook his head. "Speaking of which, I'd be careful with the field rations; I found mouse turds in the latest batch. In my opinion, war profiteers should be stood up for a last cigarette and shot without any rubbish about trials."

I won't repeat what else he said on the subject seeing as how you're a lady and my wife on top of it, but he had some strong feelings on the subject. He relaxed a little when he was satisfied I was harmless enough, just caught up in the bedlam of warlike the rest of them.

Maybe he was a fairy deep down, you heard that about some career military; goes back to the Greeks they say. A brigadier on leave got cashiered when he was arrested in Bath for public drunkenness. He was dressed up in high heels and a frilly dress, lipstick as well and a beauty spot on his cheek. His wig was snatched off by a woman in a fight over a man while a bobby watched from across the street. It got a big splash in the tabloids when I was living with Churchill; even the *Times* had a mention.

There was bolt-to-the-sea pressure in the War Office, which Brooke barely beat off in favor of orderly retreat. They fell back 127 miles over nine days in good order, and then the French and Belgians had lost their nerve and things went to hell.

The colonel could never forgive them. "The men who survived the Great War sired a generation of weaklings and cowards." He had a flask and offered me a swallow of first-rate brandy. "Liberated from a fine cellar; I've got two cases in a lorry that would cost a fortune in London."

We stopped for a few hours by a big, silent barn with the vehicles parked in a tight circle and guards posted in twos to keep each other awake for German infiltrators. I slept soundly as usual, too soundly to judge from the colonel when morning came. We were on the road nearing Armentieres when we began seeing people in brown corduroy suits by the side of the road.

"My God," Nelson said, "they've let the lunatics out of the asylum."

There were dozens of them grinning, drooling from the corners of their mouths and dripping from their noses. "Catastrophes on all sides," he said, "a dozen new rumors every day, bombed from low levels, the French army disintegrating, and now this. Sometimes it gets to be too much."

I thought that might explain the crazy thinking I kept hearing that the War Office had sent an American to spy on them. The division was worn out and when you're like that the mind plays tricks, I know from my own experience. One time I…there I go again, wandering off course.

The GHQ was at a schoolhouse where the people outside were jittery and pacing or heads in hands; there didn't seem to be any in between. The Belgians looked panic-stricken and the French as stunned as cows at the slaughterhouse. Inside, the brass were arguing over a map, but their loud voices quieted down when Brooke walked in all business with me tagging behind Colonel Nelson. The map on the wall had long arrows and little ones in between.

"Good Lord," the colonel said to me in a low voice, "the general told me it was bad, but I didn't quite grasp how bad. German armor will cut us off from the coast if it's not stopped."

A French general had a stupefied expression as he turned from the map and said a few words to Brooke, who patted him on the shoulder.

"That's General Blanchard, commander of the French First Army since Billotte was killed," Brooke said when he came back. "His brain has ceased to function. Nothing is registering and he might as well be staring at a blank wall as that map."

I went over and saw from a closer look at the arrows where the heavy fighting was and where it wasn't but soon would be. Getting those dog-tired troops on the move was going to take time, and that map showed the Germans moving fast.

As I left with all the roads straight in my head, I heard Brooke telling Nelson the German army was wonderful at waging war and they'd be lucky to save a quarter of the BEF. "I think I must burn my diary."

I kept going, trying to look like a man out for a bit of fresh air. Outside, I searched for General Blanchard's car. I figured if he was as out of it as Brooke said his would be the easiest to snatch. An enlisted man senses when a commander loses his grip—it's like dogs smelling fear in people—and he'd be goofing off somewheres.

And sure enough, there it was under a tree for the shade, a polished black sedan with a *Général de corps d'armée* pennant and license plates with the keys in the ignition. Nobody would expect a car would be pinched in the middle of an armed camp with guns everywhere, so it was as easy as stealing candy from a baby. I drove past the guard post with a wave and I'm guessing I was thirty miles up the road before they discovered the Citroen was gone.

The road was clogged with the refugees, of course, and I was afraid I'd burn the horn out before I reached Dunkirk. Shields the truck driver was right about them being sleepwalkers, hunched down under heavy loads, putting one foot down after another, not looking right or left, they were like a people herd, too tired to talk or anything but shuffle. I probably passed twenty or thirty thousand, laying on the horn even when it got feeble and wavering. Maybe a hundred thousand as I think about it now. I know from your face what you're thinking, but I couldn't give anybody a ride. Stop even for a pretty young woman and she'd want her whole family to hop in like I was driving a bus.

There were military police in their cars at intersections or along the road, not doing any good at all that I could see. A general riding with refugees? It would be suspicious as hell, whereas a single officer on special business blastin' away on a horn was to be expected. The French police had a pretty high opinion of themselves, at least before the Germans rubbed their nose in the dirt. They were symbols of the Republic, all of them little de Gaulles in their way.

Another thing that might be minor to some but wasn't to me was the French aren't over-fond of baths at the best of times; imagine the smell after days of slogging on the roads. Even with all the windows down…well, no need to waste more breath because you're not convinced, so we'll have to agree to disagree, darlin'

I BELIEVE our conversations, begun as an oral history and his vow to be honest, were helping Lowell understand himself better even though there was little change in his manner. As I wrote before, he was not someone to whom reflection came natural. He was like the water bug that skims the skin of a pond unmindful of the depths and currents below.

It was twilight when he drove into Dunkirk with the stinging sleet still falling. It was not yet the chaos it became later when English and French soldiers by the tens of thousands stood in lines that reached into the sea waiting for rescue, but Lowell said it was filling with dejected troops.

CHAPTER 9

MADE MY WAY THROUGH A CROWD OF WET AND COLD TOMMIES ON THE JETTY AND told a lieutenant that decided who got on the next ship and who had to wait that I was on a special mission for Winston Churchill.

"Get in line," he said with a real cold look. I headed off to find someone easier to work with and pretty soon felt like a rag-and-bone man going door to door with more sneers and snarls for my trouble. I repeated it so often I began to half believe it myself.

I reached a Captain Leigh with dark circles under his eyes from no sleep, but he livened up as I started my story about being a special observer bringing a fresh eye from the front on the orders of the prime minister himself.

"Hold on," he said, "we got a rocket to look for a wandering Yank."

"That's me!" I said.

I was digging for my military I.D. when he grabbed a bunch of my coat front and yanked me down. I remember thinking is this necessary as the ground rushed up? I figured I was being arrested and believed it could be done without him showing off for the crowd.

A Focke-Wulf 190 streaked overhead at roof-top level with guns blazing, only a glimpse as it was going so fast. The destroyer just nosing through the gray mist let fly with its fifty-calibers and four-inchers, tracking the plane as it went out into the channel dropping pieces and starting to smoke.

"Sorry I had to be so rough," he said, helping me up and dusting me off, "they're on you before you realize it."

Ten yards on from us, a dozen or more men waiting for embarkation

didn't get up. If the German pilot had pulled the trigger a split second earlier Captain Leigh and I would be standing before St. Peter. The men looked
like heaps of dirty clothes set out for laundering. My knees were so weak I
had to sit down.

"It wasn't our time," Leigh said with a funny kind of laugh. "First time
under fire?" he asked, squatting alongside me.

I nodded dumbly.

"You get used to it," he said.

The fact of the matter is I never did. What kind of screwball says that anyhow? I work all the angles to keep safe and still I'm nearly killed. It made me
wonder what's the use of all my scheming When I could stand up I put my
hands in my pockets to hide the shaking. Men around us were already joking, crazy as it sounds.

"You nearly bought it that time, Charlie," one says.

"At least you'd be going with me," the other answers.

Everybody roared like they never heard anything so funny. I'm thinking the oil must not reach the dipstick with these guys. That's a Southern
saying.

"Special recce for the prime minister, eh," Leigh said. "Must be hush-hush,
so I'll ask no questions how you ended up in this miserable mess."

He led me past the dead ones and the men kicking and howling on the
ground to the front of the line where he dressed down the lieutenant for not
reading the order of the day down to where I was mentioned

"So sorry." Lieutenant Snow looked as guilty as a dog caught sucking a
hen's egg, and I felt a murderous hatred. I would have been protected by layers of steel if he'd let me on in the first place. Captain Leigh said young Snow
was a good man who showed promise.

Smiling like a prince sticking out his ring to be kissed, I acted like I was
big enough to forgive. Why, anyone can make an honest mistake, I said, I've
made a few of myself. The captain told Snow to carry on and he saluted and
stamped, glad to get out of range.

"Officer coming through," Leigh shouted, and the mass of men waiting
for the gangplank to lower parted nice as you please. He waved me up with
a "Cheerio."

Who should be standing at the top but Captain Phipps-Howard, who gaped like I was still in the giant's suit.

"I never thought I'd see you again," he called.

That makes two of us, I hollered back, taking off my hat and pretending to wipe away sweat. Coming up, I reasoned that modest and humble was the best course until I got myself together, my nerves shot to pieces like they were.

He gave me a handshake at the top and we climbed the ladder to the bridge. I was as slow as the circus fat man due to my shaky legs. Phipps-Howard opened a locked desk drawer in his cubbyhole of a cabin and brought out a bottle of gin and a glass.

"A bracer for special occasions," he said, holding the glass up to the light to see if it was clean. "I think a narrow escape from death qualifies."

He left to watch over the embarkation and I tried to pour a dollop into the glass; I couldn't do it, my hands were shaking so much, so I took a long gulp straight from the bottle. It hit my empty stomach right away and there I was, reeling drunk on legs I already couldn't depend on.

I was afraid I'd fall and injure myself, so I sat in the chair and put my head on his desk. Everything that had happened seemed to hit me all at once; I don't know how long before I got woke up by the ship's high-speed turn that slid me hard against the bulkhead. Quick-firing four inch guns and pom-poms fired, followed by the .50-inch machine guns.

I can't think of a faster way to sober up except for what happened next. The hatch blew open and a warrant officer flew through on the shock wave from a monster explosion. I figured out later he saw the bomb coming and was making for the protection of the captain's cabin. I was saved by the steel bulkhead that bent in with a clang like it was hit by a huge sledgehammer. Lucky I was only hit by little stuff and not the flying furniture.

The man was flung against the rear bulkhead and his head was cracked open like a coconut. Dead as a doornail, groggy as I was that was obvious. I staggered out to what was left of the bridge. I was bleeding from my ears and a giant ringing was all I heard.

Twisted steel with body parts and guts hanging everywhere, a face sliced from its head as neat as by a scalpel hanging like a rubber mask on a shaft of steel—Phipps-Howard's it was—a leg without pants, a hand missing two fingers. I could go on but I won't. I saw as bad or worse in the Pacific later on, but this was the first time. I don't want to talk about it anymore.

CHAPTER 10

I FELT REMORSE THAT MY ENCOURAGEMENT HAD TAKEN LOWELL BACK TO THAT TER-rible scene, every detail unearthed from his prodigious memory as sharp and clear as if it had happened that morning. His natural jauntiness left him and we discontinued the interviews.

We walked on the beach in sun hats in the days that followed, mine floppy and his a dapper Panama, and we sat on folding chairs under an umbrella in our bathing suits reading books or newspapers. We talked of inconsequential things

Lowell was a great fan of Westerns, preferably by Zane Grey though Louis L'Amour was "coming on strong," while I slowly worked my way through *Remembrance of Things Past* by a Frenchman named Marcel Proust. A co-worker at the Smithsonian had told me it was a literary masterpiece few outside of Paris knew of, but my interest was that it seemed a tremendous feat of memory and might assist me with Lowell when we resumed his story…if we did.

We became very tan on the beaches and the tensions of fugitive life lightened. Lowell gradually lost the habit of going to the window several times an hour to steal looks from behind the curtains, and I didn't jump as much at sudden noises.

Most nights we drove to picture shows and afterward to dinner at one of the many fine seafood restaurants along the Pacific Coast Highway. We saw "High Noon" with Gary Cooper, "The Quiet Man" with John Wayne, and "Singin' in the Rain" with Gene Kelly and Debbie Reynolds. Sometimes it took an hour or more to drive inland to a theater where a movie played we wanted to see, but neither of us cared as it took our minds off things. We saw "My Cousin Rachael" with Olivia deHavilland, "Pat and Mike" with Spencer Tracy and Katharine Hepburn, "Sudden Fear" with Joan Crawford.

The destroyer had limped the rest of the way to Dover, steered amidships from the secondary conning station. The bomb made the tragedy worse for those who'd gone through hell and believed were headed home to the arms of loving families and thinking of steak-and-kidney pie if the makings could be found on the black market, and looking forward to pints and darts at the pubs.

Those are my suppositions, of course; Lowell's mind did not run in that direction. As time passed, I began to think we would never return to our work and, to be truthful, my naïve belief that we had a duty to History had begun to fade in the face of the obstacles that perhaps always rise in the path of Truth. Lowell's narrative that disputed an event now embedded in national mythology would be assailed from many quarters, including influential pen-for-hire notables in the academy who had close connections to officialdom.

As I showed earlier, the Smithsonian—for all of its lofty claims of independence—would be only too happy to pitch in with a nimble hornpipe to the piper's tune. Lowell's recollections would be dismissed as the work of a publicity-seeking crank, and I inwardly shrank when I pictured the expert abuse and scorn heaped from on high by credentialed experts snug in their tenure and endowed chairs. And then would come the unbearable vulgar laughter. He would be the butt of jokes by Bob Hope and other comics on the radio.

His poker winnings and the unfreezing of my bank account in Montana by a judge over the government's objections allowed the continuation of a comfortable life of leisure and travel. The possibility of arrest or gangland reprisal were the only clouds on our horizon.

My brother told me a man with a broken nose who stood out in his city clothes and lower-class Eastern dem-and-dose accent turned up on the doorstep one morning to ask how to get in touch with me for an important message; neighbors said he had also called on them.

That bald, last-ditch approach to family and friends seemed to assure all other possibilities had been exhausted. A quiet life led as unobtrusively as ours would with the passage of time further lower the likelihood of threats materializing. One morning as I made breakfast, Lowell in pajamas and slip-pers lugged the tape recorder from the closet.

"We might as well get on with it. Looking back, if I'd known things were going to be as hot as they were on the beachhead I'd have hired a Frenchie to row me across the Channel."

■◣■

A CAR with a junior diplomat who looked like a kid and a Marine Corps driver old enough to be his pa waited behind a bunch of ambulances lined up when *Amazon* came in. Their faces told me I looked as bad as the rest of the walk-ing wounded as we came down the gangplank into misting rain in our bloody bandages and splints. The worst cases had gone before on stretchers with nurses alongside. Their rain capes glistened in the lights and the white faces under dark hoods looked like sad little flowers; there's a bit of detail you're always squeezing me for.

For morale reasons no crowds were there to cry out Oh My Lord and so on at our beaten look. Orders straight off were not to evacuate any more stretcher cases because they took up as much space as seven men standing cheek-by-jowl. The Royal Navy lost six destroyers and twenty-five got beaten up at Dunkirk. The Germans could have raised even more hell, but they pulled back most of their fighters to hound the French on the roads. Take a wound bad enough to be a stretcher case and then your country leaves you behind at the mercy of the enemy; it don't seem fair, does it, but that's war and peo-ple should know when they sign up.I

"Would you like to clean up a little, sir?" asked the State Department pip-squeak, not looking me in the face. Squeamish was my guess, the smelling salts type. At least I think he said that, I couldn't make out words because of the roaring in my ears. I asked him to keep repeating what he was telling me until he gave over the job to the corporal. He was Old Breed and used to bel-lowing at recruits and his words came through, but only barely.

"There's dried blood all over your face and down the front," he yelled through cupped hands. Your average Marine puts a high store on appear-ances; it's drilled into them from boot camp. "You want to clean yourself up?"

Nope, I said, thinking the worse I looked the better. The Royal Navy on the look for a stray Yank told me Washington had put a lot of heat on. That would be the work of my mother; I wouldn't be surprised if Eleanor Roosevelt herself was pulled in. The Senator would turn the burner up full blast on all parties concerned to get through the storm he'd be going through with Mother.

It wasn't hard to picture the fit she'd throw when he said her fair-haired boy not only was sent off to the battlefront but missing in action. If the Senator wasn't blind, he would've run out of the house with hands on ears, but instead he would have to feel his way from room to room with her dogging his every step screeching like a parrot. I saw those scenes many times. He said a flogging around the fleet like in the old days was easier on a man.

She snatched his blind man's cane from his hand in one of these blowups and gave him a good crack on the head; raised a lump, that one, and he wore a hat indoors and out for some time. The trouble then was for bringing a few of his backcountry pals to a garden party for her high society friends. The men had big chaws in their jaws and spewed tobacco juice on the ground, and whooped and swore like they were at a roadhouse back home. It was the moonshine, of course; they distilled it till it had a kick like a mule.

The Senator said afterward it was an invite given in the spirit of fellowship with men known as steady voters. Mother said she knew what kind of spirit it was and gave a yank to his thick, snowy-white hair that people always admired. The Senator spent three nights in the cellar on a camp bed before she took pity on account of the damp being hard on his rheumatism.

When Mother passed away, I was given pictures of me as a toddler in a dress and curly blond hair. Photos like them was common from that time and some might've saved theirs, but mine went directly from the album to the fireplace. I don't believe any mother loved a kid more than me when she remembered she'd born me. As I told you before, her social schedule and foreign travels and so forth ate up time and months passed without me seeing her. Taking care of me was the job of nannies and tutors that came to the plantation and lived with us in the big house.

Plantation was what the Senator called it before he went into politics. He told voters then he had a little ole patch of ground with a truck garden down by the kitchen door and a bit of land for cotton scarcely worth mentioning; the truth was it ran as far as the eye could see into the next county with a dead cousin's name on the title to throw off the scent. He ripped into bankers and railroad interests when he mentioned his little ole patch in those stemwinders at county fairs where he got the yokels all in a lather about the Republicans. He raised his foot to show the hole in his shoe, proving he was as down to earth as any of them. Those shoes were kept in tissue paper in a box in the closet when he wasn't out on the campaign trail.

Mother was always pleased to see me when she came home, of course, kissing and cuddling and all that; I was brought out by a nanny when I was little for grand ladies to coo over when they came a-visiting. I didn't like being crushed into bosoms that smelled of powder or lavender water, but I was little and could only cry and wave my arms. When I grew teeth it was a different story.

"Be careful," the nanny would warn, "he's a biter."

The female secretaries and clerks at the embassy looked sick with horror when I came through the door; they put hands to their mouths and I heard a scream. I asked for the Navy photographer and he got shots from all angles, including me grinning with both thumbs up in case there was a use that came up for that in the future. You should always look ahead in life. Then I went upstairs to look Admiral Deveral in the eye.

"He's not here," said Commander Logan Mather, his adjutant. "He got a high priority message from Washington and flew out this morning." Mather had sandy hair and blue eyes that said he found a lot of things in life funny, which meant short of war he wasn't going to rise higher in rank against the humorless types, steely men with muscles knotted in their jaws to show they mean business.

"You look like hell," he wrote on paper when he saw I couldn't hardly hear. "You can wash up in the admiral's private shitter. I've got a spare uniform so you can be a commander until you get squared away."

It didn't take a genius to see there was a connection between me being sent into danger and Deveral yanked home. I put a call home that went through right away.

"Praise God," Mother cried. "Senator, he's on the phone!" Mather was listening in to write down her words for me. I told her I was fine and dandy and went on a bit more before a look from one of the communications people reminded me the line was for highest priority calls. I said I would write a letter, which to be honest I never got around to.

Mather was glad the admiral was gone and looked about to bust out laughing. I washed myself off and changed clothes. I had lots of bruises and little nicks and dings, but except for my hearing I seemed to have come out okay, at least physically. I kept seeing Phipps-Howard's face in my dreams and the nurses ran to shake me awake because my yelling bothered the other patients.

I went back to thinking how unpredictable life in war is. I was hardly on the front at all compared to the BEF soldiers, but whose picture gets in the papers and is called a hero? I'll take unfair anytime as long as I'm on the long side of it.

The embassy doctor said I had punctured eardrums but my hearing might come back and I wouldn't need an ear trumpet the rest of my life; he found that funnier than I did. He got me into a posh private hospital where I lounged around being coddled and always being asked was I feeling better? I don't know how, but word got around that I went to France to help the Tommies and people acted like I was up for a medal; not a VC but in that neighborhood.

You'll think I started the talk, but I didn't, Scout's honor. But I didn't deny it, either; I just looked off into the distance and said the weather is nice today for a change or ain't it raining hard? I believe people thought more of me for that in light of the tabloids showing that picture of me all bloody and thumbs up. "Hero Yank," one headline said. "Mystery Mission," said another. That Navy photographer probably got plenty for the picture; those London tabloids lay out big money.

Colville offered me the use of his country home in Suffolk to recuperate and sent his Rolls and driver around to the hospital; I lolled in the back seat and looked out at the countryside. The fields had all been plowed up to grow food so ut wasn't as pretty as before. We rolled through picture postcard villages now and then where people looked healthier than London. The shops had goods in the windows instead of being empty or having some pitiful display that gathered dust.

Still wearing his rear admiral's uniform with the sleeve pinned up on his missing arm from his meetings with important people, Colville showed me around his home, which of course was centuries old and a bastard to keep warm.

"General Cornwallis slept in this bedroom," he said. His foxy face got sharp like he was wondering would I recognize the name, which no doubt was in all the history books. Of course I didn't; the Ironwood School for Boys not being much for learning. I expect I would've come across General Cornwallis in a regular school and taught to talk with proper grammar and such that you call me on instead of one that hired out its students to work at the sawmills and farms. It fattened the bottom line while making us too worn out for the troublemaking that came natural, that being the reason we were there.

Colville had a painting on a wall of a fiftyish man in a redcoat uniform with a big gut that stretched a white waistcoat tight as a drumhead. I nodded at him in a sage way. Put on some weight by then, didn't he. That gave the idea I knew General Cornwallis forward and backward and could talk about him until the cows came home.

Coleville nodded. "That was painted long after he surrendered our army to you Yanks at Yorktown. He was Governor-General of India at this time, creating the foundations of the British Raj."

When I thought about it later, I wasn't so sure I'd buffaloed him. He might have seen through my bluff, good as it was, but didn't let on so I'd think I outsmarted him. He was a tricky man, Colville; you had to be on your toes all the time. He had been recalled to active duty despite that missing arm and being old as the hills, but I never had a clear idea what he did other than being seen everywhere and knowing everybody who counted and a lot who didn't. He got extra gas rations for his Rolls, which must have sucked up gas like a camel at the oasis.

As a guess, I'd say his job was finding out what people didn't want known and passing it on to MI6; he was a God and Country man willing to give his all. I'm pretty sure he saw me as just a handsome dog—he always said that—with only dust and cobwebs upstairs. But he calculated I might be of use through my influence with the Senator because of Mother, and also her being a friend of Eleanor Roosevelt whose nose was in everyone's business. Even then the British knew we blabbered top-secret stuff at Georgetown cocktail parties they wouldn't give away if their fingernails were torn out by the Huns or Japs.

Everyone gets looser with alcohol, but Colville nursed his drinks at parties and dinners and receptions, silently taking in people. When a few smarter ones wised up, he'd notice and right away spin out some funny behind-the-scenes story that cracked people up. Throwing off suspicion, you see. A good many were about cuckolded husbands and deceiving wives in royal courts over the centuries.

He showed me his beautiful gun room one morning and said he was off to London for a week and I should use any weapon I had a mind to; not to bother cleaning and oiling afterward as he had a man for that.

"The rabbits are terrible this year," he said. "Please shoot as many you can, but not to the point of over-taxing yourself, you're here to rest. The Winchester Model 20 is quite good if you're a .410 smoothbore man; though some of the hearty types say it's a touch feminine. My personal favorite for rabbits is the Wesley-Richards sporting rifle, but you do have a choice here."

That didn't do justice to it; there must have been forty rifles up to an elephant gun laid out on black velvet in showcases like in a museum. The only other person in the house after he left was the old housekeeper Moira who also cooked. She put out good chow, nothing fancy but enough so your ribs didn't show. While I'd still been in the hospital, Mather came by with a report wrote out in pencil about what went on with Admiral Deveral in case I was still deaf.

"There was a hot time in the old town when the White House tried to reach you for Harry Hopkins. I don't know if it was Hopkins himself on the line or the CNO, but the admiral jumped up at his desk pale as a sheet. I happened to be there briefing him on the next convoy coming from the states when the priority phone rang. He told whoever it was he wasn't quite sure where you were.

'Well, yes sir, he's in Europe all right, but I just don't know where exactly. I merely passed on an order I received. Sir, I never quite knew what his duties were. He seemed to spend a lot of time talking to young women on the embassy staff when he came around, but apart from that I couldn't...He didn't tell me what he was doing over here. He came close one time, but I said I didn't want to know, I made it an order in fact. No, I didn't know his work was important. Close to Churchill? No, I certainly didn't know that, sir. If I had...I received the order from the Bureau of Navigation. Captain Charles, sir. Yes, it seemed unusual to me, conditions what they are, but I didn't think it was my responsibility to question...Somebody's joke? No, I certainly didn't think that. Tomorrow? Does it have to be that soon, Admiral, I mean I...yes, sir, I understand."

Mather busted out laughing when he saw I had read to that point and hollered he'd almost felt sorry for the old bastard. I reckoned he didn't want to leave me what he wrote out in case of blackmail if I was that sort. He put it in his pocket and walked out with a wave. I heard later Deveral was reassigned to run training depots in the Midwest. From London to Lake Michigan, quite a drop. Ain't revenge sweet?

Colville was right about the rabbits, which the local people said was a plague laid upon them. Between rabbits and the rats, forty percent of the crops got ruined. In the best growing areas where there was fine, dry soil like at Colville's estate, there were sixteen rabbits to the acre. In a certain kind of light it looked like the ground was moving.

I went out the following morning with the Winchester and Albert the handyman, who had a withered leg that kept him out of the army. It was bitter cold and our breath hung in the air like we were smoking cheroots. I shot fifty-three before lunch and would've got more except Albert liked head shots because of housewives not wanting to dig out lead and fur buyers preferring pelts without holes. He'd give out with a sigh if one moved just as I squeezed the trigger and took the round somewhere in its body.

Gamekeepers and poachers used to keep them down, but most of those were gone off to the war. Crop rotation, which the farmers didn't do so much of before, meant the females dropped more than one litter a year for they had more to feed on. The females born in the spring had their own litters come the fall.

The horse population never came back from being wiped out by the Great War, but lucky for the farmers we sent over Allis-Chalmers tractors by the shipload to make up for them. They came in one color, bright orange.

I reaped another seventy-two varmints in the afternoon before the light began to fail; Albert said his gammy leg was giving him trouble and the hand cart was full anyhow. There is a lot of walking with rabbit hunting, that and sitting in blinds to pick 'em off until you move on to the next patch which might be some considerable distance away.

The rabbits were supposed to be given up at the farm gate when the government man came collecting, but Albert kept back easily half for the black market. The going rate was two shillings each; he said he'd offer me a cut if

I wasn't an officer and a gentleman who'd rise up in anger at such insolence. He was a simple man in many ways, but crafty too.

After dinner, I hitched the pony to the dog cart and drove to the Drover and Plowman's, which was full of chatter when I came in. The silence that dropped was because I was a stranger, country folk not being friendly until they get used to you, which takes living among them for ten years. One of the Land Girls came giggling up to where I was having the pint I more than earned that day and asked was I a movie star from Hollywood?

Not the last time I looked, I tell her.

She turns to a table of them, half a dozen or so, and says, "No, not the last time he looked."

They laughed and laughed, making me wonder not the first time if maybe there was a future for me in radio someday with writers hired for funny stuff to say.

Go ahead and laugh, but I was being serious. If I didn't locate a rich woman to marry, still my first choice, I'd have to find some kind of work after the war and why not cracking jokes on radio? I'd hire some over-the-hill comic who worked cheap as my straight man. Of course, that wasn't my only idea.

Uncle Sam bought a round of gin and orange and I carried the drinks over myself, pretending to stumble and making them squeal. Land Girls were young city gals who signed up for work on the farms because of the labor shortage. They were good looking from hard work in the fields and taking in the clean air; blooming as the poets say.

"They're on their own and looking for a bit of fun," Albert had told me when I asked about the female situation. He was all for them, but Moira didn't like the idea of strange young women floating around free as birds and no one to look after their morals. You could tell Land Girls from the locals by what they wore, jodhpurs and work shirts.

I spent many a pleasant evening with them as Colville stayed longer in London than planned and even after he came back. I asked Mather to send a cable to the Navy Department saying my recovery was taking a bit longer than the doctors thought, but I'd be fit as a fiddle in fairly short order so they didn't order me home on convalescent leave.

I kept a blanket in the cart to spread on the ground in case one of the ladies wanted to join me studying the stars after the pub closed. For those whose interests didn't stretch to astronomy or thought it was too cold on the ground even with the blanket and too risky to invite me into the farmhouse, I'd whip up the pony and drop them off with a kiss on the cheek like a brother. I got a reputation for being a gentleman that way, not someone who pawed them… there's that look on your face again.

It got so I was as familiar with the countryside as a native. I'd pass a member of the Home Guard now and then who was on watch for spies dropped by parachute with Nazi deviltry in mind, though burning down a barn or stampeding the milk cows were the only possibilities around here. The guards worked the farm in the day and between the two jobs they were usually knackered, too tired to even say hello although surliness might have entered into it. The government knew how much land you had and told you what to plant. The neighbors snitched if you tried to sneak in another crop for cash on the side; you got fined for that or the government might even take your farm. The farmers had to meet production quotas, too, or their land was requisitioned.

Moira was early to bed and early to rise like most old people and didn't like it when I rattled up in the dog cart in the wee hours. I put the pony in the barn with feed and came in with a sharp appetite . She showed me what she was thinking with dark looks and muttering somebody was headed to the Lake of Fire as prophesied in Revelations.

Colville having the right connections in the rations department, she laid on a full fry-up with three eggs, sausage, back bacon, baked beans, fried tomatoes and fried bread. I usually managed to get a smile out of her when she passed to and fro grumbling how times had changed for the worse.

'Deed they have, I would say, I often notice myself.

But I'd come around to thinking what's the use of worrying unless someone with harm on their mind is right on your heels, which means at that point worry is called being careful. The devil takes the hindmost; that's not me and won't never be if I have something to say about it.

I'd hit the sack after breakfast and sleep like a baby until it was time to pick off more rabbits. Moira sent us off with a flask of coffee and a heavy picnic hamper for lunch; raised pies, Scotch eggs, boned and sliced chicken,

English cheeses, bread, and sweet butter. We brought it home empty because that weather up there makes a man hungry.

Shooting rabbits gets to be a drag like going to a regular job; I got a callus on my trigger finger like I'd been digging ditches with it. Rabbits were known as the poor man's chicken before the war, but people were happy enough to get them when the fighting started; even offal if that was in the shops. When things really began to pinch, the dukes and duchesses and other quality folk ate rabbit stew if there were no guests to impress, though I doubt Winston did. And, as I mentioned, in the cities they ate even worse. I don't believe any part of an animal was off limits there.

Albert told me when he visited his family in Birmingham he never asked what it was they put in front of him at meal time and closed his eyes like he was praying so as not to see. His family was struck by how devout he had become and believed it was the war. They told him not to worry because England would muddle through like they always did.

CHAPTER 11

I WAS HAVING A HARDER TIME MAINTAINING A DETACHED MANNER WHEN LOWELL mentioned the women he had known; pain and jealousy and other emotions showed all too plainly on my face to judge by the surprise on his. Neither of us could help it; I had encouraged truthfulness from the beginning and now was pulling back as he spoke about romantic conquests. One had "big kissable lips," another had beautiful blond hair "thick as a bear's pelt" down to her shapely hips. This one had "sparkly blue eyes" and that one had dark eyes "you sank in like quicksand."

Part of my response to these descriptions was the unfairness of the double standard. A man who goes from one woman to another is a Romeo or a Lothario. He is a Casanova or a Prince Charming, a lady-killer or a playboy, all words implicit with admiration for the skills of seduction. Women in contrast are condemned as sluts, tramps or floozies when they are not outright whores; they are fallen women for having adopted the same promiscuity Casanovas embrace without a second thought about what the world might think of their wantonness.

This cannot be said even in a neutral manner for purposes of argument without seeming to endorse a fast and loose life with a consequent lowering of one's own reputation for even bringing it up, but that doesn't make it less true. I was truly in a bind—I wanted Lowell to describe that period in fullest detail…except for those many liaisons. I wished that he skipped over these encounters rather than having to listen, not that he dwelt on them with lubricious detail; they were narrated briskly and even with matter-of-factness as women passed through his life as if through a turnstile.

This delicacy of mine made me an unreliable part of our narration if for no reason than his amorous adventures were the background and even the foreground of so much that went on. Often, they began and ended stories with the military and diplomatic developments hazy in the telling or passed over in summary fashion until my questioning returned him to what History would find important. Lowell would be in the rhythm of recollection only to be checked by a flicker of emotion I could not conceal, or in honesty perhaps more than a flicker.

"Do you want to know what happened or not?" he asked once with knitted brow as if trying to reconcile my contradictory expectations—the truth but, please, not all of it some of the time—was beyond his power. When he was caught up in the full flood of recollection, it was hard to resume with the same fluency after being brought to a standstill by my look of reproach or impatient sigh that slipped out before I could stifle it. The number of women with whom he'd had affairs, flings, one-nighters and other such dismissive characterizations could already be reckoned in the scores. I could not help the undercurrent of tension entering our marriage that even Lowell noticed.

I'M GLAD to see the cat doesn't still got your tongue as the saying goes. That fat Italian waiter came over twice at dinner to see if everything was all right, the way you sat stone-faced not touching a thing. He caught me when I was coming back from the gents to ask if there was trouble with the turbot that was flown in special on ice, but I told him I noticed you get like that sometimes for no reason. He threw an arm around my shoulders and started in about his wife's female problems, that maybe being the cause you get so quiet. Real emotional, he even got tears in his eyes. When his wife was low, he was low right there with her. She sometimes sat not talking or even looking at him. He's the strong kind of fat guy and needed to talk, even if it was to a total stranger like me. We grappled like a pair of college wrestlers working on a takedown before I broke free.

Let's see, where were we? When Colville came back from London he looked weighed down by worry like the fox that hears the owl hoot. That's an Algonquin story; the Indian tribe not the Algonquin Circle in New York City. They were backstabbing authors I met through Clare Booth Luce; they hated each other as much as they did her. Poisonous as adders in her way of telling, pens instead of fangs to inject the venom. They drank more than sailors, as fast too. Passing out or needing help to walk was common. She was married to Henry Luce, the magazine man; I told you about that before.

Colville sank into a chair in his heavy overcoat not saying a word. I offered to show him some new card tricks, which he'd always enjoyed before, but he shook his head slowly.

"We stand naked before the barbarians," he suddenly cries out, dramatic-like an actor on the stage.

Moira screamed from where she was working on a highboy with a cleaning rag and he told her to leave the room at once. She had an almighty fear of the Germans; I haven't mentioned that. Of course, everybody did down deep even if they were stiff upper lip on the outside. The newspapers scared them to sell more copies, not that the news wasn't bad enough and even worse according to what Colville said the censors cut out.

"Hundreds of small boats crossing the Channel in the days after your salvation was an epic feat never to be forgotten, but we must remember all of their supplies and equipment were left behind. Artillery, tanks, trucks, armored cars, automatic weapons, even a fully loaded train in Cherbourg—my God, everything an army needs to function. But you know all this from the BBC and the papers...don't you?"

Some of it, I said, a little uneasy from his sharp look at the pile of the Times stacked neat as a pin by his reading chair. The truth was that between rabbit hunting and evenings buying rounds to develop good will for Uncle Sam, I'd fell behind on the news. Oh, I'd catch a word here and there from the regulars talking low over their pints when I brought the tray to the bar for more gin and orange, but my hearing being not up to par as yet kept me from full understanding.

Colville appeared to sense I hadn't been paying close attention to all that and let out a sigh, a big one considering how good he controlled himself, but then after a minute he squared his shoulders and put on a face like someone with a job to do. I feel bad looking back that maybe I let him down; I could've been more up to the mark on the big picture. But it wasn't our war and I thought the Navy Department would be recalling me before long and I'd get plenty of that at work and at dinner listening to the Senator boast to Mother about how people in "the power circles" hung on his every word.

She'd tip her head and gaze admiringly at him, which she learned to do when they were courting and still kept it up. Though he was blind, he was smart about voices and could tell if she was reading a magazine or looking out the window at her garden as he talked. She winked when he'd tell me to step from the room because what he was going say had to stay there.

"There are a good many admirals at the top who don't know this," he'd say, all puffed up. If the Germans sent a spy in the bushes outside our window for a week there wouldn't be anything the Third Reich didn't know about our military plans, or Roosevelt's lady friend for that matter.

"Winston has asked the president if he would allow you to remain," Colville said, getting out of his overcoat with my help, "and the president graciously agreed with the stipulation you will not be exposed to war zones."

I was too stunned to say a word.

"Your 'letters' to your stepfather will be sent in our overnight diplomatic pouch to the British embassy to prevent leaks to the isolationists in your country. I believe you know General Alan Brooke? You made a...an impression on him in France. He has been named commander of the Home Forces on the strength of his sterling performance in France. He is taking a short break from his demanding duties to watch our breeding finches. He'll spend the night in the Cornwallis room and return to work after lunch. You don't mind switching rooms? I'm not a bird fancier myself but they're nearly as common hereabouts as the birds; it seems at times every man and woman in the neighborhood lurks behind a tree with binoculars."

I told Colville I could take or leave birds the same as him. He yanked a pull bell and Albert showed up so fast he was probably listening at the door. "Light the fire," Colville said, "and then help the driver wipe down the Rolls. Tell Moira to bring us tea and scones."

He held up a finger to me to say he didn't want Albert hearing what we said.

We meandered a bit about the weather and rabbits; I stated that I liked the Winchester Model 20 rifle even though some like he said might think it a touch on the dainty side. When Moira and Albert were gone, Colville said how I wangled my way back to England showed him I was cunning.

"Cunning is a word that does not inspire admiration, but I'll take a man with cunning over the man of action nine out of ten times. The cunning man looks ahead, sees opportunities the other man doesn't and seizes them by whatever stealth and deception is required. He slips around obstacles rather than battering through them for the acclaim of the mob. The cunning man doesn't care about the laurel wreath on the hero's brow; no, not at all. He knows that only excites envy and sets machinery in motion for the hero to be laid low . The cunning man is buttery and avoids conflict; the man of action is blinded by the prospect of glory."

What's this got to do with me, wonders I, as Colville looks at me over his tea cup. Naturally, he was already one or two steps ahead.

"I have a certain native cunning, which is why I recognize the same in you. I am other things of course; I like to think I am kind and generous, but I am not soft. It is a hard world and one must be hard in return. Yet I am a peaceable man and like people and prefer that they succeed if their intentions are honorable. I am a patriot and want my country to prevail against its enemies, which, if I am frank, your country was thought to be both before and for a time after the Great War. I came out of retirement to put such gifts as I have to the use of Britain that it might survive a threat graver than any it has ever faced. I was a good strategist at the Admiralty as well as an able tactician when afloat, but my highest gift was guile, that property which you and I share. I navigated past the rocks and shoals and ascended by guile to a position of importance."

He walked to the window where beyond I saw rabbits hopping about in the cabbages; so much for my brags to him about how many I put on dinner tables for workers and their families.

"That field used to be for flowers," Colville said, "and butterflies came by the thousands. When the grass grew long, the flowers and grass would fall to the tractor's cutter bar and clouds of butterflies rose into the air in every size and color. I shall never forget that."

He went on remembering; I suppose that's what it was because he didn't say anything for a while.

"But then the nitro-chalk was applied to the soil to grow food and the flowers were suppressed. Once you turn the earth over on a natural field, that is the end of the flowers and they never come back."

He poured himself more tea, looking sad. Flowers and butterflies; it takes all kinds, doesn't it? He offered me more tea, but I waved him off. Destroyer duty made me a coffee man, the stronger the better. If you can stand a spoon up in it…well, there I go.

Colville said, "The career of many a good man founders due to malice and sabotage at the Admiralty, which, I expect, is like your Navy Department, a seething cauldron of ambition. Every hand turns against the man of promise lest he be the ruination of their hopes as his career matures. The raised nail gets the hammer and the man of promise is everybody's raised nail. What you and I do not share is a sense of purpose."

I didn't know what "guile" was until I looked it up, and to be honest thought it wouldn't be all that great to be known for it. Slick and tricky are words that mean the same, but on the other hand so does shrewdness. Shrewd means you can't be fooled easy, which is a good thing, right? So I judged that Colville was buttering me up at the same time he was saying he saw straight through me.

He didn't know it wasn't "guile" got me where I was but Mother's power over the Senator and his over the Navy on account of being chairman of a big committee. That's not the sort of thing you generally want getting round unless you're me, in which case you let it be known to send a shot across the bow of the higher-ups. Of course you heard people saying Mamma's Boy behind your back, but I never paid any mind except to put them on a mental list for paying back if it was ever in my power.

As a matter of fact it was for a time and a lot of those wise guys ended up bossing crews building dirt airstrips in the diseased tropics with zero chance of a ship command and forget about medals and glory. It was their jealousy of me that landed them there, yet I have to admit I would have done the same in their shoes. People talk, damn them, and they'll throw anything at you they can dig up. Colville had that much right. But getting a step or two on the guys who want the same job doesn't mean it's all roses from there on, as that business in France showed. Maybe I used guile now and then; like stealing the general's car, but it was mostly blind luck that got me through the hot spots.

The other thing was, what was Colville leading up to? Here was a man who looked like Reynard the Fox talking about cunning. He must have had an extra helping of that guile to pull down others while raising himself up. Wouldn't people be on guard just from his looks?

"The prime minister needs your help," Colville said. "How well do you know Ambassador Kennedy?"

I'm just a face in the crowd at the embassy, I said. Why?

"Winston believes he bears closer watching. Apparently, Mr. Kennedy has a connection with the Cliveden set."

He watched for that to sink in. "Well, of course you wouldn't know the Cliveden set," he said, impatient-like. "They are a group of powerful people in this country who believe we should give in to Hitler's demands to end a war we cannot possibly win, thereby allowing the Germans to turn their might against the Bolsheviks, our common enemy." He patted the shoulder where his missing arm used to be. A habit of his, like I said.

"Whether the ambassador is influenced by their views is the question. If so, it is inevitable that he is bending your country in that direction with the help of allies like Colonel Lindbergh who more publicly share his isolationist sympathies. We're aware also that he has presidential aspirations, which is why he hired a *New York Times* reporter to act as his personal publicity man at the embassy. Not a week passes when he or someone in his family is not in the newspapers. He sends weekly Private and Confidential reports to highly-placed journalists like William Randolph Hearst and Walter Lippmann and others who might be useful to him. His power behind the scenes is immense.

"He got wind of a long Fortune magazine article about him that was to be published that described him in very unfavorable terms. When he objected to Henry Luce himself another was written for his approval. That one was as laudatory as the other was critical and referred to him among other flatteries as 'a legendary man of action.' I have spoken to Harry Hopkins, who sends his regards by the way; he agrees it is vital that we find out what Joe is up to over here."

What's it got to do with me, I asked. I doubted I could even get an appointment with Kennedy with all the aides and secretaries that screened visitors.

"Oh, no, you misunderstand," Colville said, "all this is to be behind the scenes, totally hush-hush. Joe, as he wants us to call him, knows the president would be angered if these maneuverings were known. Harry and I believe you must do some detective work, worm your way into the Cliveden set and hear what they say when he and these people get together."

That sounded so crazy I laughed out loud and Colville's face went pink and his eyes sparked like electricity.

"Please understand, Lieutenant, this is no laughing matter."

I wiped off the smile.

"You will have heard of the famous Lady Astor, the American who sits in Parliament." I hadn't but nodded anyway.

"She and her husband were known for their recherché parties and famous guests at Cliveden in the Roaring 'Twenties. As they grew older, they became involved in reactionary politics, she more than he. They have connections high in government and the aristocracy, and it appears Joe has been drawn to them by the snobbery that is one of the vices of the self-made man. He is the son of a barkeeper and yet was the wealthiest Irish-American in the world by the time he was forty-two. There is no doubt something to the rumors he was a bootlegger during Prohibition, but he amassed his fortune by being a swindler, an insider trader and market manipulator. He told people he'd rather hand over half his fortune in taxes than lose it all to socialism, so he backed FDR.

"He went all the way out to San Simeon to argue Roosevelt's case to William Randolph Hearst. At a key moment during the Chicago convention his telephone call persuaded Hearst and the California delegation to join the campaign."

I said you sure know a lot about the guy.

He smiled slightly. "That's just the tip of the iceberg. I know many people in the states and they tell me things that are in the interest of His Majesty's Government to know."

I bet they do, I'm thinking, and don't know how much they're letting out of the bag

"Joe had a very ambitious mother who wanted him to break through the barriers that kept the Irish from the highest rungs of society. She saw to it he was sent to Harvard as a step toward that goal, but he soon determined that a Harvard association meant little to the Boston Brahmins; only money did and it had to be old money. I have it on authority that J.P. Morgan Jr. called Joe 'an Irish papist and Wall Street punter.' What contempt in those words. He was denied admission to Harvard club life and later the Cohasset country club despite his gregarious nature. It was not only because he was Irish in the latter case, but because his reputation as a ladies man and shady businessman was well established. I spoke to one of his classmates once. He said if Joe wanted something bad enough 'he would get it and he didn't much care how it got it. He'd run right over people.' The exact words. He and his wife Rose turned out children like a mill even though he never lost his taste for chorus girls."

Colville smoothed back his hair, another habit that I didn't mention. You like the really small details. "He was not impressed by the hard-working and cunning glove salesmen, furriers and junk dealers who rose to power in Hollywood. 'That bunch of pants pressers,' he was heard to say. 'I could take the whole business away from them.'"

Colville got up to get his pipe and fussed around a bit to get it going. "It's getting harder to find the tobacco I like."

He sat back down and spoke through the smoke. "He had already fathered seven children when he met the most famous woman in the world, the actress Gloria Swanson. He wanted to divorce Rose and marry Gloria, but the church objected. Cardinal O'Connell of Boston came to her in full clerical vestments to say each meeting deepened Joe's sin and asked her to discontinue for the sake of his soul. She saw him off by saying to take it up with Joe. And here is the Kennedy touch. The cardinal was told if he didn't stop interfering, a homosexual liaison of his would be revealed."

I'm thinking wouldn't the newspapers like to get hold of that?

"Our intelligence service has been following the Cliveden set," he said, "but what is needed are American ears to hear Kennedy when he speaks freely. Our need is desperate because the White House recognizes we are capable of any deception to sway opinion our way, even lies to impugn the motives of their ambassador to the Court of St. James."

Why Colville kept throwing out those ten-dollar words was beyond me, "impugn" being the latest; I thought at the time he was showing off to keep me on my back foot, but that's really the way he was; over-educated to a fault as the Senator said about the rich young pups from the Ivy League hired for the senate staffs. If he was outside, he'd hawk one up to leave no doubt where he stood regarding them.

"We have a female agent, wealthy from titled parents, both dead, who has insinuated herself into the Cliveden set at our request and attends their gatherings, one of which is next weekend. She is Cordelia Bunduck; you will accompany her as a romantic interest, the good-looking hog magnate from America."

I knew Colville was passing on an informal request from Hopkins, which we both knew this would be an order at the drop of a hat.

What's she look like, I demanded to know. I'd been in England long enough to notice rural wealth often as not turned out strapping lasses who ran to big rumps and noses with arms big as stevedores. Those strong frames come natural in bloodlines where generations worked farms, which was a hard slog even with all the servants and tenants under them. Delicate children didn't survive hard winters in those cold houses.

These young women must think they're slender beauties from what they hear from the penniless young aristocrats who throw themselves at their big feet. Women will believe almost anything a man says if it's a compliment, and you better bet the average heiresses heard plenty from those poor devils. I reeled them off pretty well myself in my time. You had to keep a straight face to pull it off.

"She is a lovely woman but Sapphic, I'm afraid," Colville said. This time I asked him straight out what he meant. "She is sexually inverted and does not like men."

As I stared he added, "She is a lesbian scornful of the attentions of males, favoring her own sex for such intimacy as she allows."

You mean a lizzie, I said, knocked back a step.

"I knew her parents, killed by poachers in Kenya," Colville said. "She was a tomboy growing up, causing people to wonder even then. She would have nothing to do with dolls and the ordinary things girls like; she preferred boy's clothing to frilly dresses and sports to hopscotch. Now that she has reached her majority, she has the mental arrogance of a male and none of the shyness natural to her sex."

I grinned after thinking a bit and said maybe she just hasn't met the right man yet. Colville gave me a dry look.

"I understand how a man like you would take pride in your allure for women, but a few unnatural specimens may lie beyond even your reach."

He suggested a walk outside where the rabbits were filling their guts with his cabbage.

"I'm sure you did your best," he said, "but the second litter in one year goes from simple arithmetic to the multiplication table."

He was going to go on, but I said Albert told me all about it. How are we supposed to pull this off, me and this Cordelia, I asked.

"It was the very question she put to me," Colville said, "her aversion to men is quite strong. I made a frank appeal to her patriotism; she has traveled extensively in Europe and what she saw in Germany made her despise Hitler and the Third Reich with all her being. Queers apparently are mistreated as badly as Jews. She knows you are American, but not a naval officer in counterintelligence. You are a member of the idle rich as far as she knows, someone unaware of her mission. You will be seen by your hosts as the Extra Man, frequently homosexual, who accompanies wealthy widows or divorcees to social events so that seating arrangements are not awkward. She will pass on whatever she hears to MI6. I don't believe your clothes, from what I've seen of them, are quite up to the mark for Cliveden. I've made an appointment for you tomorrow at my tailor for weekend attire. They promised a rush job when I informed them this was for the country's sake and no questions asked."

His tailor was a nimble little guy named Oswald, bald as a cue ball, who had a tape around his neck and pretty soon a mouthful of pins that he talked around as he worked away

"If the suit you wore here is representative of your wardrobe, you haven't kept up with the times."

When I said I was just a simple sailor, he said, "Thank you, sir, but I've already heard too much according to what Mr. Colville told me, so I'll pretend you didn't say that."

Oswald and a silent assistant measured me up and down, front and back. Oswald worked fast and talked just as fast regardless of the pins; I would have been afraid of one ending up in my gizzard.

"You could model clothing with your build and appearance, but in modish circles your look is too slimming. Saville Row today take inspiration from the British Guard officer's overcoats. Their shoulder line spreads past the natural shoulder to line up with the bicep with pads to keep the shoulder shape"

■◥■

THE MAN knew his business, no doubt about it. "Our coats angle down to the waist to create a V shape from neck to waist. Very wide pointed lapels are now *de rigueur* for the man of fashion. They cover half the width of a man's chest, the lapels extending down to not the first but the second set of a four-button double breasted closure. The elongated lapels again emphasize the V shape."

He left and returned with an armful of shirts. "Sleeves repeat the V shape by starting out very roomy at the shoulder and narrowing down to the wrist. Trousers spread farther up the waist, about three inches or so above the naval, and hang down in long column-like shapes."

He squatted to show me. "Pant legs are cuffed at the bottom for more casual wear and are straight hemmed for professional attire. This being a weekend occasion, there will be no reason for those. There, you see the strong pressed pleat down the center finishes the look. The overcoats that go with your ensemble are big and baggy with large, square pockets rather high. It's designed to beef up the man inside and make him appear larger and more masculine, not that you need those touches. I personally believe it's the effect of the Superman comic books, sir."

I don't look at them myself, I said, but I know plenty who do. There wasn't much book reading went on in the peacetime Navy and a good many men who did read a little had to sound out the words. "We'll get right on these; if you return in the late afternoon we'll see to final fittings."

I felt like a new man in those outfits and looked like a circus strongman in the mirror. They throwed in shirts and ties, four sweaters, shoes and silk socks, skivvies—the works! Even a fedora and that flat cap called a newsboy, plus two sets of cufflinks. I didn't ask, Oswald being the secretive type, but I figured the government must have coughed up a truck load of ration coupons for all that stuff; it was Colville's doing, of course. You remember the shit storm the Navy auditors kicked up over my tailor bills when I went to live with Winston. It shows what side of the Atlantic knows how to do things right; our people didn't understand you have to dress for the part or people don't let their guard down.

Colville knew the Cliveden people were clothes snobs; it's their class thing, of course. When someone is sized up as an outsider people clam up, but I mentioned all this before. Funny how fast my other clothes, which nearly got me a court martial before Harry stepped in, went out of fashion so quick, leastwise in London. Speaking of that, General Brooke out of uniform had the look of an ordinary sort of man when he arrived in an old saloon car, but no mistaking his air of command. His eyes twinkled when he took my hand with an iron grip.

"Quite a coup, that," he said to Colville. "Did he tell you? He stole a French general's car and drove it to Dunkirk where it was found a week later. It took a while for them to put the puzzle together and then they rather firmly demanded we surrender Lieutenant Brady to their custody. Imagine such pettiness in the midst of war, but apparently it was a question of French honor. Our people told them that Brady was killed when a destroyer was bombed, and that seemed to satisfy them."

Colville said the French were peculiar when it came to national honor. "Even the meanest triumph takes on an exaggerated value when a nation with the proud tradition of France is humiliated."

We went inside to lunch, which was baked grouse seasoned the usual way… who cares what the usual way is? All right, you're the one writing this up. Salt and pepper, eight crushed juniper berries, eight sprigs of thyme and eight rashers of bacon, a couple handfuls of chopped carrots, and a little fat to cook them in. I learned this when I asked the cook to jolly her along for more pie. There was gravy and bread sauce and deep fried potato chips. Just one man's opinion, but I think you want too much detail.

"Moira," Colville said sharpish when we dug in, "this grouse needs more cooking, mine is pink inside."

Albert and her took the plates back to the kitchen, Moira hot under the collar. The general and I had another glass of Syrah while he went on talking; Colville as usual only sipped and watched.

"The French army was a surly rabble at the end," Brooke said. "General Blanchard against my order planned to withdraw his troops to La Planne for embarkation, which would have uncovered my left flank and created a hopeless traffic jam. I instructed the liaison officer to say I would have him shot if he did." He shook his head. "I've been so busy those days already seem long ago."

It is one of the mercies, Coleville said, that bad experiences vivid at the time diminish in memory.

"When I got home after Dunkirk," Brooke said, "I slept for more than thirty-six hours. That told me I'd come close to physical collapse after three weeks of constant strain, although thank God my mind remained clear. When at last I was restored thanks to my wonderful wife and children, I drove to the War Office. I was overcome in the countryside by the wonderful transformation from war to peace. The awful load of responsibility had been laid aside, the nightmares from anxiety were gone, the roads were free from refugees, demoralization no longer surrounded me on all sides, and it was another beautiful English spring day.

"From every point of view life had suddenly assumed a very rosy outlook, and I walked to General Dill's room with a light heart to ask what my next assignment was. He said I must return to France and form a new British army to fight alongside the French. It was one of the blackest moments of my life. I said the French army was in the process of disintegration and there was no hope it could stand up against the Boche. Dill told me it was a political decision, a point repeated by Anthony Eden when we spoke. I said we had narrowly escaped disaster in France and to return would be to guarantee it. He was sympathetic but that was all; it was not his decision to make."

The grouse came back from the kitchen black and so tough and dry I needed one sip of wine per forkful to get it down after a good deal of chewing, and Brooke had trouble with his dentures. Colville's look was bitter, but he said nothing to Moira. You don't want to get on the bad side of a cook, particularly the Irish who are famous for their grudges.

"So back I went," Brooke said, "to take command of all the British troops in France under the orders of General Weygand. He was old and wizened and had a stiff neck from a car collision the day before. Saying he was speaking very frankly, he said they were no longer able to offer organized resistance. He had no reserves and Paris had been given up. He said he'd had a good military career up to that point but now it was in ruins. I stared at him in amazement. His country was going under and the most important thing to him was his reputation. The plan cooked up by the War Office to fall back in front of Bennes to cover Brittany was pure fantasy. I told General Dill this over a poor telephone line and recommended that further reinforcements be halted and that the service personnel—we still had a hundred thousand men there, line of communications people and other non-combatants—should be embarked at once before they were captured.

'The prime minister does not want you to do that,' he told me.

"What the hell does he want? I said.

"'I'll let him talk to you.'"

Churchill's voice came on the line and he asked various questions that led me to believe he thought I was behaving almost in a cowardly manner. 'Cold feet' is the phrase he used more than once. I had been sent, he told me, to show the French we stood beside them shoulder to shoulder.

There is no shoulder to stand beside, I said, trying as best I could on several occasions not to lose my temper. In the back of my mind was his disastrous blunder at Dardanelles in the Great War and that rag-bag expedition to Norway pulled back after a travesty of a campaign. We went at it hammer-and-tong for a half hour over that faint line and just as I was exhausted, the prime minister said, 'All right, I agree with you.'"

I understand from Winston, Colville said, that our home defenses could scarcely be worse. The general lifted his eyebrows and tilted his head at me. "It's all right," Colville said, "he's an unofficial emissary of President Roosevelt."

"We have two hundred artillery pieces and a few understrength divisions, Brooke said. "There is the Royal Navy and the RAF, but this war has shown how vulnerable warships are to bombing, and the German air force is far greater in numbers and nearly our equal in competence." Colville's gloom got thicker as he went on. We ate spotted dick for dessert and then Brooke went off to look at birds.

CHAPTER 12

COLVILLE GAVE ME HIS ROLLS AND DRIVER AND I PICKED UP CORDELIA AT HER place in Mayfair. She was striking looking but could have been gorgeous in jig time with that English peaches and cream complexion and a figure like a goddess on urns you see in museums. High cheekbones and green eyes a bit slanted, which Colville said were from her Russian side, her grandmother being a mistress of the czar. Light brown hair cut short, jodhpurs, boots and a plain blue silk blouse.

"God," she said, "a foppish gigolo with oiled hair, couldn't they come up with something more original?" She started to close the door in my face and then stopped. "I said I'd do it." This was more to herself than me. "Come in, then." She moved off with a stride like a man to a drawing room where a young woman built for rugby fussed with luggage.

"This is the man," she announced, "what's your name, Lowell Brady—is that it? This is Hazel. Say hi, Hazel." She did with a dirty look my way and hefted all the suitcases with no effort at all and we went out to the Rolls. Cordelia flounced into the backseat and crossed her arms and looked out the window. My comment about the weather not getting anywhere, I unfolded *The Times* that came with the car and wished it was *The Mirror*, a favorite of the ordinary blokes as they say over there. An hour passed as I read down to the amateur cricket scores and she still said nothing, just looking out the window. Knock, knock, I said. That's when those jokes were new. Cordelia turned to me with a scornful look, but sort of puzzled as well. I said you're supposed to say who's there?

"Who's there?" she comes back after realizing she had to say something. Orange, I said. You say Orange who? "Orange who?" Orange you going to let me in?

"How stupid," Cordelia said but with a snort like she was trying stop a laugh. It broke the ice and she loosened up a bit.

"Sir Peregrine said you are in livestock," she said. That's right, I said, we raise pigs and sell everything but the squeal.

That got another laugh and before long she was talking about the Cliveden Set. "They were anti-German in the beginning but then decided Communism was more threatening to our way of life. They're as Victorian as the old queen herself, imperialists who would have backed slavery at the time and still believe in keeping a boot on the Irish neck. Are you Irish yourself with a name like Brady?"

Scots-Irish from way back, I said.

Brady is my stepfather's name; they were papists before going Baptist like most everybody else in the southern states where they ended up. My side brought distilling whiskey to the New World over the local opposition up north. You maybe heard of the Puritans? Dead set against fun except for dancing around the Maypole when winter was over. Like the Bradys, my own folks had the sense to move on to where winters weren't so bitter, or it might be they were driven out on account of trading in whiskey.

"Meaning no offense," I said, "but don't you think she should've dressed up a little to meet the Astors instead of looking like a Land Girl.

"A strange man I just met is the last person I'd ask for fashion advice," she said very sharp. "And what do you know about Land Girls anyhow?"

Quite a bit, I said, mentioning them in Suffolk I'd met and telling a little bit about each; I said they were right fine young women as far as I was concerned. That put her on her back foot, those gals being people she valued as of right living without ever meeting one because of the class wall.

"I like the way the Land Girls dress," she said, "It is sensible and comfortable and doesn't encourage remarks about appearance."

I was about to say what's wrong if a woman's good lookin' but caught myself. By now I judged her as much in need of special handling as a stick of sweating dynamite. I got into her better graces by telling her about the fighting in

France and coming back on the *HMS Amazon*. I improved the story so I was carrying a wounded man as bullets chewed up the ground, saying it in a matter-of-fact way like it was just another day at work.

"I thought you were one of those rich Americans hoping to suck up to an earl," she said, softening a bit. But then those fine eyes flashed. "There wouldn't be war if the world was run by women, nor ninety-five percent of the crime and violence and misery and hatefulness."

I said you just might have something there, little lady.

"Oh, don't patronize me," she cried, "I hate it when men do that."

I turned to studying the Buckinghamshire countryside and the Chiltern Hills coming up on us. As impressive as Rutland Castle was, Cliveden House put it in the shade. It wasn't a house at all, of course, but a three-story mansion, pale yellow and way wider than a football field is long as you came up to it through the park. I counted thirty-three windows just on the front side but there might've been some I missed.

"It's lovely, isn't it," Cordelia said. "Italianate is the style and the grounds are described as without equal; on the other side they slope down to the Thames River. You can see Windsor Castle from the roof."

A flunky in a swallow-tail coat named John Hurdy hurried with two assistants to collect our luggage and lead us to the grand entrance.

"This has been home to an earl, three countesses, two dukes, a Prince of Wales and now the Viscounts Astor," Cordelia said as we were walking, "if that sort of thing impresses you."

I said it most certainly does and asked if Cliveden had a ghost hanging about, but her reading hadn't touched on that point. "Only ignorant people believe in that today," she said.

The entrance led into a great hall which she said was made by knocking three rooms together to make one. My new shoes with their leather heels sounded on the flagstones like a judge rapping for order.

"One of the Astors wanted to make it look as much like an Italian palazzo as possible and I think he succeeded, don't you?"

Never having seen a palazzo, I just said *Mm* like I was a veteran of a hundred and I'd put this up near the top.

"That huge fireplace is sixteenth-century," Cordelia said, "it's from a

Burgundian chateau that was pulled down. That portrait to the left is our host, Nancy Astor, painted by another of you Americans, John Singer Sargent."

Take away the wall hangings, furniture, suits of armor and so on and it was like a really nice railroad station in a big city. We were led up the grand staircase and along a wide corridor.

"Do these doors lock from the inside?" Cordelia asked John.

"Yes, ma'am," he said, giving me a little wink she couldn't see. I paid no attention, Colville having advised me not to encourage familiarity with the servants. He showed the key in the door, which looked heavy enough for a prison.

I changed shoes and took a stroll outside while my gear was being unpacked. You'd have to go up to the Hamptons in our country to match those grounds or maybe one or two places down south Sherman didn't get to. It has more gardens than you can shake a stick at; one is around an Oriental temple and another next to a hedge maze. The Long Garden had thousands of yellow and red daffodils starting to come up. It was quite the sight I can tell you.

I eventually came upon an older woman on a stone bench looking like it was from Roman times. "Well now," she said, "who's this handsome stranger?"

I told her my name and said I collected from her accent she was a Southerner like me.

"Yes, I was born in Virginia and what about yourself?"

Georgia, I said, the Peach State.

"I have traveled in Georgia and love it nearly as well as my own state." She said to call her Nancy and I did, taking her to be one of the staff. She had a merry way that put a man right at ease and soon we were talking away to beat the band. When I told her I was in the pork trade, she said she liked nothing better than a ham steak with orange marmalade on it like we have back home. I said the only thing I'd put up against it was chicken with dumplin's cooked right. She nodded and looked off dreamy like.

"You're here with that notorious Cordelia Bunduck," she said all of a sudden and her eyes were slits.

Yes, ma'am, I said, sensing I was already on thin ice and not an hour gone. As to notorious, I told her I'd have to think about that as some people called that in a certain light were not understood correctly as a result of…I was blathering away not knowing how or where I was going to end up, but luckily she busted in.

"Oh, you know what I mean," she said, flaring up. "I've heard she's a secret Communist, and her parents, who I knew well, would be turning over in their graves in Africa. Do you have Red sympathies yourself and, come to think of it, are you Jewish? No, with a name like Brady it's unlikely. Are you a Roman Catholic, which is just as bad?"

I told her no, ma'am, I'm neither that nor a Communist either as I don't care a snap about politics and that settled her down. We shot the breeze more, spending considerable time on the Civil War where both our families were on the losing side and hated Northern carpetbaggers like sin. Then she looked at her watch and said it's shore been nice hasn't it but she had to get a move on.

I sauntered around until I spotted a barn where twenty or so horses were stabled, big hunters for hacking around the countryside. I patted a few nuzzles and Harry, a wall-eyed stable hand no bigger than a jockey, said was I an American and did I want to take one out for exercise as some of the horses hadn't been rode and were getting fat.

I said I hadn't brought my riding stuff, but he said no problem and showed me a tack room where there were all kinds of rigs hung up for guests. "This looks like it would fit," he said. He looked at a log. "Last worn by William Humble David Ward, the 4th Earl of Dudley. It was cleaned afterward as he was quite the one for flying off a horse at the jumps."

I put on a sturdy tweed hacking jacket with three buttons, buff breeches, blue shirt and tie, a tattersall vest, brown field boots with matching garter straps and blunt spurs worn high on the ankle than worn sloppy at the heels, black leather gloves, a bowler I clapped on my head, and there I was, a dapper gent ready for a canter in the fresh air. While I changed, Harry and another groom brought out a huge, black stallion, easily eighteen hands high with rippling muscles under a glossy hide and eyes showing white as he skittered around, nearly lifting the man at his halter off the ground. I noticed hostlers were trying to hide grins.

"Satan don't get rid much on account of his iron mouth," Harry said, looking like he was trying to hide one himself. I was a good rider growing up, but I was about to ask was there a gelding handy with less piss and vinegar, but pride stoppeth my mouth, which I believe is a Bible expression. I gathered the reins and got a leg up and Satan took charge at once. We shot out of the barn into the sunlight like in a race with a goodly fortune to the winner.

Harry was right about his iron mouth; I've always been pretty strong, but Satan paid no attention where I wanted to go except to try to bite my leg when I pulled to turn him. We thundered along the bridal path with me hoping he'd tire out. He galloped under low hanging branches twice trying to brush me off, but I saw them coming.

A small figure on the trail far ahead turned into a man in a scarlet jacket on a pretty bay cantering along smooth as a rocking horse. Satan pinned his ears back and picked up speed like he knew an enemy when he saw one. The rider heard drumming hooves and turned to see what was coming. I shouted, Look Out! That glimpse he had of us before the collision must have been a sight, a wild-eyed stallion with teeth bared and the rider with his own gritted in a fiend's grin as I tried to control the beast.

They were knocked ass over tea kettle, the rider thrown head-first into a hedge; Satan lunged at the bay thrashing on the ground and bit him on the belly. He was aiming to do more damage until I stood in the stirrups for a superhuman yank that made him rear and nearly take us over backward. He settled back down on all fours for some lively bucking in a circle and off we went on the mad gallop again.

When the knockdown was far behind us he slowed, sucking air like he was blown. I was panting myself like I'd been the one doing the running. I pulled Satan—never an animal better named—to a stop, but likely it was his more idea than mine. I got him pointed back toward the barn, but he was still skittish and threatening to bolt. There was no sign of our victims except for a hole in the thorny Shrub Rose hedge, as I now saw it was. My mother growed them in Georgia to keep the tramps from coming to the house for handouts.

I felt the steam rising in me as the barn got closer. Bring out Satan for the Yank and watch him thrown off soon as he sticks a boot in the stirrup, or walk back all dirty if he still can walk—I figured that was their joke. They probably really didn't expect me to last as far as the barn door when they'd rush up and dust me off and say are you alright, sir? He's sure a handful, ain't he? But there's a mare gentle as a lamb that's right down your alley, sir.

Like I said many times, they never forgave us over the Great War and bragging we won it for them. The upper class hides it pretty well, but the lower orders as they call them ain't as good. Harry was probably nervous we were out so long because he looked real relieved when I walked Satan into the barn snorting and all lathered up. A horse will run until he dies, most folks don't know that.

The others were listening where they hid and expected me to whinge about the trick played on me, but I was damned if I'd give them that satisfaction. I told Harry that Satan was good enough, but I was used to a horse with more spirit. I ordered my clothes sent up to the house and walked away with great dignity.

I was glad they didn't see me climb the stairs to my room because my thigh muscles seized up from gripping Satan's flanks. I made it the rest of the way hanging on a footman's shoulder. I sank into a hot bath but still needed a walking stick when it was time for Cordelia and me to go down to drinks and dinner. A servant had brought me some canes to choose from and I picked a carved blackthorn from Scotland.

"What's wrong with you?" she asked when she knocked at the door. "They're waiting for you to come down."

She acted huffy, like she had been blamed for holding things up. I said my injuries at Dunkirk flared up now and then, but I'd be all right if she didn't walk too fast. She was in sleek evening clothes that would turn any man's head even if all he got back was a stormy look.

"Coco Chanel," she said without me asking. I believed that had to do with her outfit, but didn't comment for fear she'd spot another gap in my knowledge, which she'd done quite regular in the Rolls.

We came down the grand staircase slow on account of my underpinnings. Every other step I'd feel a stab of pain and have to blow out my cheeks. "You sound like a puffer-belly engine," Cordelia hissed.

Fifteen or twenty people in fancy dress stopped the party chatter and peered up at us as if we were coming down from Olympus for a visit with them mortals. Funny the ideas that pop into your head sometimes, ain't it? I thought of twirling my blackthorn like a propeller to put them at ease, something the Senator did with his blind man's cane on jolly occasions, but I worried Cordelia would think it wasn't dignified. The glittering diamonds on tiaras and bosoms and dangling from ears reminded me of winter in Minnesota, which is known as The Land of Ten Thousand Lakes even though there's actually a couple thousand more than that. There's a little-known fact for you to put in the book.

Nancy, the woman on the Roman bench, turned out to be Lady Nancy Astor, married to Wally, one of those poor saps who live in the shadow of their wives. "This is my friend from Georgia," she said.

How d'you do, Wally said in that tired-out way the upper crust has like all interest dies as soon as the words come out. That was all I got from him all the time I was there, which I think suited him as much as it did me.

"And you know Cordelia." It was like she was mentioning a small dog at her feet.

Leaving her behind to pull some conversation out of Wally, Nancy and I went around the room as she introduced me to Lord this and Sir that, some of them retired admirals and generals; the old salts had ruddy faces from years of squinting into keen winds at gray seas was how Nancy put it. That woman had a way with words I didn't see equaled until I met Clare Booth Luce. And you, of course, you're no slouch, either.

Admiral Fitzhugh asked where the main attraction was, meaning Ambassador Kennedy.

"It's the strangest thing," she said. "Windsor Castle telephoned to say his horse returned to the stables without him. They sent out a search party at once and found him walking in a state of high dudgeon. He told the head groom he and his mount had been ridden down by a madman. He landed in a hedge with thorns and was taken to the surgery in Maidenhead. We expect him any time now. I'm anxious to hear his story; we can think of no one who would do such a thing. The incident was reported to the police."

Kennedy was announced shortly afterwards and walked in wearing what they call sticking plasters on his face. He's a tall, wiry guy with round glasses that make him look sort of owlish; not the wise kind but the powerful ones with sharp beaks to tear apart the things they catch. They surrounded him with questions.

"I really can't say much because it happened that quick," he said and snapped his fingers. "One minute I'm riding along thinking about things and the next

I know I'm thrown into bushes with thorns. A man on a horse barreled into us, tried to trample the both of us, and then galloped off; that's all there is to say. It's the strangest thing that ever happened to me and believe me I've seen some strange things."

Nancy said the head groom at Windsor reported that it was a smiling man on a black horse.

"I wouldn't call it a smile; he looked like a savage and his horse was a terrifying beast. Huge teeth on both of them."

People stood with their drinks saying they never heard of such a thing and what was the world coming to, it could have happened to any of us, and then the party went back to talk of the war. Kennedy seemed to know everyone as he prowled around the room. Colville had told me he stayed so often at Cliveden it was like a second home for him in England. Rose Kennedy sat next to the king at a dinner there, and I expect the ambassador was ogling the women pretty openly while she pretended not to notice.

"Joe," Nancy said, "meet one of your countrymen, Lowell Brady from Georgia." Kennedy gave me a sharp look, sizing me up. I didn't smile when we shook hands for fear my teeth would connect me with the man on horseback.

"You're a long way from home," he said.

Yes, suh, I shore am, I said, laying on the accent.

"What brings you here?" I said I was in the hog trade and…but he cut me off. "No, I mean here, tonight? I was in pork bellies on the exchange for a stretch and there's no money in it. Half the country can't afford to eat any part of the animal but the knuckles, nose or guts, and that's if they're lucky. I mean, do you have a political interest in what's happening in the world?"

Nancy cut in to say I was here with that young woman over there, Cordelia. She waved her over and Cordelia looked glad to break free from the tycoon I'd met earlier, a minerals and ore man with a square head on a pile of chins. Nancy introduced her to Joe and he almost licked his chops. I was no flushing violet myself—*blushing* violet, that's the word?—but he got right down to business like a man in a hurry. Her color rose like she got a lot of this kind of attention from men like him and hated it. She took my arm like she was mentally pulling the drawbridge up.

"Cordelia is the political one," Nancy said, "a reformed leftist."

Really, said Joe, how interesting. "What brought you over to our side?"

Cordelia told her cover story of how she had been to the Soviet Union and from what she saw she wouldn't let her dog live there. It was more polished the way she said it, of course, but that was basically it.

"Hitler is the only one who will stand up to the Communists," she said. "The democracies are too feeble and rotting inside."

"I couldn't put it better myself," Kennedy said with a big smile. "I wonder if our friend here—what's your name again?"

Yes, suh, Lowell Brady from Georgia, I said.

"We got a good peach brandy from there when I was in the liquor business. I wonder if you'd mind if Cordelia and me discussed the Red threat."

Her hand squeezed my arm. I figured he'd already heard some Extra Man talk and put me down as a sissy. Even if I was, it seemed aggressive as hell, which a lot of women might like but not Cordelia, and put an underline under that.

To be honest, for me being careful always was the better part of valor as the saying goes. If somebody wanted a woman enough to fight like back in caveman days, I was happy to bow and step aside. Look, the world is full of pretty gals; there's enough to go around without risking your nose will get twisted sideways for good by somebody's fist. But this was a special case. If he zeroed in on her I wouldn't hear what he was saying without doing something ridiculous like tip-toeing back and forth with my hand to my ear.

No, suh, I told Joe, I would mind.

I sensed Cordelia's swift look up at me, but I kept my eyes steady on him. He was surprised; the man was used to having his way as Colville said, and here was an Extra Man leaning on a walking stick of all things between him and something he wanted something fierce. His eyes behind the round glasses got mean.

"Is he speaking for you?" he asked Cordelia, not taking his eyes off mine.

Try and imagine; it was the worst nightmare for a modern woman like her. Two guys squaring off the same as back when women was male property and there was no bones about it.

"Nobody speaks for me," she said, but her voice shook a little.

She didn't drop her hand from my arm, which would have let me step aside in a graceful way and blame her for messing up the plan. We both had jobs to do contrary to our natures, Cordelia and me. If she packed up and left in a man-hating huff, she wouldn't be doing her job for England. If I gave way to Joe to avoid trouble it would be the same story as far as Harry Hopkins was concerned. It was a damned uncomfortable moment all the way around I can tell you. Fortunately, Lady Nancy arrived to say it was time to take our seats at dinner and there was a *bong* from somewhere that told the others.

I was seated way below the salt between a frail, elderly duchess who was a vegetarian and a barrister so old he had wrinkles on his wrinkles but was still smart as horseradish. Once the first dishes were cleared, I cut into the Beef Wellington like a lion that had learned the use of knife and fork. The duchess and I had got along well enough until then, but she turned to the person on the other side for the rest of the meal.

Sir Charles Lofton with an Esquire behind his name was on the other side of me. "I represented Mr. Kennedy's movie business in Britain for a time," he said. "He is quite the raconteur."

Is that so, I said, not knowing what the word meant.

"Oh, yes, he can go on by the hour, story after story. A very shrewd man and hard as anthracite. When he saw that your Prohibition experiment was on its way out, Joe locked up all the Haig & Haig and Dewar's output. Working through Jimmy Roosevelt, the president's son, he got permits to import enormous amounts of what they called medicinal liquor. There was talk in parliament when Joe used precious cargo space to ship 200,000 cases of scotch. Do you know Jimmy?"

I motioned to one of the footmen for another slab of beef and said I hadn't had the pleasure.

"The popular newspapers here play him up as the American counterpart of the Prince of Wales. Of course, they are nothing alike. Jimmy has that Yankee can-do spirit while Edward is an indolent dog who dreads the very thought of work and doesn't care who knows it."

He excused himself to go to the thunder box as he put it, and when he came back he said, "You'll have this problem when you get old like me. I see Joe changed his seat to be next to that young woman of yours."

They were on the same side of the long table, so I couldn't see unless I stood up to look. "You want to be careful there," he warned. "The man gets any woman he sets his cap for, married or unmarried. He'll shower them with flowers, expensive gifts, and whatever else it takes."

I said that won't work with her.

His wrinkles were worked into a slow wink. "Good show, I admire your confidence, young man."

After we rose from our chairs after dinner, Cordelia rushed to my side and grabbed my arm with Joe just a few steps behind. "That unspeakable pig," she whispered angrily.

When the ambassador saw we had joined up, he turned back and blended into the crowd. From the flush on her cheeks, she was mad as a hornet.

"I said I would do this for my country, but I won't again; I'll find another way to help the war effort." I Joe had come on too strong, but it was a winning style for him most of the time.

Because of my legs, we were amongst the elderly folks lagging behind to the great room with a painting of scenes from ancient times on the ceiling. There were oil portraits on walls of women and men in powdered wigs pointing at things far off or on rearing war horses leading soldiers into battle. Shiny suits of armor stood around with swords and shields. We sat in gold French chairs and purple sofas from the time of the French kings. Joe was already clearing his throat to speak.

"Ladies and gentlemen, my thanks to the hospitality of my dear friend Lady Nancy and her husband Wally, one of the great men of the world."

Wally looked sheepish, knowing that wasn't within a mile of the truth.

"These are desperate and tormenting times for the world and particularly this island nation that has not been in such straits since the Spanish Armada. I backed Neville Chamberlain to stay in office, and I'm sorry he lost. Churchill is not the man to reach a peaceful agreement with Hitler, I'd bet my last dollar on that. He's pugnacious, a fighter. I'd admire that ordinarily, but what's he got to fight with? All your army's equipment was abandoned in France and your troops escaped capture by the skin of the teeth. I'm reliably told you left behind 64,000 vehicles, 76,000 tons of ammunition, 2,500 guns, and more than 400,000 tons of supplies."

People said "Good Lord" and "Oh, my God," so I guess Joe spilled beans that were supposed to be secret.

"It will take years to make up those losses," he went on. "Who would blame the Tommies if they are demoralized and ready to give up? They and a great French army everybody thought was the strongest in the world got licked by the greatest war machine in history that fights in a new way. There is no standing up to it. And it is coming after you next, ladies and gentlemen, right across that little channel that's been your moat through the centuries. This is why our embassy has advised all Americans to leave the country. There are no more moats in the world, the bomber changed all that. My understanding from l sources I cannot name is that Hitler is willing to let you keep your empire if he is allowed a free hand in Europe and Germany's former colonies."

He looked around the room, wise-owlish like in those glasses. "Hitler admires the English and hates the Communist anthill society that wants to enslave the world. Why not give him that free hand and buy the time you need to rebuild your military? Churchill seems to think America will come to your rescue, but he doesn't know how weak we are. We're weaker than you!

"We're rearming and conscripting young men as fast as we can, but we're years from being strong enough to protect ourselves let alone help you. I can't state it too strongly; you're on your own. A lot of people believe it's the Jews stirring up trouble in the world today, and I've told my Jewish friends in Hollywood if they want to keep selling movies to the world they better take Jew names off the screen, and they're smart enough to do it. Chamberlain was using appeasement as a way to buy time to make up for all those years when you were asleep—and us too for that matter. Churchill won't do that; he's been a war monger all his life."

There were nods and agreement from people throughout his talk, which went on for a half hour. To be honest, I agreed Britain was kaput and should do whatever it took to get Adolph to smoke the peace pipe. Joe said the people in this room had to find a way to force Winston from office before it was too late.

"He will lead this country to the graveyard of empires. I'll bet you five to one, any sum, that Hitler will be in Buckingham Palace in a matter of weeks." Sometimes his eyes went to Cordelia as if talking straight to her.

"The ogre!" she whispered. "The horrid swine."

Give the devil his due, the man was a damned good speaker and got a rousing hand. Other people got to their feet to agree Churchill had to go if the country wasn't to be destroyed by German bombs.

"The bombers will always get through," said one old duffer who stared around the room like he hoped to find somebody to argue with. "The bombers will always get through," he said again before sitting down. Actually, that idea was nothing new to me; the RAF people I brushed up against said the same. I figured they'd be talking for hours more, but I'd heard all I needed. I told Cordelia I was going upstairs.

"Not without me," she said and made a big show of helping me to my feet and walking arm and arm out the room. Once we were out of sight, she dropped her hand and hurried down the long corridor that led to the grand staircase big enough for eight men like at Rutland. When I was halfway there, Lady Nancy caught up to me.

"What's going on between you and that young woman?" she asked. Nothing, I could say with complete honesty.

"Then let him have her."

Fine by me, I said, and she smiled and went back to her guests. When I reached the stairs, I climbed with the help of the balustrade and the walking stick. It was painful as hell despite the wine I threw back at dinner and brandy afterward and I swore at Satan all the way up. I had a wee dram in my room, changed into pajamas, and climbed into bed.

I don't know how much time passed, a couple of hours maybe, when I was woke up by arguing next door. Cordelia sounded as angry as a spitting cat, but her voice was cut off suddenly as if a hand was clamped over her mouth. I threw my legs over the side of the bed and hobbled on my stick to her door, which was slightly ajar with a key in the outside lock. A small light was on and I saw a man and woman struggling on the bed; he's in a bathrobe half peeled off that shows he's naked as a jaybird and her nightgown is ripped down to the waist.

Joe was pinning Cordelia down with a hand over her mouth; she bit it at the same instant I brought the blackthorn down on his back. His brain must not have been able to sort out two sharp pains at the same time because he was like paralyzed while I drew back for another one across the shoulder blades. Man, that one must have hurt, wood on bone with good force. He spun off her body as erect as a stallion and saw me. My hair was mussed up from bed and I must have been gritting my teeth for the next blow.

"You!" he cried. "The man on the black horse!"

I was aiming for his head this time, but he ducked and took the stick on the knob of the shoulder, you know the one. He yowled and scuttled like a crab across the bed and ran out with the robe flapping around skinny white legs bowed like a cowboy's. Cordelia was pulling her nightgown up over magnificent breasts and beginning to shake. I held her in my arms until she began to calm down.

Then she said in a gentle voice, "Thank you and now please go."

As you might imagine, I was so charged up I had trouble falling asleep; my main worry was what would happen if Kennedy found out I was attached to the embassy? It would be something terrible bad, I knew that much. I'd lose my commission at the least and maybe even drafted as an Army grunt despite Mother. There were plenty who'd be happy to see to that. I twisted and turned in bed until at last I drifted off and didn't wake until Lady Nancy herself knocked at the door with a tray of strong coffee and sweet buns.

"What happened last night? Both Joe and your Cordelia left separately hours and hours ago."

There was no reason not to tell her that I could see.

"I hope you don't say this to anyone else," she said. "You appear not to know or care much about politics, but the future of England depends on getting Winston out of office. We need Joe working for us."

I swore I wouldn't tell a soul, but that afternoon I was laying it all out to Colville as a foxy smile spread on his face. "Dictate this to my secretary as you told it to me, including the thrashing you gave the ambassador. We'll put it in the diplomatic pouch and President Roosevelt will be reading it by lunch tomorrow. What you told me is just what Winston wants the president to know."

He wasn't a bit surprised by Joe. "Friends in Boston tell me he encourages his young sons to find women to dine with. He is charming when they are around, but turns lewd and lecherous when the sons are gone. Jack warns his female friends staying overnight that the ambassador likes to prowl at night. One of the girlfriends believes there is something incestuous about the whole family."

CHAPTER 13

LOST QUITE A BIT OF WEIGHT DUE TO THE LEVEL OF STRESS—MINE ANYHOW; LOW-ell is as larky as a man on holiday. I am sure nervousness is the reason I haven't had my period. Irregular menstruation and, sadly, lack of fertility are common to the women on my mother's side of the family and cost some their husbands. Again my apologies to those scholars of the future whose fate is to disentangle my wanderings from Lowell's rambling narrative that skips back and forth in time. I know from my own research how disappointing it is to come upon a promising lead and follow it to the disappointment of a blind alley.

Music to relieve the tedium of repetitive labor, for enjoyment, and for religious purposes has been made by ordinary men and women over the centuries. Singing and chanting kept the rhythm of synchronized pushes and pulls and set a pace for such manual and communal activities as planting, weeding, reaping, milling and so forth. Because variants proliferate, it is wrong to think there is such a thing as an authentic version of a ballad like *Barbara Allen*, to choose an example at random. Field researchers before me discovered countless versions of this throughout the English-speaking world, and often they differ greatly from each other. It is possible the original version ceased to be sung centuries ago. The competing variants of a traditional song may undergo a process of improvement similar to biological natural selection in which only those ones most appealing to ordinary singers would be transmitted onward. We would expect each traditional song to become ever more aesthetically appealing — it would be collectively composed to perfection by the community…there, it would seem through osmosis I have picked up my husband's rambling habit. As tightly as we have been bound over these months, it would be a surprise if something had not rubbed off on me though I am sure the opposite is not so.

We headed north along the stupendous Big Sur coast where on some curves I couldn't bear the vertiginous views. How did they ever build a road on little more than the face of a cliff? Sometimes Lowell would take a hand off the wheel to point out a lonely outpost of rock tossing up white spumes and spray as if the leaping ocean was already celebrating victory.

"Watch the road," I implored.

"Don't be a scaredy cat," he returned in his cheery way, "I can steer this with my knees."

"Please don't!" I cried.

At points the majestic redwood forests growing nearly to the highway were cloaked in fog that the wind suddenly blew apart for a brilliant show of sunshine. It was exhilarating but also exhausting to so closely witness the eternal battle between the elements. I was glad to cross the Carmel River and enter the little village where we found lodgings.

This is a nice little place, Carmel-by-the-Sea. Quiet, maybe a little too quiet. People don't have anything to do but wonder who strangers are and where they came from. There's a lot of old money around here, I can smell it. Back when I was on the prowl for a rich widow or divorcee, I would've set up shop for a month or so and wiggle my way into the social scene. I couldn't have had worse luck nosing around the Hamptons season after season. I think they're more alert there for guys like me. When I look back, I might as well have worn a sign on my back that said Fortune Hunter.

They're thick as fleas on a hound certain times of the year in the Hamptons and we spotted each other right away and steered off on a different course, but the rich have loads of experience holding the line. Some instinct tmust kick in.

As a last resort they pay those young bucks off to get lost, but I never saw any of that money. Too much pride, I guess. If the family didn't want me, I wasn't going to crawl unless it was a name like Vanderbilt or DuPont. The mothers liked me as a rule, but not the fathers. I probably was the mirror image at the same age, though they wouldn't be as tall and good looking if they were honest with themselves. I shake my head at the young fool I was back then. I should've been looking for someone like you, but of course you'd have been just a little girl at the time Most men are fools at some point or other, usually over a woman; it's like its a law of nature and there's no fighting it. I'm very happy with my sweetie pie that'd be worth more to me than a king's ransom even if you didn't have a pot to piss in or window to throw it out of. Old Southern saying.

That was a big lunch you tucked away. I'm glad you're back on your feed; it was starting to worry me when I noticed though I didn't let on. You mentioned on the highway back there when you were hiding your eyes that I'd skipped over Winston's time at the Admiralty, which I did because it was only eight months and most people are more interested in when he was prime minister.

You remember Quentin Reynolds? He just popped into my head. He was a *Colliers Weekly* guy and a big shot on American radio during the war. Ed Murrow, who was even bigger, said Reynolds didn't go outside to do his radio reports when the bombs were falling on London, which was Murrow's specialty. Instead, Reynolds held the microphone close to his mouth and talked in this gruff whisper like the enemy was close by.

People thought he was the real goods, but Westbrook Pegler, another big shot in the press, said he was yellow and never left the hotel bar. I didn't see what was supposed to be wrong with that myself. If nothing else, you could be killed by shrapnel dropping down from the anti-aircraft guns blasting away.

Murrow and his wife invited me for drinks one night after I watched him do his broadcast at the BBC where the announcers wore tuxedos to read the news. Very stuffy people, great voices though. We were meaning to go to the pub across from their apartment where they'd made a lot of friends, but the wife says no let's go upstairs to our apartment because I got a funny feeling all of a sudden. He was pumping me for what Joe Kennedy was up to as if I knew anything worth a minute of his time. I was throwing him stuff any messenger boy at the embassy could give him when I heard a sound that made me dive for the floor.

"What's wrong…" Ed started to say when the bomb hit.

They were thrown against the wall by the blast wave that blew in the windows. The pub was destroyed and all their drinking pals killed. See, you just never knew back then. You could be scratching your ass one minute and dead the next.

The nightclub below the Rialto theater was supposed to be bomb proof, but one night when Ken "Snakehips" Johnson was leading the band and the crowd in "Oh, Johnny" it got hit. His head got nipped off as neat as a guillotine could do and shot out on the dance floor. Somebody who was there told the papers that the couples stood for a few seconds as if still dancing, leaned a little and then toppled over on top of each other. Looters came in straight away yanking necklaces off women and even cutting off fingers that had rings. They were always in a race with the police to get to the scene.

Ed chain-smoked and paced frowning while Mrs. Murrow kindly picked bits of glass from my hair. Well, I'm off on a tangent right out of the gate, ain't I?

The Tories turned on Chamberlain for how unprepared the country was for war though Sir Percival told me it was really the fault of the prime minister before, Stanley Baldwin. Europe thought another war was unthinkable, but Hitler was planning for it hard. Nobody saw this except guys like Bill Stephenson peeking around corners and under rugs. One tip off was the Krauts were buying huge amounts of steel. I'm going to open that window and get some fresh sea air in here. Ah!

Like a lot of politicians in Britain, maybe most of 'em, Chamberlain thought Churchill was a charlatan according to what Colville said, but he'd been warning about Hitler for years and that was his ace in the hole. So the way they work over there, Neville swallowed his pride and brought him into his cabinet to quiet the mob. See, that kept Winston from sniping from the outside. Neville surprised everyone by making him First Lord of the Admiralty *again* instead of putting him in some two-bit job where he wouldn't do no harm. Okay, *any* harm. I told you; blame the Ironwood School For Boys.

The first thing Churchill did, as I said before, was the Norway blunder that would have gotten him fired from the Admiralty all over again if things weren't already so bad. His idea was good, stop the Germans from getting Swedish coal for their war machine and they'd throw in the towel. But the way it was handled by the War Office committees? Big mistake. The bigger the bureaucracy the more gummed up the wheels get and the slower they turn; anyone with the brains God gave a stomped-on piss ant knows that. The army in Norway was squabbling with the navy so much that Churchill told an admiral he could arrest a general if he kept dragging his feet.

It was the Dardanelles flop all over again like I said. Back then when Churchill ran the Admiralty he brought a famous sailor out of gardening or whatever he was doing in retirement as First Sea Lord. Jackie Fisher was a famous legend, second only to Lord Nelson. The man's career went back to wooden sailing ships and you can throw in rum and the lash. He modernized the Royal Navy against the old guard so that steel-hulled warships with big guns got built and even one of the first carriers in history. A ball of fire like him made enemies right and left the same as Churchill in politics, but he was worshipped by the public and even Winston himself.

The problem was the old sea dog's nerve failed him when the fleet tried to force a passage through the Dardanelles strait. He ordered a retreat because he couldn't stand the heavy losses just as the Turk forts were down to their last shells. If they'd pushed on a little more and bombarded Constantinople the Ottoman Empire would have given up, the Germans would be outflanked, and there'd be help for Russia, which was on its last legs with the Reds circling like wolves. A lot of history would be different.

But Fisher couldn't know the Turks were that low. The way he saw it, losing a sea battle was far worse than on land. You could raise a new army fast compared to building another fleet, so a war could be won or lost at sea in a day. Winston's opinion was if ships had to be sacrificed so be it so long as the battle got won. The old fellow turned out to be a millstone, arguing and threatening to resign over everything.

Sir Percival knew Jackie, of course. "He was a man of immense energy and drive; you could see it in his letters full of exclamation marks, four and five in a row. He was short and ugly with a round head and a yellowish face that led some to believe he had Asiatic blood, but it was from the malaria that almost killed him in his younger days. He had a fixed and compelling gaze that said you had his full attention to the exclusion of the rest of the world. I can tell you from personal experience it was quite unnerving. When he spoke he got so animated that the King once asked him to stop shaking a fist in his face."

He had a fond tone as we were being driven to the War Office to show me around. "Fisher was a wonderful storyteller. He joined the Royal Navy when he was thirteen; the only qualifications at the time being a recommendation from someone of influence, the ability to jump over a chair naked, and to recite the Lord's Prayer, though the latter two need not be simultaneous."

He laughed at his own little joke and I chuckled along to keep him company. You have to do that sometimes.

"His first assignment was on an 84-gun ship-of-the-line with a crew of seven hundred men and a hard-faced captain. Fisher fainted when he witnessed eight men flogged on his first day. Even much later some senior officers held strong to the belief men were more likely to learn from a blow than any word and were sorry it wasn't allowed anymore."

I said I saw good arguments on both sides of the question.

Colville gave me a funny look and kept going. "Fisher became obsessed with ballroom dancing at some point in his later career." We were led into the War Office across from Whitehall by a polite lieutenant commander; Royal Marines standing guard smartly stamped and saluted as we walked the hallways. "He was so taken with it that he forced the officers of his ship to learn how. The midshipmen who dug in heels had leaves cancelled, which brought them round in a hurry. When the band was playing for the wardroom dinners of the senior officers, the juniors were expected to practice their steps on deck, a custom that spread through the fleet. The older Jackie got the more autocratic. He famously said, 'Anyone who opposes me, I crush,' and this was not limited to matters terpsichorean. Officers were promoted for ability rather than seniority, which embittered those passed over and was responsible for much of the hostility toward him."

Two men coming toward us were going on with an argument they were having. "The small man is Commander Tom Phillips, who some say has the best brain in the Royal Navy," Colville told me in a low voice, "and the other is Commodore Arthur Harris of the Royal Air Force,"

"Phillips, you make me sick," Harris was saying. "I will tell you what will happen. One day we shall be at war with Japan and you will be sailing across the South China Sea in one of your big, beautiful battleships. Out of a cloud there will come a squadron of Japanese bombers and as your ship capsizes you will turn to your navigating officer and say, 'That was a mighty mine we hit.'"

Phillips had a good laugh, thinking like me at the time that battleships were invulnerable to warplanes, but that's exactly what happened three days after Pearl Harbor got it. Tom Thumb, as they called him below decks on account of his size, was on the bridge of the new *HMS Prince of Wales* when she sailed into a trap the Japs laid south of Malaya. Bombers attacked and she went down with the old battlecruiser *Repulse*.

He had been after the transports but they'd already disembarked the troops and weren't worth bothering with, though Tom Thumb couldn't know that. That was Winston again, telling everybody full speed ahead and damn the torpedoes. But in a way it was nobody's fault because the carrier that was supposed to give them air cover had run aground and was being repaired. There you have it, the fortunes of war. I heard about the blunder on the ship to Manila the Navy put me on when they caught me trying to warn Pearl Harbor. I still can't believe that bone-headed stunt of mine.

Colville said hello and we watched Harris push on still hot under the collar. Phillips was head of the Plans Department, which meant he was a desk admiral. It's a mistake to send those professor types to sea in wartime; they're over-thinkers. Instincts, if they still have 'em, don't kick in fast enough. Gallant commander, though, I give him that. He went down with the ship.

Colville told him I was an American naval officer in London on hush-hush business. "Believe it or not, Sir Percival," Phillips said with a chuckle, "I guessed he was American from the accent. We hope to see more of you chaps," he said to me.

"I'm afraid I got up Arthur's nose again," he told Colville. "He will go on about his bombers."

I said we had that type too. I told about Colonel Billy Mitchell who got fired for preaching air war. He'd get all steamed up and fiery-faced like a backwoods Baptist preacher calling people to Jesus.

Phillips said, "Rather a bad show, accusing fellow officers and superiors of treason."

"It seems Mitchell was something of a hot head," Colville agreed. "A man of conviction, however."

"Aren't all fanatics?" Phillips said.

Tell me you don't want me to go into *that* business, darlin'.

All right, long story short: Mitchell came out of the Great War saying air forces would play a big role in the future, maybe the biggest. He pushed until he got the okay to show what he meant. Back in 1921, an exercise was held where bombers attacked a bunch of ships taken from the Germans and anchored off the Virginia coast. They were beat up bad and one or two even sank, but naval officers like Phillips and most of our guys—except the aviators who the rest of us treated like lepers —said the ships were sitting ducks and if they'd been able to maneuver it would have been a different story.

"I don't deny aeroplanes have their role in war," Phillips said to me. "In one of your own Fleet Problems it was shown that the fall of shells from twenty-nine thousand yards could be accurately observed six times better by aircraft than by spotters aloft with field glasses."

I was sort of behind in my study of Fleet Problems, dull stuff as a rule, so I just put on a wise look like I'm doing now, hawr, hawr, hawr. The three of us fell to yarning about the new class of heavy cruisers a-building in the shipyards to replace the pitiful things allowed under the Washington Treaty.

"Tinclads we called them," I said. "Destroyers with six-inch guns and even smaller pop guns would be a real danger to them, but they say these new heavy cruiser classes have more armor without losing any speed."

That was proved by the way in the Battle of Savo Island, the one I was in, when *San Francisco* took several hits from 16-inch guns and kept on fighting.

"I was telling Lieutenant Brady about Jackie Fisher and Winston Churchill and the Dardanelles cock-up," Sir Percival said.

"Immovable object versus irresistible force, those two," Phillips said. "Fisher was the great innovator; he took 150 ships out of active service at the start and saw to it sailors got fresh bread every day instead of the biscuits full of weevils they'd been eating for centuries. Wonderful strategic mind as well, but he should never have been brought out of retirement, his best days were past."

"Clemmie told me he thought Winston would never get over the Dardanelles," Colville said. "She thought he would die of grief. After they kicked him out of the Admiralty, he was given the lowest cabinet office, the Chancellorship of the Duchy of Lancaster, whose only duty is appointing magistrates. A tremendous blow to his pride."

Phillips wanted to jaw a little longer and stood with his arms crossed, uncrossing them to return salutes as men passed by with the same worried looks as at the embassy. He had a strong presence for a pee-wee.

"The planning under Admiral Carden went wrong somewhere," he said. "Gunnery experts should have explained that great warships used to firing large shells very long distances were not suited to bombarding forts close up on shore. And the trawlers manned by civilians for minesweeping were not up to the Dardanelles current."

Colville was gazing into the distance. "Admiral Carden must have realized the expedition was doomed. He had an ulcer attack and was removed from command two days before. It was like General Hotblack dropping from a stroke on the steps of his club as he left for his command in France. They saw the writing on the wall. Tragic events unfolded and soon Commonwealth troops were dying with ours in the trenches at Gallipoli. God, what a disaster it all was."

"Fifty thousand dead and wounded, wasn't it?" Phillips said. "And all that disease."

"Wastage it was called, a word that put human cost out of mind then as now," Colville said. We thought about it in silence for a bit and then Phillips said cheerio, back to work I go.

"There's someone I want you to meet," Colville said to me. He led me to a door where he knocked. A voice inside said come in. One man sat behind a desk while another was at the window looking out.

"Take a chair, gentlemen," said the capable-looking man at the desk who had a well-fitted suit with chalk stripes, Oswald's work maybe. "We will use no names if you don't mind."

The man at the window did not turn. "Would you like to meet a beautiful woman?" he asked. An alert look about him even from where I was sitting.

"If you're talking to me," I said, "give me the name and address and I'll take care of the rest." The words were no sooner out of my mouth then I thought hold on a minute here. "Well, it depends."

It was Colonel Stewart Menzies of the Secret Intelligence Service who turned to us. A good-looking man as sleek as a beaver coming out of the water, he had silver hair and a neat moustache. If you wanted to meet somebody at the top of English society, Menzies was your man. The family money was from Gordon's gin, and they had an estate next to the king's in Scotland. He was in the horsey set they called the mink and manure crowd; Guards regiment and all that. I remembered him from the weekend party at Adsdean where Edward and Wallis Simpson showed up and so did Charlie Chaplin, Charlie being the bigger draw.

Like I said in your other writing, Winston, a private citizen at the time but already thinking he'd be running the show at some point, wanted to prove to FDR that he was an open book and Britain wouldn't try to bamboozle us like they did in the Great War. He had me hide behind a yellow screen there to listen in on a private meeting with spy types on how to influence our public opinion. Stephenson was there, the star attraction for the serious types who came from London for the meeting.

Menzies was in a bad mood because he put a shoe in a cow pie up to his sock where the cars parked. He cleaned up the shoe as best he could and wore a mismatching sock a servant gave him. A few city types brushed their noses with fingers pretty regular, but those of us raised with farm animals didn't mind the smell so much.

"You made the right decision not meeting with Lady Catherine Howard that night," Menzies said at the time I'm talking about. "We have had her home under observation for some time. Some men, the seedy sort, are seen to enter but do not come out."

"Surely the police should be told?" Sir Percival said.

"Yes," Menzies said smoothly, "when the time is right, but that time is not now." Shifting his look to me, he said, "Do you know an American named Tyler Kent?"

Never heard of him, I said.

"He works at your embassy," Menzies said.

"There's two hundred people work there," I said, "and anyhow I don't spend much time at the embassy."

"Yes, we have noticed you pop in one door and shortly after pop out another," he said with a friendly smile. "Tyler Kent is a cipher clerk who works in your code room. He will introduce you to the beautiful woman."

"For what purpose?" Colville asked.

"Seduction most probably."

"This man doesn't need any help in that regard."

"We have noted that," Menzies said, sort of leering. "My compliments, lieutenant. Well-born ladies to shop girls and scullery maids, quite a diverse lot. That Wanda is a beauty from every point of view."

He meant the nude model in Fitzrovia where I found that drunk poet, Dylan Thomas, spewing out his guts in the gents. I dunked his head in the toilet, getting back for a smart-ass remark he made to me in front of people. I told you about that.

"What's this about?" I asked Menzies stiffish-like. Some might not mind being spied on, but I'm not one of 'em.

"Kent is associating with pro-German sources and we believe he is giving them copies of your embassy's cables which are then passed on to Berlin. At this point, we unfortunately have no proof. I wonder if you would help us."

"The American government must be informed of these suspicions," Colville said real sharp.

"The problem is," Menzies told him, "we don't know how high this goes in the embassy."

"Good Lord, you don't mean Kennedy?"

"Is it beyond the bounds of possibility? We have seen cables that hint against creating a closer alliance against the Nazis. What if he is playing a deeper game and there is a leak to the isolationist faction in the United States?"

"The shit would hit the fan," I said.

"That colorful expression is also what we believe," Menzies said, moving from the window and taking a chair. "Kent spends his off hours at the Russian Tea Rooms in South Kensington, a center for spies and double agents of one sort or another. He met a woman named Irene Danishewsky there and they became lovers. She was under surveillance by MS and through her we became aware of Kent. He has fallen under the influence of Captain Archibald Maule Ramsay."

"He is an aristocrat and Member of Parliament from Scotland," Colville explained to me, "a bit of a reactionary. Well, perhaps more than a bit. Like many in the upper class, he believes Jews are behind everything. He had a head injury in the war and some say he's not been the same. The highest he's risen in the government is the Potato Marketing Board, but he is in the forefront of those demanding a negotiated settlement to end the war."

Menzies gave an annoyed look at Colville for butting in. "Your Colonel Lindbergh also thinks that Jews have too much power in the world," he said to me.

"The newspapers say he doesn't want us to mess with Germany," I said.

"He worships their strength," Menzies replied. "He is convinced Britain can't win this war unless the United States is 'dragged' into it. His very word, 'dragged.'"

I thought "worships" was a little strong from what little I knew, but he might know something I didn't. "Anyhow, what about this beautiful woman?" I said, "And how does this guy know me?"

"You are something of a mysterious figure at the embassy, and for that reason Kent has been asked to find out if you could be of use."

"Does Winston know about this intrigue?" Colville demanded, his face reddening. "Without saying more, I suggest you approach him on this matter."

"Whatever for?" Menzies said with surprise, shooting a look to the other man.

"He very certainly will have an opinion."

"He is lord of the admiralty, not prime minister or home secretary. This falls under the remit of MI5, MI6 and the Special Branch of Scotland Yard."

"Nonetheless, I suggest that you seek his views." They stared at one another until Menzies gave in. "If you feel so strongly, Sir Percival, we will speak to Winston."

"I suggest you do so unaccompanied," Colville said with a look at the other man.

"Very well."

Colville was on fire after we left. "Menzies is a greatly overestimated man, an amiable sportsman out of his depth, and here he is blundering into the very delicate relationship we are trying to create between Winston and your president. He will be set straight directly."

Colville said he was the Number Two man in the SIS, the top guy being sick. "I had no idea this was on his mind when he asked to be introduced to you."

"The beautiful woman sounds good," I said.

Colville gave me a warning look. "Margaretha Zelle was a beautiful woman, a famous exotic dancer; I saw her perform in Paris in the nude, or as good as. A bit heavy in the legs I thought. She is better known now as Mati Hari, the seductress and spy. The French executed her at dawn by firing squad."

"I saw the movie with Greta Garbo and Ramon Navarro," I said.

"I hope you take my point."

Later that night, I left the gambling table at White's after a run of bad luck that cheered up the regulars I'd been bleeding white. Nothing was said, that's not the English way, but looks told all. They didn't mind losing to one another because things evened out in a rough way over time, but for a stranger to pocket their money and an American at that.

To be fair, I might have joked around too much, you know—kidded them for being stuffy. I've noticed what people think is funny in one country they don't always in another. You expect a laugh and get a cold stare. I went into the bar for a bracer before bed at Winston's, hoping Randolph wasn't there to threaten me with eviction again. Who should I see but Menzies himself. I nodded and meant to leave it at that, but he waved me over to his table.

"I owe you a drink for today," he said as I took a chair. "I certainly didn't mean to stir up the old boy; I thought he'd pop his top. I was hoping for your help in a matter of vital concern to both our countries. I'm to see Churchill tomorrow, a forbidding prospect these days."

"You were just doing your job," I said, sinking my drink and signaling to the waiter. It looked like I was going to have to hit up Mother again and the Senator was bound to find out. "You better talk to our intelligence guys. They handle that stuff."

I was replaying poker hands in my mind. The problem was I didn't have enough in my poke to match the raises of the ones with castles and miles of countryside. I bet small and threw in my cards when I should've called bluffs. It didn't take long for them to realize I was as broke as the Ten Commandments compared to them and they changed their game. I would've done the same if I was them.

Menzies was humming and drumming his fingers on the table as if deliberating how to say something. "If I may speak frankly, our people don't have a high opinion of American capabilities in the intelligence field."

"Speak away," I said, "no skin off my nose."

In our pecking order naval intelligence didn't rank high; it was understood them folks weren't fit for ship command. I reckoned I fell into that category myself, not that I minded. The weight of the world is on your shoulders when you're CO, and guess who gets the blame when things go wrong. The skipper and navigating officer on that British carrier that went aground knew their careers were over the minute it happened. Imagine what they felt like when they got the word that those two warships were sunk.

"Not your embassy's fault, of course," Menzies went on. "You people are new to this level of foreign intrigue, which takes a certain kind of mind that is not always very nice. We and the Continental powers have been at it for time out of mind while you fought your way West, crushing the tribes and bully-ing people south of your border as we would have done ourselves. You had no need for carefully calculated alliances with deceitful partners that require slyness and espionage. That, sadly, is a way of life on this side of the Atlantic."

I said I didn't know anything about that, being a simple sailor and all, and then a sudden thought struck me. "Lend me a thousand pounds for an hour or so."

Menzies rocked back like I landed one on his chin. "Are you joking!? A thousand…why would I give that a second's thought, a man I just met today?"

"You know all about me, I wouldn't be surprised if you were going to black-mail me."

He looked like I'd caught him going through a woman's underwear drawer.

"The thought had occurred to us, of course," he admitted. "We must con-sider every option in counterintelligence, and your gambling and womaniz-ing would surely be of interest to your superiors. Why do you want a thousand pounds—to gamble more? You've taken a pretty good thumping."

Someone had been watching the game for him.

"I'm going to win it back and more," I told him.

That was pure gambler's talk, of course. You think you can do anything if you've got the money. I know this is making you think about that poker game, darlin', where we ran into the night and never looked back. Am I right? Ha, I thought so.

"Here's the deal," I told Menzies, "the loan of a thousand for an hour, maybe two, and I help you with Kent. You're a rich man and wouldn't miss it, and anyhow you've got the government behind you. If I lose the dough, which I won't, they're good for it."

He thought about it and called over the man with him earlier in the day; he'd been standing by the fireplace with a drink in his hand eating nuts from a red bowl. They stepped aside to talk and a minute later he climbed the stairs to the gambling room. When he returned, he nodded.

"You have credit in the amount of a thousand pounds," Menzies said with a small smile. "Good luck."

The bluebloods and captains of industry licked their chops when they saw the pigeon was back humming Yankee Doodle. I put a little wobble in my walk so they'd figure I'd knocked back some Dutch courage and was ripe to throw good money after bad. At first I held back from raising much like the over-cautious player I was before. Then I hit a hot streak every gambler worth his salt knows when it happens. I hauled in the chips like I was a pirate pointing a blunderbuss at 'em.

By the time I cashed in I added five hundred pounds to that thousand. I paused at the door to sing out "...and called it Macaroni." You should've seen the faces! The color of rare roast beef or white as a fop's handkerchief. Hawr, hawr, hawr. I bet they talk about it still.

I took my stack of Bank of England hundred pound notes with that flowing handwriting on fine paper and peeled off ten for Menzies. "We're square," I said.

Menzies was impressed, no doubt about it. "You should resign your commission and take up life as a professional gambler."

I told him I thought about it from time to time, but nobody knew better than me how luck comes and goes. What rich man would let his daughter marry a gambler? They're low as circus barkers, the way they see it. She'd be cut off without a cent and no way would I keep her on a lieutenant's salary.

I slowed my usual breezy stride through the embassy corridors to give Kent a chance to introduce himself. One day as I sat in the cafeteria drinking coffee and pretending to read a file like I spent every minute on work, a dark-haired man with good looks and a smile asked could he join me? Shore, I said, closing the file.

He introduced himself and said he understood I was a Southerner like

202 | JERRY JAY CARROLL

himself. He reminded me of a feed store clerk I knew back home in Georgia but he boasted about a Virginia pedigree going back to Colonial days. His grandfather was treasury secretary in the Confederacy.

"What do you do around here, if I can ask?" he said after we talked some about his ancestors and prep school and Ivy League education. I shook my head and said I couldn't tell him and patted the file.

"I work nights in the cable room myself, coding and decoding telegrams," he said. He looked around carefully. "I've come across your name a few times. You don't seem popular with your colleagues."

There was my opening, handed to me on a silver platter you might say.

"That's because I don't like how the country is drifting toward this war when we couldn't stop Mexico if they decided to take back California." I looked around myself and dropped my voice. "The way I see it, if Hitler don't stop Communism, who will?"

That was just how he saw it and why didn't we get together for a drink sometime? I said that was okay by me and we met at the Wheatsheaf on Rathbone street so I could take a peek at Wanda for old time's sake. She'd dropped me because I didn't have what she liked in a man, which was talking about books and art and that stuff.

She respected painters who had wild, tangled hair and smelled of sweat because that showed they were close to nature, and also shabby poets opposed to punctuation who were pretty ripe themselves. I bought them dozens of drinks because Wanda insisted and I never got a single thanks in return. They saw beer as a fee Wanda's boyfriends paid while they raved on about the working man under the iron heel of capitalism until she was drunk enough to take home. I smiled and passed them their pints; even an "up yours, mate" now and then would've been a nice change.

Undercover coppers made sure the models didn't move a muscle as the law required, but Wanda maddened you just sitting on the stool when the curtains opened to cheers from her fans giving off that honest smell from armpits. His handkerchief held to his nose in the tight-packed crowd, Kent's eyes bugged out.

"Look at those...she's better than Venus de Milo" he said with awe. "She was your girlfriend!?"

"Yeah, until I got tired of her," I said carelessly.

"I don't think I could ever get tired of that. Of course, a man like you must have his pick of women."

"More or less," I said. "I prefer 'em with money, though."

The curtains closed and opened for the next nude model, a junk-wagon nag compared to Wanda's show horse look. I told Kent we'd have to wait for her next show for another look and were expected to drink up pretty regular or lose our seats. I saw right away he had a weak head for liquor. I had to help him to a cab as he babbled on about Wanda.

He got sick at the curb and I moved away smartly, dodging the hand he held out for support. It seemed the cab driver took him to some low dive, Kent couldn't remember whose idea it was, where he was beaten and robbed. Luckily, he didn't blame me for walking away.

We sometimes met for tea down the street from the embassy on account of I didn't want to spend more time there than I was used to, deal or no deal. Out of sight out of mind like the saying goes. Kent ranted on about the Jews hoodwinking everyone and I nodded and put in a line now and then from *The House of Rothschild* starring George Arliss, Loretta Young and Robert Taylor, who Howard Hawks said I resembled, Taylor I mean, except he might give me a little edge on looks. I'm not kidding, Sugar, I'm just saying what he told me.

"Exactly!" Kent would say when I tossed out some dialogue from the movie, "I couldn't put it better myself." The Nazis liked that movie so much they spliced some of the scenes into one they made. There's some little known history for you and those scholars of the future you talk about.

One day as I was running low on lines and starting to repeat myself, he invited me to the tea room to meet his friend, who turned out to be that Irene Danishewsky, a dumpy shrew with red hair. I couldn't see the attraction except maybe her Jew hate scored high even for that crowd.

The place was full of foreigners jabbering away, White Russians I was told, followers of the Czar when he ran the country. There was a big golden eagle on one wall and pictures of Imperial officials with beards and waxed moustaches and uniforms nearly as good as Italian leaders, who always top the league in that regard. A waiter brought us tea from a samovar bubbling away in a corner and what they called smetannik cakes with honey and sour cream. One bite was enough for me.

"Be careful what you say; there are many undercover Soviet secret police here," Irene said with a look around the room at people whispering with heads close together. That was when they were drinking tea; later in the day they switched to vodka and roared away at each other full volume. They waved arms and shook fists in their faces. My ears always rang when I walked outside.

"Look, there is that awful Anna Wolkoff! I will not be in the same room with her." Irene got up to leave.

"But darling," Kent said, "she's the daughter of the owner. She has a right…"

Irene marched out as Anna swayed over with a smile I'd call mean. Dark-haired, better looking and curvier, but still nothing to write home about. "Why did you bring that harlot here?" she asked Tyler, taking Irene's seat. "And who is this fine man?" It turned out both were his mistresses, a sure-fire recipe for trouble even for a man with experience.

Kent introduced us. "I'm going to ask him if he wants to join the Right Club," he said with a kind of timid look. I got the feeling he was seeing if it was okay by her.

"You are interested in politics?" she asked me. She had high Slavic cheek-bones, honey-blond hair, and dark, suspicious eyes that made you think you'd done something wrong even if you couldn't remember what it was.

"I read the newspapers every chance I get," I said.

She threw her head back and laughed. "You can't be that naïve. What the newspapers print is mostly false, and in any event they know nothing except what they are told by the government."

"Well," I said, putting on like I was ashamed of not knowing, "I wouldn't know in regards to that."

"He is a simple sailor," Kent said, "he has told me many times."

"And the Jewish influence over the world, their conspiracies?" she asked

"That goes without saying, don't it?" I said.

She already sized me up as a bonehead, but she said to Kent, "If you want him to join our club, how can I say no? Your black eye and bruises are much better, darling."

We sat there for an hour drinking tea from small cups and them eating the cakes brought by waiters with flapping white trousers and short black vests as Kent and his lady friend gave Jews and Bolsheviks hell, which I gathered were mostly the same people. A trio walked around strumming balalaikas as fast as we do banjos. Fortunately, she hadn't seen *The House of Rothschild*, so my lines worked pretty well when I pitched in.

After a while, I felt Anna's leg press against mine under the table. She wasn't up to my standard in women, but I was thinking of maybe dropping them a peg or two on a temporary basis. I had to avoid her eye for fear Kent would notice when she started up with long, smoldering looks my way.

A week later, he and I took a taxi together through the blackout to the meeting of the Right Club in a big hall upstairs from the tea room. Three or four dozen people were there, not dressed as good as the Cliveden crowd but saying pretty much the same things. Churchill was a war monger and aiming for Chamberlain's job; Hitler might seem against the English but in his heart he wasn't; Britain should throw in with the Germans to crush Stalin; nobody trusted Jew-run America, and so on and so forth.

Kent bent forward in his chair giving full attention like a rabbit in the cage with a boa constrictor, but I had to keep fighting off the kind of yawns that make your face look like a manhole. I winked at Anna when she looked my way. That and jumping up to cheer a speaker when the others did was all that kept me awake. Two hours of it!

Irene had boycotted the meeting because of Anna, Kent said, giving out with a long sigh. The man wasn't up to the juggling act otherwise neither woman would know about the other. Anna was more pleasant to be around and Kent said he thought of dumping Irene but was afraid of her temper.

"She carries a small pistol in her purse in case she is attacked by a Soviet agent," he said. "She is capable of emptying it at me in a blind rage."

When the meeting broke up, I suggested a drink at a pub. "Let's make it the Wheatsheaf," he said as eager a dog pulling at the leash.

I lied that it was Wanda's night off and suggested some place closer. On busy nights, waves of German bombers were overhead like buzzing bees. A steady boom, crump, crump, crump of bombs came from where people and buildings were being blown to pieces.

Without light from fires or the little bit from the searchlights swinging back and forth, you needed the curb to find the way. Four streets this direction, three streets that direction, hoping one wasn't blocked to throw you off course. Then you counted down the number of houses to the one you wanted if it was still there. If you paused to light a match to see at an address an air raid warden shouted. Power had gone to their heads, of course. Give a man a uniform.

We found the pub in the dark when the door opened and let out a crack of light. It was a silent place with people hunched over drinks. We knocked back whiskey until Kent was happy as a kid with a new toy and I helped him stumble to his flat. He broke into the Boola Boola song from Yale along the way. His place was a bed-sitter without a kitchen up two flights of stairs, about what you'd expect for a bachelor working as a clerk.

"I got some whiss-kee round here somewhere," he slurred with a wave of his arm. I poured him a stiff one hoping to get him to say something that would wrap up my deal with MI6. But he chug-a-lugged it like it was water for a fire burning inside and toppled onto his sofa and began a snore that made his lips flutter.

I poked around some and came across boxes and boxes of paper stacked in the closet crammed with carbon copies of cables from the embassy. I pocketed a handful and said goodnight and goodbye to Mr. Kent.

"How many would you say?" asked Maxwell Knight, the agent that Menzies passed me on to after his talk with Churchill; I'd have liked to be a fly on the wall for that meeting. Knight was a man with a deep voice perfect for the stage or radio. The man could read the phone book and make it sound like God talking.

"Hundreds, maybe over a thousand," I said.

In fact, it turned out to be more than twelve hundred decoded cables, from run of-the-mill office crap to stuff so secret the State Department had to change the code for embassies and consulates all over the world.

Kennedy pulled Kent's diplomatic immunity and he was tried in a closed court and hauled off to a British prison. He might still be rotting there for all I know. I went round to the tea house to give Anna my sympathy and sniff out what I could, but they said she was in custody herself. Don't know what happened to her, either.

CHAPTER 14

AS WITH SO MANY FIGURES IN MY HUSBAND'S NARRATIVE, JOSEPH KENNEDY had popped up at odd times in the newspapers in my old life, but in researching him at the very good local library I realized how important he was in the interwar period in politics, banking, finance and the movie industry. He had been recalled as ambassador from London in 1940 for his defeatist attitude.

"I heard he tried to make it sound like it was his idea to come back," Lowell said with a laugh. "Half of what people know is wrong if they get it from newspapers."

Joseph Kennedy Jr., the eldest son, was killed in the war and another son, John, the junior Senator from Massachusetts, won a medal for bravery in the South Pacific.

"Colville told me it was no secret Joe wanted Junior to run for president and already was lining things up," Lowell told me. "He'd figured out he would have to come out of the war as a hero to make up for being a Catholic. The way I heard it, young Joe would've had a chestful if he'd come back from a special bombing mission so risky it was almost like suicide. I don't know why a man would volunteer for it, but I suppose he heard his father's voice in his head when they asked for a pilot. It's up to John now and I wouldn't bet against him. The old man is probably arranging it behind the scenes the way he did with the other son."

Cordelia was one of the few women in Lowell's stories able to resist his charms, and her Sapphic nature was the explanation. Women figured in so many of his stories, and again I couldn't help wondering if I was just another he could leave without a backward glance. He enchanted women without effort except for that prize he most wanted, a rich one.

The money I had, supplemented by his coup at poker in Hot Springs was more than adequate for our needs, but far from the princely measure he had imagined was required for a good life when a young man. He had pictured a compliant wife of good family, stately homes, travel abroad and a yacht for weekends, healthy children he would shape up like a ship's crew, household servants "and all the trimmin's" as he put it. He would have time and money to pursue whatever fancy took him; he once even spoke of an expedition to South America to look for the father who disappeared in the jungle. A reconciliation he would bring off between his mother and real father was part of the fantasy; the hateful Senator being pushed out into the cold.

"That would have squared matters some," Lowell said, "but the old devil would still owe me for Ironwood School."

I sometimes asked the question many do in the quiet moments of a marriage. "Do you love me?"

Of course I do, he would reply with a touch of asperity as if the matter was settled and nothing more needed saying.

"You think I'd buy you all that Mother Sees if I didn't?" He ate the choicest pieces as he had a sweet tooth, but believed this token and other small attentions were dispositive.

After an evening at the motion pictures or dining out, we liked to stop for a nightcap at a friendly place on the oceanfront called Al's Anchorage before going home. We became known to the Italian owner and the regulars and would nod and say hello, but Lowell said we should do nothing to encourage familiarity.

A burly, blue-jawed man called Turk who worked in shipbuilding, a very loud man, was usually there in various stages of drunkenness that ranged from morose to loud hilarity and horseplay. One stage was to impose his louche company on others, sitting down and calling for another round on him.

"We're just going," Lowell would say good-naturedly and we would rise and leave. "He might be a good customer, but if Al is smart he'll tell him to beat it," he told me in the cold salt breeze outside. "I've seen plenty of his kind and they're kegs of dynamite with lit fuses."

Turk made a lot of money as a civilian during the war and wanted people to know it. "Somebody had to build the ships for the sailor boys," he said, making it sound like it had been a sacrifice.

He brought in hard-faced floozies from time to time that made you think of the phrase "painted woman," but never the same one more than twice. He made joking passes at wives and girlfriends when he came by himself, but nobody seemed to think anything of it except Lowell. "He'll go too far sometime."

One night after we had swordfish down the street at the Fisherman's Net, we dropped by Al's. We heard Turk's jackhammer laughter all the way out on the street. It was a Saturday night and more crowded than usual, and Turk was at that stage of inebriation where he was host-like, gliding importantly from table to table buying people drinks so they would listen to his boasting.

"Hello, sweetheart," he said to me when he came to ours. He began kneading my shoulders like a baker with dough.

"Hands off," Lowell said in a genial voice.

"Aw, she don't mind, do you sweetheart?" Turk said.

He bent to whisper in my ear and as I turned from his horrid breath I saw the beer bottle coming down. Turk hit the floor, conscious but only barely, and covered with foaming beer. We walked outside to applause from the other customers.

"Lucky I only took a sip," Lowell said, "you need a full bottle for a good conk. A chief petty officer told me that back when I was an ensign in charge of a shore patrol. You come across some almighty hard heads on the waterfront, a good many of the guys feeling no pain as the saying goes. A hickory nightstick was best, but in a pinch you made do."

I was upset and trembling on our way home. Perhaps there are some women not distressed by violence, but I'm not one of them. I asked why that had been necessary. "Well, he's younger and probably stronger, so I had to take advantage of the opportunity."

No, I protested, why couldn't we just walk away?

"It's a man thing," he said. When we were in bed, I recalled to him that he had said many times he made a point of walking away from fights over women, there being so many of us to pick from.

"That was then and now is now," he answered. "Give us a kiss, darlin'." Of course, I did.

The next morning, Al worriedly called to say Turk needed stitches on the crown of his head and had made a police complaint. Lowell held the phone out so we both could hear. "They're looking for you, so maybe you better stay away for awhile. I told Turk I didn't want to see his face again; he bought a lot of liquor but the guy's a pest. Maybe when things cool down you and the missus can come back."

We packed up and within an hour were on the road for Santa Barbara, a sleepy little beach town far north on Highway One. When I raised the possibility of writing the owner to get back some portion of our lease in Laguna Beach, Lowell smiled. "Not a good idea."

He was in the highest of spirits, but I had a hollow feeling because we were once again tumbleweeds at the mercy of the wind. Other than love for one another, the only fixed point in our lives was putting his story down on paper for posterity. I wanted our wandering over more strongly than ever; call it a nesting instinct awakened. I had lost whatever interest I had in what lay over the next horizon, experience having shown it little different than on this side. Wherever you go, said some sage, there you are and the problems are the same as ever. I plugged in the tape recorder at the Barbara Hotel, which Lowell said had gone downhill from what he remembered in the 'Thirties.

THEY USED to get a lot of Hollywood people here for weekend hanky-panky. Okay, where was I? Joe Kennedy moved himself, his wife and the nine kids to the countryside with all their nurses and nannies when the Germans began bombing. The Krauts mauled the British airfields first to control the skies come fall when the invasion barges crossed the channel. I mentioned before that if they got their armor past the beach defenses, which was nothing more than barbed wire and a few mines most places, Brooke planned to have troops hound the tanks day and night, not giving the crews a chance to gas up or even get out for a piss. That sounded pretty thin to me and I dropped a hint to Harry Hopkins over the trans-Atlantic line that my talents could be put to better use back home.

"What?" he said. "Oh, no, no. The chief needs your eyes and ears over there more than ever. If there are any signs of giving up, we want to be the first to know. Don't forget the Duke of Windsor."

The worry was the ex-king would head up a peace party and parlay with Hitler, a possibility I'd passed on to him from Colville. I didn't remind him of that because you had to make your points fast with Harry. You would end a sentence and before you could start another he'd hang up. I told you about all the phones in his bedroom, every one of them ringing off the hook.

"Yes," he would say to whoever was on the other end or "no" and bang, that was it. I don't know how Harry kept all those decisions straight in his head, but he was a smart one and no doubt about it.

Business at the embassy picked up considerable and there were lots of new faces in the hallways looking stern and worried like it was an order from the top. There was a new crowd of staff officers and other flunkies who wrote up reports for Washington. They got written longer there and passed to new departments of this and that. Government had gone hog wild and the filing cabinets grew by the mile.

I stepped up my visits to the embassy, making sure I walked fast with a file and the official look of concern so as not to seem like I was slacking off. The old hands told new people what I did was a mystery, and Admiral Deveral showed what happened when somebody looked at me too close. The man who brought Deveral down! I suppose I was a hero to some, the admiral being hated by every decent man and woman.

I usually left the embassy inside ten minutes by another door. You had to sign in and out, but nobody who was important looked at the logs. It was just paper and smart people avoided paper when they could. Some yawning flunky might run an eye over the logs before they got put in a drawer, never to be seen ever again. You learn this stuff if you work in government.

One morning on my breeze through the premises my name was shouted out from behind. My hearing is back, I told Commander Mather, so no need to bellow. He said he was glad to know it and asked if I had time for coffee. I made a show of looking at my watch and said I could give him fifteen minutes.

"They're keeping you hopping, too," he said in the embassy cafeteria where the food was not fit to eat. "All noses to the grindstone these days. I go home at ten or eleven, eat supper and hit the rack; I'm back here at six. Betsy and the kids went home a week ago. I'd hardly have any time for them anyhow; they'll be safe, that's the important thing. Admiral Howard replaced Deveral. He's a nice guy, not so much an asshole. I told him how Deveral got yanked home fast as jack rabbit running from a fire and he thanked me for the warning. I doubt he'll bother you."

I put a dreary look on and said there were plenty of times I wished for regular duty instead of…I let my voice trail off.

"I know," Mather said with merry eyes, "you can't talk about it."

It made me wonder if he was on to me, but I pushed on with a shake of my head and said if I could only talk to someone it might relieve the pressure. "But I've already said too much."

Looking like he was holding in a laugh, damn him, he asked had I heard the War and Foreign affairs offices made a place on the Horse Guards Parade for a bonfire if it was necessary to burn secret papers. This was news to me, probably just another rumor if you cut to the heart of it, but I spread my hands like it was one of the things I couldn't talk about. He said we must get together for a drink sometime, us old bachelors, and I said what a fine idea. But I had no interest in that; the man was no fool and I'd have to watch every word.

Besides, drinks with him would be a big drop off from what I was used to. A lot of the fizz had gone out of the London social scene, but a few hostesses were trying to keep spirits bucked up. I was invited out every night, cutting quite the figure in my new uniform as the ladies told me. It was tailored in Oswald's shop on Savile Row and was nearly as stylish as the Italian rigs; like I tell you the dagos have a flair for military appearance even if they can't fight a lick. I had him send the bill to the Navy Department. They wrote me that the cost was six times what regulations allowed and the difference would be taken out of my pay. I mentioned it to Mother in a letter she gave it to the Senator to take care of.

"Rather than quibble over such a small matter, he said he would pay it out of his own pocket," she wrote back. "He was not gracious."

The Duchess of Rutland and her husband, Duff, were welcomed back at the Savoy from their trip to the Far East at a "glittering gala" as it was called by the tabloids. They didn't approve of the swells having a high old time with a war going on.

There was a quote about the Duchess of Richmond's ball the night before Waterloo that Wellington himself came to. It seemed almighty casual to me to go dancing before a battle to decide the future of Europe, but they were different times. In our war, terror gripped your guts the night before action. Dry throat, constant yawning, hands shaking; it was almost even worse than the fighting.

A big dance orchestra was playing when I got there after sharing a bottle of champagne with one of the chumps who filled my pockets with so many ten pound notes I crackled when I sat down. The walls had patriotic posters with spotlights on 'em. "To Victory!" said one that showed Hitler's skull on two bayonets. "Don't Waste Oil. Not a drop, Not a Splash," said another. A cartoon of Hitler with a huge listening ear said, "Careless Talk Costs Lives. Mr. Hitler Wants to Know!"

Diana came straight over like she had been looking for me special. "You're an awfully good dancer, aren't you? Please say yes!"

I said I couldn't answer for how things might be nowadays, but when I was at the academy a young midshipman was expected to know the social graces for the debutante balls and not tripping over your feet was one of 'em.

"Oh, tosh," she said, "don't be so modest. I want you to meet a friend of mine."

Anastasia Abramova was a Russian ballerina, older looking than when you were up close instead of out there in the theater seats. She had a swan neck and a formal way of standing and moving, stilted I heard a catty woman say. She was wearing a light blue whispery dress with a high collar. She gave me a curtsy that forced me into an awkward bow, not being used to them. Like snapping off a smart salute to impress the brass, it takes practice before a mirror to get it right.

"She is on a goodwill tour," Diana had said. "I can't imagine who approved it; Duff says when Stalin hears the guilty party will be shot. It is rare for a dancer of her ability to come abroad for any reason, and she brought a new waltz from the brilliant composer Shostakovich. He has a first name, but dear me I seem to have forgotten it. The orchestra was practicing the music this afternoon and it is too, too wonderful. The problem is the dancer who came with Anastasia is having trouble with his stomach. He blames our food, the

214 | JERRY JAY CARROLL

beast. But you see Anastasia needs a partner and there is no one we could find on such short notice."

Both women looked at me brightly and it dawned that they expected me to step in as his replacement. Ha-ha, I said, you're not serious. When the terror began to show, Anastasia patted me on the shoulder and said in her heavy accent, "It be hokay-dokay. Do best you are can. I do rest."

The orchestra was already putting music sheets on their stands as the dance floor was clearing. I thought of bolting but Anastasia clung to one arm and Diana the other. They pulled me out on the floor and Diana called out that everyone was in for a rare treat. Her words came to me like in a dream as I gaped at all the smiling faces, hoping someone would step out and raise a hand to say the joke had gone far enough.

"The great Shostakovich...the great prima ballerina Anastasia Abramova... music never heard before outside the Soviet Union...goodwill tour...her partner taken ill...gallant and handsome Yank kindly offered..."

And then Diana walked off the floor.

The lights went out and a single spotlight was on us. A bass drum was stuck, a lone saxophone tootled, and we were off to the races. After some stiffness from stage fright, I got into the swing of things and even started to enjoy sweeping around the floor with her with what people afterward said was elegance, but it was all thanks to her. Anastasia smiled into my face and gave extravagant tosses of her head like she was my adoring lover. The Second Waltz it was called and damn fine music when I look back; I could whistle it today.

When it was over, the crowd cheered as we bowed to one another and the orchestra struck up that waltz again and the dance floor filled. I danced most of the night away with women wanting a turn with the dashing Yank to tell their grandchildren as several said to me.

Anastasia left with two unsmiling men in dark suits, pausing at the door to throw kisses to the cheering crowd. "Thanks for being a good sport," Diana said when I got winded and dropped in a chair at her table. I told her my heart nearly stopped at her nasty surprise, but I hoped no permanent damage was done. She was beautiful in a gown cut low to show her...well, never mind.

"See the elderly ladies dancing with dear old prancing partners, jangling with their orders and decorations and coattails flying," she said. "I'm afraid gamboling does not go with weary faces and unlimber limbs."

That seemed hard on the old gents when I looked up "gamboling," but if you've got enough years on you the dance floor should be off limits; the old boys would rather be sitting and smoking their cigars anyhow.

So you've been in the Far East, I said to her, blotting my forehead with my handkerchief. Lordy, I felt like I'd run a race.

"Yes, Duff was sent to inspect the state of our defenses. Between us and not to be repeated, he found them lamentable. While he was inspecting troops and forts, I went out to the bazaars. I love the native people and their colors They're warm and everything we're not. But not all is perfect in paradise. In Singapore they have what is called a brain-fever bird, have you heard of it? It has a rising three-note call they repeat six times that ends in a scream. One was in a tree outside our bedroom window and poor Duff went into an insane rage."

I doubted she was much bothered, what with her bedtime morphine.

"There's the vulpine Sir Percy Colville," she said, "the man is everywhere; I don't know anyone who isn't his closest friend. He has a genius that is positively occult for drawing out one's secrets. I've told him things I wouldn't dream of telling anyone else, even Duff."

I took a glass of champagne from a waiter, wondering what "vulpine" was, and asked off-handed how the ghost at Rutland Castle was doing. I still had bad dreams from that time, worse even than from *HMS Amazon*.

"Oh," she said, sitting up straighter, her tits jiggling. "Actually, there is a new ghost. The household staff think it is the footman who went missing."

Went missing, I repeated in a weak way. It felt like a hand was on my windpipe.

"Of course, you were there the night it happened! Did you 'bump him off' as you say in America?"

Colville slipped into a chair at that moment and she turned to him as I'm thinking with a chill up my spine it could be me wandering those cold corridors for eternity. I gulped down my champagne and waved the waiter back for more.

"Tell us news!" she begged Colville. "Something that isn't in the newspapers."

He took a guarded look round. "We have it on very good authority Comrade Stalin is displeased over his war with Finland. Even though the Finns had only two French cannons from 1871 that fire black powder charges, the Russians suffered staggering losses at Tolvajarvi. A quarter million, so we understand. Generals are being executed right and left even though they do everything they can think of, even forcing soldiers at gunpoint to walk into minefields to find paths for the tanks. They go singing hand-in-hand to death; it is the Russian fatalism and their infinite capacity for suffering. The enormous loss of life is not important to the Kremlin because they have five million men under arms, but this ineptitude is bound to interest Herr Hitler."

Oh, Diana cried, that is too horrible to be true. "It must be German propaganda."

Colville said he was prepared to believe anything about either power. "People don't realize this is a new kind of war."

"What about Hitler?" she said. "They're allies now; he signed a treaty with the Soviets."

He gave her a pitying look. "It's worth no more than loo paper from your corner grocer."

More news was Stalin was dumbfounded how fast the French and English folded. "He thought there would be a million casualties and two years to prepare for Hitler's attack. We are informed Mussolini made a similar miscalculation; he hoped the Germans would win but be seriously weakened. He didn't want them all-powerful and counted on enough of his own losses, say a few thousand or so, to buy a seat at the peace table."

The Second Waltz struck up again and a dark-haired beauty in a diamond choker and a blood-red gown, a former lady-in-waiting I was to find out, begged the favor of a waltz. That is how she put it. From her burning look, I had a good idea the favor would be paid back with interest. Lady Catherine Howard danced better than any of 'em except Anastasia herself, and we went whirling around the floor to the admiration of all.

"He's taken," she said in a haughty way when other women asked to cut in.

Over her shoulder as we spun past, me sweating like a dock worker, I saw Colville with his head close to Lady Diana. Pumping her about the Far East, was my guess. When the dance was over, Lady Catherine gave me a leather coin purse.

"This is for you," she said.

It was light enough so if it was a tip I figured she thought I came as cheap as the dago counts with oiled hair that hang about rich women. I was going to give it back with some strong language, but she was already disappearing in the crowd.

When I looked at it in the gent's room where the old coves were mopping their red faces with hand towels, I saw it had a door key and an address in Kensington Palace Garden. I wondered if it was usual for her to invite strangers home. Howsomever, I wasn't one to look a gift horse in the mouth. To stray off the point, I remember as a kid the Senator skinning a horse's lips back to inspect its teeth from someone who said he was giving a present.

"Get out of here," he said, cursing the man. "My vote don't come that cheap." I was watching with open mouth like little kids do and got a cuff on the ear. "Mind your own business."

Colville was alone at the table when I got back, Diana being out on the floor with her husband. "He was detained by his mistress, a very jealous woman," Sir Percy said. "You're surprised? I keep forgetting how unsophisticated you colonials can be. Diana has a lover, an educated man with poetic tastes who shuns the city. She goes in summers to him and comes back quite brown and professing the virtues of rural life. People listen patiently, she is a duchess after all, until it is gone from her system."

He looked down at his vacant sleeve, remembering how handy that arm used to be. He had a tidbit for one of my letters home he thought the president might find interesting.

"We call Singapore the Gibraltar of the East, an impregnable citadel and fleet base to suppress uprisings, and now of course as a deterrent to the Japanese. Diana was entertaining a young diplomat waiting to speak to Duff when in the course of idle conversation he told her he didn't know why they called it impregnable. He spent his weekends getting to know all he could about Singapore; he must be a quite conscientious fellow to go to that trouble. He acknowledged that the south of the island is defended by powerful naval guns and is indeed impregnable, but to the north there is no defense except the strait a man can swim across. I was in Singapore a few times myself and visualized the withering fire those mighty guns were capable of delivering to a hostile fleet foolish enough to approach, but it never occurred to me or it seems anyone else to wonder about the back side."

I mentioned this in my next letter to Washington, but nobody said anything one way or the other, which was pretty common. I sometimes felt like I worked in a vacuum, but that suited me just fine. If no one paid attention, all the better. Weeks later when I casually mentioned this to Commander Mather, he said, "Isn't it jungle all the way up that peninsula? You'd have to be a monkey to get through, and anyhow that's an English problem."

It sure wasn't a Japanese problem. They swarmed up that peninsula taking 50,000 prisoners on the way and then another 80,000 when Singapore surrendered in seven days. Worst disaster in British military history, Churchill's own words. He got the news at a White House meeting; a note an officer brought in was silently pushed across the table. You can imagine how broken and humiliated the old boy was.

Around four o'clock as the gala was winding down I hopped into one of the tall, black London taxis in the line outside and gave the driver the address. "You're the Yank from Dunkirk," he said, "I recognize you from the newspapers."

A short man with a horseshoe of white hair under the cap he put on, he started up the cab and we crept off into the darkness; the slits in the headlight for the blackout only showed the street a few feet ahead. "We appreciate what you did over there for our boys," he said over his shoulder.

Glad to help, I said automatically.

I got a lot of that, strangers coming up to silently grip my hand or bless me, which is unusual as the English are shy around people they don't know. Flower ladies at corners in London would skip up to give me a flower for my lapel and rounds were bought at pubs. When I lifted the pint with a grin they cheered my heroism, as they thought it was because the papers said so. They called out hear, hear and there's a jolly good fellow.

"I 'ope you don't mind, sir, if I say something about this 'ere address," the cabbie said.

Eager for the adventure ahead, I said say away. A little something to eat washed down by a rare wine and then off to bed where I'd show her what a tiger I was between the sheets.

"It's a fine neighborhood, the best," he continued, "but I've taken strange men there. Men from low places a decent person wouldn't go in, if you don't mind my saying so, sir. None too clean, either. I had to open the doors to get the smell out."

We drove along in silence as I'm thinking about it.

"I'm saying, sir, if it's a leg over you have in mind, I would recommend a knocking-shop or even them street slags that flashes torches in doorways as the safer course, not that all them is clear of disease from what I 'ear. I wouldn't say anything as a rule, a gentleman's business being his own, but because you were so 'elpful to our boys across the channel…"

She must be a nympho, I thought; that didn't sound so bad, being in my prime and ready to gallop with the best. I'm just being honest here, darlin', letting the chips fall where they may. But as I thought about it, I didn't like the idea of lying in the same bed where some bum had been no matter how many times the sheets were changed.

"I talked to a constable familiar with the address," he went on. "There it is, right over there." It was one in a beautiful row of mansions. "The place has a spanking room for them as like that sort of thing, as some gentlemen do I'm told, but 'e said it seemed more than that. It has a rack and shackles on the wall and 'e saw some nasty looking whips with dried blood on 'em. It was about the time that Hungarian diplomat went missing you may have read about."

Take me back to the Savoy, I said.

He was astonished when I gave him a couple of my crisp ten pound notes as a tip. "Oh, no, sir," he said, "that's not necessary." But I raised my hand like a lord silencing a man servant.

Colville had moved to the bar when I got back and was talking to a couple of older men, general officers in dress uniforms. I got his attention and he broke loose from them.

"Lady Catherine Howard," he said with surprise, "where did you hear that name?"

I was dancing with her tonight, I said.

"Here!" he said with amazement. "She has been ostracized from society for years; no home will receive her, let alone the royal court where she was one of the queen's favorites. Her husband divorced her over her liaisons with countless men. It appears she has uncontrollable sexual desire and is destined for a bad end. I hope you…" He paused delicately.

No, I said, the cab driver warned me off; I gave him twenty pounds as a tip.

"You should have given him fifty pounds—nay, a hundred!—for what he saved you from."

Hold on, I thought, I might have turned around anyway after I sized up the situation. To change the subject, I asked who the brass hats were. "Those old buffers are up kinda late, ain't they?"

Colville was silent for a moment. "They've been to a senior officers' conference in York where Anthony Eden said the government wanted to find out if our troops could be counted on to continue the fight in all circumstances. There was a gasp around the table. He explained the time might come when the government would be forced to leave if the Germans gained a lodgment, and he asked how many would respond to an order to embark for Canada. It was understood from their responses that most officers, NCOs and single men would obey, but the ordinary soldier would choose to stay behind with his family. Like the French, they would lay down their arms rather than undertake the uncertainties of continuing the struggle in exile. No one had considered the possibility that fighting on to the end might mean from a foreign country. Churchill expects people to accept the same severities of sacrifice that he would."

He nodded at the generals finishing their drinks and pushing off. "They are very frightened for our country." He made a funny sound then and his cheeks were wet.

"Please tell the president how desperate the situation is, I don't know if he and his people fully understand. The president's distrust of Ambassador Kennedy might be a filter that keeps the truth from getting through."

Not wanting to be around a man crying—you start to snivel yourself if you're not careful—I said I'd do my best but I had to be running along now.

He wrung my hand, which was wet from tears he brushed away, and gave me a ride to Churchill's flat. He said he was sorry for such a damned show of emotion and hoped I didn't hold it against him. Fearing he might start up again, I told him breezy-like don't give it another thought and popped out before the chauffeur got round to open the door.

The flat was empty now except for the housekeeper because Randolph was off training with the 4th Queen's Own Hussars, his father's old regiment. A funny story I heard at the time: Randolph was one of the oldest of the junior officers and not popular—big surprise. He was on the flabby side from the booze, and his brother officers let it be known they didn't think he was in good enough shape for the regiment. A lot of them had fathers who hated Winston and that was part of it. Anyhow, Randolph bet several of his brother officers he could walk the hundred miles round trip from their base in Hull to York in under twenty-four hours.

Followed by a car with somebody as witness and in case he got blisters, he made it back with twenty minutes to spare. And then they wouldn't pay up! Hawr, hawr, hawr. You don't think that's funny? Women look at these things different. I'm ready for dinner, how about you?

IS THAT thing on yet? That wasn't a bad lamb chop for four bucks. You can pay twice that and get no better. They mix a nice martini at the Blue Onion, too. It's sad the Santa Barbara Hotel has dropped so far, it was right spiffy in the old days. I bet these drapes haven't been cleaned for years, and State Street looks like it should be called Cheap Street. Everything has its rise and fall, and it'll come back one day, mark my words. You can't beat the weather or the scenery, even prettier than Laguna Beach I'd say. Me and Bill Stephenson, who I told you about before, spent time here when Roosevelt sent us out to soften up Hollywood for the English side. Some preferred Palm Springs for their romancing, but you could usually find a studio bigwig here hiding out from the press guttersnipes with his starlet of the week. Women will do anything for a movie career and those guys knew it.

That dining room downstairs is dingy and the waiters look like slackers. I wouldn't trust 'em to get ham and eggs right, but it was top-notch back then with starched linen, silverware heavy in the hand, and so forth and so on. There's a table in a corner where me and Stephenson and a screenwriter named Budd Schulberg watched Louis B. Mayer and Georg Gyssling having dinner as they went over scripts Gyssling brought in a satchel.

Schulberg told us Gyssling was Hitler's man in Hollywood and tipped us to the meeting and then decided to come along. Good-looking, fast-talking guy. I drove a borrowed Packard as big as a coach and four while they talked, Stephenson leaning forward to hear Schulberg, whose story was he got car sick if he rode in the back. He gave us a rundown like machine-gun bursts at the windshield or at me, sometimes craning around to riddle Stephenson. He was quiet in between like he was reloading.

"Hitler is a terrific movie fan," he said, "he watches them every night; they say Laurel and Hardy in *Way Out West* and *Swiss Miss* are his all-time favorites, so I wouldn't say his taste is exactly sophisticated. Hollywood pumps out twenty to sixty movies a year that make big money in Germany. Lines of people outside theaters, photos of Hollywood stars on magazine covers, glowing reviews in the newspapers. Say, turn up the radio, would you. I like that song.

"German films are crap, dull and humorless; even Hitler says so. He told a newspaper that German propaganda in the Great War made a big mistake. It tried to make the enemy look ridiculous when it should have made him look dangerous. The Führer is a smart guy in his way and cunning as a shit-house rat. Screw books, he says, people are too dumb and lazy to read them.

"He wrote in *Mein Kampf* that the best way to get ideas across is movies at night when people are relaxed and open to the message. I'm one of the few guys I know who read the book; he wrote it in prison when he had nothing else to do. Give the man his due, he's a great orator. You've seen him in newsreels whipping huge crowds up to hysteria. If you were making a movie, you would do a quick cut from the crowds yelling for blood to a quiet library where a few people are silently reading books and stroking their chins, learning stuff to undermine Deutschland.

"It would be understood by the audience that those weaklings with their sly eyes behind thick glasses are the enemy, they're intellectuals and probably Jews. Yarmulkes and side locks to emphasize the point might be too over the top, but maybe not! Those aren't geniuses in those theater seats. They're the masses needing manipulation by smarter people. *Wanting* to be manipulated."

He was quiet as he lit another cigarette and put another belt in his machine gun.

"On the business side, plenty of dough is lost if Germany slams the door to Hollywood; some studios would be forced to hang out the For Sale sign. When my father was vice president of Paramount, he saw a private study that was circulated among the studios after the Reichstag passed Article 15. It was a law that if they objected to any film distributed anywhere in the world, *anywhere*, it couldn't be shown in Germany, which is the third biggest market in Europe. And that was *before* Hitler.

"They were tired of seeing themselves as the villains in World War One. Carl Laemmle at Universal agreed to make twenty-three cuts on *All Quiet on the Western Front* to get it approved. If they weren't made, Gyssling said in a letter to him and sixty other people who worked on it, even including the wardrobe people, that no future movie with any of them involved would be shown in Germany. Their diplomatic service kept track of showings over the world to make sure Universal didn't sneak the scenes back in. It's still a great movie but it would have been better."

The road to get to Santa Barbara was Highway 1, which was pretty but slow, especially if there was an accident to hold you up, which was common with all those curves. We crept past an overturned truck at one point with cantaloupes scattered all over.

"The poor guy," Schulberg said, "it's probably his whole crop. Look, he must be Italian the way he's stretching out his arms and looking up at the sky. Mama mia, why me? He's crying! I could build a whole movie around that scene; I'd write it in four days and you could begin shooting on Monday.

"Excuse me if I get excited; a lot of Jews are like Italians that way. Imagine what it's like to be an *Italian* Jew. You wave your arms all day arguing with everybody and go to bed exhausted from emotion." He lit another cigarette. "It doesn't seem like smoking would be healthy, but you see all those doctors in white smocks in magazine ads saying a smoke relaxes them, and they're the experts, right?" Stephenson rolled down his window.

"Anyway, when Hitler comes in he turns the screws even tighter. The first thing was he knew how much leverage he had and how to use it. Eight days after he was voted in the studios were told from now on work with Gyssling on upcoming movies if they want to show them in Germany. Script approval and cast approval so no Jew names are on the screen.

"Can you imagine the arrogance, Germans telling Americans what to do? In Yiddish we call it *khutspe*. But the studios went along with it! Early on, the sequel to *All Quiet on the Western Front* was cancelled. The latest twist is the Third Reich doesn't want the studios to employ Jews to do anything; I suppose that includes sweeping up at the end of the day.

"From the *shmendrik* bosses, not a peep. They were even told not to go to the newspapers about it. They went along! *Give Us This Night* had a Jewish composer so Paramount agreed to dub in a score written by a German." He went on and out about the studio bosses, what cowards they were.

When we checked in, Stephenson gave the guy running the restaurant ten bucks for the corner table and said leave the one blocking our view empty for another ten. Why do I have to explain who Stephenson is again? Okay, have it your way, but it's all in the other writing you did.

Stephenson is a Canadian who was a hero in both wars, knighted by the Brits and given one of our biggest medals. He got pilot training with the RAF in the Great War and shot down twelve Germans in his Sopwith Camel. He riddled troops and stampeded horses, shot up a staff car that overturned, and then got nailed himself. He was wounded going down in his parachute and got shot by a Frenchman on the ground.

He escaped from prison camp after a few months. He was a captain with a Military Cross and a Distinguished Flying Cross when he mustered out. He is exactly the kind of guy I told you about, the ones you want to be a thousand miles away from when the shooting starts.

He had a golden touch between the wars and made a bundle in radio, airplanes, construction and other stuff, and married a tobacco heiress from Tennessee to round it off. He did a lot of business travel in Europe and tipped off Winston that the Germans were secretly building an air force; Chamberlain didn't want to hear what he dug up. Typical ostrich, head in the sand, didn't want to know the truth.

Stephenson is a charmer in Colville's league, and when Winston became prime minister he sent his master spy over to tell Roosevelt how to build up our scrawny intelligence operation. Roosevelt liked him of course, and on

Stephenson's say-so hired Bill Donovan to set up the OSS, which grew into our friends the CIA. I was a naval aide at the White House there with an office the size of a closet I shared with a fat guy. If one of us wanted to go out the door the other had to get up and flatten himself against the wall. People would just about kill for a spot anywhere in the building.

Harry Hopkins sent me out to Hollywood with Stephenson so the studio people would see me in my immaculate whites and take it the administration was squarely behind him. At least that's what they told me; more likely it was to be a dog's body whose duties included driving Stephenson to his appointments. This stuff is old so I'm getting on with the story.

While Stephenson silently watches and sometimes turns my way and says something about golf to pretend he's part of the conversation, I give Schulberg the play-by-play so Mayer doesn't recognize him unless he has the back of his head memorized. It went like this, word for word the way I said it:

A distinguished looking guy in a smart dark suit is at the door and he's being led to the table. Must be Gyssling. He's got a leather suitcase, heavy by the looks of it. He's ordering a drink and taking out screenplays, a big pile he stacks on a chair. He's lighting a cigarette in a long, black holder, which makes him a phony in my book. Looks over here but thinks I'm talking to you, Budd.

A little guy, Louis B. Mayer himself with a pot belly comes in with a taller, younger guy. The younger guy, a flunky is my guess, stops at something Mayer says and goes to a table by himself. A friendly hello between Mayer and Gyssling, handshakes and pats on the back. The waiter comes over with a martini in a stem glass for Gyssling. Mayer orders something. They are chatting away; the waiter brings Mayer a cup of coffee. Gyssling screws in a monocle and they are looking at their menus. Now, they call the waiter over. The young guy is looking at his, too. Gyssling takes one from the pile and shows it to Mayer, he points at a page and Mayer nods and writes in a notebook. Skips to another page, another nod and writing. Skips to another page, another nod. Same thing. Same thing. They're done with that screenplay and Gyssling takes another from the pile. Shows a page, gets a nod and Mayer makes a note. Over and over it goes. Do you want me to keep this up?

"We get the idea," Budd says. "They are scenes the Heinies don't like and

MGM will take them out. The writer, that poor bastard, will blow his brains out if he still has any."

"He does this with every studio?" Stephenson asks. "Why do they put up with it?"

He has the perfect look for the spy. Medium height and weight, dark hair, regular features. If you were asked to describe him you'd say what I just did. Travel ten floors in an elevator, just you and him, and he'd be forgotten ten seconds after one of you got off. Make it five.

"Moola," Budd says. "It's all about money in this business whatever bullshit you hear from liars on the so-called creative side like me. Money and screwing beautiful women on the casting couch. Mayer was putting the make on Shirley Temple's mother when they came to MGM to sign a contract at the same time Alexander Freed, who produced *The Wizard of Oz*, was showing his schmeckel to the little kid in another room. Twelve years old! The mother strides out of Mayer's office head held high, Shirley starts laughing at him, so Freed slams out of the room in a fury. How do I know? All Hollywood knows! It must have been some conversation between mother and daughter on the ride home."

That's the way it went, Gyssling passing the screenplays as his pile gets smaller while the one on Mayer's side gets bigger. In between they ate; lamb chops for Mayer who has something to say about them to the waiter that doesn't look like a compliment and grilled salmon for the German. Red potatoes for both and green peas. Hamburger and fries for Stephenson which he barely touches, and Porterhouse steaks two inches thick for me and Schulberg as I'm passing all this on. Gyssling pats his lips delicate-like with his napkin and Mayer starts doing it, too. Sometimes it looked like Mayer was arguing over a scene; Gyssling would listen for a bit and then give in with a smile and shrug like it never hurts to ask.

"I bet most won't get made anyway," Budd whispers, "but Mayer can tell his production people he's got advance okay and maybe somebody can make a silk purse from one of those sow's ears. I wouldn't be surprised if he got a sadistic thrill from making Gyssling spend hours looking for something that might get him in trouble with Goebbels. And MGM isn't the only studio in on the deal; all the majors are shoveling screenplays to him for an okay. How's he got time for anything else? You wouldn't believe the drek screenwriters grind out; they ought to be walking dogs not writing them."

They have pie and coffee like us and then get up from the table as Mayer waves over the flunky to carry the pile of screenplays out to the car. More handshaking and back patting.

When they cleared out, Stephenson shook his head and said one word. "Unbelievable."

Like I told you before, we called on all the studios and Stephenson begged them to show England in a better light and Germany in a worse one. He said the government would help with money, free screenwriting, and even strong arm big British actors into working cheap. The studios were tempted but still scared stiff, like Schulberg said. Even so you began to see changes in the big costume movies; sinister dueling scars on Germans talking in that guttural way and the English looking plucky.

Jack Warner and his brother the silent partner who tagged along as close as a tail on a dog—the guy never said a word I heard except hello and good-bye—almost went along with the deal, but then Jack said they would have to get all the profits their movies made from the British market. That was the richest in Europe, ten times bigger than Germany, and it was a deal breaker because...Hey, did you fall asleep? You did! Why am I telling you all this if you're not listening?

CHAPTER 15

LOWELL WAS RIGHT, I DID FALL ASLEEP, BUT NOT BECAUSE I HAD LOST INTEREST. When I replayed the tape, I saw I nodded off at the dinner description as he talked to the ceiling in the trance-like state that he went into recalling the past. As I transcribed the tape later, I wondered is there anything people won't do for money or power.

Mayer was knowingly letting himself be manipulated in the interests of an evil regime that hated Jews like him and wanted them annihilated. Even cursory research showed that reports were trickling out in the newspapers about what the Nazis were doing, but the public paid little attention. Sequestered in a library carrel in the nation's capitol deep in my research, I admit I was only dimly aware of passing events.

According to Schulberg, Hitler's obsession with movies was because he understood early their power to move public opinion. Had Hollywood made movies about the Third Reich a decade earlier, it might have affected how people thought. As it was, ninety percent of our population held firm to the isolationism we had reluctantly given up in the Great War with nothing to show for it afterward.

Jews in Hollywood were divided over whether the movie industry should get involved; some argued it would just make things worse for Jews in Germany. Herman Mankiewicz, who later wrote *Citizen Kane*, wanted to show Hitler's malevolence by making a movie with the title *The Mad Dog of Europe;* Sam Jaffe, the celebrated actor who played the water boy in *Gunga Din*, quit RKO to work fulltime as its producer. Then came another threat from Gyssling that was supported by the Hays Office, the industry trade group.

He said if the movie was made, *all* American film companies might be banned from doing business in the lucrative German market and that was that. What Lowell related about Hollywood's contemptible connivance with Hitler will be of interest to future scholars who combine this manuscript with what is publicly known.

I have always been an active person both physically and mentally, which made the strange fatigue I began to feel disturbing. We would return from morning walks along the beach and I would be so overcome with sleepiness that I would nap for an hour or more. I was dull and yawned frequently; even Lowell noticed.

"You used to be a lot livelier."

Yes, I said, forcing a bright smile and promising to do better because illness had the effect of exasperating Lowell, though he saw humor in a shoulder-shrugging way when our pursuers forced us to that Kentucky cave in the dead of winter. He should have been in a hospital with a bronchial infection, an event described in the earlier manuscript.

I was in my thirties, young enough for that sense of invulnerability common to the young, but a corner of my mind was aware that some diseases in early stages settled in with symptoms that included weariness and mental listlessness.

We drove farther north on Highway One after a few days, an old sailor like Lowell more comfortable with the ocean near. Those long years of penury had confined him to the interior of the country and he had sorely missed the smell of salt air. He would roll down the window or stop the car for a deep breath.

"Smell that!"

I would make a game try at matching his zestfulness, but lethargy seemed to weigh me down more every day. I no longer took his dictation by hand as we drove because my attention strayed and with a start I would realize I was woolgathering. He was sympathy itself when I confessed my lapses.

"You're a little under the weather, that's all. Sit back and enjoy the view, we'll get this on tape tonight."

I fell behind transcribing the tapes after he dozed off nights because I could not keep my own eyes open. We stopped for lunch at a burger shack at Avila Beach though I had little appetite. I found unbearable the smell of the little baskets of sandwiches and limp fries almost cold and glistening with grease. When Lowell opened his hamburger bun to make sure the onion was in, I was nauseated by the glistening, pulpy slice of tomato that made me think of flesh flayed from bone. Holding my hand to my mouth, I hurried to the ladies room. He was reading a newspaper when I got back; after a few minutes' perusal of the sports he folded it.

"You haven't touched your food," he said with surprise.

"I'm just not hungry," I said wanly.

He had the waitress put it in a bag for later. "I didn't think about it before, but my time in Russia and those years as a tramp made me hate to see food wasted."

As days passed without any improvement in my condition, I began to wonder how to break through his carapace of solipsism—which upon reflection explained how he survived all his trials—to tell him what was happening. He owed his freedom to swift movement from potential and real threats in different ways, even running from it in some cases, and that meant traveling light. This would no longer be possible burdened with the anchor of an ill wife. More emotional than ever in my life, I imagined heart-breaking scenes of parting.

I pictured him dropping me at the doorstep of my brother Buck with a look back and saying, "I'll be in touch." Sometimes, clinging feebly to Buck's arm, I imagined him saying it casually as if to a slight acquaintance, and other times with a quavering voice. But either way and with all the permutations in between it was soul crushing. He misread my sadness.

"Yeah, that place in Laguna Beach was okay. Too bad we had to haul ass out of there."

It was impossible for him to imagine someone who did not find pleasure in the highway stripe that led to the horizon. As I watched with dull eyes, the white line rushed under the car and then dwindled to nothing in the rearview mirror. Over and over.

And his own health became a worry for me; his "bum ticker" as he put it. What would happen if he had a heart attack and I wasn't there? He would hold on against the pain until it was too late. He wouldn't call for help because it would mean questions asked by officials, and his several bogus identifications would be found in a search of car and luggage. The thought of him alone at the mercy of strangers made me burst into tears.

"Look, we'll find another place just as good or better," he promised.

Night in another auto court, this one farther up the coast at Moro Bay.

WOW. THAT moon on the water is beautiful, ain't it, darlin'? Where was I before we swung off course to that Hollywood stuff? You call them digressions, a new word and a pretty darn good one; it rolls right off the tongue and sounds important. Right, the brass were knocked back on their heels when Eden asked would the army keep up the fight from Canada. That was around the time I was recalled home because Admiral Standley stepped down. It could've been from overwork as he was also filling in as Navy Secretary because Claude Swanson was a long time dying of cancer.

Standley was liked by all hands but didn't have the time of day for me the few times I came in range. He'd heard the talk about me I suppose. He was born and raised on the Russian River in California up near Ukiah. His pa the sheriff was called Iron John because of how he enforced the laws, including some made up on the spot. His favorites, brown-nosers to the man, said the admiral liked to yarn as much as any Southerner.

He had stories about the second generation of Russians that settled those parts up there still living like they were back in the old country; log cabins dug into the ground, cooking over pits, and stepping into the woods regardless of weather when nature called and so forth. But they made their kids talk English and kept them in school to the eighth grade, which was uncommon for then. Good people, the admiral said.

A British special operations officer I was with once topped him on primitive. He told me when he was sneaking around Yugoslavia lining up saboteurs and spies that the Yugos lived like people did five hundred years ago. Their huts had rushes and bracken instead of floors and women wore hand-woven dresses cut down to the navel so their titties flopped out; they greased their hair with butterfat and parted it in the middle. They stank to high heaven even without that, not being partial to washing. Most stuck to home and had never even visited the local village; they're probably not much changed to this day.

Okay, I'm drifting a few points off compass. Admiral Leahy took over as CNO and I got a cable telling me to report to the Navy Building on the next ship coming home. That was a Mizar class reefer built for the United Fruit Company, a banana boat if you want to call it that, with nice cabins for nine paying passengers that they hadn't got around to tearing out yet for storage space.

What a relief from the bombs in London! You could never totally relax there even in the countryside because the Germans sometimes lightened the load flying to London or saved something for farmers on the return trip. They mostly fell in pastures, but now and then a farmhouse or some quaint little village got blasted. It happened enough so a person was kept on edge, it did me anyways when I shook loose of London. There was always something to worry about back then.

The top speed of the reefer was 17 knots and no need to go that fast as there was nothing in the hold, so the skipper took a while to cross the Atlantic to ease the strain on the engines. I arrived purring like a cat now I was out of the danger zone. They were poor card players and I took nearly a thousand bucks off the crew. We dropped anchor at Wilmington on a drizzly gray morning and I took the train to D.C. to give Mother a surprise. I knocked at the door of the fancy Federalist house built in 1830 on the south side of N Street in the heart of Georgetown where all the home numbers were in buffed brass.

"Senator! Senator!" she cried, "Our boy is home!"

Always the stately grand dame who made strangers feel as small as elves, she always showed her warm side to me on T the rare times when she wasn't touring the country or the world with the Senator. She hugged and kissed me and led me to a gilt chair the Senator wasn't allowed to sit on account of it was a precious antique.

"Senator, come see, it's Lowell, praise God!"

After some time, he grudgingly tapped into the room with his blind man's cane, his great mass of white hair impeccably combed as always by Burton the valet.

"You put yourself in a good mood right this moment," my mother ordered when she saw his look.

"Well, this is a surprise," he said, not quite sullen but right on the border. "What brings you around?"

Mother said it was enough I was there and they should count their blessings. She said how good I looked as the Senator looked round to where he remembered the window was.

"My handsome, darling boy." She demanded I tell her all that had happened since she saw me last and it took a good hour to cover all the ground as the Senator blew out his cheeks from time to time like he wanted to interrupt but not daring.

"I don't believe that ghost story," he said when I finished, "and some of the other hooey if I comes to that."

Mother turned on him with her voice rising. "Oh, you don't know, you weren't there. Why would my boy make up such things?"

He looked like he was going to say something, but knowing he was beat from the start he asked, "Is that rain I hear out there?"

Mother went off to order refreshments and we sat in silence. The Senator took out his false teeth, making his face collapse like one of the buildings hit by a bomb in London. He turned them in his hands as if feeling for something from dinner. He knew from what Mother said that it disgusted me, which is why he did it when it was just the two of us.

"When do you go back?" he said at last, hearing her footsteps and putting them back in.

"I hope never," I said, "it's a damned risky place."

I was always nice as pie to him because of the need to draw on his power when they tried to give me duty in the blazing tropics, a weather station in the Arctic wastes, or whatever else they might dream up. They were very clever in the Bureau of Navigation, evil too, and had the memory of an elephant when it came to me.

"You took your time, Lieutenant," Leahy's aide said when I reported in. He was Commander Barkham, a banty-rooster kind of guy with red hair and a pug nose that was just about asking for a punch. My guess was he had a grudge against anybody over five foot seven. Buttocks like a woman.

I said I took the first ship home as orders stated. "You could have left Portsmouth at 0700 aboard *Brooklyn* and been home three days ago instead of that slow boat from China."

He didn't really mean China, darlin', that was just a saying. I pointed out the reefer left at 0600 and my orders said the first homeward bound ship.

After a good reaming out about obeying the spirit and not just the letter of an order if I wanted to get ahead, he led me into Leahy's office, that busy rump of his begging for a kicking the same as his nose did a punching.

The CNO waved off my crisp salute and said take a chair. He was a lanky, friendly kind of guy, not one of the ogres that normally land in that job. He wanted to know how I thought things were going across the pond.

"The RAF just kicked the hell out of the Italian fleet at Taranto," he said.

I explained I'd been crossing the Atlantic in recent days and wasn't fully in the picture as yet.

"Their old Swordfish biplanes flew off a carrier and torpedoed battleships getting up steam for Crete. Big victory for the Brits and they sure needed one."

I said there's the Italians for you. We talked along until he saw I didn't have any interesting insider stuff.

"When Admiral Standley handed over to me he mentioned that ruckus in London with Admiral Deveril," he said. "What the devil was that about? I had somebody ask around at naval intelligence and they said you didn't belong to them. Who was your boss?"

I said I'm not at liberty to say, sir.

He was knocked back a step and then the lightbulb went on. "I've been friends with the president since he was assistant secretary of the Navy. This is one of his deals, isn't it?"

He laughed when I grinned like a monkey and gave a shrug.

"The chain of command never meant a damned thing to him; he was always up to his games and I guess nothing has changed. Go on and get out of here, and when you see him say I'm on to his game."

I paused at the door and said real casual, "Who should I see about my new assignment?" I was thinking he would say look in at the Bureau of Navigation for my orders but instead he said, "Your boss is the Commander-in-Chief, talk to him. Until you do, London is your billet and you better get back ASAP. Have Barkham set it up."

You won't be returning by another leisurely ocean voyage, Barkham told me.

"The admiral said ASAP so we'll get you on Pan Am's Yankee Clipper tomorrow morning; a thirty-hour flight to Lisbon and from there KLM will fly you to Whitchurch near Bristol."

When I told Mother, she burst into tears. "Oh! So soon?"

The Senator sensed trouble as soon as he walked in the front door, but she waited until he tapped his way to the rosewood dining table with Mother's silver candelabras set out in my honor. As he was spooning in thick pea soup and smacking his lips, she explained the problem.

"You must do something, Josepha. Lowell says he would like an assignment on the Gulf around New Orleans where the weather is nice and he can come to see us regularly."

The Senator lay his spoon down. "A good many officers would like that duty, perhaps most of a certain kind." He sent a look where he thought I might be sitting. "But there's nothing I can do; the president is down in Warm Springs with his mistress and Harry Hopkins is back in the hospital. I'm not going to the Navy Building and piss away my influence asking for that kind of favor. No, siree."

I saw his point, damn it all, and so did Mother. She began to cry.

When I was still a midshipman, he explained to her the way it worked. Influence in Washington was built like a beaver does a dam, a little at a time until the current is blocked enough to make the quiet little side pools where deals got done. He would have to meet with Admiral Leahy over cocktails at a reception or at one of Mother's parties where she entertained the cream of society. The admiral would expect something in return and the Senator was miserly that way as in others.

Still, she threw down her napkin and ran from the room. All the power the Senator had breathed in during the day from all the ring kissers dancing around telling him what a great man he was left like air from a balloon. We finished the meal in silence except when the banana pudding was put before him. "She'll be like this for days."

I found out from my friend on the White House switchboard, I told you about her before, what hospital Harry was in and put on my dress uniform. Even the guys who hated my guts said nobody looked smarter on the parade ground. Coming through the entrance, I caught the eye of the gray-haired woman at the desk that said Administration and advanced on her chin up, shoulders back, arms swinging like the Navy Band was behind me.

I'm from the White House to see Mr. Hopkins, I said.

"He is not allowed any visitors," she said in a scared way.

I said I was on the nation's business and then my silence left it up to her to interfere if she dared. After a few seconds, she called over a young nurse to show me to Harry's bedside.

"You don't look so scrawny flat on your back," I told him.

He gave a weak laugh. "You silver-tongued devil, I see how you get all those women." He looked like hell—something was gnawing at his guts but they couldn't figure out what. "What brings you over from the Blitz?"

I explained the changeover in CNOs and his interest in what I was doing. We talked for a bit more and then his eyes closed and stayed that way for ten minutes while I leafed through a National Geographic on his bedside table. Wonderful pictures but a sight too many words for my taste; I'd cut back in favor of more photos.

"You still here?" he said when his eyes opened.

Sir Percy Colville sent me with a message, I said, which is they're really worried if they can hold out. There's talk about moving the government and army to Canada.

"They can't do that," Harry said, rising up on his elbows. "They have to stay and fight or all is lost."

"Well, yes, Harry, but they're pretty shaky after Dunkirk," I said. "All their gear got left behind and..."

"We're going to give them all they need," he said, lowering himself back down with his skinny arms shaking from the strain, "and tell them we don't rule out sending troops after the election."

It sounded like they were afraid the election was nip-and-tuck. I was surprised to hear Wilkie was putting up that kind of a fight, the party of Hoover and all, but many didn't think it right for Franklin to go for a third term, it being greedy in a way. But you don't need me to tell you that, your little finger knows more about politics than I got in my whole body. You'd a thought I'd pay more attention to it, being raised in a senator's household and all, but it seemed I always had better things to do. More interesting to me, anyhow.

"The chief has to lay low about getting involved in Europe's mess," Harry said. "He's promised the mothers of America he won't send any of our boys to fight overseas."

I hadn't heard about that, I said.

"He had to say it for the voters, but he doesn't mean it. Pass that on to Mr. Churchill."

I told him I didn't see much of the prime minister these days.

"In that case, tell Sir Perceval."

I said I'd send off a telegram as I expected the Navy Department had a new job in mind for me.

Harry shook his head. "No, there's a danger someone would put it in the hands of the Republicans. And forget that stuff about another job the chief wants you right where you are."

I said anyone could do what I was doing in London, maybe not as good, but...

"Forget about it," Harry said, turning on the side with his back to me. In less than a minute, his raspy breathing told me he was sleeping. My last hope gone, it was back to the Blitz.

I told you before what Lisbon was like—everyone a spy or working for one. I fell into conversation with a good-looking woman with a nice smile and a classy chassis who gave me goo-goo eyes at the hotel bar. We were getting along so swell after a couple of drinks that I'm thinking she was in the pay of some intelligence service, maybe even ours, so I excused myself to go to the gents and didn't go back. The bartenders working for the Germans, English, French, Russians, Dutch, Danes, Portuguese or all of them and us at the same time would report I didn't fall for the bait. It was a good time to be a bartender in the better hotels; they made out like bandits and bought olive farms.

When my train pulled up at Waterloo station the sirens were just beginning their mournful howl, *ooooOOOOOOOOoooo*. Rising and falling like they ran out of air and had to catch a breath to cut loose again. People were running for the shelters, me among 'em with the suitcase banging my leg. Even with that I beat the better part of the crowd to the shelter and elbowed a couple of old guys out of the way for a spot with a pillar to lean on.

Those places were like paintings of purgatory painters did in the old days, the ones in museums I got dragged to. The smell of bodies packed so tight made people faint, but it was nothing compared to when things were bombed to smithereens and families had no choice but to live underground. The papers kept out word about the smell so morale didn't drop any lower. A lot of things were kept out, and I didn't blame the government. What you saw with your own eyes was bad enough.

Things were comfortable enough when I got to White's after the all-clear; a crowded bar, wealthy lords in deep leather armchairs, and a crackling blaze in the fireplace. You wouldn't know a war was on the other side of the plush purple curtains. I had thrown back my first brandy and about to rattle the dice with the bartender for another when Colville seemed to come from nowhere.

"When do you leave for America?" he asked. I told him I had gone and come back again already.

"And?" he said. "Were you able to communicate the anxiety we feel?"

I said the president is off with his lady friend in Warm Springs and Harry's in the hospital, but I bluffed my way into his room. "He says there's nothing to worry about if FDR wins, and don't believe his talk about not sending America's boys overseas, that's just for the dumb voters."

"Winston tells me we can't lose once you Yanks are in the affray." The haunted look he'd had lifted. "It says a lot about you that you returned so quickly in our hour of peril. You are a true friend of Great Britain."

I told him wild horses couldn't have kept me away.

CHAPTER 16

BEARING A CHILD TURNED MY WORLD UPSIDE DOWN AND REORDERED ALL MY priorities. What scholarly interest and even sense of virtue that remained in correcting the historical record melted away. Lowell's avid speculations about the evil genius behind our troubles now held small interest. I felt an ever greater need to put an end to our parlous passage through storm-tossed seas. I longed for a quiet harbor where I could prepare for our baby's birth.

We stopped at a mom-and-pop general store with a vegetable stand out front at a sleepy, sun-drenched crossroads called Oakville to inquire about a place to stay. We were told an Italian couple named Nichelini took in guests at their small winery on Howell Mountain.

It lay in swelling hills enfolded in undulating rows of Pinot Noir grape vines reached by a dirt road in the Vaca Range near Angwin northeast of Napa Valley. We stirred up a dust cloud worthy of a stagecoach chased by Indians before reaching a two-story stone building with a red tile roof and ivy climbing the sides. The stillness and natural harmony all around struck me as the dust slowly settled. The loudest sound was the ticking of the cooling car engine. It seemed heavenly, but Lowell said it looked like Dullsville to him.

A tall, middle-aged woman generously proportioned in a green, white and red sun dress was like a barefoot goddess of bounty in an opera. She wiped floured hands on her apron before spreading arms wide, beaming with warm welcome. Three small children tumbled after her with happy shouts.

"Hello!" she called out in a cheery voice. "The store say you come to stay."

She had a strong Italian accent. In a low voice, Lowell quipped, "You'd expect a good grapevine around here."

When I look back, it was one of the most important days in my life.

"My name is Sofia Nichelini, please, please come in, come in. We don't get many visitors this early in the season." She was a handsome woman, dark-haired, full of joyfulness and an Earth Mother presence; she had dancing eyes with smile lines at the corners. I felt my spirits rise at once.

"I see you're expecting," she said, hugging me. "How wonderful! I have five, but no more, no more." Her laughter was throaty and robust. "And you, sir, what a distinguished man. You must be very important."

"Well, I…"

"When are you due, *tesoro*?" she asked me, grabbing my hands and kissing me on the cheek. I told her the early fall. "You too thin! We fatten you up." She turned to Lowell. "Tell me your name, signore."

"Worthington," he said unhesitatingly. "Lowell Worthington and this is my wife Harriet." I wondered what new fabrication he would come up with. "I work in Hollywood," he said. "I'm a location scout."

"Ah," she said, smiling. "What's a location scout? My husband, he will ask."

"I look for places where movies can be made. Interesting scenery and all that, places for cast and crew to stay while they're shooting. Several studios hired me to check out this part of California for upcoming projects. Their people don't get up this way very often."

"How exciting, Hollywood coming!" Sofia cried delightedly. "What movie stars?"

"Things are just in the talking stage so that's hush-hush. The only thing that's set is they want pretty scenery."

"Just look around, signore." The sweep of her arm took in the vineyard, the mountains and the flawless blue sky.

My elation faded and I felt dislike settle in, dull and heavy, for the lies Lowell must tell told this generous, open woman. But of course he had no choice.

"Do you like my dress?" she said to me, turning and making it swirl. "The colors of the Italian flag; I wear it every year for the Festa de San Marco which we celebrate here, but only in a small way, not like Venice. Oh, that is such a thing. It's in honor of Saint Mark, but also it is the rosebud festival." I said I would love one like it. "We'll make one while you are here!" Sofia exclaimed.

"What does a little fib hurt?" Lowell asked as we unpacked. "It gives us an alibi for laying low, doing nothing but driving around the countryside, seeing the sights, and having a good time. Look, you don't have to say anything, leave it all to me. You're the dumb wifey a little vague about her husband's work. Just say 'Ask him' and I'll make it up like they do in Hollywood anyway."

DAMN, THESE Italians eat good don't they? A salad picked from their garden, home-made pasta with a Bolognese sauce, and we must have put away two bottles of wine even though you hardly took a sip. And that stuff called cassata for dessert—*hoo-wee*, I thought I'd died and gone to heaven. The husband seems like a nice guy; a little quiet for me, but it takes all kinds. He might have a suspicious side so we have to watch out. Sofia likes to talk, don't she? Nice, though, I like her; a good woman, you can see it in her eyes. Not much of an Eyetie accent compared to most you see. Well, let's get rolling before my eyes get so heavy I can't keep 'em open from all that chow and the vino. It's not as good as French wine, but don't tell them.

THE TIME I'm remembering now was when Winston was still at the Admiralty in April of 'Forty. Colville told me he thought the war couldn't be fought unless one man was both prime minister and defense minister. Norway had showed that plain as the nose on your face. Beaverbrook convinced him to go a step more and take on the job as party leader to keep parliament in line. In a month he was more king than the one in the palace.

I passed all this on as it was happening and it seemed Roosevelt and Hopkins saw it as good news, which of course they would. A lot of people thought FDR was a dictator and Harry was like his Rasputin. You know who that was, a Russki from way back when? I should've known you would, smart as you are.

He told Thompson the bodyguard he wished he'd got the job in better times. Winston said, 'All I hope is that it is not too late. I am very much afraid it is.'"

Saying that put Colville in the dumps again. "Perhaps you shouldn't pass that on to your people." I swore I'd never dream of it.

The Senator's voice was waspish through the static. "He's afraid it's too late, eh? Sneak around and see if they'll agree to send the fleet to Canada. The president mentioned it off-hand just the other day." I guessed he thought he was paying a compliment with that "sneak around." Mother would've rung his bell with her wood spoon.

Colville and I had lunch at the Savoy a couple of days later, Welsh rarebit with a dry Riesling I drank most of while Colville sipped and listened to me rattle away; being under his eye made me do that. I was thinking how to bring up the fleet when he suddenly said, "Winston would like to see you."

I choked on the bite of rarebit I just forked in, the last for me by the way— it's so cheesy it binds you up for days.

"Are you all right?" Colville said. "Your face is purple."

I took a long drink of water and a longer one of Riesling. "Why does he want me?"

"Winston needs a sense of what is in the President's mind. I told him of the lengthy visit you had recently with him and Harry Hopkins."

"Lengthy?" I said, caught in the lie. "Well, yes, it was long, but the president sort of rambles around, tells jokes and stuff about the past. Good luck trying to figure out he's thinking; even Harry says he doesn't know half the time, which he thinks is doing better than the president himself."

I saw how the Roosevelt operated when I worked at the White House. He'd give the same job to three or four people and see who did the best. The losers that worked their asses off for nothing weren't seen again. I told you about that before.

I was undressing after a so-so night of poker at Boodle's when there was a knock at the door. I opened it in my bare feet and two men showed MI6 credentials and said Churchill wanted to see me toot sweet.

"It's almost two o'clock," I said, tapping the crystal of my watch.

"The prime minister keeps irregular hours," said the one decent enough to look sorry about bothering me. I put my clothes back on and they drove me to the Cabinet War Offices that were underground at Whitehall. It was a cramped and crowded place with small rooms and narrow corridors.

We passed an officer I recognized from the newspapers as General Ironside, the new commander of the home forces that were supposed to turn back the invasion with knives on poles, hunting rifles, and a few tanks and trucks with steel plates bolted on them.

"I've been to nine meetings today," General Ironside said bitterly to an aide as we passed. I was asked by the MI6 men to wait in the hallway as the word was the prime minister was running behind.

Winston was snappish to the people who came and went through the door left open for air. I sat in a straight-back chair in the hallway and yawned, regretting the Veuve Clicquo I put away with a few of the club members waiting for the all-clear to push off to their country homes for the weekend. We were telling jokes and stories to keep up spirits, but they were as sad-looking as dogs back home that get mixed up with skunks. They envied I'd be called home before the Hun stormed the beaches at Clacton-on-Sea and Ramsgate.

Clouds of blue cigar smoke drifted out of Winston's office pretty regular and people hurrying back and forth made it swirl. A young woman pulled a black handkerchief from a ventilator sucking in air from outside. "This was white when I came on my shift," she told me. "And to think we're breathing this."

Time passed and my head started jerking. Then I heard Churchill say real sharp, "Where the hell is Lieutenant Brady? He should have been here long ago."

"I don't know, prime minister," a male voice said. "There's a man sitting outside, could that be him?"

I heard the scrape of a chair. "Someone will pay if it is." Churchill peered around the doorway. "Lowell Brady! Come in, old friend." The aide hurried out, shooting me a look of fear.

"Old friend" was on the strong side, but you know politicians. I followed him into a bare room with a low ceiling and patches of damp on the wall and took a seat in chair as uncomfortable as the other. His desk had three telephones and was drowning in papers and files.

"I was not prepared for the sloth and incompetence at the War Office," he said, "but I should have known from the conditions at the Admiralty. I sent General Ironside on his way a short time ago after I had a look at his plans for the defense of our island. A 'thin crust' of defenders on the coast with fallback

244 | JERRY JAY CARROLL

lines to be more robustly contested by what troops we have. They are to be assisted by mobile units of untrained volunteers astride horses or in private cars or double-decker buses. They'll wear armbands in lieu of uniforms. The way Ironsides has drawn it up, our airfields will be abandoned at once, giving the Luftwaffe dominion in the skies. You can imagine what they would do to those buses and the men on galloping horses. I'm going to make Ironside a field marshal and send him off to retirement with a peerage. General Brooke will replace him; I believe you know him from France. He speaks amusingly about the encounter." He looked at me with a twinkle in his eyes as he relit his dead cigar, sending up more blue smoke to circle and drift for the door.

Then he got serious. "As before, I will be as open to you as to President Roosevelt if he sat in his wheelchair where you are. We've lost ten destroyers in eleven days to U-boats and other attacks. We can't continue the war at this rate. We can't feed ourselves without imported food and our convoys depend on destroyers to get through."

"That's hard," I said, shaking my head. I decided it was better to hold off mentioning moving the fleet to Canada. It was a damned awkward position to be in, a lowly lieutenant talking to the prime minister of the greatest empire in the history of the world.

"Hard?" he said like he couldn't believe his ears.

I saw he thought that didn't do it justice. "Really hard," I said. "Awful."

"Despite all its riches, the English language doesn't have the power to describe our condition at this moment. 'Catastrophic' might come closest." He peered at me through the smoke as if he had misjudged me.

"It's terrible for sure," I said. I was straining forward in the chair like watching a runner round third who'd get home the same time as the ball. I think that more than any fancy word I might come up with convinced him I got the picture.

"Do you believe this feeling is shared by the White House?"

"They're plenty worried, I can tell you that."

"Worry is an emotion any casual bystander can feel. Do you think your country would give us fifty or so destroyers in this our time of greatest need?"

I was about to say I doubted it, but then I had a flash of inspiration. "We've got plenty of four-pipers left over from the Great War in our reserve fleet, why not ask for them?" Then I blurted, "While we're on the subject, what about sending the Royal Navy to Canada if…you know…if it comes to that?"

Churchill glowered and it felt like the walls were closing in and the floor squeezing up toward the ceiling. "If it comes to what?"

I stammered in a high voice. "Well, you know, if…if…if the Germans looked like they were winning and…and…"

"Sending the fleet from our shores would be an admission of defeat," he roarerd with a thump of his fist on the desk. "We would never, never do that. As I said in my speech, we would rather die choking on our own blood than surrender."

"Times change and nobody could blame you…" If I'm honest, that wasn't my finest moment. If my voice got any higher only a bat could hear me. It was nerves, of course.

He got that bulldog look you see in pictures. "Nothing has changed!"

He poured brandy into two tumblers and pushed one to me. "I think you need this." I gulped mine down as he diluted his with water from a carafe.

"I can formally request the destroyers through diplomatic channels, but I would first like to determine if such a request would be received with sympathy in light of the power of your isolationist bloc. The President and I have had a few informal exchanges, but they have been little more than expressions of good will." I felt the presence of someone in the open door behind me; Churchill waved away whoever it was.

"I know the President is concerned about the upcoming election, but I wonder, Lieutenant, if you would be so kind as to privately and quietly plumb your sources in Washington. I would hate to have a request through official channels be declined with every polite expression of sorrow. The newspapers inevitably would find out and it would have a dampening and even fatal effect on the morale of our people. I possibly would be forced to leave office for someone more conciliatory toward the Germans."

The brandy steadied my nerve. "I'll ask as soon as they open up shop." I banged the desk myself with my fist. But then I realized I couldn't tell the Senator because he would be on the phone to his newspaper friends ten seconds after he told the White House.

"Let me know the answer as soon as you can." He drew on his cigar. "Action

246 | JERRY JAY CARROLL

this day is our motto now." He smiled. "That is why you see dignified civil servants known for their stately pace now running in the corridors."

"There are several people with appointments waiting, Prime Minister," said the voice behind me.

"Yes, yes, yes," Winston said impatiently. "Show the first of them in. God bless you, Lieutenant Brady, our hopes ride on your shoulders."

I squared them and marched out in step with one of Churchill's secretaries, a thin guy in a wrinkled pinstripe suit, loose tie and a shirt he hadn't changed for days from the look. He was dead tired, almost out on his feet. Bags under his eyes, his pip-pip Old Boy voice gone hoarse.

"Good Lord," he said, looking at his watch, "it's almost four o'clock."

"How does he do it, a man his age?"

"A two-hour nap in the afternoon," he said wearily, "while the rest of us slog on. We eat standing up and snatch a few minutes of sleep in a chair when we can. People are breaking down from the pressure. The worst is his shouting at us; Mrs. Churchill promises to speak to him." He took a deep breath of early morning air only a little smoky compared to others lately.

"Well," he said wanly, "back to the salt mines."

My hope was Harry Hopkins was back to work, but if he wasn't I'd have to try the Senator. He usually took his sweet time getting back to me. I had spent hours at the embassy chatting up girls with I admit pretty good success waiting for his call. He wasn't interested in most of the political developments that Colville told me were highly important.

"I get enough of that horseshit here," he said.

Lately, it was the next day that he called back, or even two days later. Never a word of apology for wasting my time. I could try to get through to the president myself, but I was bound to be blocked by Pa Watson, who didn't like me as I said before. He guarded Roosevelt's time like it was the gold at Fort Knox.

I felt my way in the darkness for a long stretch, being extra careful where I stepped, until I found a pub open early for workers round-the-clock at a factory for military uniforms. I had three cups of strong tea and ordered an old fashioned English breakfast.

"Pitiful, ain't it?" the young waitress apologized when she put the plate in front of me. "One banger, one egg—and that a blessing—one rasher of bacon and a little bit of beans. The only thing wot's the same is the price. Well, we better get used to it and worse if I'm to guess." She said it with a tired smile, English pluck for you.

The night porter let me into White's and I caught a few winks in a leather armchair until the snap and rustling of newspapers by early risers woke me. I walked around outside and killed time looking at the shell of a bombed building. Its insides were opened up to show sitting rooms, bedrooms and toilets like stage sets in a theater; you expected an actor to pop through a door and utter some drivel like in those modern plays nobody understands. The Marines opened the gate for me before the embassy opened and I put in a call to the White House. Luckily, I got one of the operators I knew and she found out Harry was awake.

"Hopkins," he said when he answered the phone.

"Harry, it's me, Lowell Brady."

"What do you want?" I told you he didn't spend much time on a phone conversation those days.

"I talked to Churchill a few hours ago. He wants to know if we'd give him fifty destroyers."

Harry laughed.

"No, I'm serious Harry. We've got them in our reserve fleet."

"Those rust buckets? He wouldn't want them."

"They're desperate, Harry. They lost ten destroyers in eleven days he tells me."

"Holy shit." He was silent for a minute. "We'd have to get something back for it. The stingy Yankees up in New England will throw in with the isolationists if we don't."

"There's something else. Sending the British fleet to Canada? No deal, Winston says."

"How'd he hear about that?"

"My stepfather asked me to feel him out. Winston said no and he meant it. It would look like they're throwing in the towel."

"I'll run the destroyers past the President when I see him, and I'll tell Senator Brady to keep that bottle nose of his out of this. This town leaks like a bucket they use for target practice."

248 | JERRY JAY CARROLL

That night I was at the Savoy dining with a shop girl I wanted to impress. She was saying I was the handsomest and best dressed man in the room when a moon-faced Marine lieutenant named Rod Howard came up the table and asked for a private word. I introduced him to Miss Williams and we excused ourselves.

"Ambassador Winant told us to find you as quick as we could," he said at the bar. "Yes, I will have something, thanks. A double Scotch if it's on you; I'm off duty now that I've delivered the message. You're to call your stepfather as soon as possible. He's at home."

"How'd you know I was here?" I asked.

"Someone said go to the most expensive restaurants in London and you're bound to find him. A bunch of us went out looking. I was just at the Dorchester Hotel." He looked around. "Impressive, but not quite as nice as this."

I asked would he mind seeing Miss Howard home and he said do monkeys shit in the jungle?

She didn't have the time of day for me after that. Howard must have had had a terrific personality because he wasn't much to look at. Ordinary is the best you could say, but down-right homely was closer. A moon face, like I said, and liver lips. Maybe I'm being too hard on the guy out of jealousy, but I didn't lose many gals and it pissed me off.

When I telephoned the Senator, he asked straight off why I'd reversed charges. I explained the embassy was closed and I was calling from White's because it was urgent.

"Never mind, there's crazy rumors going around that that Churchill is going to ask us for some destroyers. The man must be out of his mind. The president was surprised I hadn't heard about this and it was goddamned embarrassing. I'm supposed to be giving him the inside stuff on what's happening over there."

"It's news to me, Senator, I'll find out right away."

"Don't bother, this will be handled by the Navy and the cookie-pushers at State and I'll be..." His poisonous tone changed to nice as pie. "Why, hello, dear. Oh, no, it's nothing important. I'm talking to someone about a post office for one of our smaller towns." He whispered to me, "Get on the ball or you'll find yourself at the Buffalo dry docks."

If you've ever been there in winter with icy winds cutting through your clothes like you don't have any—well, it would put the fear of God in an atheist. I knew an ensign sent there as punishment who said a gust forced open the buttons of his watchcoat and it billowed out and snapped behind him like a sail torn from the main. He was nearly pulled off the deck into the following sea and a watery grave. He…there I go, off course again.

A mass of military officers and diplomats was sent over to London and kept coming; the British cleared out entire buildings around the embassy for their offices. It was like a little village of Americans got turned into a mid-sized city right in the heart of London.

The bureaucracy grew faster than a mushroom on horse manure. Helped along by people just like them at Whitehall, soulmates you might say, things slowed so committees could split up into sub-committees until the subject whatever it was got talked to death and there was nothing to do but take action.

Then there was the paperwork people had to put initials on to show they'd read it. From bits of conversation I heard most would touch a match to nine out of ten reports stamped "Classified" for all they were worth. Seeing all these new people left no doubt we'd be in the war no matter what baloney the White House was feeding the people back home.

The destroyer deal went through in March, giving us ninety-nine year leases on British bases in the Caribbean and other stuff in return for the hulks from our reserve fleet. You could almost build a new one in the time it took to make them sea ready. Colville told me bitterness was so thick at the Admiralty you could cut it with a butter knife. Screwed again by the Yanks was the feeling.

But Roosevelt in his devious ways built on the deal until it became Lend-Lease and the thousands of shiploads of weapons and food we sent saved the British. Harriman was sent from home to lord it over everyone. I told you about that before.

One afternoon I met Colville to take a turn as he called walking around one of London's squares. He pointed with his walking stick at the plane trees where the leaves were beginning to turn. "Each year I wonder if I will live to see them change again."

We walked in silence, me wondering how to move the subject on to something more cheerful. "I'm changing next week from my summer wardrobe to the fall one," I said, meaning civilian clothes of course. He gave me the sort of disappointed look he did now and then as if wondering, I don't know, like was I a serious enough person?

Contrails made patterns in the sky way above. "The dog fighting is at its highest pitch," Colville said. "All three air wings are up, leaving no reserves. The Germans are paying a heavy price to knock out our airfields, but captured pilots have that strutting arrogance of Prussians and say their detention will not be for long."

It gave you a queer feeling watching those life-and-death fights going on like they were silent movies.

"The prime minister has written the president to tell him the hour of decision is near at hand, but who knows what effect that will have? Our air defenses are buckling and reconnaissance show a thousand barges in Channel ports waiting to bring the invasion. Our intelligence reckons about a hundred thousand battle-tested soldiers are ready for embarkation; if they get their panzer divisions ashore it will be the end for us. Winston says he won't be taken alive and has Clementine learning to shoot a pistol in the event Germans come over the garden wall."

"There's the Royal Navy to get past," I said faintly. Even I didn't know things were this bad, let alone the White House. Maybe Colville had been holding out on me.

"Yes, the Royal Navy," he said sadly. "Who knew warships would be so vulnerable to air attack before this started?"

Nerves at the embassy were stretched tight as piano wire. A big new Stars and Stripes was ordered for the flagstaff so Germans would know this was American soil if they even cared when they came tearing across St. James Square. People were told to get sensitive files together for burning.

"Mine are up here," I had said, tapping my temple and looking round with a smile. It came back later to bite me in the rear. I suddenly wasn't allowed in the room with the scrambler phone. The man in charge, a middle-aged commander with a high forehead dimpled with old shrapnel wounds, didn't hide this was fine by him.

"I've got an important message to get off," I said.

"Try the OSS boys, but get it in writing," he said. "There is a meeting tomorrow in the Secure Room at 0800 and you're to be there."

I sent off five overnight cables to Harry via different companies with the same message. "We must talk. Urgent. B at breaking point."

The OSS people from the Ivy League schools made themselves stand out trying to look ordinary; trench coats and hats pulled low was what they came up with. The Britons had a good laugh at them. "They mean well but they are such innocents," Colville told me.

I was led into the Secure Room like a criminal from the holding cell. A fiftyish, pompous sort in civilian clothes sat in the chairman's chair looking so full of himself he'd burst if he took a deep breath and we'd all be ducking flying guts. I pegged him as an investment banker or Wall Street lawyer giving his services to the nation for a dollar a year. The embassy's naval and military intelligence bosses and their deputies faced each other across the table with stone faces.

He told me, "I'm with OSS" and motioned to take a chair. "Lieutenant Brady," he said, "who is your source in British intelligence?" His glance at the others said this was the question they'd agreed on. I learned more spooning soup with Colville than the OSS crowd did grubbing away for weeks. It must have stung more than I thought when questions were asked in Washington and got repeated in London.

"I can't tell you that," I said nicely. "Orders."

"We understand you have learned that 'B,' as you call it, is at the breaking point. That obviously is the British and evidently refers to air defenses. Is this true and how do you know it?"

"I can't tell you," I said, beginning to feel uneasy at bucking the system like this. It came to me under those hard stares that if Harry faded away for good, it would leave only the president in my corner and he'd give me up as easy as a pawn on a chessboard. "Orders," I repeated.

"Orders from whom; surely you can say. Captain Waters here was told by the CNO himself that he doesn't know whom you work for." Two "whoms" in a row; a simple sailor like me couldn't help but feel small.

"His information is essentially accurate," Captain Waters said in half-hearted defense. We Navy guys stick together, right? Nope. Everybody's out for himself. "But I think you should answer the question, Lieutenant."

"The fact is," Mr. OSS said, "nobody in the Navy is higher than the Chief of Naval Operations."

"There's the Secretary of the Navy," I said.

He brushed that off. "I understand you have had a very nice little life here, coming and going as you please and spending government money like it was water. I know that you are Senator Brady's son..."

"Stepson," I corrected.

"Very well, stepson. The Senator is a fine man and I have the utmost respect for him, but a patron even as important as he is not enough to explain the freedom with which you operate." He paused to see if I had an answer.

"You're right," I said. "It wouldn't."

"So then, the question is..."

At that moment like in a radio drama there was a knock at the door and a young Army shavetail stuck his head in. "Sorry, sir," he said to the brigadier at the table, "but there is an urgent telephone call for Lieutenant Brady."

"Inform them that Lieutenant Brady is at an important meeting and will return the call when it has concluded," Mr. OSS said, his jowls darkening. He wasn't a man used to being interrupted. The brigadier nodded okay at him and the lieutenant closed the door.

Mr. OSS looked at the ceiling to simmer down or get his thoughts together again. He cleared his throat and was about to speak when there was another knock and the lieutenant was back. "Sorry, sir, but it's the White House and he is to come to the phone right this minute."

I would have liked to stay to enjoy the sight of all the dropped jaws, but I followed the lieutenant to the scrambler phone and closed the door behind me. "What's going on?" Harry said. "I got a strange telegram from you."

"Only one? I sent a bunch."

"I'm looking at the one that got through."

"The OSS is reading your mail."

"They are?" He sounded irritated.

"That's what this meeting is about. They want to know what the message means and how I know."

"*I* want to know what it means," Harry said.

"The RAF is almost out of fighter pilots."

After a long silence, Harry said, "That's very bad news."

"You know about the German armada across the Channel?"

"Yeah, we've known that for a while. Not about the pilots, though."

"I'm getting some heat, Harry. The OSS doesn't like our arrangement."

"How did they find out?"

"They haven't said but they're grilling me about it right now. There's a fat guy who didn't give his name, he only said he's with the OSS."

"Put him on the phone. Don't say who's calling."

I went back to the Safe Room. "They want to talk to you," I said to Mr. OSS.

"Who is 'they?'" he said, rising from his chair with indignation.

"I can't say," I said. "Orders."

I looked around the silent room with a pleasant smile after he left. He was back in less than a minute breathing deep and his jowls a richer burgundy. Harry must have been pretty rough on him.

"This meeting is adjourned," he said, "thank you for your time."

This should have put me in deep clover, feared by both the Navy and the intelligence boys, but life seldom pans out the way you think it will. You could travel the world and not find anybody who knows that better than me.

A huge storm blew up in Washington over this two-bit event in the Secure Room. I told you J. Edgar Hoover was still trying like hell to pull foreign intelligence under his control and was being fought by Wild Bill Donovan and his OSS with the backing of Stephenson and M6, which did all the training of Donovan's agents in the beginning. They were thick as thieves those two, with enough medals for courage between them for a whole division.

Also in the fight were naval and military intelligence and even the spooks at the State Department. It all came to a head in that little Secure Room in London where I waltzed out thinkin' I was king of the hill when I was no more than a rooster crowing on a dung hill. The upshot was I was ordered home in a compromise that saved everybody's face.

"I suppose it's all for the best," Colville sadly said at our last dinner together. "I'm being shunted to the sidelines myself by young blades coming up who don't see much use in an elderly admiral poking his nose around where he shouldn't.

254 | JERRY JAY CARROLL

Something to do with 'security concerns.' Winston was most unsympathetic when I approached him. 'The old gives way to the new,' he told me in a dismissive way. 'It will happen to me one day and I hope I go with equanimity before they use the hook like in the music halls.'"

"I did the best I could for you," Harry told me when I was called to the White House directly when I returned, "but you were the one thing they could all agree on. Franklin did his soft shoe away from the fight like always. "You boys figure it out.' I'd say if there was a winner, it was Wild Bill. The president is going to keep you on his bench for the odd jobs that come up if that makes you feel better."

Harry was in bed, pasty-faced and weak, eating bread dipped in a saucer of milk; the man had strength hidden to the naked eye, to mine anyhow. He always looked like he was at death's door, but it wasn't long before he was flying across the Atlantic with me carrying his bag of medicine to get introduced to Winston and then go on to meet Joe Stalin. You already wrote that stuff up.

I guess that's it for now, I don't want to keep you up any later. A mama-to-be needs plenty of sleep.

CHAPTER 17

I HAD FORGOTTEN THE PLEASURE TO BE HAD IN THE COMPANY OF OTHER WOMEN, their liveliness, warmth and sensitivity, their bright laughter over absurd little things, their rolled eyes over the impossible but endearing men in their lives. I don't mean the silly chatterboxes that were my roommates in Washington, D.C., when all this started, but real women like Sofia who made beautiful and loving homes for their families instead of withering away in dead-end office jobs wondering when Prince Charming would come to spirit them away.

Our bedroom and sitting room were part of the house and the air was filled with the mouth-watering aromas of simmering sauces and stocks for dishes favored in the Abruzzo region of Italy where Sofia's people came from. "It is between the Adriatic and the Apennines," she said. "It is beautiful but hard country, cut off from the rest of Italy by many steep mountains."

Beginning with the antipasti, the food from that kitchen matched or bettered any of the fancy restaurants where Lowell and I ate in Washington or during our wanderings. Bruschetta was spread with salt and oil with sausage and tomato or with zucchini and mozzarella, or it had chicken livers with onion, peppers, vinegar, sugar, dry wine, pepper, salt, and oil. When the truck came from San Francisco, the spread was steamed mussels with parsley, onion, bay leaf, white wine, olive oil, and seasoned with saffron sauce. The Abruzzo version of mortadella, called campotosto, was made from lean pork with a small amount of bacon, smoked fifteen days and aged three months.

"I could eat them all day," Lowell said, pushing away his appetizer plate with regret, "but you have to save room for what comes next in this place."

The pasta peeled from drying frames and shaped on cutting boards might be any size or shape, including *maccheroni alla chitarra*, long thin noodles served with a tomato-based sauce flavored with peppers, lamb and on one memorable occasion goose. We gloried in Sofia's tortellini, ravioli, lasagna, risotto and a tiny lentil with a long name (*Lenticchie di Santo Stefano di Sessanio*) that is so permeable it doesn't need soaking before cooking. Her cooking was so effortless as to seem a form of magic. She prowled back and forth from storeroom and ice box to the big restaurant-size stove with pots and kettles simmering, even as she kept on eye on the children before and after school. She managed the winery and household accounts in a tiny office, fed her silent husband Ampelio and the half-dozen farm workers a plentiful lunch, and did a thousand other things while she kept up a cheerful conversation with visiting friends and neighbors and whoever else was in earshot. That included me a good part of the day after I begged off from accompanying Lowell on his restless drives through the wine country, offering my condition as an excuse. I was drawn irresistibly to her kitchen, the beating heart of the house, and loitered like a gossip at a gate until she began to put me to work.

"Sitting is not good for you," Sofia said, agreeing with my decision. "You must walk around and be busy. Sit when you are tired, but not a car seat all the day long."

I had assumed I was a fairly good or at least a competent cook when I made meals for my housemates in the Capitol, but I learned in Sofia's kitchen that I knew next to nothing, including the use of garlic which before I only associated with Bela Lugosi of the movies. I had never heard of frittata, let alone eat it.

She threw her hands up. "Never!? It is unbelievable. Ampelio, she has never heard of frittata." Her husband merely shrugged. "I talk enough for both of us," Sofia said with a laugh. He was short and stocky with farm-hardened muscles and calloused hands and was so hairy his eyebrows met and his jaw was blue an hour after shaving. I sometimes wondered if theirs was an arranged marriage.

"We will make a breakfast frittata tomorrow, Harriet, you and me. I will show you everything."

She had bowls, a skillet and other cookware laid out on a table when I straggled to the kitchen, still drugged from my long sleep. It seemed I could never get enough because the child growing within sapped my energy. I left Lowell singing "I'm Popeye the Sailor Man" in the shower.

Sofia explained as she went. "In a large skillet, we sauté the broccoli, mushrooms and onions in butter until tender. Ten minutes, say. Johnny, your shoelaces are dragging, tie them so you don't trip. We add this cup of cubed cooked ham until it's heated through. Michael, you can do a better job combing your hair, look in the mirror this time. We take from the cook fire but keep it warm. In a bowl, beat these eight eggs I opened while you were still sleeping—ha, ha, never mind, I did the same thing every time—a quarter cup of water and some mustard, a little Italian seasoning and garlic salt. Keep beating until it's foamy. Stir in the shredded cheddar cheese, the chopped tomatoes, the broccoli florets, mushrooms, and green onions finely chopped."

Her hands moved as smoothly over the dished ingredients as a card dealer's. "We pour it into this greased shallow baking dish and bake in the oven at 375 degrees for twenty-five minutes."

The children had gone off to school after their breakfast cereal and toast when Sofia pulled the frittata out of the oven and Lowell followed his nose into the kitchen. "Something smells awful good," he said. She went off to find her husband who was working near the house and we all sat down to a breakfast that included bread baked earlier, fresh-squeezed orange juice and strong coffee. The frittata seemed light as air but was as filling as pancakes.

"You will be hungry again for lunch," she said.

"You're a lucky man to eat like this every day," Lowell told Ampelio with an admiring shake of his head.

"Yes," Ampelio said. He always ate quickly, rarely looking up from his plate; he kissed his wife and went out outside. "They are looking for plant disease and which vines to graft," Sofia explained. "There are so many to do."

"He's hiding something," Lowell said when I walked him to the car. When I scoffed, he insisted. "No, really, it takes one to know one."

Thinking about this, I wondered if Ampelio had concealed something about the age gap between their children, the little ones and the ones in their teens. Had he been lured away by another woman and returned to be forgiven? No, I thought, they are too Catholic. The house showed every sign of it with crucifixes on the walls, little statues of the Virgin Mary and saints in alcoves, and paintings of sacred subjects, including in the roomy living room that had an oil in a gilt frame of a gentle Jesus praying on Mount Olive; under it a small candle burned during the day. The church was too far for them to go to daily mass, but like other growers the Nichelinis rode their farm truck to town on Sundays with the youngest in the cab with mom and dad.

Standing before the painting with his morning coffee one Sunday when the family was gone to church, Lowell said, "They got the wrong idea about Jesus if you go by the old commodore." He was the strange farmer he met in the middle of nowhere when he was at the end of his rope. He worked in return for food and shelter and received daily instruction in the Bible, which was a condition of the job. Though armor-clad against religion in his former life, it seemed these teachings had some effect on Lowell in his weakened state.

"We'd drop to our knees in the fields whenever the commodore said, day or night and in all weather, while he called out a verse from memory. According to him, Jesus wasn't a gentle milquetoast like that picture but a tough cuss who came with a sword to turn things around in this evil world. The commodore wouldn't be comfortable in a house like this with all its idols and such; he said a church should be bare as a bone. He didn't care for foreigners, either."

Another reason I was so sluggish some mornings was Sofia and I had begun staying up late talking. At her suggestion we began to knit and sew baby things. "Pink or blue, it make-a no diff'rence to little ones." Naturally, we began confiding and as we became closer I came to see her as the wiser and more experienced older sister.

"You have been traveling all this time?" she said, bent over her needle. "What a lot of movie pictures they making!" She glanced at me. "But never to have a place to come home to, it would be hard for me." I said some of our travel was for pleasure. "Same difference, you not home. We take in guests in the summer which we enjoy and they nice people, but at the same time we never relax because always strangers in the home. But the money..." She sighed. "Some year the grape prices are good and some year not so good. And if you don't have an honest company to sell what you grow it is bad. Some of them are criminal people, cheats that live off the sweat of the honest people." She pressed her lips tightly together.

One night I asked her about the gap in the ages of her children. I wasn't prying; it just came up naturally when I was talking about my own family in Montana where there was a similar gap with my sister Helena who went eleven years between her first and second children because of the fertility problem I mentioned.

"My husband was away in the war like your mister." Sofia was silent for a moment. "He went back to Italy after his grandfather's death to sell land and take care of other business and was force into the Italy army."

"How could they do that to an American citizen?"

"Well, that's just it," she said looking out the window. "You never say, even to Lowell?" No, I said, and kept my promise until all these years later. "He was illegal in this country since a little boy, sent on a ship bringing marble to America. Italian crew, Italian stevedores; such things were easy to fix up. The carabinieri looked away for a little money and people this side for a little more. He told the soldiers you can't put me in the Italy army because I'm American. 'Where is the proof?' they said, and of course he had none. He was years in the army, fought in Abyssinia and was captured in North Africa. He swore on the Bible he never fired one shot at the American soldiers but in the air always. He was afraid to say he was American when his regiment gave up because they might think he was a traitor and hunged on a tree. He escaped from a prisoner-of-war camp in Fort Smith, Arkansas, and found his way back here. He was silent with others for not to give something away and now is his nature." Telling her secret seemed to bind us even more closely.

Lowell complained about me not joining him on his rambles, lightly at first and then more insistently. "I got used to talking to you and it's kinda lonely driving along without you."

"We have to think about the baby," I said firmly.

"And when I do get back, you spend so much time with Sofia talking and laughing away t I might as well be invisible. All I've got is the radio and the newspaper. Hell, I almost opened up a book the other day."

"We're sewing baby things. It's more fun when you do it with another woman, and she knows so much about children and has so much experience." Chiara, a wizened ancient from the old country who was the most trusted midwife in the community, told Sofia and me she believed I was carrying a boy, but she worried about his position in the womb.

"But maybe that will change," she said, patting my hand.

"Poor little feller growing up without a pappy," Lowell said gloomily one day.

"Why do you say that?" I was impatient with him more often as the due date approached. He'd always had all attention focused on him, but circumstances had changed and I felt he should too.

"Look at all this gray hair I'm getting. I'm an old man on his last legs, no denying it. I've had a hard life as you know better than anyone and it's beginning to show."

I told him he was just being dramatic, but I had begun to notice small changes. It was as if moving from one place to the next and needing always to be on his toes had been essential to keeping him youthful. But the birth of our child would mean an end to life on the road; that and the loss of my single-minded concentration on him seemed to weaken what I can only call his Life Force. Most tellingly, his faultless memory began to weaken.

I WAS still feelin' poorly in Darwin after Corregidor, trying to get back the forty-three pounds I lost. I could've cleaned up at the nightly poker game in the bachelor's barracks, but I just wasn't up to it. A Navy commander all spit-and-polish whose name I can't remember knocked at the door one night with two beefy shore patrol guys behind him. He had orders to put me aboard a freighter headed for Vladivostok with Spam. Soldiers joked that it was ham that didn't pass the physical.

"These men will pack up your gear seeing as how you're not looking so hot," he said, looking me up and down. "The shipmaster is in a hurry to get out of the harbor because of the Japs."

Planes from the carriers that clobbered Pearl Harbor had bombed hell out of Darwin the month before and nobody knew when they'd be back. Most people skedaddled for the interior, including the Australian army, which turned into a rabble worse than the French. They had a high old time, drunk on beer no doubt, looting as they went. They took furniture, refrigerator, pianos, stoves and even kids' toys. Half of Darwin's population and a lot of soldiers were still in the Outback at the time.

In my weak condition, I had to sit down when the commander handed me the envelope with orders for Russia. "Whatever it is they have planned for you must be important because this was delivered by hand of officer all the way from San Francisco. He flew out again on the Catalina held for him even though an admiral was not happy about it. You'd think they would give a man more time after what you've been through."

They'd been treating me like a hero for being with MacArthur on Corregidor, which was in the news a lot there. People were always shaking my hand and patting my back. The Aussie papers didn't know what was really going on. Like the poor devils we left behind they thought a relief expedition was on the way. I told you all about that before. I'm trying to remember the name of that commander.

My nemesis as you call it found out I had wangled a spot with the general's party and started dreaming up the next frying pan that would pop me into the fire. Russia, they must have been thinking, *let's see him get out of this one.* The orders said I was to look Siberia over, the roads and so forth, in case they became allies and we needed to ship over materiel. You couldn't say, "I am a spy, please arrest me" more plain than that.

"Look, they're already raising anchor," that commander—damn, what *was* his name—said as we approached *Boringia,* an old tramp steamer overdue for the ship breaker's yard. Buttrick Hammond, that was it. He looked like his name now that I think about it; podgy, the Brits call it. The shore patrol guys climbed up a ladder with my gear as I followed, resting after every step. The minute they were back down to the admiral's barge, *Boringia* belched out a big black cloud and wallowed into the Indian Ocean at her best speed, which was ten knots with a good wind astern.

The skipper was a wiry man with a thin, patchy beard named Simmons. He was so jumpy it looked like an electric shock gave him a regular jolt. "Sorry I didn't meet you when you came aboard," he said up on the bridge where he was pacing back and forth, "but she's temperamental and I've got to watch every little thing. This crew is none too smart, the dregs of three waterfronts if you want to know. Even at that, it took ten times the normal hazard pay for them to sign up, which most did with an X. I've got Catholics and Buddhists fingering their beads and a man with an amulet he moans over. They'll be wealthy men by their standards if we survive, and I'll be well off myself even by our way of thinking."

We sailed to the Arafura Sea and through the Torres Strait to the Bismarck Sea, passed between the Philippines and New Guinea with lights out by night and flying a Japanese flag by day until we reached the Sea of Japan when Simmons broke out the red Soviet flag. They had been fighting little battles at the border of Mongolia and Manchukuo for a long time but signed a neutrality treaty the year before on account they each had bigger fish to fry.

Vladivostok was a primitive place like pictures of wooden towns from our Wild West days. Horses and wagons, dull-eyed peasants, raggedy and some of 'em barefoot, and merchants with sly eyes coming to their shop doors to watch us clump along, that was my first impression. I was marched to the police station by half a dozen NKVD agents that met me at the bottom of the gangplank. They took me to a bare room where Sergeant of State Security Anatoly Vasiliev stood at a table with two chairs. He was an ugly sort, brutish with red hair real short on a bullet head; a fair hand with the knout was my guess. He wore a green cotton tunic and pants and heavy boots with cloth windings 'cause they were short on leather. He had a canvas cartridge belt and pouches for grenades and food and a water bottle. It wasn't a smart uniform but it was clean, which seemed rare from the Russians I'd seen so far.

"Welcome to Siberia, Russia," he said in a thick accent. He pointed to my uniform. "You Americn navy. Why?"

Right to the point. I could have said I'm here to see the condition of roads and bridges and rails and so forth. What the average sergeant in the Soviet army would take that to mean is "Tell me your secrets, stupid soldier man."

The inspiration came in a flash. "That is for Stalin's ears only."

Fear showed in his eyes. "I am telled…food only." He called to someone. A woman built like an ox in a baggy uniform with a skirt that showed big calves came in and they spoke in Russian. Her dark hair was pinned back in a spinster way and she had suspicious eyes.

"The sergeant know nothing," she told me.

"That surprises me," I said pleasant but at the same time aiming for a look that said don't mess with me.

Your average Russian is more obedient than even Germans from being serfs through the ages. "Are the telephone and telegraph lines down to Moscow?"

Looking surprised, she explained what I said. I saw Vasiliev's big hands begin to tremble. He must have screwed up in a major way to be sent to Siberia in the first place, and the next stop was slopping pigs if he was lucky. With regular beatings of course, that's how they and the Japs kept the lower ranks in line. He'd given more than a few of them himself, I reckoned, and knew what to expect.

I said I must see the commanding officer and she translated that for him before saying, "He not this place." More back and forth between them. "He hunt wolves with political officer," she said. "They will be gone..." She held up four fingers. "That day come back." There was sweat on the sergeant's forehead.

"I must go to Moscow at once," I said loudly. "I know Comrade Stalin personally."

That was not a lie because you remember I went to the Kremlin with Harry Hopkins, which you wrote about before. He doodled pictures of wolves while Harry talked and as he waited for the translation. He was like a wolf himself with those half-Asiatic slanted eyes that froze your blood when they turned your way. Millions died on his personal orders, *millions*. Saying I knew him was like a thunderbolt struck the room. The story was unbelievable but my arriving with the Spam was so out of the blue it had to be true. They jabbered back and forth with each other.

"You wait Colonel Petrov?" she asked fearfully, blinking her eyes rapidly. The sergeant sent a quick look to the ceiling like shooting a prayer to heaven even though they were all supposed to be atheists. I heard a train whistle not far away.

"Immediately!" I shouted.

"Colonel he say..."

"There's no time," I shouted louder. "Hurry! Hurry!"

They were frozen by the fear of higher authority that was never far from a Russian's mind. "That *choo-choo*. Where go?" I said harshly.

"Tree for Novosibirsk City," she said.

"I take that train." I pointed at Vasiliev. "You go with me."

When she translated that, his mouth fell open. After the smallest delay like he had to put in the clutch and change gears in his mind, he clomped out of the room yelling orders as me and the other agents trailed behind.

The engine was chuffing with a long train of overloaded flatbed cars carrying trees that smelled of pine pitch. It was about to start off when we pulled up in the battered old pickup from the police station. Vasiliev climbed the steps of the cab and spoke to the engineer who shrugged his shoulders like it was all the same to him.

We drove down the train to the rickety wooden caboose and I followed Vasiliev inside where three train workers stared with astonishment. He said something that made them cower and then thumbed out the one in the best seat for me to sit. The sergeant looked to me for my approval and I gave a nod.

The train jerked and slowly picked up speed out of the bad part of town, which from what I could see was just about all of it. Dirt roads hovels and outhouses, goats, chicken pecking at the ground, shabby people staring as if this log train was the most interesting thing they'd seen all month, which it probably was.

I was surprised I'd got this far, let alone plan a next move. Remembering the Soviet Union on maps, I knew endless forest and then the steppes and days of travel were between me and Moscow. Time passed slow as we crept along, never breaking twenty-five miles an hour. The monotony would have driven me nuts if it weren't for the deck of cards in my sea bag. I taught the sergeant and the crewmen poker and one or two other games, losing as many matchsticks as I won to stay on their good side.

I also showed them how to pull cards from behind ears, but they could never master it because their hands were beaten up by work and missing fingers pinched off on the job. The caboose swayed back and forth with only a couple of kerosene lanterns for light after the sun went down.

Heavy drinkers, those Russians, and their vodka is as strong as it gets. Vasiliev got drunk every night, probably second-guessing himself about leaving his post back in Vladivostok on the order of a foreign officer. He sang sad songs in a real deep voice that had crewmen crying. If I'd known the language I'd probably have tears running down my cheeks myself. Very melancholy people, those Slavs.

There was a stove in the caboose and we ate okay considering it was Russia.

Kasha, cabbage, turnips, radishes, peas, and cucumbers raw, pickled, steamed, boiled or baked. We opened the windows regular because that diet churns up the stomach and I'll say no more on that subject. Ever now and then crewmen cooked chickens with necks wrung on the spot to show freshness when the engine took on bunker oil and water. There was a boy in the crew who plucked them clean.

The weather turned from spring back to winter and the snow got deeper in the trees along the track as we headed into the interior. Then late one afternoon in some nameless mountain range the brakes suddenly screeched and less than a minute later the engine way up ahead ran into a rock slide and cars left the rails all the way back to the caboose, which tipped over on its side with a crash I can hear to this day.

I cracked my head a good one and saw stars, but that was my only injury. The overturned stove burning day and night to keep us from freezing set fire to things and we crawled outside except for Vasiliev who was caught in the wreckage. There was nothing we could do to save him so we put our fingers in our ears until he stopped screaming.

I had pulled out a blanket out of the jumble and put it over my shoulders as me and the others walked along the jackknifed cars to the front of the train. The engine was buried under huge rocks that had bounded down the mountainside, probably from a little earthquake we didn't notice in that rattling caboose. I guessed the engineer saw the avalanche coming and tried to stop, but there wasn't time. As soon as the sun set behind the mountains, the cold got bitter and we hiked back to the caboose to warm ourselves at the flames still leaping up there. Everyone was stunned by what happened and we sat in silence except for the crackling of the fire.

The crewmen were used to taking orders and I got the idea as time passed they expected me to take charge. I didn't mind, generally being the sort as I said who favors giving orders than taking them unless a lot is at stake and the wrong decision can cost a man his head. It's better in those cases to have orders to blame if things get screwed up.

So when dawn broke colder than a well-digger's…with the smell of snow in the air, I considered the decision. Try to hoof it back to the last bunch of hovels calling itself a village or go on to the next that was who knew how far ahead? None of the crewmen knew as far as I could make out trying to pry something out of them in spite of not knowing their lingo. My guess was we wouldn't make it back with no food or winter clothes, so buggering on as Winston would say was the only choice. I started walkin' along the railroad track with the blanket over my shoulders and the men shuffled behind.

Snow started falling, light at first and then worked its way into a full-scale blizzard inside of fifteen minutes. If it hadn't been for the railroad ties under our feet we'd have been lost in no time. We stumbled along, heads low, each man with a hand on the shoulder of the one ahead except for me at the front in the teeth of the wind. About midday I saw a dark shape from the corner of my eye barely visible in the white-out. I led my human chain to a shack the railroad built for keeping tools from thieves when it was laying down the rails. It was a shelter from the wind but not much more. We stuffed snow in the cracks and gathered in a tight circle for body warmth and that's how the rest of that day and the night passed.

Come the dawn, we went outside to deep snow and deeper silence that took about one minute to get on your nerves. Bone-chilling cold, of course. The men looked scared and I wasn't feeling all that bold myself. The Russians had hacked a narrow track through the wilderness to get to Vladivostok and left it at that. It seemed from the gabble of the men and the show of fingers that Vladivostok got one train a week coming and going, so no hope from that quarter.

We better call it a night, the way you're yawning. You're making me do it too; I almost dislocated my jaw just now. This stuff is boring to the both of us, me because I went through it and don't have good memories from then and you because you have other things on your mind, not that I'm criticizing. It wouldn't be natural if you didn't.

CHAPTER 18

THE SERIOUS SCHOLAR CAN TAKE HIS LEAVE NOW FOR THOSE WERE THE LAST words that passed between us. The remainder of this account is of a personal nature with not the slightest interest to History with the capital letter. My apologies for trying your patience for so long.

I didn't get out of bed until late in the morning, feeling very unwell. "Mister Lowell, he drive off so early to look for places to shoot the movies," Sofia said, looking at me sharply. "You no are feeling so good?' Her eyes filled with concern. "Not morning sickness, not this late. We go see Doctor Worthington in Napa."

After an examination and a grunt that said he didn't like what he saw, he put me in the hospital for observation over my protests. He was the kind of doctor whose word was law.

"You must do what he says," Sofia said firmly. "I tell your mister and he will come."

But he didn't that day or night and I wondered if he was angry over my increasing inattention, but worry about my baby crowded out everything. The following morning Sofia hurried into the ward where other expecting women lay with complications or waited for the blessed event. Her grave expression made her the cynosure of all eyes.

"What's wrong?" I whispered, fear constricting my heart.

"Your husband upset by men who ask about the motion pictures, chamber of commerce men. All smile, they are hoping to help. They talk to Lowell and everyone happy for the business coming. 'This put us on the map,' the police chief said."

268 | JERRY JAY CARROLL

"There was a *policeman?*" I whispered. My heart leaped and the baby shifted in my tummy as if in alarm.

"He said police force will cooperate every way and the sheriff also. Why do you look that way? You have pain? I call the nurse."

"No, no," I said. "It's just that…" I beckoned her closer to tell the true story. "I don't think he will be back," I said when I finished, beginning to cry. "He thinks he will be found out."

Sofia was silent, disappointment in her face. "Why you not say before?" Then with an effort she was her usual brisk self. "No, doesn't matter. So, no pain? You can come home?"

Home. So much meaning in such a small word, especially for someone without one for so long. I yearned more than ever for a safe place for the baby's sake. "You stay with us until he comes and after," Sofia said decisively. "We love babies, my family. They make homes to come alive."

"Your blood pressure was dangerously high," Doctor Worthington told me on his rounds the next day. "We have got it down but you must stay off your feet as much as possible."

"We wait on her hand and foot," Sofia said dramatically. "Bed or chair, she be in one or the other."

"Bed would be better," he pronounced and moved to the woman in the next bed. He was tall and distinguished and had great authority. The eyes of the women followed him admiringly as he passed majestically on his rounds.

The days passed slowly after I left the hospital, the baby's kicks becoming more robust. I sewed and knitted and worried. "Oh, he is a strong one," Sofia said, witnessing one of the thumps inside. "Or she," I prompted.

"Or she," she said with an indulgent smile, "but Chiara is never wrong."

A thin envelope in Lowell's handwriting arrived two weeks later with no return address. I remembered as I opened it that he was a poor hand at correspondence; other women in his life had complained about their sketchiness and brevity, including his mother.

"I knew we stayed too long. I gave those guys a line of B.S. about the movies and they seemed to believe me but they'll check up. The phone is probably tapped and I wouldn't be surprised if they opened this letter. I will get in touch when I got a place for We Three. Ha Ha. Keep your chin up, darlin'."

Who wouldn't be disappointed at that, what woman and wife? I knew he hadn't abandoned me and the baby, not permanently anyhow, but the jokiness so typical of him in ordinary times smarted now that things were so different. What were the claims on his time that he couldn't say more and far sooner?

The envelope had a Merced postmark, but he could be anywhere by then. On the road again—that was where he was happiest. He had told me he would have been a trucker if not for the deeper official interest in a commercial license than for the ordinary driver's license. Having me alongside listening had made a peripatetic life the ideal existence for him, and sometimes for me as well, I must admit, when I became used to it and still believed I must help correct a major historical error. What scholar, however lowly, does not dream of finding a conspiracy that alters the course of history? But the thrill I felt over the acclaim that would enhance my professional standing had vanished little by little like morning mist as the day stretches out.

Lowell didn't care about the events he had observed and in which he played a role. They were just things that happened to him, however momentous as they unfolded. They might as well have been no more memorable than card games where he had won or lost sums of money. In me he had found someone who believed his personal recollections of great value to History and was willing to uproot her life to listen to hundreds of hours of reminiscences and indeed urge him on in plumbing memory for the smallest details.

I was sure he would find his way back for the birth of the baby, but as the time drew nearer for my confinement—as if the vexation of being bedridden for weeks didn't already qualify for that word—I began to lose heart. Even Sofia's confidence faltered. "It strange," she admitted, frowning. "Maybe he not knows when? Or maybe he think the police watch when baby come? You know, tip off by hospital people."

That would explain his absence, but so could a lot of other possibilities including ill health. His heart gave him trouble and had for a long time. He wouldn't see a doctor about it, of course. This latest close call would have put additional stress on him, perhaps enough to be fatal. If he was driving and went off the road with a heart attack, the local coroner's office would not be able to make heads or tails of the many forms of bogus identification they would find. If it was a poor county, they wouldn't even place a marker where they laid him to rest. His disappearance would finally be a complete success.

Sofia had whispered consultations with the old midwife, Chiara, which she brushed off as unimportant when I asked about it. I saw the old woman shake her head as she was leaving. "What did she say?" I asked Sofia when she came back inside.

"Oh, we were talking about…her knees. They are stiff." I knew from how the corner of her mouth turned down that wasn't true and it was me they talked about, but she didn't want to say what Chiara told her. I was enormously pregnant by now and the smell of her simmering soups or sauces that once made my mouth water now made me feel ill.

My worry about Lowell turned to dull resentment. I dwelt on how his life had been shot through with his evasions of responsibility, acts that paradoxically landed him in hotter water than if he had done his duty as he should have. His duty now was to me and the child that fussed to get out.

I visualized him with yet another woman drawn by his charm and handsomeness, jollying her along with his stories. Perhaps it was the wealthy woman who had always eluded him, a recent widow used to having a man around. He would make short work of it; they would fly to Las Vegas for a quickie marriage and he would impress her with his ease around the gaming tables. I doubted he thought of us—just another thing that had happened.

"Oh," Sofia said, her hand on my brow as I sat listlessly, "you burn up with fever." Her voice seemed to come from a long way. "Ampelio, come quick!"

In fairness to my husband, I was half-crazy from the fever when I had those thoughts, but I wrote them down to give a picture of my state of mind. Millions of women experienced the loss of their husbands because of the war not so very long before, sometimes for years and sometimes for good. By that sterner standard I failed the test. The Nichelinis bundled me into their rough, old pickup with Sofia riding in the bed because I was so big she couldn't fit in the cab and we rattled to the hospital in Napa. I was put in a room of my own because of the worry I might have something contagious; the next couple of days were a blur and on the third I gave birth to Lowell Jr.

He had a lot of dark hair and the squinched up face all babies have, but Sofia said he looked like his father. *"Esattamente,"* she said.

THE GREATER LIARS | 271

When the drugs wore off and I held him, I saw that she was right. Every time the door opened I half expected Lowell's smiling face. I felt ashamed of the hard thoughts I'd had about him, though I suppose they were natural enough. Even these years later when I hear the crunch of tires on the gravel my heart beats a little faster.

Sometimes I find myself wondering how he had crossed the vast expanse of the Soviet Union and then found his way to the West through the storms of war. Was it before or after the fall of the Third Reich?

His White House background would impress the Soviets if he fell into their hands. He would have exaggerated his importance and mentioned the meeting with Stalin at the Kremlin with Harry Hopkins. Although Lowell only went to carry Hopkins' medications in a satchel, only he would know that. The jeeps and trucks and other war material that came out of that meeting helped the Soviet Union survive; there would be gratitude for that. Or maybe he found his way to some Baltic port where he linked up with one of the bands of pro-Western guerrillas. It could be any one of infinity of scenarios that Lowell could be trusted to invest with color and interest. What stories they would be!

Lowell Jr. often asks me about his father and I tell him he was a hero in the war, which is true. The other parts I don't speak about but he will know when he reads these words published by a university press. Your father was no saint, I will warn him then, merely a man placed by fate in extraordinary circumstance who did the best he could.

Lowell Jr. is a quiet and serious boy, very handsome like his father. I think it is good that he seems to have inherited my quiet personality instead of the rakehell ways of his father and grandfather, the gambler and adventurer who disappeared in South America. Still, I wouldn't mind if he had some of the outgoing charm that made it such a delight to be around his dad. But that would make him perfect, wouldn't it?

Sofia and Ampelio made us a part of their family, and aside from summer visits to Montana to see my people he regards them as co-parents and their children as his brothers and sisters. He likes the farm life and I wouldn't be surprised if he became a vintner. I do not want him to join the Navy and see the world as the recruiting posters say. The world is a hard place.

ABOUT THE AUTHOR

Jerry Jay Carroll is a former feature writer and columnist for *the San Francisco Chronicle*. Nominated twice for the Pulitzer Prize, he is the author of *Top Dog*, a *New York Times* bestseller that earned an "A" from *Entertainment Weekly* ("A captivating romp".). Recently revised, it is available in print and as an ebook. He also wrote *Inhuman Beings, Dog Eat Dog, The Great Liars* and *The Horror Writer.* His most recent book is *End Times.*

www.ingramcontent.com/pod-product-compliance
Lightning Source LLC
Chambersburg PA
CBHW020311200626
46814CB00006BA/2192